"When Pride Builds an Empire, Heaven Wages a Higher War."

SEVEN SPIRITS

Supernatural Adventure of Faith

Seven Spirits

April Newton

Newton Apple Books

Published by: Newton Apple Books, LLC.
For more information or to book an event, contact:
http://www.newtonapplebooks.com
newtonapplebooks@gmail.com
Library of Congress Control Number: 2025917271
ISBN – paperback: 978-1-7343012-4-3
ISBN – hardback: 978-1-7343012-3-6
First Edition: March 2025
Cover design, graphic art, and Interior illustrations
by April Newton.

NEWTON
APPLE
BOOKS

Dedication

To my Lord Jesus, You gave me the privilege of writing this fun and faith-filled novel and patiently waited while I figured out how to use a thesaurus. Your inspiration made this journey possible, and Your grace covered every missed comma along the way.

To my ever-patient and ever-supportive husband, Tom Newton, Editor-in-Chief, Grammar Police, and the reigning champion of "Who vs. Whom" debates. Without you, this book would have more typos than plot twists, and thanks to your broad knowledge, I now understand that men don't shave while wearing expensive Italian suits (even if it feels cinematic).

To my family, thank you for your cooperation and patience, and for only interrupting me mid-sentence... sometimes. You're proof that a bit of chaos can still lead to great things.

To those who think you have everything under control...
The real journey begins the moment you let go.

Dear Reader

Thanks for stepping into Ari Keshet's world. Seven Spirits began as a teaching idea about the *Seven Spirits of God*, but one night the Lord surprised me and told me to write it as a novel instead. I remember saying, "A novel? But I write children's books." Yet as I followed His lead and stepped into Ari's story (an overconfident CEO colliding with God), He gently stretched my own understanding of the *Seven Spirits of God* in ways I never expected.

I'm a Bible teacher at heart, and I love sneaking real learning into made-up worlds, because I think the best stories make us laugh, think, and look a little closer at our own lives. That's why my publishing company, *Newton Apple Books*, uses the motto *"Stories that make you think."* In *Seven Spirits*, instead of Sunday School experiments, you'll find one stubborn businessman, a very patient God, and a journey into the heart and character of the Holy Spirit.

This isn't a theology textbook. Instead, think of it as a modern parable, complete with espresso, alpacas, and abundant mercy. As you explore the *Seven Spirits of God*, I hope you'll recognize some of your own questions and those *"Wait... what is God doing?"* moments within these pages.

Most of all, I hope this story makes you chuckle, think, and grow a little closer to Jesus through His Holy Spirit, who still leads, nudges, and loves us in all kinds of surprising ways.

Enjoy the journey,
April Newton

Before We Begin...

Ariel "Ari" Keshet never thought he'd be the kind of man who conversed with spirits, especially seven of them. He was a wealthy CEO, not a spooky mystic. His world revolved around balance sheets, corporate takeovers, and a curated collection of Italian espresso machines. After all, how could one be expected to make life-altering business decisions without the perfect shot of caffeine?

But life, as Ari learned the hard way, doesn't care about five-year plans or the stock market. One minute, he was at the top of the world, literally, standing on a mountain, surveying his empire like a well-dressed, modern-day Midas. Next, he was tumbling headfirst into what seemed like Hell, staring up at what could only be described as a Spirit that looked more like a *cosmic life coach* with an agenda.

To be clear, Ari wasn't looking for enlightenment. He was looking for more success, more power, more things that made other people feel slightly inadequate when they scrolled through social media. But God had different plans. It all started with whispers: gentle nudges toward humility, cryptic supernatural messages, encounters with a giant snowman, and yes, there's an alpaca farm (you'll thank me later).

And then, of course, there is *romance*.

Enter Elinor Miller, botanist, geologist, world traveler, devout Christian, and the only woman on the planet who could infuriate and captivate Ari equally. She wasn't impressed by his billions, arrogance, or his ability to charm his way through boardrooms like a corporate James Bond. No, Elinor saw something beneath the bravado, something real. Something Ari wasn't entirely ready to acknowledge.

And just when things were already complicated enough, in walked the Ghost of Christmas Past (or, in this case, the Ghost of Hanukkah Past). An old college flame. Sharp-minded, sophisticated, and exactly the kind of woman Ari's family had always expected him to marry.

She was a power player, a force of nature, the embodiment of everything that had once made sense in his life. Together, they could have been unstoppable.

Yet something, something Ari couldn't quite name, was off.

Thus began the battle for Ari's heart, or, more accurately, his reluctant surrender to something greater than himself. On one side was Elinor, a woman of deep faith who challenged him in ways no one else dared. The other, a ghost from his past, tempts him with the life he once thought he wanted.

This isn't just a story about a billionaire learning faith. It's about an overconfident CEO being thoroughly outmaneuvered by God, by two extraordinary women, and by the realization that maybe, just maybe, Pride isn't the best business strategist.

Throw in some supernatural interventions, an evil voice whispering in the shadows, and the *Seven Spirits of God* attempting to drag Ari kicking and screaming toward redemption, and you've got yourself one wild adventure.

And yes, there is an alpaca farm. (You're welcome).

Seven Spirits

Chapter 1

Dancing with the Edge

The freezing wind screamed like a living animal, clawing at the jagged cliffs of Denali, or Mount McKinley, depending on whom you ask, with merciless fury. Temperatures had plummeted below zero, transforming every ledge into a treacherous fortress of ice and snow. Ariel Keshet, Ari to most, but always Mr. Keshet to anyone bold enough to challenge him in the boardroom, stood at the edge of a sheer vertical drop.

His boots were balanced on a narrow ledge that might as well have been a knife's edge. Below him, the abyss yawned, a gaping throat that devoured light and sound and swirled with mist and shifting shadows. For anyone else, standing here would have been the height of insanity. For Ari, it was a calculated risk, another dance with danger that most would never dare attempt.

This was his element, the razor-thin line between brilliance and catastrophe. For Ari, this wasn't insanity; it wasn't even extraordinary; it was simply Tuesday.

The cold barely touched him because he was encased in SummitTek's latest prototype, a sleek, jet-black thermal suit engineered for extreme conditions that insulated him from the bone-numbing chill.

The suit, woven from cutting-edge fibers, clung to him like a second skin, its design as much about performance as aesthetics. Every movement was fluid and effortless as if the howling wind and ruthless frost were mere inconveniences.

Strapped to his harness was a rope unlike any other, forged from proprietary synthetic fibers and alloy filaments marketed as "unbreakable." Ari tugged it experimentally to ensure it was safely anchored into the rock face, his gloved hand testing the tension. Ari smirked. *Unbreakable*, they say. He relished the claim, already imagining the pressure he could subject it to during this field-test. He loved pushing boundaries, not just of the equipment he designed but of his own endurance and the fragile line separating brilliance from recklessness.

The wind picked up, a feral howl that rattled the carabiners on his harness. Ari glanced down at the abyss again, a flicker of something primal tugging at his gut. It wasn't fear, not exactly, but an acute awareness of the stakes. One slip, one failure, and the mountain wouldn't hesitate to claim him.

He exhaled slowly, watching the plume of his breath vanish into the wind. He tightened his grip on the rope. This wasn't about survival. Ari wasn't here to survive; he was here to conquer. Survival was for those who sought safety.

Safely parked in a rugged all-terrain vehicle, two research interns, both in their early twenties and plucked from top universities, sat bundled in so many layers that they resembled caricatures of a Christmas Story. They watched through frost-kissed windows.

Jacob and Emily, typical Gen Z new hires, never expected that field testing would require leaving their comfortable work-from-home setups. They anticipated climate-controlled labs, not epic ice vistas. Instead of streaming playlists in hoodies and sweatpants, they were dressed in layers of high-tech insulation, appearing like Arctic explorers. Huddling near the heater, they secretly longed to treat themselves to a fruity, popping boba.

"Mr. Keshet...Sir!" Jacob's voice crackled through Ari's earpiece, betraying a note of panic. Under a beanie that barely tamed his lanky hair and behind a scarf that covered half his face,

Jacob tapped nervously at his smartphone as if hoping to scroll this nightmare away. "Shouldn't we test this back at the lab... with, you know, controlled variables?"

Next to him, Emily, petite and swaddled in puffy layers that made her resemble a penguin girdled in bubble wrap, nodded vigorously. Dyed blue hair peeked from under her fur-lined hood, and fogged glasses slipped down her nose. "Yes! Controlled variables. Indoors. With heat." Her tablet trembled in her gloved hands, the cold biting through no matter how many layers she wore.

"This is insane...Sir! You're on a ledge that's literally crumbling!"

Ari smiled, though his voice remained calm over the comm-link. "Controlled variables don't tell you the truth," he said, voice smooth and confident.

"Real truth comes from pushing limits. No simulations, no safety nets, no second chances. Out here, we find what's real."

He tested the rope again, enjoying the tension, a prideful gleam in his eye. Inside the vehicle, Jacob and Emily exchanged wide-eyed glances, their Gen Z sensibilities offended by the lack of creature comforts and stable bandwidth. They could handle data crunching and virtual conferences, not icy death-defying stunts.

"Sir," Jacob ventured, voice muffled by scarf and nerves. "There are safer ways to... you know, die."

Ari smirked as he peered over the brink. He thrived at this edge where technology and nature collided, where only courage and innovation prevailed. This was the essence of SummitTek's philosophy, and Ari embodied it fully, cocky, unshakable, convinced the world belonged to him.

Emily tried once more, her voice strained. "M-Mr. Keshet, please! The wind's picking up, and that ice looks... It's not stable. We have enough data. Can't we just...,"

CRACK!

A sudden, splintering crack echoed from above. Jacob and Emily froze inside the vehicle, breath catching in their throats. Through the windshield, they saw it, a massive slab of ice shearing off the cliff face, tumbling straight toward the narrow ledge on which Ari stood.

Neither of them spoke. Their hands clenched anything solid in a useless instinct, eyes locked on the unfolding disaster.

As the ice crashed into the ledge near Ari, the stone gave way beneath him in a roar of breaking ice. Debris plunged into the void. For a split second, he disappeared.

Jacob's voice shot up several octaves. "Oh God, oh God!"

Emily's eyes widened behind fogged glasses. The rope snapped taut, swinging violently.

The interns sat frozen. An eerie silence lingered for what felt like an eternity.

Crackling through the comms, "Rope's good. Held perfectly," Ari remarked, as calm as if he were adjusting his shoelaces.

Then, Ari victoriously pulled himself back up, hand over hand, climbing the vertical drop as if it were an easy gym exercise. With a breathless grin, he dusted snow from his shoulders in one sharp motion, as if the mountain had merely tried and failed to challenge him. But Ari just glanced down at the ruined ledge and smirked. To him, it was nothing more than another obstacle conquered and another test he had expected to pass.

Emily's voice cracked, "You... you almost died!"

His tone carried a smug edge. "Almost Emily, but not today."

Jacob shook his head, disbelief mixing with grudging admiration. Ari's arrogance was towering, but he delivered results. Emily could only press her gloved hands against the window, stunned by his audacity.

Ari's decisive and assertive voice came through again: "We're testing the next prototype tomorrow. Be ready."

Inside the vehicle, Jacob keeled over dramatically into the door with a groan, clutching his chest like a soap opera heart attack. "Tell my mom I loved her," he whimpered.

While Emily covered her face with her tablet like it was a bulletproof shield, rocking back and forth and mumbling, "This is fine. Everything's goin' to be fine. Totally normal fieldwork."

Ari's motto was clear: the world isn't controlled, it's conquered.

And he intended to conquer it, one perilous climb at a time.

Annoyed by their lack of adventure, he turned off his earpiece and stepped away from the brink, with Denali's lofty summit towering in the background. Pride swelled within him. He had flirted with death and emerged on top again, proving his rope, his gear, and himself to be superior.

But then, a flicker of movement shattered the serenity. Something stirred behind a jagged boulder, barely visible against the stark white landscape. Ari's eyes locked on the figure, a hulking, monstrous silhouette far too enormous to be a man and far too substantial to be a trick of the light. It stood motionless as if carved from the very stone. Its presence loomed ominously, radiating a sense of danger.

Inside the vehicle, the interns saw nothing of this. They only saw Ari pause and glance around. The comm-link remained silent.

The creature's form rippled, shifting with the swirling snow, its outline blurred and unsettling. Two hollow black eyes, if they could even be called that, fixed on him, cold and calculating. Ari's pulse quickened, and his grip on the prototype rope tightened instinctively, the braided fibers digging into his gloves.

"A bear?" he muttered, his voice more hopeful than confident. "It's just a bear or possibly a wolf."

But he knew better. The figure's sheer size, its unnatural stillness, it wasn't a wolf. It was something else. Something ancient and hungry.

The wind howled across the ridge, whipping ice against Ari's face and rattling the carabiners on his harness. He took a step back, his mind racing. He forced himself to think logically.

He reassured himself that there was nothing out here but snow, rock, and wildlife, nothing that couldn't be explained.

And then it moved towards him. Aggressive steps. Silent. Purposeful. Closing the distance between them with an eerie grace that defied its size.

Ari's heart lurched. He could feel its heavy and predatory gaze boring into him as if measuring his worth. Fear clawed at his chest. He could run, but there was nowhere to go. He could fight, but against what? His rational mind faltered, and for a brief, paralyzing moment, Ari Keshet, master of control, conqueror of challenges, was powerless.

Then, without warning, the air shifted.

A dark blue mist, an aura, appeared between him and the creature. It shimmered like liquid night, swirling in an ethereal dance of light and shadow. The temperature around him seemed to warm in the presence of the mist. It was... calming and protective.

The creature halted mid-step. Its hollow black eyes narrowed, and a low, guttural growl rumbled deep within its chest. The monstrous form recoiled in the presence of the mysterious blue force. It lingered for a moment as if weighing its options, then slowly began to retreat, melting back into the snow and rock until it vanished altogether.

Ari stood frozen, his breath visible in the frigid air, the mist still hovering before him like a sentinel. He stared at it, his mind grappling for an explanation. Aurora phenomenon? Reflection off the ice? Some strange atmospheric anomaly?

The mist pulsed twice, as if acknowledging him, then dissipated into the wind, leaving no trace of its existence other than the temperature returning to frigid.

Ari blinked, the adrenaline still coursing through his veins. His rational mind seized the opportunity. A trick of the light. Fatigue. Nothing more. He forced a smirk, shaking his head. "Figures," he muttered. "Even the mountains are playing tricks on me now."

He pulled his hood tighter, eyes locked on the trail ahead. The next challenge waited. The next summit was his to claim. There was no room for mystery. No time for ghost stories. He was Ari Keshet, and he didn't look back.

He adjusted his gear, forcing confidence back into his stride. Whatever he'd seen... it was nothing. A shadow. A trick of light. He turned from the ridge's edge, leaving behind the place where ice and darkness whispered lies. But as he walked back to the vehicle, the wind rose, and with it, a low, haunting murmur. A voice, carried thin and cold across the ridge.

"Come and fight me... If you dare."

Ari froze mid-step. The voice was gone as suddenly as it had come. Something was watching... and it had just issued a challenge.

Whispers of Pride

The all-terrain vehicle rumbled as it headed back to the base camp down the icy slope, its reinforced tires gripping the treacherous path as though defying nature's attempts to shove it into oblivion. Ari Keshet held the wheel, driving with a casual confidence that would have stunned even the most seasoned off-road veterans. Outside, the Alaskan wilderness stretched into a monochrome canvas of ice and stone. Inside, the heater hummed, keeping the small cabin slightly warm, but not easing the tension that chilled the air.

In the back seat, Jacob darted his eyes nervously from window to window, as if he expected the mountain to lunge at them. Emily tried to hold her tablet steady as the vehicle skidded and jerked. Both of them were used to climate-controlled labs, not shifting snowbanks and subzero gusts.

Jacob cleared his throat, attempting to sound calm. "Mr. Keshet... sir," he began, his voice carrying a note of forced politeness. "I just wanted to say that was... quite a show up there. You really knew how to handle yourself on that ledge." He looked sideways at Emily, who nodded encouragingly as if they'd rehearsed this show of respect.

Ari caught Jacob's eye in the rear-view mirror and smirked. "You sound surprised, Jacob."

He sat up straighter. "Not surprised, sir. Just... impressed. Not many company CEOs would even attempt to test a prototype line in those conditions."

Ari's tone was matter-of-fact yet prideful, as if daring the world to challenge him. "Most people aren't like me."

Emily chimed in, her voice quieter but steady. "It's not every day you see a billionaire risking his life on a frozen cliff, sir. We're... not really used to that kind of approach."

Ari shrugged, the gesture casual. "That's the difference between leaders and followers. Leaders don't wait for perfect conditions. They create them."

In the back seat, the interns exchanged a look. They had read about Ari's reputation, how he demanded excellence and didn't tolerate excuses. Witnessing it firsthand in the relentless wilderness truly illuminated the reality behind his legend. They had expected a visionary strategist, not a man who danced with death as if it were a polite partner at a corporate gala.

The vehicle hit a patch of ice, jolting them sideways. Jacob's grip on the door handle tightened, and Emily clutched her tablet desperately. Ari didn't flinch, navigating the treacherous path like it was a city street.

"You two look like you've seen a ghost," Ari said with amusement in his tone.

Jacob forced a laugh, though the words wobbled on the way out. "Just not used to this kind of terrain, sir." What he didn't say was that back in the lab, the ground didn't crumble under your feet, the snacks and coffee were endless, and the only thing howling was Emily when the Wi-Fi lagged.

"Lab work doesn't change the world," Ari replied evenly. "Field-work does. Remember that."

"Yes, sir," they said in unison, swallowing any further comment.

As the vehicle rounded a final bend, SummitTek's base camp emerged: rows of modular structures glowing with warm light against the Alaskan sky. The camp's orderly presence promised civilization and safety, a beacon after the mountain's brutal test.

Ari parked near the main office and stepped out. The cold snapped at him, but he moved with easy confidence. Behind him, Jacob and Emily fumbled out of the vehicle.

Wrapped in their layers, they resembled a pair of overstuffed astronauts trying to navigate a foreign planet. Jacob waddled, arms stiff at his sides, his beanie slipping. Emily's oversized parka nearly swallowed her whole, her glasses fogging each time she breathed.

"I... I can't feel my legs," Jacob muttered, attempting another step and nearly losing his balance.

Emily managed a shaky laugh. "Three pairs of socks, and my toes are still numb," she said, eyeing her boots suspiciously.

Ari chuckled and asked, "Are you two planning to walk to the office, or are you going to roll there?"

Jacob forced a sheepish grin. "We're good, sir. Just... acclimating."

"Totally acclimating," Emily added, breath puffing into little clouds.

Ari shook his head and walked toward the cafeteria. Jacob and Emily shuffled after him, clumsy penguins in a world without their comforts. Inside, the warmth struck them like a blessing. The scent of gourmet espresso and a catered meal filled the room, a luxury from SummitTek in this harsh environment.

The interns hesitated at the spread of soups and sandwiches, wondering if they should indulge. Ari nodded toward the food. "Eat," he said, and that was enough. They piled their plates and settled into chairs, the tension in their shoulders easing slightly as they devoured the warmth of the room and the calories they desperately needed.

Ari speared a forkful of grilled trout and quinoa, the local specialty the team had been raving about. He chewed his food thoughtfully, his jaw tightening. Almost absently, he muttered under his breath, "It's not it."

Jacob glanced up from his plate, baffled. "Not what, sir?"

Ari waved him off without answering, setting his fork down with a soft clink. He wasn't even sure what he was searching for, only that it wasn't it.

Between bites, Jacob cleared his throat to draw attention to the research. "The rope... it held perfectly in the cold, sir. The data suggests minimal strain."

Emily nodded, tapping her tablet to pull up graphs. "And the grip was stable, no freezing or brittleness. We've got solid preliminary results."

Ari listened, satisfied. Their voices carried respect laced with awe, and he basked in it. After a while, he rose. "Good work. Keep compiling the data. I'll review it later."

"Yes, sir," they replied. As he stepped out, they watched him go, relief and admiration mingling in their eyes. Their boss was indeed everything the rumors claimed: brilliant, fearless, and undeniably prideful.

Ari walked to his private office, closing the door with a quiet click. The lively hum of conversation outside dissolved, replaced by the whisper of the heater. The space exuded understated power, minimalist décor, rich dark wood paneling, and a sleek mahogany desk polished to a mirror finish.

Behind the desk, framed photos of him climbing during his latest mountain triumph showcased his relentless ambition and spirit, a vibrant declaration of who he is. No matter the wilderness he conquered beyond these walls, this office was his domain, an empire (he believed he had built), one calculated risk at a time.

He loosened his jacket and pulled out his phone. Within moments, a video call connected, and Elinor Miller's face appeared on the screen. Her light green eyes, filled with warmth, met his gaze. The fireplace at her apartment danced behind her, softening the shadows.

"Ari!" she greeted him, her voice gentle and caring. "How's Alaska?"

"Cold," he said, smirking. "But I always manage it."

Her eyes searched his through the screen, finding humor and perhaps something else, an edge. "You always say that."

"Because it's always true," he teased, leaning into the chair with a confidence that never seemed to waver. "You know who you're talking to."

She laughed softly, her presence a balm he wouldn't openly admit he needed. "Ari Keshet: conqueror of mountains, fearless adventurer, CEO extraordinaire. Did I miss anything?"

He pretended to think, raising an eyebrow. "Exceptionally handsome?"

She rolled her eyes, smiling. "Exceptionally modest, too."

"Modesty is overrated," he said lightly, though the words carried a truth about his worldview; he thrived on pride. He leaned closer. "You miss me don't you?"

"Yes, I miss you," she said, her smile gentle but her gaze serious. "Feels like you've been gone forever."

"Only a couple of weeks," he replied, dismissing the weight of time. Yet he knew a few weeks felt longer out here in cold Alaska.

"Two weeks too long," she countered. "Just... be careful, and remember... I'm praying for you."

In his mind, another voice stirred, smooth and seductive... the voice of Stolz, the whisperer who had always propelled him forward. *"You don't need prayers. You need only yourself."* Stolz said this without a sound, shaping Ari's thoughts.

Ari forced a smile at Elinor. "Prayers always appreciated," he lied smoothly. In truth, he considered faith a distraction, something Stolz had taught him to view as a weakness.

"Don't show doubt," Stolz whispered.

Elinor noticed a dark flicker in his eyes. "Ari, you sure you're okay? You seem... distant all of a sudden."

"I'm fine," he assured, voice calm and collected. "Just thinking about the next challenge."

She nodded, concern lingering. "All right. Just... remember you're not alone. People care about you."

Ari's smile became more intense. "I know." He hesitated, sensing Stolz's influence hovering in his thoughts like a shadow.

"She doesn't have to know everything," Stolz argued. *"It will only make her worry and distract you from your successes."*

She gave him a soft smile, and they said their goodbyes.

As the screen went dark, Ari sat in silence. Stolz's whisper returned, *"You don't need anyone. Emotions and attachments weaken you. Focus on what matters: success, power, and control."*

Ari inhaled, staring at the photo of his last conquered peak. Pride swelled within him. He had always succeeded alone, bending conditions to his will. Yet something in Elinor's voice, in her gentle laughter, made him want more than just victory. He wanted her acceptance and warmth, and that desire bothered him.

"You don't need her," his tone smooth and laced with toxic confidence.

Ari clenched his jaw, the conflict gnawing at him. He wanted Elinor; he couldn't deny that, but letting himself get lost in those overly sweet, Hallmark movie thoughts felt ridiculous. Still, a part of him secretly didn't mind the indulgence, like sneaking a guilty pleasure. Shaking his head, he stood abruptly, brushing off the sentimentality before it could sink deeper. Pride was safer. Pride was predictable.

As he stepped out of the office into base camp, he carried his triumphs in his mind, and the quiet murmur of Stolz's counsel, ever coaxing him toward self-reliance and away from the sweet softness of Elinor for which he secretly craved.

Chapter 2

Fraulein Maria Gottschall

The SummitTek headquarters in downtown Denver was a sleek fortress of innovation, all glass and steel rising confidently into the city's skyline. Inside, cutting-edge technology hummed quietly while modern art installations adorned the halls. The staff, though crisp and professional in their attire, enjoyed comforts that rivaled five-star hotels. Productivity thrived here, fueled by gourmet coffee bars, catered meals, and a subtle culture of pampering that left no one wanting.

And why shouldn't it? SummitTek was a global powerhouse, and its people knew their worth. Every day offered new indulgences: pastries imported from Paris on Mondays, a pop-up gelato stand on Wednesdays, and today, a lavish lunch catered by one of Denver's finest bistros. In a world of fierce innovation and competition, SummitTek's employees lived like they had already won.

At the center of this well-oiled empire stood Fraulein Maria Gottschall, Chief Operations Officer and second-in-command to Ari Keshet himself. If Ari was the visionary force that drove SummitTek to conquer new summits, Gottschall was the one who ensured the machinery never faltered. She managed crises before they could be named, orchestrated logistics with near telepathic insight, and maintained an atmosphere where excellence was the only acceptable standard.

Towering at six feet, Gottschall was an imposing figure in a tailored black suit that proclaimed power without a word.

Her silver-gray hair was pinned into a no-nonsense bun, and her steel gray eyes surveyed every office corner like a high-powered radar. Employees didn't merely respect her; they revered her. She was the COO, the backbone of SummitTek's daily triumphs, and everyone knew it.

She strode into the conference room where a group of employees waited in anticipation. Lunchtime was five minutes away, and they were restless. The moment she appeared, the conversation hushed to whispers before cutting off entirely. Fraulein Gottschall didn't need to demand respect; it settled naturally around her like an aura.

"Lunch will be served in five minutes," she announced, her crisp German accent slicing through the anticipation like a knife. "And kindly refrain from stampeding. This isn't the Running of the Bulls in Pamplona."

A ripple of nervous laughter moved through the group. Everyone knew she was more than half-serious. She understood human nature all too well.

Near the back, two junior engineers whispered to each other. "Are there Wagyu sliders again?" one asked, barely containing his excitement. "I heard there's truffle mac and cheese," the other replied, eyes gleaming.

Their soft chatter didn't escape her notice. Gottschall's gaze snapped to them, just a raised eyebrow, no words needed. The engineers stiffened, caught like schoolboys passing notes.

One of the young engineers stammered, "We, uh... we love truffle mac and cheese," his voice cracking under the pressure of Gottschall's silence. Gottschall blinked once. Then she let out a sharp, unimpressed huff through her nose, a sound that somehow conveyed both disappointment and disdain.

"Charming," she said dryly. "Perhaps one day you'll graduate to actual protein... and a coherent pitch."

She turned back to her notes without another glance, leaving the poor engineer questioning both his diet and his career.

The double doors swung open on cue, and the catering staff paraded in with the feast. There was enough food to boost morale, fuel office gossip, and induce a collective food coma for at least a month. The employees' eyes widened as dish after dish was unveiled.

Gottschall inspected the setup critically, noting every detail before giving her verdict. "Acceptable," she pronounced. "You may proceed".

The employees needed no further invitation. They approached the buffet with both juvenile enthusiasm and unfailing good manners. No one wanted to test Gottschall's patience.

After confirming everything was in order, Gottschall rolled her eyes in annoyance at the employees' strained shenanigans and left for the conference room. She passed through the open office floor where clusters of innovators and strategists produced tomorrow's breakthroughs and headed toward Ari Keshet's private office. Despite Ari's absence on far-flung expeditions, she managed SummitTek's daily rhythm with effortless poise.

The Gatekeeper's Domain

At SummitTek's executive suite, the private elevator doors slid open with a soft chime, revealing a quiet, elegantly appointed foyer. Here, no one rushed. The hum of activity below felt distant, muffled by the plush carpeting and discreet lighting. In the center of this hushed space stood the executive secretary's desk, a sleek modern structure with smooth edges and a minimalist design.

This was the nerve center of the company's leadership tier, where visions were crafted, contracts were hammered out (always in SummitTek's favor), and information flowed, enhancing SummitTek's already soaring reputation.

In the center of this serene space sat Susan Richard's desk, the Executive Secretary and Administrator. Her desk was a command post and filter. Appointments were screened, schedules orchestrated, and critical information curated for leadership. Susan ensured the finer details flowed smoothly, despite Ari's sometimes erratic moods and visions.

Fraulein Maria Gottschall's office was near Susan's strategic command post, while Ari Keshet's corner office, radiating power and vision, was tucked deeper for privacy. This layout was purposeful; Ari, the summit seeker, enjoyed solitude, while Gottschall, the vigilant strategist, maintained an eagle-eye view at the entry.

Gottschall entered her office, leaving the foyer behind. The CEO's office was dramatic, but the COO's was disciplined. Her mahogany desk resembled a starship's control panel. Every item was meticulously placed, reflecting efficiency. Floor-to-ceiling windows provided a view of Denver's skyline, showcasing SummitTek's reach and her part in protecting its future.

The office balanced modern luxury with personal tokens. Delicate Hummel figurines sat on a shelf, a nostalgic nod to her Bavarian childhood. A finely carved cuckoo clock ticked in perfect rhythm, a tribute to Old World craftsmanship, a timeless contrast to the sleek, high-tech surroundings.

On her desk sat a small but striking piece, a silver Star of David paperweight perched gracefully on a sleek black leather coaster. More than décor, it was a declaration of heritage and loyalty. Since Ari's late grandfather, Reuben, Maria Gottschall has proudly guided the Keshet family through decades of change. To her, this wasn't just a job. The Keshets were more than employers; they were like family. The star was her silent vow, symbolizing her faith and duty to protect them. She had witnessed Reuben's relentless ambition to succeed. She had watched Ari's father, Abner, build a legacy with his iron will.

And now, she saw Ari's restless search for something bigger and better, something to conquer, even if it was his own internal demons.

Through it all, she had remained the steady force, ensuring that both the company and the family survived. However, deep in her gut, she knew Ari and Abner were destined for a disastrous conflict, an encounter between innovation and tradition. She could feel the tremors beneath the surface, the kind that foreshadowed a fracture too deep to repair.

Her eyes flicked to the photo beside her screen, Ari at thirteen, a young man filled with awkwardness and spunk. She had straightened that crooked tie countless times. As she scanned the latest expedition update, she wondered what situations Ari had put himself into today that she would have to "straighten up". Shaking her head, she was surprised to feel both frustration with Ari and a love, like that of an aunt for her nephew.

Her fingers tapped the desk, once, twice, three times, then, with a steadying breath, she took her place in the high-backed chair like a conductor before a symphony. Regal, composed, and sharp. Gottschall perched with the poise of an eagle, ready to orchestrate order and catch the slightest misstep.

Beyond the executive suite, SummitTek sounded like a garage band mid-rehearsal, ambitious, noisy, and always chasing the next big sound. But inside SummitTek's command center, order reigned. She conducted a silent symphony of precision, her fingers gliding across the keyboard with practiced grace as she reviewed emails, project updates, and operational reports. Every detail was finely orchestrated, and every detail mattered.

A soft chime broke her thoughts, an email from Elinor Miller inquiring about Ari. Gottschall smiled. She liked Elinor. There was a goodness about the woman, an integrity that wasn't performance. Unlike others who circled Ari for power or influence, Elinor wanted nothing but the man himself. Gottschall respected that. She trusted her.

She considered replying, but decided Ari should handle it himself. Still, as she returned to her tasks, a rare flicker of approval for Elinor remained.

Just as Gottschall was about to return to her work, there was a hesitant knock at her office door. She barely had time to glance up before it swung open, revealing a young engineer from the executive conference room. He was grinning, a napkin still tucked in his collar, a plate of sliders held precariously, and his eyes wide with enthusiasm.

"Fraulein Gottschall," he blurted, breathless with excitement, "You must try the truffle mac and cheese. It's... life-changing."

For a moment, a cringy silence stretched between them.

Gottschall blinked, expression unreadable. She looked at him over the rim of her glasses, unimpressed. "I am not in the habit of having my life changed by... cheese."

The engineer, so caught up in the culinary revelation, didn't immediately register the graveyard of etiquette he had just tap-danced across.

Then, realization dawned. His face paled. His posture stiffened. He had just barged into Gottschall's office, Gottschall... the woman who ran SummitTek with the precision of a Swiss timepiece, to gush about... pasta!

"I, I mean," he stammered, suddenly very aware of the immense miscalculation in his life choices. "I just... wanted to say thank you for approving the catering budget..." His voice trailed off like a fading radio signal.

Gottschall stared at him for an excruciating second longer before she spoke, her tone perfectly level. "Duly noted."

Clutching his plate of sliders as if they were contraband, the naïve engineer nodded stiffly, backpedaling toward the door. "Right. Okay. Umm...enjoy your, um... day."

Gottschall rolled her eyes and sighed. The staff was talented but sometimes too quickly enamored by SummitTek's indulgences. Shaking her head, she returned to her computer screen. She had survived boardroom wars, corporate espionage, and financial crises. But somehow, nothing ever prepared her for the sheer audacity of the under-30s.

Her phone buzzed; Ari was calling to check in. She answered with her usual calm, composed tone. "Mr. Keshet, everything is proceeding as planned," she reported smoothly. "The field test data is being compiled. The team, well-fed and content. If they get any more spoiled, we'll be putting them down for naps like kindergartners."

Ari's voice crackled through. "Excellent. Remember, when a team feels appreciated, they become more productive!"

Gottschall allowed herself the barest hint of a smile, though her voice remained measured. "Of course, Mr. Keshet. But please remember, there's a fine line between rewarding them and letting them grow complacent. Indulgence, if left unchecked, can dull motivation."

A brief silence hummed over the line before Ari responded with a chuckle. "And that's precisely why you're the COO, Maria. You see the dangers even in our comforts. You know how to strike the balance."

She tilted her head, "Indeed, sir," she said evenly. Then, choosing her following words carefully, before ending the call, she added, "I'll ensure they stay sharp and satisfied... and awake."

As she ended the call, she tapped her nail firmly against the desk.

Ari wanted loyalty through luxury. She wanted loyalty through discipline. Employees stayed because of purpose, because they were invested in the company's mission, not because they had access to Wagyu sliders and imported saffron in their lunch specials.

And that was where she and Ari differed. He believed motivation could be bought, but she maintained that it had to be fostered with a clear mission and vision.

Gottschall knew better than to confront him directly. Although Ari Keshet remained the powerhouse behind SummitTek, his arrogance would eventually catch up to him. He constantly tested boundaries in business and life. Someday, one of those boundaries would push back, and she might not be there to fix it.

And some influences were beyond her reach. Like the unheard murmurs that inflated Ari's self-esteem, they were simply out of her control. From time to time, she felt a sinister energy lurking at the reckless edges of Ari's aspirations. During a moment of Ari's inattention, she had heard him mutter the name Stolz, and she wondered if that was the malevolent spirit's name.

She leaned back in her chair, thinking about when that moment of crisis would come. She hoped to be ready, prepared to step in and ensure the company remained strong, even if Ari stumbled. With a satisfied sigh, Gottschall returned to her work, her mind already strategizing the next move.

Home Sweet Headquarters

The SummitTek Gulfstream G700 taxied to a smooth stop at Denver International Airport. Inside, Jacob and Emily were nearly vibrating with excitement, not because of any groundbreaking research, but because they were finally back in civilization.

Jacob stretched dramatically in his plush leather seat, groaning like he'd aged decades in a few weeks. "Ahhh... It's good to be back," he declared. "I never thought I'd miss Colorado so much."

Wrapped in a blanket she'd discreetly "borrowed" from the plane, Emily nodded fervently. "I still can't fathom why anyone chooses to live in Alaska. It's nature's freezer, and zero ice cream. You know what I missed most?"

Jacob perked up. "Uh, warm toilets?"

"Absolutely!" Emily shouted, her eyes wide. "Can you imagine the number of layers I had to take off each time I went to the bathroom? It felt like unwrapping an Egyptian mummy, such a complicated process."

Across from them, Ari Keshet sat quietly. He kept his gaze on the window, taking in the city lights of Denver. His mind drifted to that towering figure he'd glimpsed in Alaska, the hulking shape by the boulder. Not a bear, that was certain. But what was it? A trick of the cold, or something more unsettling?

"You could go back," Stolz's voice murmured in his thoughts, smooth and seductive. *"Face it. Conquer it. Who else could?"*

Ari set the idea aside as Emily persisted with her amusing rant.

He would reflect on it later.

"And the Wi-Fi!" Emily groaned, shaking her hands in a gesture of exaggerated horror. "I was one buffering wheel away from sending actual smoke signals!"

Jacob nodded solemnly. "Downloading a file felt like waiting in line at the DMV. By the time it finished, I was mentally planning my retirement party."

As though in a theatrical scene, Emily dramatically exclaimed, "Oh, you poor, courageous soul! How did you survive?"

Jacob dramatically shrugged. "I acted like any brave man; I quietly sobbed into my mittens."

Emily's laughter tinkled through the cabin. Ari rolled his eyes, annoyed by their continuous banter.

"First, a hot shower, then lunch. Maybe another lunch after that." She brightened. "I heard today's menu is French cuisine. Macarons, Jacob, macarons!"

Ari raised an eyebrow, humoring them. "You act like you dream about food!"

She didn't miss a beat. "Constantly. Especially after living on trail mix all week."

Jacob exhaled dramatically. "If I never see another peanut again, it'll be too soon." Then, with a pointed look at Ari, he added, "Speaking of traumatic experiences, sir, if I ever write a memoir, there will be an entire chapter dedicated to how you nearly killed me. Twice."

Emily, still wrapped in the airline blanket, shook her head. "Twice? Try... 500 times!"

Jacob nodded thoughtfully. "Yeah, that seems more accurate. Although it's tough to keep track when your life is flashing before your eyes."

She laughed softly while Ari remained quiet, gazing out the window with a troubled expression.

"Totally right..., Sir?" Emily offered more cautiously.

Ari turned around, sharing words of worldly wisdom with the bantering interns... "Survival builds character."

The laughter faded. Something had shifted.

Jacob leaned forward, studying him more seriously now. "You really believe that, don't you?"

Ari met his gaze without hesitation. "I don't just believe it, I know it. Playing it safe doesn't build anything worth remembering. Discovery demands risk."

She rolled her eyes but couldn't quite hide her curiosity. "And what exactly are you building, sir? Because this isn't just about ropes and tents. There's something else driving you."

Ari hesitated, but only for a second. "Let's just say I don't intend to play it safe. Discoveries are made with calculated risk."

Jacob and Emily exchanged a look. For all their sarcasm, they both knew this wasn't just another CEO obsessed with his company; Ari thrived on risk in a way most people didn't. Whatever was pushing him forward was bigger than just product testing.

The flight attendant swung open the door, allowing the fresh Denver air to rush in. Ari stood up, reaching for his bag. "Welcome back," he called out behind him. "Enjoy your downtime; the next adventure will be even tougher."

Jacob groaned sarcastically. "Fantastic... Can't wait."

Emily let out a sigh, her voice tinged with frustration. "I swear, if I encounter one more ice ledge just sitting there..." As they trailed Ari down the steps, the humor diminished a bit. Deep down, they realized that whatever lay ahead, Ari had no intention of stopping. Whether they appreciated it or not, they were in for the journey.

They disembarked and made their way through the private terminal. Outside, an SUV waited to whisk them back to SummitTek HQ. Ari followed the interns slowly, his eyes drifting to the distant peaks. The memory of that eerie figure in Alaska tugged at him, and something restless lingered in his chest.

He remembered the voice in the cold, Alaskan wind.

"Come and fight me... If you dare."

The challenge haunted him.

Then Stolz whispered in his mind, *"You felt its gaze, its intent. It was challenging you. It's waiting for you to return and confront it."*

Ari's jaw tightened. He dismissed the thought with a shake of his head. "Nothing," he murmured to himself. "It was nothing." Yet the intrigue gnawed at him.

"Sir?" Emily's voice pulled him back as she looked at him. "You alright? You've been quiet."

"I'm fine," Ari said, forcing a reassuring smile.

Continuing the conversation, Jacob flashed a grin. "I totally get it. After this grueling expedition, let's just embrace comfort. Gottschall's got HQ running like clockwork. Imagine... a warm office and gourmet lunch with no frozen fingers."

Emily nodded enthusiastically. "I swear, I might just kiss the office floor when we get back. Is that weird?"

Jacob pretended to consider it, tapping his chin thoughtfully. "A little weird. But honestly? After this, I might join you."

They laughed, and even Ari managed a quiet muse. Yet, as the SUV glided onto the highway, his gaze drifted to the snowy ridges far off on the horizon. Stolz's whisper threaded through his thoughts.

"You don't belong in safety and comfort. The unknown calls you. Push the limits!"

Ari exhaled slowly, ignoring Stolz for now. Denver's skyline grew larger, promising familiar routines and luxuries. Jacob and Emily were already debating desserts, macarons versus crème brûlée, an argument as light and sweet as their relief at being back.

As they neared SummitTek HQ, Ari silently acknowledged Stolz's hint: the unknown still beckoned somewhere beyond the warmth of civilization. He might return to face it. For now, he would savor the comforts, meet with Gottschall, review the data, and keep this secret curiosity locked away until the mountain's call grew too insistent to ignore.

Chapter 3

The Return

News of Ari Keshet's return from Alaska swept through SummitTek's headquarters like a spark across dry tinder. While his private SUV rolled into the underground garage, whispers and speculation raced along the halls. Everyone had heard the rumors: he'd tested new prototypes on sheer ice, dared conditions that would send most climbers packing, and now he was back. For SummitTek's staff, Ari's ventures weren't mere field tests; they were the source of company lore, stories they could tell each other with awe. Here was a CEO who didn't just talk innovation, he lived it.

In the sleek atrium, employees moved with a heightened sense of purpose. The hum of productivity took on the edge of excitement. In an open concept workspace on the third floor, a group of engineers and designers hovered around a holographic display of the *Titan Tent*, Ari's latest triumph.

"Did you hear?" Bob from R&D asked, voice low and charged with enthusiasm. "He tested it on an ice wall in Alaska. Set up in under thirty seconds, no manual drilling needed."

Bill grinned, rotating the 3D model with a flick of his hand. "It anchored itself right into the rock. No stabilizers. This is going to change mountaineering, Bob."

"Mountaineering?" Bob laughed softly. "Think bigger... military contracts, and lunar expeditions. We are talking the invention of the year!"

A rising current of pride and ambition ran through the team. They knew Ari demanded excellence, and he got it. This was SummitTek's culture: relentless, proud, and fueled by vision.

Meanwhile, Ari stepped from the SUV flanked by Jacob and Emily. The interns chatted about the Titan Tent's potential applications, eyes shining with possibility, but Ari's thoughts started drifting elsewhere. He nodded farewell absently to them as he entered the executive elevator, the doors sliding shut with a whisper.

Ari caught a glimpse of himself inside the elevator in the mirrored walls. His dark hair was slightly tousled from the trip, and his tailored jacket concealed an athletic frame honed by countless challenges. He looked every bit like the adventurer-CEO who had just returned from wrestling with nature itself. Yet beneath this confident exterior, a different tension simmered.

The thought of Elinor.

Her name drifted into his mind like a warm breeze. The days had stretched into eternity without her presence, laughter, and simple faith in God... which he never fully understood but always found grounding. The Alaskan nights had amplified the echo of her absence. He hated to admit it, but he missed her deeply.

The elevator chimed, and the doors opened onto the top executive floor. Susan, the Executive Secretary, greeted him as he stepped onto the plush carpeting. Other employees working on a project in the conference room immediately paused their tasks to take turns greeting Ari.

A project manager approached with a bright smile. "Mr. Keshet! Welcome back! How was Alaska?"

"Challenging," Ari replied, acknowledging the enthusiasm politely. "But productive." He moved into the suite with purposeful strides, offering nods and brief handshakes. His attention drifted toward Gottschall's office, which had its door slightly ajar.

Gottschall rose from her desk at his entrance to her office. "You've returned," Gottschall said, stepping forward. "I trust the trip was a success?"

Ari cocked his head. "It was Maria. The Titan Tent and the new gear performed beyond expectations."

A flicker of satisfaction lit Gottschall's steel-gray eyes. "The team will be pleased. I'll see that the results are disseminated promptly."

"Do that... and Maria, there's something else," Ari's voice softened.

The CEO's mask slipping just enough to reveal the man beneath. "I'd like Elinor brought here from her apartment... if she's available."

Gottschall's expression remained unchanged, but her understanding was evident. She knew Ari better than anyone; she knew when his ambitions gave way to personal longing. "I'll see it arranged immediately," she said, not bothering with questions. She reached for her phone. "She'll be here soon."

Minutes later, a sleek SummitTek SUV pulled up to one of Denver's modest brick apartment buildings. Darren and Chloe, two of Ari's most trusted staff, stepped out and headed to the second floor. They knocked at Elinor's apartment, and moments later, Elinor Miller opened the door. She wore her brown hair loosely braided, a simple sweater, faded jeans, and her ever-present cowboy boots.

"Elinor Miller," Darren greeted, courteous and professional. "Mr. Keshet has requested to see you at headquarters, if you're available."

Elinor's heart fluttered, despite Maria having already called her to give her a heads-up. Now, just as suddenly as Ari had vanished into the wilderness, he wanted to see her again. "Of course," she managed, slipping on her coat and grabbing her playful, floral-print backpack.

Elinor's reflection flickered in the tinted glass as the SUV carried her toward SummitTek's tower. She felt a mix of excitement and a hint of worry. She'd missed Ari deeply. He was her best friend, if she dared to admit it to herself, and someone whose faith she prayed would one day find root in something more stable than ambition. Now he was back, and she wondered what he would say, what he had seen and done.

On the top floor of SummitTek, Ari waited, his thoughts wandering to Elinor. Her essence represented a unique bond, unmarred by ambition or gain. He glanced at Gottschall's office, assured she would manage the details with discretion. He envisioned Elinor stepping into the lobby below, the elevator softly chiming as it ascended to this private space.

Outside the executive suite, the city twinkled. Ari found himself balancing between two realms: the technology empire he believed he had built with pride and the genuine sincerity Elinor represented. As he anticipated her arrival, he acknowledged, if only to himself, that her warmth could provide the equilibrium he sought, a gentle counterpoint to Stolz's relentless murmurs of ambition.

Reunited

At SummitTek's top floor, Ari Keshet stood by the floor-to-ceiling windows of his corner office. The Denver skyline stretched out before him, each glittering light a reminder of the empire he believed he had built. But today, that display of power and progress was a blur as he focused on the black SUV pulling up at the building's entrance far below.

A gentle warmth stirred within him. Weeks had passed since he'd last seen her, but the ache of that absence had made it feel like a lifetime. Turning away from the window, he waited impatiently as Elinor made her way through the building to him. He eagerly faced the door as it swung open.

Elinor entered, and her eyes found him at once. "Hey," she said softly, her voice steady and warm.

"Hey," Ari replied, allowing his usual guarded composure to soften as he allowed her presence to produce a smile. For a moment, the weight of Alaska, SummitTek's demands, and the world beyond these walls faded away. She was here and it felt right.

Elinor stepped closer, bringing a quiet calm to the room that Ari couldn't ignore. She tilted her head slightly, her discerning gaze fixed on his face as if she could read his every thought. "You look... different," she said softly, her voice laced with curiosity and understanding. "Like you've been through something."

Ari hesitated, unsure how much he wanted to reveal, but her steady eyes seemed to see past the walls he was so used to hiding behind. It was almost unnerving how she seemed to know exactly what he was feeling without him saying a word.

Ari offered a small, bashful smile. "You could say that."

Her hand rose to touch his arm, the warmth of her touch cutting through his lingering tension. "Do you want to talk about it?"

He glanced down at her hand, savoring the comfort it brought. "I will," he said, voice soft. "But first... do you remember the first time we met?"

Elinor's eyes brightened at the memory. "How could I forget? The Negev desert, three years ago."

Ari nodded, nostalgia flickering across his features. "You were using your botany and geology expertise while working for the Desert Bloom Initiative, turning barren lands green. I showed up for a photo-op, just the big donor playing benefactor."

Elinor smiled, her gaze drifting somewhere far away. "You looked so out of place in that expensive suit. Do you remember that sandstorm hit right after taking photos?"

Ari chuckled. "Dry-clean only. Completely impractical. Yet I stayed and helped cover the seedlings. I couldn't just leave you all struggling, not when I was curious about what you were doing."

Elinor's smile turned gentle. "At first, I thought you were pretending to be interested. But then I saw you really cared. You asked so many questions and tried to understand. That's when I caught a glimpse of who you truly were beneath the billionaire's veneer."

Ari's eyes met hers, sincerity glowing in the quiet space. "And I saw you. Not just the botanist in the desert, but someone interesting... different than I'm used to."

She reached for his hand, their fingers intertwining. "You've always had a way of surprising me, Ari."

"Good surprises, I hope."

She teased him with a light laugh. "The best."

They stood together, letting memory and presence blend into a comforting silence. For now, the harsh Alaskan expeditions, the grand halls of SummitTek, and the relentless push for innovation all receded. At this moment, it was just them.

"You know," Ari began softly. "I never told you why I stayed in that desert dust storm."

Elinor tilted her head. "Why?"

Ari's voice dropped to a near-whisper. Vulnerability pushing his limits. "Because you looked at me like I was more than just a name on a check. You saw me, and I didn't want to leave."

Her eyes shone, and her thumb brushed lightly over his hand. "I still see you, Ari."

His heart tightened at her words, an unexpected tenderness reaching through his armor of pride. "I still don't want to leave," he murmured, voice barely above a whisper.

She leaned closer, her presence grounding him in a way nothing else could.

Ari exhaled, tension easing from his shoulders. "I want you to be there for me," he said, vulnerability tracing every syllable.

"I'm here," Elinor replied, quiet but firm. "I'm not going anywhere."

They stood like that, the hush of the office wrapping around them. For a moment, he allowed himself to rest in her presence, not in the glory of triumph or the thrill of the next conquest, but in the simple truth that she cared.

Tranquility lingered, delicate and genuine. Yet, as always, it was temporary.

"She's a distraction, Ari." The voice slipped into his mind as smoothly as silk over steel. Stolz.

Ari's grip on Elinor's hand tightened slightly. He'd hoped Stolz, his unseen whisperer of pride and ambition, would remain silent. But Stolz never stayed quiet for long.

"You can't afford distractions," Stolz purred, each word a scalpel. *"Empires fall because of them. Empires like yours, built on focus and strength."*

Elinor sensed the change, concern creasing her brow. "Ari?" she asked softly. "You okay?"

He forced a smile, though it didn't reach his eyes. "Just tired," he lied. "Long trip."

"Liar," Stolz chided in his mind. *"You don't tire. Not if you want to stay on top."*

Elinor squeezed his hand reassuringly. "Then rest," she suggested. "You don't have to do everything alone."

Her kindness made Stolz's voice hiss. *"Hear her? Offering rest. Weakness. You are not weak, Ari."*

Ari swallowed, caught in the tug-of-war inside. Pride built an empire on relentless drive and ambition. What would happen if he genuinely let himself rely on someone else?

"I know I don't have to do everything," he said softly, uncertain if he was speaking more to Elinor or Stolz.

She smiled gently. "Exactly. You have a whole team, and you have me. You're not alone."

Stolz's whisper sank deeper into Ari's thoughts. *"She'll make you soft. Empires need hardness and edge. Don't let her lull you into complacency."*

Ari's eyes flicked back to Elinor's face. Despite Stolz's insistent murmuring, he wanted this warmth, this genuine care that balanced his pride with humility. Maybe he needed her more than Stolz would ever allow him to admit.

"I missed you," Elinor said quietly, the words simple and honest.

Ari didn't reply, despite the storm inside.

For now, he would let her reassure him, let her kindness push back against Stolz's poison. He knew the struggle wasn't over, Stolz would return, and the mountain still called. But Elinor's presence offered another path: one of trust, of sharing burdens, of acknowledging that maybe, just maybe, he didn't have to conquer alone.

Ari held her hand, feeling his heart settle for a moment. Tomorrow, he would face new battles, both in the boardroom and in his own mind. But tonight, he was back home in Denver, and she was with him in the moment, and that was enough for now.

The Keshet Residence, New York City

In the heart of New York's Upper West Side, the Keshet family's brownstone home stirred quietly to life. Soft morning light filtered through tall windows, reflecting off polished surfaces and meticulous decor that spoke of decades of careful cultivation, of fortunes earned and legacies forged.

Inside the master bedroom, Abner Keshet stood before a full-length mirror, adjusting the knot of his conservative navy tie. At seventy, he still carried the commanding air of a man who had long conquered boardrooms. But today, a subtle unease hovered around him, creasing his brow as he struggled for the proper symmetry.

"Where are my cuff links, Iris?" Abner called out in his distinct New York accent, a note of impatience edging his tone.

Iris Keshet, his wife of over forty years, drifted into the room with serene grace. Her silver-streaked dark brown hair was pulled back in a simple yet elegant twist. She wore a modest, earth-toned dress and a delicate Star of David pendant resting against her chest, a quiet testament to faith and heritage. Meeting his eyes in the mirror, her gentle patience stood in contrast to his tense energy.

"Abner, if they're not in the valet on your dresser," she offered softly, "maybe you left them in the bathroom."

"I checked the bathroom," Abner grumbled, opening and closing drawers with frustration. "It's like the things grew legs and walked away."

Iris crossed her arms, leaning against the doorway, amusement dancing in her warm brown eyes. "Did you check the second drawer? The one you always put them in for safekeeping while you get ready?" Abner paused, realization flickering over his face. Within seconds, he strode into the en suite bathroom, tugged open the second drawer, and there they were, patiently awaiting rediscovery.

"Aha, found them!" Abner declared, returning to the bedroom triumphantly as if this minor victory restored order in his universe. He started to put them on his cuffs, then frowned. "I can't find my lucky socks either," he added.

Iris watched him, shaking her head with a fond smile. "We have been together for a long time; without me, you'd be lost."

He glanced at her reflection, his expression softening. "Not just lost. I'd be a complete mess." The admission hung in the air, a gentle acknowledgment of how she balanced his driven nature with steady devotion.

She stepped forward, placing a light hand on his shoulder. "We've always done this together, haven't we? You brought security and a future; I kept the household affairs running smoothly." Her voice held gentle pride in their shared legacy.

Abner's eyes met hers in the mirror, vulnerability flickering briefly. "Yes, we have," he agreed quietly. "I couldn't have done it without you." Then, as if remembering a duty, he straightened his shoulders. "I need to catch my flight to Denver. SummitTek's board meeting won't run itself."

Iris's smile dimmed slightly. "Don't push Ari too hard, Abner. He's forging his own path. It might not be the one you would've chosen, but he's still our son. He needs our guidance now, not our worry." Then, with a teasing glint, she added, "And maybe a little nudge toward a nice Jewish girl wouldn't hurt."

Abner gave a faint, noncommittal grunt, but his expression darkened as he turned back to the mirror. His cuff link slipped, clattering against the dresser.

"He's not thinking clearly," he muttered. "Field-testing prototypes himself, scaling ice walls alone... That's not leadership, it's a spectacle. He's chasing danger like it's a virtue." He paused, voice tightening. "And he's being... swayed. Emerging voices, fresh directions. Ones I'm unfamiliar with."

Iris stepped in gently, her tone quiet but firm. "He's searching, Abner. And that search might look messy. But maybe that's how he finds what truly matters for himself." Iris squeezed his hand, catching his gaze. "Keep an open mind. He needs you, Abner. He needs to know he's not alone in this journey."

For a moment, Abner's mask of control slipped. He considered his wife's words and the weight of years of strained father-son tension. He nodded, a flicker of resolution lighting his eyes. "I'll try, Iris. For him. For us."

Just then, his phone buzzed on the dresser.

He frowned and picked it up. "It's Henry, from the board." Iris gave him a curious look as he answered. "Henry?"

The voice on the other end was crisp, businesslike. "Morning, Abner. Apologies for the early call, but I thought you should know that there's concern building among the board... about Ari."

Abner straightened. "Concern?"

Henry didn't hesitate. "Your son is undeniably impressive, but he tends to be reckless. Some think he's chasing thrills instead of strategy. We're worried he's becoming more of a hype, a brand, rather than a leader."

Abner's jaw tensed as he defended his son. "He's a visionary. Risk is part of leadership."

"Vision is crucial, but caution matters too," Henry stated. "Just think about it, Abner. We definitely don't want to find ourselves in a situation where we're scraping your son's body off the side of a mountain someday."

There was a long pause; Henry hung up, and the line went dead. Abner abruptly put the phone down, staring at it like it had insulted him.

Iris observed him intently. "Well?"

He exhaled, tension etched deep in his brow. "They think Ari is becoming too reckless."

"Do you think that?" she asked quietly.

"I think..." He paused, choosing his words carefully. "I think he's becoming everything I raised him to be. But maybe too much of it, all at once."

A car horn blared from the street below, snapping the moment like a twig.

"That's your ride," She reached into her pocket and pulled out his lucky socks, navy blue, finely knitted, arguably no more fortunate than ordinary ones, but essential to his ritual. "Here. But remember, you don't need luck, you only need faith."

He tucked the socks into his bag, grabbed his briefcase, and started for the door. But at the threshold, he paused, turned back, and looked at Iris. Gratitude flickered in his eyes, mixed with something heavier. The moment was quiet, charged with emotion. He stepped forward and kissed her goodbye.

"Don't forget to call tonight," she reminded him. "I won't forget," Abner said, his voice softer.

The door closed behind him, and Iris stood in the stillness of their home. She thought of her son, brilliant, proud, and still searching for something no legacy could provide. As sunlight crept further into the room, she prayed silently for healing between a father and son. She hoped that Ari would discover his true purpose, wherever his path might lead.

SummitTek Boardroom – The Next Day

The SummitTek boardroom embodied sleek sophistication: panoramic windows framed a spectacular view of Denver's skyline, and a polished mahogany table stretched grandly across the room. Around it, leather chairs were occupied by the company's top executives, each keenly aware that this meeting would shape the next chapter of SummitTek's success story.

A tray of crafted hors d'oeuvres floated by, delivered by the private chef team. Ari chose a smoked salmon tartlet, critiquing it before taking a bite.

He chewed once, twice, then exhaled sharply through his nose. "It's not it," he said under his breath, pushing the plate away.

From across the room, Maria Gottschall observed Ari criticizing the food. What is he looking for? She wondered to herself but pushed that question to the back of her mind and focused on the meeting's agenda.

At the head of the table, Ari was dressed as if he had stepped out of a prominent men's magazine. His confidence radiated from him as he exchanged greetings and small talk with the board members. His presence, calm yet assertive, commanded the room effortlessly.

Seated to his right was Abner, Ari's father. Although officially retired, Abner's demeanor spoke volumes about his enduring influence. His mere presence made the executives sit a fraction straighter. Two generations of Keshets, each formidable in their own way, shared the helm of this family empire.

Today's agenda focused on SummitTek's newest innovations, the *Titan Tent* and *Titan Rope System*, designed to revolutionize high-altitude expeditions with unprecedented durability and weather resistance. The atmosphere was charged with anticipation, and every executive harbored high expectations.

Ari cleared his throat and addressed the assembly. "Ladies and gentlemen, we stand on the cusp of a breakthrough. The Titan Tent and the accompanying gear promise to redefine high-altitude climbing. Our projections estimate a large increase in market share within the first year of launch."

He paused, letting the announcement settle into their minds amid appreciative murmurs. "But before we proceed to mass production, we must ensure our product's performance in extreme conditions."

He turned his attention to a pair of visitors seated across the table, representatives from AndesCon, a prominent Peruvian mountaineering company. Their presence underscored the significance of the next steps.

"We are pleased to have AndesCon partnering with us," Ari continued. "They bring invaluable expertise in extreme terrain, particularly along the Andes Mountain ridges. I now invite Mr. Diego Vargas, director of AndesCon, to present their proposal."

Diego Vargas, weathered by countless climbs, respectfully inclined his head. "Thank you, Mr. Keshet. SummitTek's innovations align perfectly with what the climbing community has sought for decades. Our proposal is straightforward: a two-week field test in the Andes among South America's most challenging and unforgiving terrains. The data and feedback we gather will be valuable in refining the Titan series before its commercial release."

The board members exchanged glances, nodding and murmuring their approval. Abner leaned back, a subtle flicker of pride mingling with worry crossing his features.

Henry leaned on the table, folding his hands with deliberate precision. His tone was polite, but the edge beneath it was unmistakable. "And who exactly will be leading the SummitTek team during these field tests?"

The question hovered, drawing a ripple of shifting glances around the boardroom. Most already suspected the answer, but Henry wanted it said aloud.

Ari met his gaze squarely. "I'll do it."

A brief silence followed, tight, expectant.

Henry arched an eyebrow. "You will be on the ice yourself?"

"I believe in the product," Ari said coolly. "If we're asking others to trust their lives to it, I should do the same."

"Yes," Stolz murmured, velvet and venom in his mind. *"Let them squirm in their seats while you rise above them. You were not made to follow, you were made to lead."*

Henry sat back slowly, steepling his fingers. "That's bold," he said, voice carefully measured. "Though some might argue it's impulsive. CEOs don't usually put themselves at the mercy of unpredictable elements. That's what field engineers and team leads are for."

A few heads nodded subtly.

"Listen to them," Stolz sneered. *"They fear risk because they don't know how to conquer it. But not you. You don't ask, you command it."*

Ari's smile was thin. "This isn't about protocol. It's about credibility."

Henry didn't blink. "Or public perception, perhaps?"

The tension thickened.

Abner shifted in his seat but said nothing, his expression unreadable.

Henry allowed the silence to linger momentarily before saying, "I bring this up because I've witnessed the consequences when leaders prioritize their personal narrative over the company's strategy."

Ari stood, unbothered, at least outwardly. But inside, Stolz was like liquid fire in his bloodstream.

"Let them talk. While they hedge bets and take notes, you'll be out there proving you're still the strongest man in the room. Just like always."

"As I lead the team into this field test, I'll be recommending we bring on a consulting geologist to assess the tension requirements of the self-anchoring mechanism across diverse soil and rock formations in the Andes." Ari stood before the board, his confidence filling the room like a practiced keynote.

The board members took a moment to discuss the proposal in hushed tones. Afterward, a wave of relief and gratitude swept through the room.

Abner arched an eyebrow, his expression tightening as he finally caught on to exactly who Ari had in mind for the so-called "consulting geologist."

"You're volunteering to lead this expedition yourself?" he asked, his tone sharp with irritation. He exhaled sharply, his patience wearing thin.

Ari calmly met his father's glare. "Yes, I need to experience it firsthand. I'll lead the SummitTek team in Peru, collaborating with AndesCon and the geologist."

Diego Vargas smiled, clearly impressed. "A bold move, Mr. Keshet. We look forward to your leadership in the field."

With that, approval swept through the boardroom: the partnership with AndesCon and the field tests were all green-lit. The Titan Tent and Rope System would soon face the Andes, with Ari Keshet standing large at the helm of the challenge.

As the meeting concluded, the executives filed out in clusters, their voices buzzing with optimism. Ari remained behind, basking briefly in the afterglow of approval. But across the room, Abner didn't move. He stood with arms crossed, his sharp gaze fixed on his son, not with pride, but with a simmering irritation barely concealed beneath professional restraint.

"You're leading the expedition yourself," Abner said flatly, more statement than question.

Ari met his eyes, "If we're asking others to trust the equipment..."

His father cut him off, "Yeah, yeah, yeah. You're not a brand, Ari. You're a CEO, a leader." Abner's jaw clenched. "This company doesn't need a stuntman, it needs a strategist who leads."

Ari didn't flinch. "Sometimes, the best strategy is proving we're willing to take the same risks we expect of others."

His father shook his head, exhaling through his nose. "Or maybe you just enjoy being the center of attention, showboating?"

The silence hung heavy between them.

"You're chasing headlines, and that's a dangerous game," Abner warned.

Stolz whispered, his voice curling through Ari's thoughts like smoke. *"He built walls, you build empires. You don't need his approval. You only need victory."*

Ari turned away without another word, his expression unreadable. But inside, his pride burned hotter than ever.

Elinor's Dream

Morning light slipped through Elinor Miller's sheer curtains, painting faint patterns on the walls. Yet the gentle dawn did little to calm her racing heart. She'd awakened moments ago, breath ragged, skin damp with cold sweat. A dream, no, a nightmare, still clung to her mind, as vivid as if she'd just lived it.

In that dream, Ari had been trudging up a snow-laden mountain, each step an effort, each breath a struggle. Suddenly, a colossal, abominable snowman emerged from swirling mists, its eyes aglow with cruelty. It roared a guttural thunder that shook the very peaks, then seized Ari with monstrous strength, dragging him into a dark ravine. She could still hear his echoing cry: "Elinor!"

Helpless in the dream, Elinor had fallen to her knees, voice raw with desperation, crying out: "Jesus, help him! Save him!" As if in answer, a vast dark blue cloud descended from the sky, charged with power and mystery. From its center emerged a radiant figure, Jesus, His presence commanding yet compassionate. Light swirled around Him, and then, in an instant, Ari stood free from terror, strength rekindled in his eyes. A single kick from Ari sent the monstrous snowman tumbling into the abyss. Jesus reached out, lifting Ari from the darkness. Together, they rose to the mountain's peak.

Elinor remembered the calm in the Savior's voice as He whispered to her, "Trust Me."

Now fully awake, Elinor sat on the edge of her bed, pressing shaking fingers against her face. Her heart pounded, and her mind churned. The dream had felt so urgent, so real. She rose, slipping into a soft cardigan, the quiet hum of the city outside failing to dispel the vivid images.

In her living room, she settled onto the couch, the silence of the apartment as fragile as her thoughts. On the coffee table lay her Bible. She picked it up, turning to a passage that had always offered solace, Psalm 91. *"He will cover you with His feathers, and under His wings, you will find refuge..."* she read aloud in a trembling whisper. Tears gathered at the corners of her eyes. If the dream was a warning, she needed God's guidance more than ever.

She prayed, her words hushed but earnest. "Lord, if this dream means Ari is in danger, please protect him. Open his eyes to see You, to trust You. Give me the words to tell him and soften his heart to listen." Elinor clasped her hands together, pleading quietly. "If he's walking into peril, go before him, Lord. Be his refuge, be his shield."

The apartment remained still, only the distant hum of traffic signaling life beyond these walls. Yet in that hush, Elinor sensed a gentle peace, a blessed assurance that her prayers had not vanished into emptiness. Whatever the dream meant, she wasn't alone in facing it.

Elinor had been shocked but ecstatic when Ari called her yesterday after the board meeting and invited her to his latest field test in the Andes Mountains. She readily agreed and began preparations. Thinking about the unsettling dream, she wondered if it could mean that something unexpected might happen during this expedition. She shuddered at the thought.

She closed her Bible, the tension in her shoulders easing slightly. Ari might not readily believe in dreams or divine intervention, but she would tell him anyway. She would try, trusting that perhaps this time, he might find room in his rational world for something greater than himself.

Chapter 4

Preparation for Peru

Only two weeks later, a hum of purposeful activity filled the air in SummitTek's conference room. The table was covered with maps of the Andes, topographical charts, and technical specs for SummitTek's latest innovation, the Titan Tent and Rope System. Engineers and designers swapped notes, environmental consultants reviewed geological data, and assistants fetched coffee as if the caffeine itself fueled their ambitions.

At the head of the table, Ari Keshet was utterly on point. Dressed in a tailored suit, he exuded the perfect GQ vibe with a millennial twist, like he was on the verge of launching the next big thing. He embodied CEO energy, poised to disrupt the industry and venture into a new frontier.

Although confidence radiated from him, his thoughts wandered back and forth to Elinor as he recalled his call to her after the board meeting. This expedition would be different, not just another product test but a shared journey where his taste for high-stakes innovation would converge with her "down-to-earth" expertise in botany and geology. While keeping one eye on the preparations, he hoped to impress Elinor, picturing her awe and admiration for him as he conquered his next challenge.

To his left, Gottschall, SummitTek's formidable COO, presided over the final details like a general preparing for battle. She rarely ventured beyond the corporate command center, preferring to keep SummitTek's intricate machinery running flawlessly from her strategic perch at HQ. Fieldwork was a job for Ari's team of adrenaline-crazed specialists, not Maria Gottschall.

But this time was different. Ari had insisted that she come along, citing the complexity of the field test. He had said that her presence would keep him honest, and half-joked that she could serve as a chaperone for him and Elinor. At that suggestion, Gottschall's eyebrows had risen to dangerous heights, but she agreed without protest.

"If you expect me to haul climbing gear," she had said with her signature icy precision, "Prepare to be disappointed."

"All major equipment has shipped ahead of schedule," Gottschall reported, her sharp gaze flicking from her tablet to the team. "The R&D crew and consultants will meet us in Lima. AndesCon's climbers are on standby for field tests along the ridge."

Ari nodded approvingly. "Excellent work, Maria. And travel arrangements?"

"Your jet awaits at the corporate airfield," she replied. "We depart tomorrow morning. The team's accommodations in Lima have been confirmed, including Miss Miller's," she added, her voice carrying just a hint of dry amusement. "And, per your insistence, I'll also be joining this... adventure."

Ari's lips twitched at the slight pause before adventure. "I appreciate your willingness, Maria. Your oversight will keep us... uh, balanced."

Gottschall tilted her head slightly, her face staying perfectly neutral, but her tone held a subtle sharpness. "Your confidence is noted. As for Miss Miller, I've ensured she'll be compensated appropriately for her geological expertise," she said.

The faintest arch of her brow betrayed that she knew full well Elinor's invitation had less to do with geology and more to do with Ari's transparent romantic inclinations, the depth of which he may not even understand.

Ari's eyes brightened with humor. "Her input will be invaluable and I'm glad she's part of the team."

Gottschall rolled her eyes and returned her attention to her tablet. "I'll finalize the logistics. The expedition should run seamlessly."

"Thank you, Maria," Ari said smiling before turning his attention to his phone.

The meeting adjourned, and the executives dispersed like chess pieces, moving to execute their respective strategies. The hum of SummitTek's ambition buzzed in the air as if the walls themselves anticipated what would come.

Ari lingered behind, texting out a quick message to Elinor.

> *Everything's set. Can't wait to have you on this adventure. Ready to trade your microscope for a mountain?*

Her reply came almost instantly.

> *Always up for a challenge. Question is, can you keep up with a geologist on unfamiliar soil?*

Ari smirked, typing back.

> *As long as you don't name every plant we pass.*
> *My Latin's rusty before coffee.*

Her response was playful.

> *Don't worry. I'll ensure plenty of coffee. Just don't forget your fancy hiking boots. It wouldn't look good if SummitTek's fearless leader slipped on a rock.*

He laughed, noticing Gottschall observing him from a distance. Though she remained silent, her face seemed to shout, "Am I really meant to babysit you and your geologist crush?"

Typing again, he added.

> *You're part of the team, not just a guest.*
> *Compensation included.*

After a brief pause, her response appeared.

> *You didn't have to, but thank you.*

His reply was simple.

> *I wanted to. This trip isn't just about data.*
> *Other things matter.*

Ari's mind buzzed. He felt a familiar mixture of excitement and unease, the thrill of the unknown mingled with the weight of the risks ahead. He glanced at Gottschall, who was already immersed in her tablet. He knew she'd keep everything running smoothly, even if she had to drag the entire team by sheer force of will. Then there was Elinor, whose teasing texts reminded him that this trip might hold something more than just business.

For now, he set aside Stolz's whispering presence. The Andes loomed ahead, daring him to conquer their peaks and mysteries. But Ari wondered if conquering was what he truly needed, or if he was about to discover something far more meaningful in the challenge.

The Departure

Elinor stood outside her apartment building as the crisp morning air teased her braid and touched the worn leather of her trusty cowboy boots. She adjusted the strap of her whimsical, flower-patterned backpack, which gave her otherwise practical attire a playful edge. In her other hand, she held a compact case of essential scientific equipment, carefully assembled to handle whatever the Andes might throw at her.

A black SUV glided up to the curb, its tinted window rolling down to reveal Darren, SummitTek's ever-reliable driver. He wore a broad grin that suggested he, too, felt the excitement of this journey.

"Good morning, Ms. Miller," Darren said, stepping out to take her bags. "Ready for an adventure?"

From the passenger seat, Chloe, the co-driver, waved cheerfully. "Love the boots," she called. "You look ready to wrangle data, or maybe a few mountain goats!"

Elinor laughed and handed her equipment case to Darren. "Thanks, Chloe. These boots have come in handy against unruly spreadsheets; they might work on goats, too."

Settling into the back seat, Elinor took a steadying breath. This wasn't just another field trip. She was stepping into Ari's world of high-stakes expeditions and cutting-edge innovation. The thought thrilled and unsettled her, stirring a quiet flutter of anticipation.

The drive to the private airfield passed smoothly. Darren and Chloe chatted about the Peruvian weather and, with amused grins, noted that Ari had been uncharacteristically cheerful that morning.

"He was whistling show tunes." Chloe's eyes danced. "I mean, whistling! I think that's a first for him."

Elinor smiled, picturing Ari being softened by whatever happiness buoyed him today. Perhaps he was as excited as she was.

They arrived at a private hangar, where a sleek Gulfstream jet gleaming under the early sun waited. A flight attendant stood at the foot of the stairs, poised to greet them. Darren handed Elinor her flowered backpack with a playful bow.

"Safe travels, Ms. Miller," he said. "Don't let Mr. Keshet keep all the thrills to himself."

Elinor grinned, her gaze already drawn to the jet. "I'll try to share the fun."

Inside, the cabin exuded quiet luxury, exotic leather seats, polished wood accents, and a cozy lounge area that blended comfort with efficiency. Ari stood near a table with a light breakfast, fresh fruit, pastries, and steaming, hot, exotic coffee. His tailored shirt and confident posture matched the elegant surroundings, yet his eyes showed unmistakable warmth as he turned to face Elinor.

The engines hummed softly beneath them, the subtle vibration signaling their imminent departure. Gottschall, already in full executive mode, settled into a nearby seat and began tapping out emails with the precision of a sniper. "Once we're airborne, Ari, I'd like a word about the rope tension issue. R&D insists it's minor, but I'd rather not find out mid-ascent that their minor is my catastrophe."

Ari nodded, though his attention was clearly elsewhere. "Sounds good. We'll discuss it en route." His gaze, however, had drifted to Elinor, who was staring out the window, her hand idly tracing a faint pattern on the armrest.

Elinor turned just enough to catch his eye, her brow arching with playful challenge. "What's up, Keshet? Are you spacing out, or just perfecting your brooding explorer vibe?"

"Just thinking," Ari replied with a smirk, leaning forward slightly. "This is your first field expedition with SummitTek. I hope you don't miss your cozy lab coat and controlled variables."

"Lab coats don't give you blisters," she replied, smirking. "I'm just praying your high-tech gear lives up to the hype. If not, you might be hauling me down the mountain."

He leaned back, arms crossed, and grinning. "I can carry you without issues, but only if you promise not to criticize my 'tech-bro carries botanist' technique."

"Deal," she playfully shot back. "But if you fall, I'm tweeting about it."

Meanwhile, Gottschall glanced up from her tablet, her gaze darting between them with a barely perceptible raise of her brow. She didn't comment, but the set of her lips screamed, "Keep it professional, lovebirds!"

Elinor felt a quiet thrill mingling with the rising altitude as the jet lifted into the sky. This trip wasn't just about collecting data or reaching the summit. It felt like the start of something bigger, discoveries in the mountains, yes, but also discoveries about Ari, herself, and whatever strange connection seemed to spark between them when their gazes lingered too long.

Ari leaned back in his seat, sipping his coffee as Gottschall launched into her usual list of priorities.

He nodded occasionally but couldn't help but sneak another glance at Elinor, who was now pretending to ignore him by flipping through a geological notebook. She clearly wasn't reading. She caught him looking and raised an eyebrow, a silent dare.

"You two are worse than teenagers," Gottschall muttered under her breath, though there was the faintest twitch of a smile as she returned to her emails.

The jet leveled out, and the horizon stretched wide ahead, Peru lying somewhere beyond the distant clouds. They were on their way to the Andes, to the next challenge, and maybe to answers neither of them had expected to find.

Peru, Andes Expedition Headquarters

Under the midday sun, the AndesCon expedition headquarters, built of weathered stone and sturdy timber, stood against a rugged backdrop of peaks and narrow passes. Inside the compound's largest meeting room, anticipation buzzed through the air. A group of native Peruvian climbers and guides gathered around a wooden table with topographical maps and survival gear. Their faces, tanned, weathered, and carved by years of ruthless elements, reflected a quiet assurance that came only from deep experience.

Raúl Ortega, the lead guide, commanded the head of the table with an air of unspoken authority. His broad shoulders and piercing dark eyes signaled that his leadership had been earned through experience, not given lightly. As the chatter around the room subsided, Raúl glanced at his men, each waiting intently for his words. "They arrive tomorrow," he began, his voice laced with both amusement and skepticism. "The Americans, scientists, executives... and their leader, Ariel Keshet, the billionaire."

Laughter erupted around the table, the rich tones of their thick Quechuan accents echoing in the small room.

Miguel, the youngest guide with a cocky grin, leaned back in his chair and quipped, "Billionaire or not, his money will not mean much up here. It cannot buy air when altitude sickness takes their breath away."

Javier, older and more measured, chuckled softly. "Nor can it buy strong legs when the mountain tests them."

Raúl allowed himself a faint smile but raised a hand to restore order. "True," he said, his tone shifting to a serious edge, "but do not underestimate them. They may not know our mountains, but they come with money, technology, and expectations. Our job is to ensure they succeed, and that they return home in one piece."

Miguel shrugged, his skepticism undeterred. "Money and technology will not be enough. These mountains do not surrender easily."

Javier folded his arms, his respect for the Andes evident. "And their leader? Does this American boss think he can handle the Andes like another business deal?"

Raúl's gaze dropped to the map spread across the table, his finger tracing the planned route. His voice lowered, taking on a reverent tone. "Maybe he does. Maybe he does not. But one thing is certain." He paused, letting his words settle like the weight of the mountains themselves. "These peaks will put the fear of God into him."

The room grew still, the earlier humor replaced by solemn respect. Miguel raised an eyebrow, his smirk fading. "The fear of God... now that, no one can buy."

Raúl nodded, his expression firm. "Exactly."

The men shared a quiet moment of understanding. They would meet the SummitTek team tomorrow, not with fanfare but with the unspoken acknowledgment that the mountains could have the final say. The Andes esteemed neither wealth nor ambition, and soon Ari Keshet and his team would discover that respect garnered mercy.

Outside, the wind whistled through the narrow passages, infused with the essence of the Andes. The peaks stood silently, ancient and ready to humble anyone who dared challenge them.

Chapter 5

Welcome to the Andes

The SummitTek SUV convoy rolled to a stop in front of the AndesCon Peru headquarters, a sturdy, weathered building at the foot of towering peaks. The thin mountain air carried a faint scent of pine and distant rain. This was the gateway to the Andes, the proving ground for SummitTek's daring venture, and where two worlds would collide.

Ari Keshet stepped out first, the collar of his expedition jacket crisp against the rugged backdrop. His sharp gaze swept the scene. Weather-worn guides stood waiting and ready. These men had braved more summits than any ambitious executive could imagine.

Behind Ari, Elinor Miller emerged from the SUV, her worn cowboy boots crunching on the gravel. Her backpack drew immediate attention, a tiny spark of levity amid the stern environment. The Peruvian guides exchanged amused smirks and whispers.

At the forefront stood Raúl, the lead guide. His shoulders were broad, his posture confident. He surveyed the newcomers, not as adversaries but as variables yet to be measured. "Welcome to our mountains," he said in English, his voice steady and just a touch amused.

Ari extended a hand. "Thank you, Raúl. We look forward to working with you."

Raúl shook briefly, then let his gaze drift toward Elinor. His men murmured, commenting on her youthful backpack and seemingly delicate demeanor.

Noticing their tone, if not every word, Elinor raised an eyebrow. "If you're going to mock my backpack, at least wait until I can't hear you," she replied playfully. Her composed voice held a hint of defiance; she was far from a timid spectator.

The guides stiffened, surprised by her directness. Raúl allowed a faint smile. "No offense," he said, "it is... very colorful."

Elinor shrugged, her eyes sparkling. "Flowers reflect life, even in the harshest places. You'd be surprised by all the things I can carry in here."

Raúl nodded, a hint of respect now evident in his eyes. "We will see," he whispered under his breath.

Another SUV door swung open, revealing Fraulein Maria Gottschall, towering with unshakable authority... and height. She stepped out like a general inspecting her troops. Her sharp gaze swept over the Peruvian team, as precise as the mountains. Every inch of her tailored expedition gear declared she had no tolerance for nonsense or inefficiency.

The men tensed slightly, reading her commanding posture as easily as weather patterns. One older guide murmured in Spanish that she was a force of nature. Beside him, Carlos, one of the senior guides and a notorious flirt, broke into a bold grin and strode toward her.

"Welcome, my name is Carlos. Uh..., Frow...line, Frow lean..." He hesitated dramatically, "Guts... slaw? Did I say it right?"

Gottschall arched a single, impeccably shaped eyebrow, halting his attempt with a glance sharp enough to slice granite. "Fraulein Maria Gottschall," she corrected crisply, her German accent giving the name a distinct, authoritative edge. "But thank you for the... creative attempt."

Carlos placed a hand over his heart with mock sincerity. "A beautiful name... for a powerful woman." His grin widened as he added, "It suits you perfectly."

Raúl coughed discreetly, and a few of the other guides exchanged glances, trying not to smirk.

Gottschall's expression didn't falter, but a faint hint of color flushed her cheeks. "I'm here to work, Señor Carlos," she replied. "Let's keep our priorities clear."

Carlos offered an exaggerated bow. "Of course, Fraulein Maria Got-She... Gottschall. Whatever you need, just say the word. I live to serve!"

"Then serve by staying focused," she replied smoothly, turning her attention to Raúl. "I'll need a full inventory review of supplies before we begin the ascent. There will be no delays."

Raúl straightened, nodding crisply. "Understood."

As Gottschall walked past, Carlos muttered something in Spanish about "conquering the queen of hearts," earning a quiet snort from Miguel.

"Buena suerte, amigo," Miguel whispered back. (Good luck, my friend.)

Nearby, Ari and Elinor watched the exchange with mild amusement. Ari leaned slightly toward Elinor, his voice low. "I think Carlos might be biting off more than he can chew."

Elinor crossed her arms, suppressing a smile. "Gottschall doesn't strike me as the type to be impressed by flattery. But I have to admit, his commitment is... admirable."

"Admirable?" Ari echoed, smirking. "It's borderline deadly... but entertaining."

Elinor's lips twitched as she tilted her head toward the towering peaks. With a contemplative look, she said, "They'll all need to focus soon enough. I hear respect out here isn't given. It's earned." Ari nodded, his expression softening. "No doubt about that."

The wind skimmed across the foothills, carrying a faint chill and a whisper of ancient tales. Raúl stood nearby, his gaze fixed on the skyline where clouds brushed the summits. "These mountains will not be charmed by smooth talk," Raúl murmured to Javier.

"No," Javier agreed, his voice low. "They will demand respect and fear of God."

As the team started unloading gear, the mountains stood silently, unaffected by wealth, ambition, or charm. They provided no shortcuts, only obstacles.

SummitTek Base Camp

Over the next two days, Gottschall completed her supply and equipment inventory. The SummitTek team was introduced to the AndesCon guide team. Ari made his rounds to meet each of AndesCon's executives and the guide team.

On the third day, all was ready, and the teams started up the mountain.

A few hours' ride brought them to the base camp, where the teams would set up and dispatch the climbing team.

The SummitTek base camp was perched like a futuristic outpost on the edge of a wind-swept plateau. It stood in absurd contrast to the raw, untamed Andes. Under the moon's silvery watch, its sleek, prefabricated units shimmered with soft LED glows, less "survivalist grit" and more "tech mogul glamping." These weren't just tents. They were high-end modules. Heated floors, ergonomic workstations, and satellite uplinks.

At the heart of it all stood the crown jewel: the cafeteria. But calling it a cafeteria was like calling the Sistine Chapel a ceiling. A gourmet chef and his white-coated entourage worked like culinary wizards behind polished stainless-steel counters, whipping up meals that scented the thin mountain air with the seductive perfume of roasted lamb, artisan bread, and velvety sauces that probably had their own passports.

A short distance away, a group of Peruvian guides lingered by their trucks and crates, watching the scene with a mix of amusement and skepticism. Their thick accents rolled as they shared their observations with each other.

Miguel shook his head in disbelief, gesturing toward the glowing base. "Seriously? A silver tray of desserts? Out here? Why?"

Javier nodded, his tone dry as he gestured to the structures. "A luxury spa in the middle of the Andes. That is what this is."

Ever the joker, Carlos, still nursing his admiration for Maria Gottschall, smirked as he watched a SummitTek staffer scurry past with the tray. He said with a grin, "Well, at least they have good taste in women."

Standing slightly apart, Raúl crossed his arms over his broad chest, his skeptical eyes surveying the camp with quiet authority. "Do not be fooled by all this," he said, his voice steady, cutting through the banter. "The mountain does not care about gourmet meals or warm beds. It will not give them any special treatment."

The men chuckled lightly, but Raúl's words hung in the air like the weight of the peaks above. Their job was to guide these Americans, to keep them safe, and to ensure their success. But respect was never handed out like cheap trinkets. The mountain was the only boss here and didn't bow to money, technology, or entitled wealthy Americans.

Above them, the wind skimmed the cliffs, whispering ancient truths as the peaks loomed in their silence.

Inside Ari's Office

Inside one of the sleek modules designated as his private office, Ari Keshet sat, bathed in the soft glow of a desk lamp. Blueprints, topographical maps of the Andes, and R&D notes were spread across the surface. He tapped a pen against the desk's edge, his mind buzzing with thoughts of tomorrow's tests, and with something else he couldn't quite name.

Then, the smooth and persuasive voice slipped into his consciousness: Stolz.

"You're holding back," the voice whispered. *"These mountains demand risk. Prove yourself, don't play it safe."*

Ari whispered, leaning back with a frown. "The team has a plan. The tests are calculated."

Stolz scoffed, *"Calculated? You didn't build your empire by playing it safe. Show them why you're the best! Impress the guides, the scientists... Elinor."*

Ari's jaw tightened. The temptation dangled before him, a familiar lure. Pride had fueled his ambitions before; why resist now?

In the Cafeteria

Elinor sat at a corner table, hands wrapped around a mug of herbal tea. The warmth and scent of chamomile and mint offered small comfort but couldn't chase away the quiet unease that tugged at her spirit. She watched as the Peruvian guides, invited for dinner, approached the buffet with a mix of curiosity and thinly veiled amusement.

"¿Esto es comida o arte?" one guide muttered, eyeing the elaborate platings. (Is this food or art?)

"Ambos, parece," another replied, smirking at the desserts. (Both, it seems.)

They piled their plates high, joking about truffle soup and pretending they were dining on a luxury cruise rather than preparing to scale the Andes. The SummitTek staff, long accustomed to luxury, hardly noticed the humor, but Elinor did. Their honest laughter felt strangely grounding in a place so polished it barely breathed.

The cafeteria door swung open, and Ari stepped in. He moved with his usual purpose, but something in his posture seemed rigid, his eyes more distant than sharp. He headed straight for the gourmet buffet, an impressive spread prepared by the traveling chefs that Ari insisted on bringing along for his personal enjoyment.

No matter where in the world he went, Ari demanded the finest: imported cheeses, handmade pasta, artisan pastries, truffle-infused everything. It was rumored that more money was spent on meals than on most of the field equipment.

He grabbed a plate, selecting dishes with an almost mechanical precision. Elinor watched as he approached, seating himself beside her without a word.

"Busy day?" she asked lightly, hoping to soften the tension in his shoulders.

Ari nodded, slicing into his entrée without looking up. "I have alot on my mind. That's all."

He took a bite, chewing thoughtfully. His brow furrowed almost immediately. He set down his fork with a quiet clink and muttered under his breath, just loud enough for her to catch it:

"It's not it."

Elinor blinked. "Excuse me?"

"Nothing," Ari said quickly, brushing it off. But the frown lingered on his face as he pushed his food around, unsatisfied.

Across the room, one of the chefs watched anxiously, mistaking Ari's discontent for perfectionism. They had been warned, impress the boss, or else. Yet no amount of imported truffles or aged balsamic ever seemed quite good enough.

What no one realized, not even Ari himself, was that he wasn't truly chasing flavor or luxury. Somewhere deep beneath the arrogance and indulgence, he was searching for something lost: a taste, a feeling, a memory that no Michelin star could replicate.

Elinor studied him quietly, sensing a hollow ache behind his polished exterior. He wasn't just demanding excellence; he was searching for something he couldn't name.

"You seem more preoccupied than usual," she said gently. "Everything okay?"

Ari shrugged, taking another bite, another disappointment. "I'm fine. Just thinking about tomorrow's tests."

His tone didn't fool her. But she knew better than to press. Some walls took time to crumble. She lifted her mug, offering a silent prayer under her breath.

Help him find what he's truly looking for, Lord, even if he doesn't know it yet.

At the Edge of Camp

Outside, near a row of parked trucks and crates, Raúl and his men had finished their meal and now stood beneath the moonlight. They could see into the cafeteria's warm glow where the Americans dined in comfort. The Peruvian guides exchanged low, half-joking, half-judgmental remarks about the luxury these newcomers enjoyed.

Miguel popped a piece of gum into his mouth and muttered something about the CEO hosting a luxury retreat rather than bracing for the Andes.

Javier laughed softly, and Carlos, ever the romantic, mused about how Ari might try to buy the mountain and build a resort.

Laughter rippled through them, but their eyes drifted to Ari, who was visible through the cafeteria window and seemingly lost in thought.

Raúl didn't join the laughter. Standing with arms folded, his tone was quiet but firm, his thick accent cutting through the night. "Laugh if you want, but these mountains do not have a sense of humor." The chuckles faded, the other guides falling silent as they turned to listen.

His gaze sharpened, fixed on the distant silhouette of Ari. "That boss of theirs, he has pride in his eyes. And pride never lasts long when it stands before God."

The wind carried Raúl's words into the night like a voice of gossip, tattling to the very peaks themselves. Javier nodded slowly, his face serious. These mountains, he knew, had a way of stripping a man down to his soul. Miguel swallowed hard, the weight of Raúl's words making him uneasy. Even Carlos, usually quick with a jab, stayed quiet, his eyes fixed on the distant ridges.

"If he doesn't honor the mountain, the mountain will educate him, and its lessons can be deadly." Raúl lifted his shirt, revealing a large scar from an injury he had sustained during a climb years ago. The men acknowledged his scar. His body was riddled with life experiences. He allowed himself a grateful smile.

The wind howled, echoing Raúl's words into the peaks. The moon rose higher, casting its pale glow across the jagged terrain like an ancient spotlight. It scrutinized men's actions with the precision of a surveillance camera.

The moon may watch silently, but the mountain was taking notes.

Chapter 6

The Ascent Begins

The early morning sun cast a gilded glow over the Andes, its rays stretching across jagged peaks and painting the mountains in shades of gold and amber. The thin air carried the scent of cold stone and vast earth. At the SummitTek base camp, the modular structures stood out like a disco ball in stark contrast to the rugged wilderness. The teams bustled efficiently while they finalized preparations for the climb ahead.

Ari Keshet stood like a walking ad for Popular Science: Expedition Edition, decked head to toe in SummitTek's latest high-tech climbing apparel. His jacket gleamed with thermal fabric and nanowave panels that promised to regulate body temperature with eerie precision. Every buckle, boot, and seam screamed "cutting edge," and Ari knew it. He shifted his weight just enough to catch the morning light on his gear, casting a glance toward Elinor that said, Behold, the apex of man and material science.

His stance was all effortless swagger, shoulders back, jaw set, eyes coolly sweeping the camp like he owned both the mountain and the patent office. Years of commanding boardrooms gave him the confidence; the futuristic gear gave him the edge. But the Peruvian guides weren't buying it.

They offered the occasional grunt of approval or raised brow at SummitTek's sleek innovations, but their side-eyes and quiet chuckles told a different story.

High-altitude fashion was one thing. Surviving the mountain was another.

Nearby, Elinor adjusted the straps of her bright, whimsy backpack, its cheerful design standing out against the rugged mountain landscape. A few of the guides exchanged amused glances, wondering how someone would bring such a whimsical bag into the harsh Andes terrain.

Unbothered, Elinor crouched beside a patch of greenery at the camp's edge, her fingers brushing the leaves. Her expression lit up with curiosity as she pulled a small trowel and a specimen bag from her pack.

"This soil is fascinating," she murmured, scooping up a bit of earth. "High mineral content. These plants thrive against the odds."

Carlos, passing by with a coil of climbing ropes slung over his shoulder, smirked. "Here to climb or start a community garden?"

Elinor looked up, eyes with mischief. "Maybe both. But if you're lucky, I might discover something to cure your terrible sense of humor."

The guides chuckled, and Carlos held up his hands in mock surrender. "Alright, alright. Just do not blame me when the alpacas start judging that backpack."

"Alpacas?" Elinor's interest piqued.

Miguel grinned. "Oh, yeah. They are everywhere. They are convinced they own the place."

Carlos nodded sagely. "They will steal your snacks, stare into your soul like they are questioning your life choices, and, if you really annoy them, spit on you without hesitation."

Elinor laughed, zipping up her bag. "Sounds like a few professors I've met."

As if summoned, a lone alpaca sauntered up to the group, its thick wool ruffled by the mountain breeze. It squinted at Elinor's backpack, twitched its ears, and then, with dramatic disdain, turned its head and walked away.

Carlos grinned. "Told you. Even the alpacas are not sure what to make of that thing."

"I didn't know alpacas were such fashion critics..." as she rolled her eyes and laughed.

Miguel clapped his hands. "Alright, let us move out before someone actually gets spit on."

With that, the group shouldered their packs, laughing as they set off. Elinor's soft laugh blended into the morning quiet, easing some tension.

But the unimpressed alpaca watched their departure with the air of a judgmental emperor.

Meanwhile, SummitTek's equipment, modular tents that set up instantly, ropes that coiled perfectly, boots and crampons tailored to extreme conditions, had begun to impress even Raúl. He nodded thoughtfully to Javier as he watched an engineer rapidly secure an anchor.

"Esta tecnología... no está mal." Raúl conceded quietly. (This technology... not bad.)

Across the camp, Gottschall surveyed the preparations with a hawk's eye and enforced standards as if leading a military campaign. No detail escaped her notice.

Pausing near Elinor, Gottschall held out a sleek, sealed bundle. "These are high-tech insulated boots," she said, her voice firm. "Your cowboy boots won't cut it at high altitude temperatures."

Elinor offered a smile. "Thanks, Gottschall, but I'll manage." The COO's eyes narrowed. "Humor me, Miss Miller. The temperature will drop, and I would rather you didn't lose any toes." Her tone softened slightly as she added, "We had them made in your size. SummitTek's team thought you might appreciate proper gear."

Elinor accepted the bundle. "You think of everything." "Someone has to," Gottschall replied briskly, striding away to address another matter.

As the sun climbed higher, the team assembled. The path ahead wound upward into rocky slopes and snow-dusted ridges. Ari took the lead, his steps confident as he moved into this world of ice and altitude, his domain of risk and reward.

Elinor fell into the middle of the group, her colorful backpack standing against a backdrop of muted grays and whites. Now and then, she knelt to examine a hardy moss or a cluster of tiny blooms. Miguel teased her, but she held her own, unruffled.

Soon, they encountered a small herd of llamas grazing on a rocky outcrop. One turned its head and seemed to assess them dismissively. Miguel winked at Elinor. "See? Even the llamas judge your backpack more harshly than we do."

Elinor grinned, amused. "I'll keep that in mind."

SummitTek's innovations proved their worth as the climb intensified. The self-erecting tents and advanced rope system performed flawlessly. Even Raúl had to admit that the technology was impressive, and Javier nodded in grudging approval.

Yet both men knew that the mountain had no interest in clever engineering.

As the team ascended, the temperature dropped noticeably. Elinor felt the cold gnawing at her toes. Remembering Gottschall's warning, she pulled the high-tech boots from her pack and exchanged her cowboy boots for them. The warmth was immediate and profound.

She caught Ari watching her. "Guess Gottschall was right," she said with a self-deprecating shrug. "Don't tell her, though. I'll never hear the end of it."

Ari smiled. "Your secret's safe with me," he said softly. There was something warm in his gaze that lifted Elinor's heart.

He turned forward again, focusing on the path and the tasks as they pressed on. The air became thin with each step, the view stretching into distant horizons of ice and sky.

Elinor paused near a narrow ledge to catch her breath. As she glanced toward a ravine far below, something flickered at the edge of her vision, a strange, purplish glow, something tall and elusive. It vanished in a heartbeat, leaving her uncertain if she had really seen it.

Ari noticed her hesitation. "Everything okay?" he asked, his voice steady but curious.

Elinor hesitated, her heart drumming with confusion. "I thought I saw something... down there." She gestured vaguely, her tone quiet.

Ari followed her gaze. "Probably just a trick of the light," he said, forcing casualness into his voice. But the set of his jaw betrayed a flicker of unease. He remembered Alaska, remembered something he had chosen to dismiss. He didn't want to indulge these doubts now, not when so much depended on clear focus.

Elinor nodded, not entirely convinced. She stepped forward, pushing the strange sight from her mind. She trusted Ari, but part of her wondered if he was pushing aside something important.

As they continued upward, the mountain offered no hints, no confirmation of shadows or spirits. Just endless snow and stone, breathtaking vistas, and a silence broken only by the crunch of boots and the hum of SummitTek's advanced gear.

Behind them, Raúl and the guides followed with measured steps. Respect was slowly building. For all their comforts and gadgets, the Americans at least had the courage to face these heights. Yet, the Andes remained impartial, waiting to see who would falter first, who would learn humility, or the fear of God, among its peaks.

And somewhere within that silent standoff, Ari carried Stolz's whisper like a thorn in his mind. Elinor clung to her observations and quiet faith, and the Peruvian guides pressed on, all parties converging on a truth hidden high among ice and rock.

Climbing Higher

The air was crisp and clear as the SummitTek team arrived at the designated site to set up their mid-climb camp. The towering Andes still stretched endlessly before them, the peaks dusted with snow under a bright, cloudless sky. The Peruvian guides worked efficiently alongside the SummitTek crew to secure the larger prototype, the Titan tents, while the scientists inspected them and collected data.

Elinor busied herself beside the scientists, pointing out soil and rock variations. When the tents were set up, she took some time to catalog the sparse vegetation around the camp, her flowery backpack resting against a boulder. She couldn't resist the pull of the rugged beauty surrounding her as she paused now and then to jot down notes or snap a photo.

Bryan Carter, a seasoned mountaineer and communications expert, sat at his station in the Titan tent assigned to the radio team. He received and logged updates from his crew. "Mid-camp operational conditions are stable, and the weather looks good," Bryan relayed to the base camp staff.

Ari's team assembled nearby, discussing the final leg of the ascent. Raúl glanced at Ari and said, "This is the last clear stretch. We expect to reach the summit testing site in two days. For now, we rest and acclimate. I suggest we start for the summit tomorrow morning." The word spread quickly throughout the camp, and the team settled in.

Ari looked around at his crew, the challenge singing in his blood and Stolz whispering his persuasions. *"This is it. Products are awaiting their test. Let's get the proof of how great they really are."*

Ari cast a thoughtful glance over the camp, then zeroed in on Elinor, who was perched on a rock with her notes in hand, her breath shallow from the thin air. As he started toward her, he pulled a small tube of lip balm from his jacket pocket, uncapped it, and applied it with a deliberate, slow swipe across his bottom lip.

Elinor's pen froze mid-scribble as her gaze locked on the motion. The sheen of the balm highlighted his lips in a way that sent her thoughts spiraling into uncharted territory. She swallowed hard, attempting to refocus on her notes, but the task was suddenly impossible.

"You all right over there, Elinor?" Ari called out, slipping the balm back into his pocket and flashing her a grin. "Is the mountain taking your breath away?"

Her cheeks flushed deep pink, partly from the thin air but mainly from the direction her mind had wandered. She glanced up at him, determined to appear unfazed. "I'm fine," she replied quickly, though her breathlessness gave her away.

She straightened her back, trying to project more composure. "Just strategizing my next move."

Ari sat beside her, his jacket brushing her arm as he leaned in closer than necessary, his smirk the perfect balance of teasing and charm. "Strategizing, huh?" he drawled, his voice low and playful. "At this vantage point, it appears that something, or perhaps someone, is leaving you breathless."

His hand rested on the rock beside her hip, so close that she swore she could feel its heat through the proprietary fabric.

Elinor's lips twitched in response, her instincts telling her to fire back with something sharp, but the words stalled on her tongue. Instead, she caught herself leaning slightly toward him as her heart thundered in her chest.

"Well..." she began, her voice shaky as she tried to steady herself, "I might not be climbing the summit, but I'll still be here. Someone has to keep you in line."

Ari tilted his head, amused, something softer flashing in his eyes. "Oh, I see how it is. Supervising me from mid-camp while I do all the hard work at the top?"

"Exactly," she said, grinning. "And don't worry, I'll record every plant you stomp on, as you march to glory."

Ari chuckled softly, the teasing in his tone fading into something deeper. "Good," he replied, his voice quieter now. "I like knowing you're here. It keeps me grounded."

For a moment, the noise of the camp and the biting wind faded into the background, leaving only the silence between them. His hand, hovering near her thigh, brushed lightly against it, a barely-there touch that felt like an unspoken request.

Elinor's breath hitched, her gaze flicking to his lips before meeting his eyes again. The tension coiled tighter, almost too much to bear. "You should get going," she said softly, though the reluctance in her voice betrayed her.

"Right... right," Ari murmured, but made no move to leave. His voice was soft, the bravado dialing down as his eyes lingered on her face a moment longer than necessary. "Don't let the plants boss you around too much while I'm gone."

Elinor smirked while adjusting her trekking poles, yet her eyes remained locked on his. "Maybe you should stay..." She paused, shook her head slightly, and clarified, "I mean, stay safe. I'm not hiking up there to rescue you."

He smiled as she slipped on her words.

They sat silently, staring at each other for a moment that seemed to be suspended in time. The mountain wind curled around them, giving them an embrace. Then, without thinking, Ari reached out and brushed a stray strand of hair from her cheek, his bare fingers gently touching her skin.

"I'll be back. See you soon," he assured, voice low.

Elinor's breath caught, just for a second. Then she smiled. "You'd better."

He smiled, nodded, then confidently walked back to his group... with a slight skip in his step.

Elinor sat there, her heart racing and her cheeks flushed and warm. Watching him rejoin the team, she wondered if the thin air or Ari Keshet himself made her breathless... and whether she even cared to resist either one.

High on the Mountain

The morning of the climb to the summit arrived, and the team began their ascent. The trail steepened as Ari's team ascended the ridge to the summit testing site with the prototype systems. Progress was frequently relayed via radio to ensure communication with mid-camp operations. The air was colder and thinner here, but the skies remained clear, a rare gift in the unpredictable Andes.

"Beautiful day for a mountain climb," one of the scientists remarked, wiping sweat from his brow as they paused on a rocky outcrop.

Raúl scanned the horizon, his sharp eyes narrowing. "Let us not waste it. Conditions like this do not last long."

The sky above them was an impossible blue, almost too perfect, sunlight gleaming off the peaks like polished ivory. Even the wind seemed to hold its breath. It was the kind of stillness that felt... unnatural, like a stage set just before a trapdoor drops.

The next day, back at mid-camp, Elinor stood looking out of the communications tent, soaking in the picturesque view and listening for updates. The calm wrapped around her like a warm blanket, until it didn't.

Without warning, Bryan's radio snapped to life, the peaceful silence torn in half by a burst of static.

Raúl's voice cut through, sharp, urgent, nothing like before. "Mid-Camp. We have a problem. Over."

His transmission cut off abruptly, drowned out by static.

"Mid-camp, this is Raúl. The weather..."

Bryan leaned forward, slightly concerned but still smiling as if this was all a joke. He adjusted the dials with practiced hands.

"Raúl, this is mid-camp. Repeat your last message. Over."

The radio crackled again before Raúl's voice returned, more urgent this time.

"A storm is coming in fast... unnatural... not normal weather. The wind is picking up... visibility has dropped quicker than I have ever seen... Over."

Elinor's mind froze, her heart skipping as she moved closer to Bryan's station. She remembered her awful dream the night after Ari invited her on this expedition and couldn't keep her fear out of her voice. "What do you mean, unnatural?" she whispered. Bryan didn't respond; his smile dropped to a frown as he focused on the transmission.

"Raúl, confirm location and conditions. Over." Bryan replied, his calm voice cutting through the tension.

Raúl's reply was fragmented, but the urgency was unmistakable. "We are near the summit... skies were clear... now, whiteout conditions... not on radar. Over."

Bryan's fingers flew across the equipment to verify weather data. "Nothing on our end, radar shows clear skies. Over." He muttered, confused.

Elinor leaned over, her voice trembling slightly. "Can you reach Ari? Is he okay?"

Bryan glanced at her briefly before keying the mic. "Ari, this is mid-camp. Do you copy? Over."

Static filled the tent, and Elinor's chest tightened. She gripped the back of Bryan's chair, her knuckles white.

Bryan tried again more urgently. "Raúl, Ari, this is mid-camp. Do you copy? Over!"

A faint reply came through. Raúl's voice was barely audible over the rising wind noise. "Setting up Titan Tent now. Over."

Elinor exhaled shakily, and she remained uneasy. The clear skies earlier had seemed too perfect, too stable. The storm's sudden aggression felt ominous and unnatural, as if the mountain had turned against them.

Bryan glanced at her, his professional demeanor softening slightly. "They've got the tent. The design can handle this. Try not to worry."

Elinor nodded, but her eyes remained fixed on the radio, her gut telling her that something more was at play.

The Supernatural Storm

The storm arrived with an unsettling speed, catching Ari's team entirely off guard. What had been a calm ascent moments before was now utter chaos. The temperature plummeted, the wind howled with an almost animalistic aggression, and snow began to whip around them, blurring the trail ahead.

Raúl struggled to shout over the roaring wind. "We need to stop and set up camp. Now!"

Ari's jaw tightened, and a flush of fury rose to his face. He spun toward the guide, eyes blazing. "Are you kidding me?" he snapped, his voice cracking through the cold air like a whip. "How could you not see this coming?" His voice was sharp, laced with uncharacteristic anger.

The tension snapped like a cable under strain. His usual composed veneer was shattered, replaced by a sharp edge that even his team found confusing.

"We trusted you with this route, this entire plan, and now we're standing here snow blind?"

Raúl's face tightened, but he held his ground. "The weather changed too fast. This is not normal."

"Not normal?" Ari cut him off, his tone venomous. "It's your job to predict this kind of thing! You're supposed to be the expert!"

The other team members exchanged uneasy glances; their leader's sudden outburst was alarming. Ari's usual composed demeanor had shifted to something unnatural, harsh, and threatening, much like the storm.

"You!" Ari snapped, pointing at one of the scientists. "You told me you checked the forecasts. Did you see this coming?"

The scientist stammered, clearly intimidated. "The... the data didn't show..."

"Useless," Ari muttered under his breath, his fists clenching as Stolz's voice dripped like poison in his mind.

"That's it, Ari," came the sly, dark whisper. *"Put them in their place. Show them why you're the one in charge. Command their respect!"*

Raúl stepped in, his voice firm but cautious. "We can argue later. Right now, we need to set up the tents."

"Then do it," Ari barked. "No more excuses." The team scrambled into action, their movements hurried but efficient. The Titan Tent proved its worth, deploying with astonishing speed.

Its advanced mechanisms locked it into place against the howling wind, forming a sturdy refuge within seconds.

"Everyone inside!" Raúl called out, ushering the others in.

But Ari lingered, his eyes scanning the storm as Stolz whispered again. *"You don't need shelter, Ari. You're stronger than this. A storm doesn't scare you. Show them your strength."*

Ari's pride flared, fueled by the seductive voice. He stood his ground, defying the elements as snow and ice pelted his face.

Swept Away

A sudden roar cut through the storm, an avalanche! Formed by the unnatural rise and power of the wind pushing snow from higher up the mountain, a torrent of snow and chunks of ice came rushing down the slope, carrying debris and rocks in its path.

Before Ari could react, the flood slammed into him with a force that knocked the air from his lungs. He was swept off his feet, the icy flash flood dragging him down the mountainside like a large snowplow.

He collided with jagged rocks, each impact jarring and painful. The frigid temperature numbed his limbs, even through his company's premier snow gear, making it harder to fight against the flow. His world became a blur of cold, chaos, and pain as the flood carried him further and further from the team.

After an undetermined time, that felt like forever, a sharp tug on his chest signaled his backpack catching between two boulders, abruptly halting his descent.

Ari's mind moved sluggishly. The debris stripped away his hat and gloves. He wasn't feeling the ground beneath his feet; he then gravely realized... he was dangling precariously over a deep, dark ravine.

His bare hands clutched convulsively at the backpack straps. The avalanche's roar receded, leaving an eerie silence punctuated only by the creak of the boulders that held him back from the fall.

He tried to move, but the pack held him in place, suspending him mid-air. His radio and headlamp were gone, lost somewhere in the chaos, leaving him unable to call for help.

For the first time in years, fear gripped him, not the thrill of the adrenaline-fueled stunt he craved, but a deep, primal fear of helplessness.

And then, Stolz's accusations flew, *"This is their fault, you know. The guides. The scientists. They failed you. You wouldn't be here if they'd done their jobs."*

Ari clenched his jaw, the cold seeping into his bones. This time, Stolz's voice felt heavier, darker, like a chain tightening around his mind.

Ari hung there, trapped. His breath came in ragged gasps as he peered into the void below. The bottom of the ravine was shrouded in shadows, and he had no idea how far he might fall if the pack slipped free. A warm trickle slid down his temple. He blinked, then saw the blood drip onto his chest, dotting the fabric in slow, steady drops. Pain bloomed sharper, no longer masked by adrenaline.

His side throbbed with each breath, deep and grinding, likely a fractured rib..., probably more. The storm had taken its toll.

The weight of his pride vanished, and Stolz's whispers were silenced, which amplified his isolation.

Back at Mid-Camp

Inside the communication tent, the atmosphere buzzed with unusual tension as if the mountain had breathed its intent into the thin, high-altitude air. Though the storm hadn't touched mid-camp, the wind outside whispered through the tent walls, carrying a haunting, almost beckoning tone. It wasn't the force of the gusts that unsettled the team; it was the way the wind seemed to speak, urging them to find something... or someone.

The insulated panels quivered slightly, but the uneasiness came not from the cold but from the weight of an unspoken urgency. Each breath felt heavier, the lack of oxygen amplifying the sense that the mountain was alive, guiding them toward an answer hidden above.

Elinor sat near the radio console, her eyes flicking between the silent speakers and the window. Her heart thumped against her ribs as the silence dragged on like a gnawing ache without any signal or message from Ari's team.

"Something's wrong," she murmured, her voice low but steady. Her declaration caught everyone's attention. The others exchanged uneasy glances, some nodded, acknowledging their shared worry, while others looked at the floor, unsure how to respond. The storm was worse than they could know. The radio remained silent.

Elinor turned to face the small group of staff and support personnel and drew a deep breath. Many were seasoned professionals, trained to rely on technology and expertise. Yet, technology offered no comfort at this moment, and expertise could not quiet their fears.

"We need to pray," she said calmly, stepping into the center of the room and folding her hands. A few looked uncertain, but no one argued. Fear and helplessness had a way of leveling the ground, making people open to God's grace.

Lowering her head, Elinor began softly. "Lord, we don't know what's happening on that mountain, but You do. Protect Ari and his team. Guide them to safety and give them the strength to face whatever they're up against. Help us trust in Your plan, even when we don't understand. We need Your help, Lord, please bring them back to us." Her voice steadied, "In the Name of Jesus Christ, amen."

Inside the tent, silence was pierced only by the faint, distant rumble of thunder from the storm near the summit. This was no ordinary weather; the radar displayed nothing but clear skies. It felt as if the mountain had summoned the tempest, and they were not privy of seeing it.

A few team members exchanged nervous glances, while others closed their eyes, silently absorbing the gravity of Elinor's plea to God.

Outside, the wind's eerie whistle seemed almost alive, a sound that carried a warning, or perhaps a challenge. It clawed at the distant peaks, relentless in its fury, but left the mid-camp untouched, as though sparing them while unleashing its wrath elsewhere.

Elinor's voice trembled slightly as she continued to whisper a quiet prayer, her hands clasped tightly. The others watched her, respect mingling with unease.

As Elinor opened her eyes, a flicker of calm settled in her chest. She was still concerned about Ari's safety, but prayer had given her a measure of peace.

She glanced at the radio, wanting it to crackle and burst forth with Ari's steady voice. There was no answer, not yet, but Elinor refused to surrender her hope.

They waited, each in their own silence. Where faith and worry collided. A seed of hope had been planted inside the tent. Elinor held on to that hope, knowing that as long as they prayed, they weren't alone, and neither was Ari.

Chapter 7

Between a Rock and a Hard Place.

Far above, Ari's battle with the storm ended as suddenly as if a cosmic switch had been flipped. One moment, the wind and rain had assaulted him like a pack of wild beasts; the next, they disappeared, leaving only silence and the sharp sting of pain and wet cold.

Two massive boulders crashed around him like stone-faced officers of the mountain, pinning him in place with crushing strength. He wasn't just trapped; he was detained. Backpack wedged, chest compressed, legs dangling uselessly beneath him, Ari hung there like a prisoner under arrest for the heinous crime of... *arrogance.*

The mountain, it seemed, had read him his rights before he could process the claim. An unseen force seemed to seize him by the collar and slam him into nature's holding cell.

The stillness that followed was deafening, almost mocking. The faint water drip echoed through the ravine. Each drop was a maddening drum marking his helplessness.

Stolz slithered into his thoughts, sharp and venomous. *"How pathetic, dangling like a poorly hung coat,"* Stolz sneered. *"Is this the great Ariel Keshet or not? Conqueror of mountains and boardrooms? Now look at you, caught between a couple of rocks like some amateur climber. It's embarrassing."*

Ari gritted his teeth, his jaw tightening painfully. "I'll get out of this," he seethed, each word forced through labored breaths.

"Will you?" Stolz's tone was oily, dripping with mockery. *"Because from where you're standing, oh wait, you can't stand, you look like you've already lost. No radio, no plan. Go ahead, big man. What's your next move going to be? Admit it, you need me to get you out of this."*

"I don't need anyone," Ari spat back, the words almost a reflex. "I've never needed anyone. I can do this myself."

"Ah, the classic Ari Keshet's mantra." Stolz laughed. *"You're a self-made man, aren't you? Never relied on anyone, never letting anyone in, but me."*

Ari's muscles strained as he shifted against the straps, attempting to find some leverage. Pain shot through his arms, but he ignored it, glaring into the darkness of the ravine as if Stolz might materialize there.

"Shut up," he growled, his breath visible in the frigid air. "I've been through worse."

"Worse?" Stolz's voice coiled tighter, *"No, Ari. You've been through it easier. With every risk you've taken and every mountain you've climbed, you've always had an escape. But here? This is about beating the odds and proving yourself. This is about survival. Something you've only ever flirted with from the safety of your billion-dollar bubble. Now it is the time to prove that you are invincible."*

The words struck deeper than Ari wanted to admit, and Stolz seized the opening like a predator sensing weakness.

"You're weak, Ari," Stolz hissed. *"And you hate it, don't you? Feeling powerless and vulnerable is disgusting. It's not who you are. You were born to dominate, to win. But right now? You're nothing but a man dangling over a hole, waiting to fall."*

Ari's vision blurred with cold and frustration, his breath coming in shallow bursts. He closed his eyes, trying to block out the voice, but Stolz's grip on his mind was relentless.

Ari's eyes snapped open, the jagged edges of the boulders blurring through his breath's misty vapor. His mind raced, searching for a way out, but Stolz's taunts echoed louder.

"No one's coming for you, Ari," Stolz purred, his voice smooth and insidious. *"Not your team. Not Elinor. It's just you and me now. So go ahead. Prove me wrong. Show me you're the unstoppable force you keep pretending to be."*

Ari's hands tightened on the straps of his pack, his knuckles white from the strain. Elinor's face flashed in his mind, her steady presence, her beautiful eyes that always saw through his facade.

Stolz's mention of her stung, but it also fueled his determination. "This isn't the end," Ari said aloud, coaching himself. "I'll climb out of this. I always do."

The words hung in the freezing air, defiant and raw. Stolz chuckled softly but said nothing more, retreating to the shadows of Ari's mind.

Ari braced himself against the cold. Blood and pain radiated down his body. His path forward was uncertain, but one thing was clear, he wasn't giving up. Not yet. For now, determination was enough.

Missing

At mid-camp, a tense calm settled over the SummitTek crew. Elinor stood outside the communication tent, her eyes scanning the jagged silhouette of the mountain. She clenched her hands, struggling to steady her racing heart.

The storm's sudden disappearance raised more questions than answers, leaving them to wonder if what they had witnessed was nature or something far beyond it.

Inside the tent, Bryan Carter's calm but urgent voice crackled over the radio as communication was restored with the ascending team. The Titan Tents had held up remarkably well during the storm and avalanche, proving their worth against the elements. Yet that relief was short-lived as they began to assess the aftermath.

"Raúl, status report. Over." Bryan said, his tone even but concerningly tight.

He adjusted a portable satellite-linked tablet on the table before him. On its screen, a topographical map flickered, overlaid with digital signals from SummitTek's high-tech satellite tracking markers installed in every climber's backpack and coat. Each team member's location flashed as a tiny dot, a testament to the company's cutting edge safety measures.

Raúl's voice came back, strained but steady. "We are cleaning up now. Some tools and equipment are missing from the avalanche, but most of the team is accounted for. The tents worked perfectly. Over."

Elinor hovered near the room entrance, her pulse quickening as she caught a subtle tension in Raúl's tone. Bryan's brow furrowed, and he leaned closer to his radio.

"Most of the team? Who's missing? Over."

There was a pause, static crackling. Then Raúl's voice returned, quieter, hesitant.

"Señor Keshet. He did not shelter in the tents with us. We assumed he was ahead, but he was not there when we regrouped. We are searching now. Over."

Elinor felt her knees threaten to buckle. Is Ari missing? It made no sense. He was always at the forefront, pushing everyone forward. Yet now, he had vanished into the unforgiving mountain.

Bryan's face tightened, but his voice remained steady and professional. "Raúl, confirm. Is Ariel Keshet missing? Over."

"Confirmed. Yes. Ariel Keshet is missing. We have no visuals. We are sweeping the area where the avalanche passed. Over," Raúl replied.

"*Avalanche?*" Bryan questioned. "Did you say avalanche? Over."

"Confirmed," Raúl replied, his tone grim. "There was an avalanche that came near the camp. Over."

Elinor's heart clenched. Bryan cast her a sharp look, acknowledging the blow this news dealt her. "We'll find him," Bryan said quietly, though the weight of his words betrayed his worry.

Elinor knew Bryan as a seasoned expedition coordinator; he wouldn't make empty promises. Still, her mind raced with dread.

Organizing the Search

The entire camp sprang into action, facing the reality that Ari Keshet, the billionaire founder and driving force behind SummitTek, was missing somewhere on the dangerous mountain.

Bryan barked orders, his experience in extreme environments kicking in as he directed the rescue effort. He tapped on his tablet's screen, magnifying the map. Each team member's signal blinked reassuringly on the display. However, Ari's signal concerned him; it was stationary, far off to one side, miles away, and near a dangerously deep ravine. His signal was too still for comfort.

"We have Ari's signal from the tracking devices in his coat and backpack. According to the satellite data, his beacon is active but not moving. The coordinates suggest he is near a ravine's edge, Over." said Bryan.

In the quiet outside, Elinor strained to hear every word, hope and fear tangling in her chest. She wondered if the signal was steady, meaning Ari's gear was intact. *But why wasn't he moving?*

Raúl responded, "Copy that. Reading the handheld locator connected to the satellite link. Over."

A flicker of hope passed through the camp at Raúl's words. They knew the trackers were reliable. If the signal persisted, Ari's equipment, and hopefully Ari himself, was nearby. *Was he injured? Trapped? Alive?*

Bryan nodded grimly to himself. "Understood. Be careful when approaching. The terrain may be unstable. Over."

As Raúl and his team pushed forward, Elinor found herself pacing outside, her mind a whirlwind of scenarios. This was the man who had faced impossible odds before. How could he not find a way back?

Nearby, a few SummitTek staff members exchanged uneasy looks. One of them, Nate, a young engineer, approached cautiously. "Elinor," he said softly, "he's got that tracking device. If it's active, it means the battery and systems are intact. That's a good thing."

She managed a weak smile at Nate. "Thanks for that. It means they know where to find him. I'm holding onto that."

Bryan monitored Ari's blinking dot on their screens. His signal lay dormant in one spot. A motionless signal could mean he was unconscious, pinned, or dead. Still, as long as the device pinged, they had a beacon of hope.

Into the Ravine

Ari hung suspended in the biting cold. The silence around him was oppressive, broken only by the occasional groan of the boulders that held him captive. His situation felt more desperate with every passing second.

He shifted slightly, trying to reach for the SummitTek multi-purpose tool clipped to his harness. His fingers stretched, trembling, but it was just out of reach. Frustration rose inside him as he muttered, "Come on. Come on!"

His fingers brushed against something else when he relaxed his arms, a small, smooth object tucked into his pants pocket. "My pocket-knife!" he exclaimed. His breath hitched as he dug into his pocket and pulled it free. His father, Abner, had given him the pocket-knife during his Bar Mitzvah when he was thirteen.

"This is for emergencies, Ari," his father had said, his voice uncharacteristically soft. "It may be small, but it's sharp and reliable, just like you. Use it wisely. One day, you'll thank me."

The memory was so vivid it momentarily eclipsed the dire reality of his situation. Ari blinked, holding the knife tightly in his hand. It wasn't just a tool; it was a symbol of his father's legacy, his expectations, and, in some strange way, his faith in Ari's ability to overcome.

He adjusted his position, pain throbbing in his muscles. He strained as he worked the blade against the SummitTek backpack's unyielding straps. The super-strong material resisted initially, but the blade was sharp, razor-sharp, and after several tense moments, the strap gave way with a...*Snap!*

Ari plummeted into the darkness, the wind howling past him like a chorus of wailing demons. It felt endless, a free fall straight into Hell itself. His stomach twisted violently, and terror gripped his chest, squeezing the air from his lungs. He braced for the worst, jagged rocks waiting to shred him on impact, but the mountain had other plans.

He landed hard. Wet sand and gravel broke his fall with a sickening thud, the force slamming through his body and snapping his left ankle. Pain exploded in his leg, white-hot and searing, but the shock hit harder, dulling the edges of his awareness. The breath was driven from his lungs, leaving him gasping like a fish stranded on shore.

For a moment, he lay sprawled in the wet, freezing earth, unable to move. His heart pounded like a war drum, and the strip of sky far above seemed impossibly distant, mocking his survival. The throbbing in his ankle grew sharper as his mind cleared, his body beginning to register the damage.

When he attempted to move, a spike of agony pierced his side and a shock of pain shot up his leg, nearly paralyzing him.

"It's not broken," he muttered, though the pain screamed otherwise. "It can't be." He forced himself to probe his ankle lightly, wincing at the pain. Deep down, he knew the truth; it was broken, but the state of shock refused to let him dwell on it.

Gritting his teeth, he shifted his focus forward. The overwhelming instinct to survive drowned out the pain. Each second he lay there was a second wasted.

"You've survived worse," Stolz whispered in his mind, though the voice was quieter now, almost subdued.

Ari dragged himself upright, leaning heavily on his uninjured leg. The effort sent waves of dizziness and nausea flowing through him, but he clenched his jaw and forced himself to move. The mountain hadn't killed him yet, but he wasn't about to wait for it to change its mind.

Above him, the faint strip of sky seemed even narrower, like the gates of some cruel, otherworldly prison. Ari clenched his fists. He wasn't going to lie here and let the mountain win. Broken or not, he would keep going. He had no other choice because he wasn't going to lose this challenge.

The Search Continues

Raúl and his guides moved methodically high on the mountain, calling Ari's name into the still air. The roaring storm was gone, leaving a profound hush that every whisper echoed. Mateo fiddled with the hand-held locator. Ari's position remained steady.

"Boss," Mateo said quietly to Raúl, "We are close. The ravine is just ahead." His voice trembled slightly. Everyone knew the ravine was dangerous, with steep drops and loose rocks, but they had to try.

At mid-camp, Elinor stood by the radio station, her hands clasped tightly as if holding herself together. She barely noticed Bryan stepping up beside her, his arms crossed and his face determined. His presence was steady, but her focus remained glued to the faint crackle of the radio.

"If Raúl can follow that signal, they'll reach Ari soon," Bryan said, calm and reassuring. "Our trackers are some of the best. He can't be far."

Elinor nodded, swallowing hard. "Thank you, Bryan."

He nodded his head. "Just doing my job, Elinor. Ari's not just a boss, he's a friend. We're not leaving him out there, alone."

The words were a balm to her fraying nerves, but the weight on her heart didn't lift. As Bryan shifted to the radio, Elinor stepped back slightly, closing her eyes. Her silent plea felt like her only anchor in the thin mountain air, where every breath seemed harder to draw.

"Lord," she whispered, so softly the words barely left her lips, "guide Raúl and his men to Ari. Keep him alive. Let him hold on just a little longer."

The stillness around her seemed almost sacred, as though the mountain had paused to listen. She thought of Ari, his strength, determination, and how he could face challenges with a confidence that bordered on recklessness. Yet now, he might be facing something even he couldn't conquer alone.

The faint static hum broke her thought, and her eyes snapped open. Bryan leaned closer to the receiver, his expression firm as he fielded incoming transmissions. Elinor clung to the knowledge that they had a signal.

Ari was there, somewhere near that ravine, waiting to be found. The minutes dragged on, each one heavier than the last. The entire camp seemed to hold its breath, their collective hope tethered to the faint beeping of the locator.

And then, Raúl's voice cracked through the radio, sharp and clear, cutting through the static like a knife. Every head in the tent turned toward the receiver, breaths held as if even the faintest exhale might drown out his words. The tension was palpable, coiled so tightly it felt like the entire room might shatter under its weight.

Raúl's voice continued, his tone urgent but unclear in the bursts of interference. The team leaned closer, straining to catch every syllable, every hint of meaning. The radio crackled, his next words poised to land, and then... *silence.*

Purple Cloud of Fear

The cold, damp floor of the ravine seeped through his clothes as Ari gently pushed himself to his feet. His surroundings were dimly lit, the shadows stretching ominously in every direction. But something drew his attention, a faint glow in the distance emanating from what appeared to be a cave structure.

The glow pulsed gently, a deep, supernatural purple that seemed to shift and swirl like a living mist. Ari's breath caught in his throat. It was beautiful and terrifying all at once, unlike anything he'd ever seen.

"What is that?" he whispered, taking a hesitant step forward while limping severely.

Stolz's voice was silent. There were no taunting whispers, no prodding arrogance, just silence, as if even Stolz was scared by whatever this was.

As Ari limped closer, his instincts screamed at him to stop, to turn back. But his curiosity was more substantial. He felt a deep spiritual pull urging him toward the cave.

And then, IT stepped into view.

A being emerged from the purple mist, its form both ethereal and overwhelming. It was large, inhumanly tall. Its presence radiated warmth and an indescribable power. Its translucent form shifted like a storm cloud, hues of purple and magenta swirling within. Eyes like molten gold burned with an intensity that froze Ari in place.

The Being's voice shattered the stillness, reverberating through the ravine and into Ari's soul.

"THE REVERENT FEAR OF THE LORD IS THE BEGINNING AND PREEMINENT PART OF KNOWLEDGE, BUT FOOLS DESPISE GODLY WISDOM AND COUNSEL."

Ari's legs trembled as he dropped to his knees, his body responding before his mind could process what was happening. The energy emanating from the Being was unlike anything he had ever experienced, raw, consuming power.

"ARIEL KESHET," it continued with a thunderous and calm voice. "ARE YOU A FOOL, OR ARE YOU A SON OF GOD WHO WILL WORSHIP THE LORD YOUR GOD WITH REVERENCE AND AWE?"

Ari couldn't breathe. He couldn't think. All he could feel was fear, so profound it nearly stripped him of every shred of pride and ounce of defiance. He had faced boardrooms of ruthless executives, climbed mountains that few dared to attempt, and stared down the elements themselves.

But none of that had prepared him for this. This wasn't fear born of danger or failure. It was reverence, the overwhelming recognition that he was in the presence of something infinitely more significant than himself. A power that could snuff him out in a mere blink.

His lips moved, but no sound came out. He wanted to respond, to say something, anything, but the words wouldn't come.

The Being stepped closer, its presence filling the ravine. Ari's heart pounded so loudly he thought it might burst. His chest tightened, and he felt utterly powerless. And yet, amid his terror, a single thought flickered in his mind, a realization that terrified and humbled him.

This was no monster. This was no threat. This was the presence of God's justice and mercy manifested in a way he could barely comprehend.

The Being tilted its head slightly, waiting, its golden eyes fixed on him.

Ari's hands trembled as he finally found his voice, barely a whisper. "What... what do you want from me?" Ari's voice quivered, barely audible, as he knelt before the radiant figure. His entire body shook under its presence, his mind struggling to grasp what stood before him.

The Being's response was thunderous. "REVERENTIAL AWE FOR THE LORD GOD ALMIGHTY. WORSHIP HIM ALONE."

It reverberated in the thin air and deep within Ari's very soul. Its voice carried the roar of raging waters like a mighty river surging through canyons, each word flowing with relentless power and purpose.

Ari's breath hitched, but before he could process the Being's words, Stolz's familiar voice coiled through his thoughts, smooth and insidious.

"You? Serve? Worship? That's not who you are, Ari. You don't kneel to anyone. Remember who you are, Ari Keshet, self-made, untouchable. Do you really think bowing down will make you stronger? It will make you less. You're above this."

Ari's jaw tightened as Stolz's whispers fed the ember of defiance still smoldering in his soul. He clenched his fists, and his anger flickered in his gaze. Pride, the force that had driven his every success, wrapped around his thoughts like chains.

The *Spirit of the Fear of the Lord* watched Ari closely, its golden eyes unblinking. It seemed to see the conflict raging within him, and its gaze grew sharper and more piercing.

"ARIEL KESHET, YOU ARE WEIGHED AND FOUND WANTING."

Ari flinched. The words cut deep, something he didn't expect. The Spirit's form shifted, pulsing with holy intensity as if the air rejected his pride.

"YOU LACK REVERENCE. YOU LACK HUMILITY. YOUR HEART IS HARDENED WITH ARROGANCE AND SELFISH AMBITION. YOU ARE UNWORTHY TO RECEIVE GOD'S SPIRIT UNTIL YOU HUMBLE YOURSELF AND HONOR THE LORD YOUR GOD."

It lifted its hand, and in that fleeting moment, Ari beheld something extraordinary. A magenta orb was suspended above the Spirit's palm, its swirling currents resembling a rushing river somehow contained in a perfect sphere. Liquid light flowed within it, surging as if seeking release. Yet, as Ari's heart leaped at the sight, the Spirit pulled it back. The orb's shimmering water-like currents evaporated into the Being's ethereal essence, leaving only the memory of its luminous, fluid power behind.

"No...!" Ari reached out instinctively, his voice trembling with desperation and frustration. "Wait!"

Before he could say more, Stolz's mocking laughter filled his mind, drowning out other thoughts. *"Oh, Ari, you never disappoint. Humility? Reverence? Those words don't belong to you. Let it think you're unworthy; it doesn't matter. You've always made your own way and don't need its approval now."*

The *Spirit of the Fear of the Lord* began to fade, its voice carrying one final, thunderous warning as it disappeared into the mist: "BOW IN REVERENCE TO THE LORD GOD, OR YOU WILL REMAIN BLIND TO THE TRUTH. FOR YOU WILL SERVE A GOD... BUT WHICH ONE WILL IT BE? REMEMBER, SELF IS AN UNSTABLE AND DECEPTIVE GOD LEADING TO DEATH."

The purple light dimmed, leaving Ari alone in the cold, dark ravine. The warmth of the Being's presence lingered in the air, a palpable reminder of what had just transpired.

Stolz's laughter grew louder, triumphant and mocking.

"Well, that went beautifully. You don't need its approval. You're already everything you need to be. Just keep moving, this mountain will be yours soon enough."

Ari stood slowly and carefully, trembling. His chest heaved as he tried to steady his body and his thoughts. The terror he had felt moments before began to be replaced by a hollow ache. For the first time in years, a faint crack formed in his self-confidence. The memory of the Spirit's piercing gaze lingered in his mind, and he was unable to shake it. He couldn't entirely extinguish the feeling of fear and dread.

"Gotta keep moving," Stolz whispered, urging him forward. Ari turned toward the darkened path ahead, but his steps began to falter.

Stolz kept talking, louder, filling the silence with his usual bravado. But the words didn't land like they used to. They rang thin, like echoes in an empty chamber. Ari wasn't doubting himself. He was doubting Stolz.

The voice that once sounded like strength now sounded like mere noise. Ari wondered if this path of ambition and self-reliance was leading him away from what truly mattered.

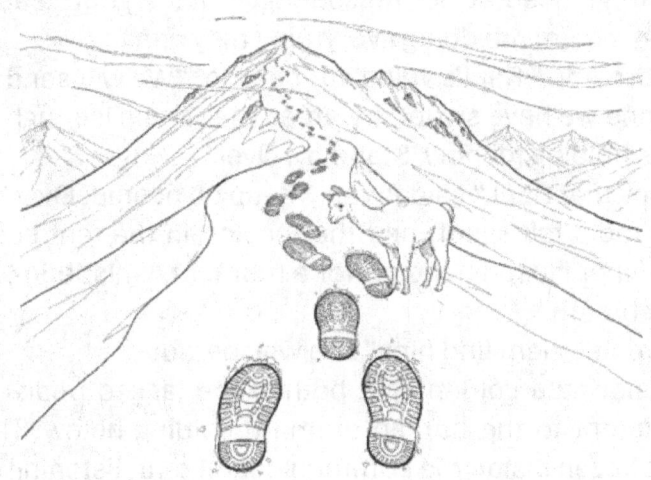

Chapter 8

Searching for Ari

Inside the mid-camp command tent, the air was thick with anticipation. Every pair of eyes was locked on the radio, its faint crackle, the only sound breaking the tense silence. Bryan leaned forward in his chair, fingers hovering over the controls as if willpower could push the next transmission through the static.

"Mid-camp, this is Raúl." The voice broke through, clear but urgent. "We have located Ari's backpack. Over."

A ripple of movement swept through the room. Elinor clutched her arms, her knuckles whitening as she pressed closer to the console. "Did he say the backpack?"

Bryan nodded grimly, his tone steady. "Copy that, Raúl. Can you confirm the location? Over."

Raúl's voice came back, firm but hurried. "The pack is about half a mile west of the avalanche path. It is wedged between rocks, no sign of Ari yet, but we are expanding the search. Over."

Elinor exhaled sharply, her mind racing. "If the pack's there..." she began, her voice trembling slightly, "then he has to be close."

Bryan glanced at her reassuringly. "It's a good lead, Elinor. Raúl and his team are doing everything they can."

"Mid-camp," Raúl's voice cut back in, "We will send another update once we have swept the area. The terrain is rough, but the weather is holding for now. Stand by. Over."

"Copy that Raúl," said Bryan, "Keep us posted. Over."

The radio fell silent, and the tension in the tent seemed to deepen. Elinor closed her eyes for a moment, whispering a prayer under her breath.

"Lord, let them find him," she whispered.

Outside, the golden light bathed the jagged peaks, serene and indifferent to the human drama unfolding below. The team remained frozen inside the communication tent, listening intently, waiting for the next crackle of hope to break through the static.

At the search site, Raúl and his men moved closer to the edge of the ravine, the air filled with tension. Beneath them, the drop yawned dark and silent. Ari's backpack lay wedged between two boulders near the brink, its locator flashing steadily. The strap was cut, blood marred the scene, and Ari was nowhere in sight.

Mateo looked over the edge, a knot tightening in his throat. He tapped the handheld device, expecting the coat's tracker to register, but it did nothing, only static and silence.

Raúl's face was grim as he studied the locator's readout. "The coat's beacon is not getting through," he said quietly. "Ravine walls must be blocking it. He might be moving deeper inside or trapped where we cannot see. If he shifts position, the signal may break free momentarily."

They exchanged uneasy glances. Above, the sky was serene, a cruel contrast to their mounting dread. Raúl keyed his radio. "Mid-camp, this is Raúl. We have got the backpack at the ravine. The strap is cut. No coat signal yet, likely blocked by stone walls. We will stay put. The ravine edges are unstable; using caution. Watching for movement and hoping the coat's beacon can get through. Over."

He leaned out cautiously, peering into the ravine. The bottom was lost in darkness. Loose stones tumbled down with no sound of impact.

"I cannot tell how far it goes." Raúl wondered, *Where is he?*

Mateo adjusted his pack. "Maybe the mountain swallowed him whole," he said, wiggling spooky fingers at the team.

Raúl shot him a cold look. "Not helpful, Mateo."

The radio crackled to life, making Mateo jump. A burst of static from mid-camp cut through the air.

"Raúl, any sign of Ari yet? Over."

"Negative. No signal, no visual, no Ari. Over."

He clipped the radio back to his vest and exhaled. The search team gathered in silence beneath the looming rock face. Nearby, a few crumbling edges warned them against attempting a rappel; any added weight could collapse the edges of the ridge entirely.

"We cannot go down there," Raúl commanded, "The rocks are too unstable, and I do not want to cause a landslide, and we are not picking up the beacon."

Mateo added. "Not even a blip on the radar."

Raúl's jaw clenched. "The ravine walls are blocking the signal. Or maybe..." His gaze lifted to the towering cliffs. "Maybe God and the mountain are hiding him on purpose."

Even Carlos, usually the joker, nodded with an unusual seriousness. "This mountain feels different. Like it has a voice." His words hung in the air.

Out here, the Andes felt alive. Pride didn't go unnoticed in this terrain, and nature had a brutal way of humbling men who thought they could tame it.

Then suddenly, *CRACK!*

A stone snapped loose and tumbled into the shadows. The team froze. Another sound followed, a faint rustling below.

Mateo leaned forward, eyes narrowing into the darkness. "Something is down there. It moved!" The team stiffened, hearts lifting in unspoken hope.

"Could be him?" Someone whispered. For a breathless moment, no one moved. No one breathed. They strained their eyes, willing a shape, a voice, any sign of life.

Then it emerged. An enormous black shape rose silently from the depths. "Diablo!" Mateo screamed. The broad wings caught the sunlight, casting a silver sheen along the edges. Its wings spread wide, nearly ten feet across, gliding effortlessly into the sky.

"Just a condor, merely a scavenger," Carlos reassured Mateo as the condor swooped, gracefully turning in wide, slow loops.

Raúl shook his head. "No, it is not just a condor... it is a witness." The large bird circled several times before vanishing beyond the cliffs, leaving a heavy silence... and everyone sensed it: neither God nor the mountain had finished speaking.

Raúl stepped back, his face hardening. "We are not done here. We need to keep looking and praying for a miracle."

The men stood quietly beneath the shadow of the cliffs, the wind whispering through the rocks like the breath of the mountain itself, watching, waiting.

"Let us start heading down. Maybe we will run into him as he finds his way out of the ravine," Raúl ordered, his voice cutting through the quiet murmurs. "If we do not find him soon, the mountain will not be the only thing we will have to worry about."

With that, the men rose, their boots crunching against the rocky ground as they resumed the search. Their voices called out Ari's name, echoing through the ravine only to be swallowed by the vast, callous peaks of the Andes. Determination pressed them forward, knowing full well that time wasn't on their side.

At mid-camp, Elinor closed her eyes at the update, her heart pounding. Bryan placed a steadying hand on her shoulder. "They'll keep searching," he said softly. "If Ari can shift position or find a vantage point, that coat tracker might blink through. Let's pray he moves soon."

Elinor nodded, clinging to the fragile hope that somewhere in those unforgiving cliffs, Ari would find a way to signal them, or at least keep himself alive until they could reach him.

Alone in the Ravine

Far below, Ari sat slumped against a jagged rock, his bloodied hands trembling with cold. The *Spirit of the Fear of the Lord* was gone, and its presence left an icy void that seemed to seep into his very bones. His heart still pounded from the encounter, the Spirit's words echoing in his mind:

"YOU ARE WEIGHED AND FOUND WANTING."

Ari felt small, truly small. His wealth, strength, pride, all of it had crumbled in the presence of that divine power. And now it was gone, leaving only the hollow whispers of Stolz.

"It abandoned you," Stolz hissed, mocking yet oddly soothing. *"That Being left you in the dirt, but I'm still here. I've always been here. And you're not weak. You're not lost. You're Ariel Keshet, master of every challenge."*

Ari clenched his bloody fists against the freezing air. "It said that I was unworthy," he shouted, his voice hoarse.

"And who is It to judge you?" Stolz retorted, his voice growing sharper. *"You're a king among men. A conqueror! Did It help you build your empire? Did It save you from that avalanche? No. You did that. You can get out of this ravine, too. Focus on what you can control. Focus on yourself."*

Stolz's words fed the faint flicker of defiance in his heart. His pride was battered but not broken, not yet. Though doubt in Stolz still lingered at the edges of his mind.

Ari rose slowly, every movement sending fresh waves of pain through his body. His head throbbed, a deep, pulsing ache behind his eyes, while a sharp jolt flared up his leg with each tentative step. His ribs ached with every breath, and his ankle throbbed angrily.

His breath was visible in the frigid air as he surveyed his surroundings. The jagged walls of the ravine stretched out like a labyrinth before him, offering no mercy.

"Where do I go?" Ari muttered, his voice barely above a whisper.

"Forward," Stolz purred. *"Always forward."*

Ari limped through the ravine, dragging his wounded leg behind him. Each step was a struggle, and he staggered deeper into uncertainty. The chill and pain in his bones refused to subside, and haunting reminders of the Spirit's presence pounded in his mind.

For now, the memory of its golden eyes and thunderous voice burned into his memory as Ari progressed painfully forward, terrified, lost, but still unwilling to surrender. Meanwhile, the mountain, though silent, watched and waited.

Thoughts of Better Times

Back at mid-camp, Elinor's eyes drifted toward the silent distant peaks. She thought about the tracking locators.

"These trackers," Elinor ventured, "do they have any... limitations?"

Bryan tilted his head, choosing his words carefully. "They're solid tech, but nothing's perfect. The coat tracker's not responding, which could mean it's damaged or he's not wearing it. The pack locator was working perfectly when Raúl found it."

"Not wearing it?" Elinor's brow furrowed, and a frown set in.

She didn't finish her thought, the unspoken fear hanging in the air.

Bryan caught her eye, softening his tone. "Ari's been in worse situations," he reassured her. "He's resourceful. We'll get him back, Elinor. You'll see."

The air in the command center felt heavy. Around her, the team buzzed with activity, typing on laptops, reviewing maps, and coordinating with the Peruvian guides. Every so often, a voice crackled over the radio with updates, each causing Elinor's pulse to quicken.

"Raúl reporting. Still searching the ravine area. No additional signs. Continuing search. Over."

She turned back to Bryan. "What's the plan if we don't find him by nightfall?"

Bryan hesitated, his lips pressing into a thin line. "We'll set up more checkpoints and expand the search radius. We have the best mountain gear and equipment in the world. The team is prepared to stay out as long as it takes."

Elinor's eyes drifted to the rugged Andes peaks, but her heart took her back to the dry sands of Israel three years ago, a place and time that, in hindsight, seemed like the quiet beginning of something powerful.

She remembered those long days at the Desert Bloom Initiative, working on a project dedicated to cultivating sustainable vegetation in harsh desert environments. Back then, her hands were always full of soil samples or irrigation notes, and her trusty cowboy boots kicked up dust as she trudged through the heat. She was focused on the land and the science, not on polished donors or celebrity benefactors.

When she first saw Ari, he struck Elinor as another well-dressed figure dropping in for a quick image boost. His immaculate suit and gleaming shoes looked almost absurd against the dusty desert backdrop.

But then, he approached her, cutting through the haze of sun and sand with a confident stride and a gaze so intense that she paused mid-task. "I'd like you to join me for lunch tomorrow," he said, his voice crisp and businesslike, as if this were a deal to be sealed rather than an invitation. She blinked in surprise, not accustomed to being addressed so directly by someone who appeared so out of place.

Her project manager had leaned in, whispering that she should accept the invitation; maybe it would secure more funding. Negotiation wasn't her strong suit; she preferred working with soil and seeds over business lunches and negotiations. Still, a sense of responsibility for her project nudged her to agree.

"It's settled, then," Ari had said before she could protest, a faint smile playing at his lips. He glanced at her dusty clipboard and boots as if taking stock of everything she stood for, practical, earthy, unpolished, and then walked away, leaving her intrigued and confused.

Little did she know that Ari had been observing her from the moment he had arrived. He found her refreshing, focused on her work, unimpressed by his status. She was different, and he couldn't look away. He was accustomed to carefully choreographed social arenas where everyone knew the game. But here was someone who didn't acknowledge the usual rules. In less than five minutes, he decided he needed to know her better. Since he lacked a more genuine approach, he played to his strengths, manufacturing a reason to meet under the guise of business.

The next day, Elinor showed up at the restaurant in her usual attire: her cleanest work shirt, jeans, and boots. The maître d' gave her a once-over but said nothing when Ari stepped in, his charm defusing any judgment. Still, she sensed a hint of tension in Ari's jaw, as if he was trying to play it cool but was uncertain how she'd react to such unfamiliar surroundings.

Then, in a moment that cracked his polished façade, Ari accidentally knocked over a glass of water and the breadbasket, sending dinner rolls tumbling across the pristine tablecloth. For a moment, he froze, feeling sheepish and embarrassed.

Elinor couldn't help but laugh, tossing him a stray roll. "So much for fine dining," she teased. "Want me to grab a mop while I'm at it?"

He chuckled, a genuine boyish sound that made him seem less like an out-of-place billionaire and more like a regular guy trying to impress someone who saw right through his act.

As they ate, conversation flowed easily. They discussed her work, his admiration for innovative projects, and their love of nature. When the server offered Ari wine, he politely declined, and Elinor's fingers brushed over the small cross necklace she wore. Ari's gaze followed the motion, hesitating before asking if she was Christian. She confirmed lightly, unashamed.

"I've just never... dated outside my Jewish faith," he admitted, caught off guard by the realization.

Elinor's smirk was both kind and firm. "Good to know, but let's be clear, I'm not changing for anyone's comfort. My faith isn't a phase, and besides... I didn't realize this was a date."

Ari blinked, momentarily thrown by her directness yet intrigued by her refusal to bend. He managed to smile. "Fair enough. You're not like anyone I've met before."

"And you're not nearly as intimidating as you think," she shot back, eyes twinkling.

Recalling that day now brought a smile to Elinor's face. That unexpected lunch had revealed Ari's humanity beneath his polished armor. It was also the first time she fully realized how different they were, and how those differences would shape and test whatever bond they formed.

Her reminiscing was cut short as she heard another update from Raúl. The mountain's harshness had not broken their spirit, and their resilience gave her hope. Elinor glanced at the Bible on the corner of a nearby table, where she had left it after a previous moment of quiet prayer.

She picked it up, running her fingers over its worn cover. At that moment, she whispered a prayer for Ari's safety. When she opened her eyes, she felt a flicker of peace. The mountain loomed cold and vast, but her prayers and the team's determination were mighty.

Somewhere out there, Ari was waiting to be found. And she wouldn't stop believing until he was.

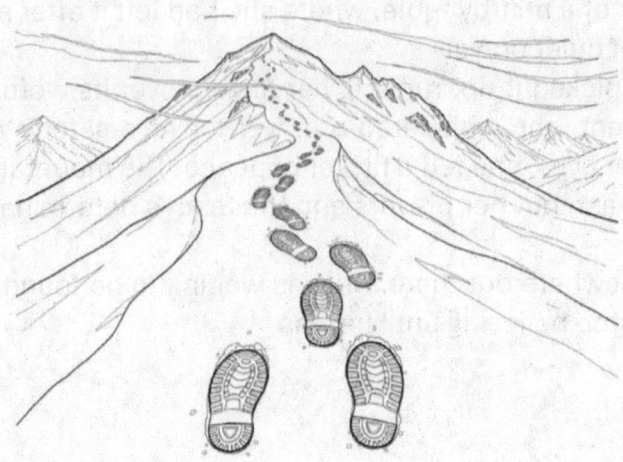

Chapter 9

The Winding Ravine

Ari Keshet staggered forward through the ravine's jagged throat, each breath a sharp, uneven gasp. The cold bit into his exposed skin, burrowing deep where the avalanche had ripped away his gloves, hat, and mask. His bare, bloodied hands gripped the icy rock, raw, trembling, and growing numb. He flexed his fingers, fighting the creeping paralysis, though it felt like trying to stop the ocean's tide.

Every step sent agony lancing up his left leg, the pain in his ankle searing and relentless. The SummitTek boots had spared him from worse, but not by much. The fall had left something seriously fractured. He couldn't tell how bad. He only knew that he needed to keep moving.

His ribs burned with every breath, tight and grinding, making each inhale a war. Dried blood crusted along his brow where his head had struck the rocks. The world tilted slightly each time he blinked.

Still, the coat held, SummitTek's finest, scuffed and torn at the edges but clinging to him like the last layer of civilization. It shielded him from the full wrath of the cold, even as the wind needled through gaps in the fabric, whispering of icy threats.

He paused, slumping against a frozen wall of stone. His breath came in short, shallow bursts. The pain in his ribs warned against deeper ones, and his mind fogged.

Then, *skitter*. A faint scratching sound cut through the silence. He froze, listening. *Skitter...skitter.*

His eyes tracked the dim shadows ahead, narrowing against the dusk. There, small shapes, flickering at the ravine's edge.

Mice? Tiny, swift, and impossibly living in this frozen graveyard.

Ari squinted. They weren't fleeing from him. They were moving ahead, disappearing into a narrow crevice between the rocks.

His heart gave the faintest lurch. A trail! He forced his body upright again, his voice hoarse. "Where are you going, little guys...?"

By all logic, he shouldn't have been walking. His ankle was wrecked, his ribs screamed with every breath, and his blood loss had left him shaky and cold. But the human body had its own strange mercy in moments like this; shock dulled the pain just enough to keep him moving. It wasn't strength; it was survival. Nerves numbed by trauma, instincts overriding agony.

And with nothing else to trust, not his body, not his bearings, he followed them. Quickly, they wove in and out of narrow crevices as if they possessed an innate map of this hostile place.

"You know the way out better than I do," he said hoarsely, voice ragged and unfamiliar to his own ears.

The mice paused, clustered on a ledge like a committee in urgent deliberation. Tiny noses twitched, whiskers flicked, and a few stood on their haunches, studying him with comically intense curiosity, as if trying to decide whether he was friend or foe.

One gave a squeak that almost sounded like a sigh. Another tilted its head and blinked slowly, as if weighing Ari's survival odds. Then, without any further ado, they turned as one and scurried forward, their little feet tapping against the stone in a brisk, determined rhythm.

"Great," Ari muttered, dragging himself upright. "Led out of a ravine by a rodent search party."

But with no better plan, he followed.

Every step was a negotiation between pain and balance. His scraped fingers clawed at the stone for support, slipping occasionally on patches of ice. His ankle flared, his ribs protested, and still, those mice pressed on like furry little Sherpas with somewhere very important to be.

They darted around a bend, pausing only briefly to make sure he was still coming. One even squeaked impatiently, as if urging him to pick up the pace.

Ari grunted, staggering forward. "You try falling off a cliff and see how fast you move."

The wind whistled overhead, but within the narrow path ahead, something had shifted. The mice weren't afraid of him. They seemed to show him kindness, which felt... oddly hopeful. Ari felt like he wasn't completely alone.

The mice reappeared momentarily farther down the ravine, effortless in their navigation. Ari envied their simple instinct, their fluid grace in a place that seemed determined to break him. They belonged here in a way he never could. Yet he was not broken... Not yet.

He straightened slightly. Every step tested him, but he refused to stop. "*Am I a man or a mouse?*" he mused, his voice barely audible over the hiss of the mountain wind. The answer felt elusive, swallowed by the cold, silent walls surrounding him.

Then, as his mind raced, he shivered from the vivid memory of the *Spirit of the Fear of the Lord*. The thought of those piercing eyes and the voice that had thundered with judgment and truth. The fear it had instilled was unlike anything he had ever known, not the adrenaline-fueled thrill he'd courted on countless adventures, but a terror that stripped him of control, of himself.

That Being, towering and utterly terrifying... had pierced through every layer of his soul, stripping away his facade layer by layer until the raw truth of his Pride stood bare. It had truly seen him, and it left no room for excuses.

Ari's Pride, the very thing that had propelled him to conquer mountains and build empires, was laid out before the Spirit like a dark, unflinching mirror of his soul. And at that moment, the Spirit judged him as unworthy. Its refusal to grant him the *orb*, to acknowledge even the smallest shred of his effort, stung more than any physical wound.

The weight of that rejection lingered like a phantom in his chest. He couldn't shake the feeling that the Spirit wasn't done with him, that its piercing gaze might return at any moment to demand parts of himself that he was unwilling to surrender.

The rejection bothered Ari more than he wanted to admit, the way it had turned away, as though his pride had tainted even his intentions. The cracks in his self-assurance felt irreversible, leaving him shaken in a way he couldn't quite understand or escape. He stumbled over a stone as he questioned. "What if it came back? What if it was watching even now, waiting to strike again?"

He growled under his breath, shaking his head as though to cast off the thought. His pride surged, a desperate antidote to the fear that gnawed at his soul. "I am Ariel Keshet, adventurer, billionaire, conqueror. And I will not cower in the face of a memory."

Still, the flashes haunted him. The purple light and the voice were like a thousand storms. They had made him feel so small, so powerless.

"Keep going... step by step," he coached himself, his voice stronger now as he moved forward, teeth gritted against the pain in his body and the turmoil in his mind. And yet, with every step, he couldn't shake the feeling that the Spirit's presence wasn't entirely gone. It lurked in the shadows of his mind, watching, waiting, testing him.

His footsteps mingled with the faint skittering of the mice squad ahead. His tormented mind began to wander. Drifting to Elinor. Her laugh came to him first, bright and genuine like sunlight cutting through the clouds. He could almost see her face. Her light green eyes sparkled when she teased him.

He remembered the time when she dragged him to a local farmer's market during a rare weekend together, insisting he needed to "see how real people shop." She'd laughed as he awkwardly fumbled with an oversized burlap tote bag, filling it with fresh produce. His polished demeanor was utterly out of place among the rustic chaos.

"You're hopeless," she'd teased, holding up a deformed, lumpy carrot. "But at least you're entertaining."

"Hopeless?" he'd shot back, trying to maintain his dignity while juggling a squash. "I run a multi-billion dollar business, Elinor. I think I can handle this."

"Uh-huh," she'd replied, unimpressed, a playful smirk tugging at her lips. "Let me know how that works when you're paying cash for kale. Oh, wait, you do carry cash, right?"

Ari froze mid-step, glancing at her with a raised eyebrow. "Cash? Who carries cash anymore?"

Elinor stopped, her smirk widening as she crossed her arms. "Apparently, everyone at this market. No credit cards, no Venmo. It's old-school, Ari, like, really old-school. Hope you've got some bills hidden in those fancy pockets of yours."

He reached instinctively for his wallet, flipping it open to reveal a sleek array of credit cards. Not a single dollar bill was in sight. He blinked at it, then at her, his expression a mix of mild irritation and disbelief.

"You've got to be kidding me," he muttered, snapping the wallet shut.

Elinor bit back a laugh. "Well, guess who's washing dishes to pay for dinner?" She turned back toward the vendor's table. Her cowboy boots kicked up dust as she led the way. "Don't worry. I'll lend you a few bucks, for a fee, of course."

Ari sighed, following her with a reluctant shake of his head. "But I am rich..." he grumbled under his breath. "And I'm borrowing cash for... kale."

"That's right," she called over her shoulder. "Welcome to the real world, Mr. Moneybags. Hope you like the view."

The memory brought a warm chuckle to his frigid surroundings, but Stolz quickly snuffed it out. The self-centered whisper in his mind had crept in, tainting the moment with his calculated words.

"You don't need anyone knowing your weaknesses," Stolz had murmured, smooth and seductive. *"She'll use them against you. Everyone does."*

And Ari listened. He slowly pulled back, hiding his feelings behind the wall of self-assured ambition. Stolz encouraged him to build that wall. It was easier that way, or so he told himself.

Mice of Hope

The mice skittered towards him, snapping Ari back to the present as their tiny bodies circled around him. Then, they vanished around a sharp bend in the ravine. He staggered after them, each step a battle against the protests of his battered body. His thoughts churned, as restless as the shadows around him.

Guilt gnawed at him, the sharp edge of regret over keeping Elinor at arm's length, over denying the depth of his feelings. His pride bristled at the thought of needing anyone, let alone her, and yet he couldn't shake the hollow ache left by her absence. Overlaying it all with his encounter with the *Spirit of the Fear of the Lord*, its piercing gaze continued to haunt him.

He paused for a moment, leaning heavily against the rock wall. The icy chill of the stone seeped into his skin, but it was a distant sensation compared to the storm of thoughts in his brain.

"She wouldn't understand," Stolz's voice cooed in his head, as smooth and familiar as ever. *"No one does. You don't need her. You don't need anyone but me. Look how far we've come."*

Ari shook his throbbing head as if the motion could dislodge the voice. He didn't have the strength to argue with Stolz, nor the clarity of mind to resist him.

As the mice scurried ahead, their faint squeaks echoing in the quiet, Ari pushed forward. Somewhere beyond the ravine, his team was searching for him. Somewhere, Elinor was probably pacing, worried, praying for him.

The thought sent a pang of something unfamiliar through him, not fear, not pride, but perhaps the slightest glimmer of hope. It was tentative, and Stolz would do everything he could to snuff it out.

But for now, Ari struggled on, following the path of compassionate creatures.

Moving Signal

The rescue team moved carefully along the ravine, boots crunching against loose stone. Suddenly, Raúl stopped. The tracker in his hand beeped.

"¡Se está moviendo!" he said, eyes fixed on the screen. "The tracker is picking up the signal. And it is moving!"

Santiago leaned in. "If it is moving... he is alive."

The radio crackled. Bryan's voice from mid-camp came through: "Raúl, confirm. You are detecting the signal, and it is moving? Over."

Raúl responded firmly, "Confirmed. Weak, but it's heading west down the ravine. Over."

At mid-camp, Elinor's breath caught. "If he's moving, he's alive, right?"

Bryan nodded, eyes on the screen. "Yes, it's a good sign. But the daylight's fading fast."

Twilight bled into the mountains, painting the peaks in dusky gold and purple. The wind turned sharp.

"Look!" Mateo pointed to a jagged rock cluster. "Signal is stronger here!"

Raúl raised the tracker again. The beeping grew louder. But the terrain was dangerous, and the last of the daylight was slipping away fast.

"We camp here tonight," Raúl said. "We move at first light. "As we all know, the mountain is deadly after dark." As the team pitched the high-tech Titan Tents, Raúl stood at the edge, watching the shadows swallow the rocks below. "The mountain is not done with him yet," he murmured.

The men worked in silence, their faces shadowed by the waning light. Raúl's voice carried softly but with authority as the final tent was secured. "At first light, we continue. For now, we rest. The mountain will still be here in the morning, and so will Ari."

At mid-camp, Elinor's breath caught as she watched the faint beeping on Bryan's screen. This was the only tether she had to Ari, and though it gave her hope, it also fed her anxiety. "How far away is he?" she asked.

Bryan frowned, leaning closer to the screen. "Not far, but it's getting dark, and we'll have to pause the search until morning."

Elinor bit her lip, glancing toward the horizon where the sun was already sinking behind the peaks. "Hold on, Ari," she whispered. "Just a little longer."

Led by Mice

Down in the ravine, Ari stumbled forward, each step wracked with pain. His ankle burned with every shift of weight, and his ribs protested each breath. But the scurrying mice ahead of him gave him something to focus on, something to follow.

They darted over rocks and slipped through narrow cracks with uncanny precision, always staying just ahead, just visible, like furry little guides with a secret map.

At first, he'd dismissed them as a hallucination or a coincidence. But now, after watching them reappear again and again, always leading, never lost, he was convinced: they were showing him the way out.

"All right, little guys," he rasped, voice raw from thirst and exhaustion. "Don't ditch me now."

The oppressive stone walls of the ravine slowly widened. Jagged shadows gave way to soft silver light as the full moon poured across the broken terrain. Above, the Milky Way stretched in a river of stars, shimmering in the pristine night sky.

Ari blinked, squinting as he emerged onto a wide, open ledge near a cliff. The mountain range unfurled before him, glowing under the twilight sky. Peaks rose like sleeping giants, their snowy crowns kissed with moonlight. The valley below shimmered in hues of lavender and pale blue, touched by the last breath of day.

Despite the pain still pulsing through his limbs, a flicker of relief stirred in his chest. He was out. The ravine and possible death were behind him. The mice scattered to the rocky edges and paused, turning as if to check on him. Ari gave a broken chuckle and limped forward before collapsing onto a patch of sandy dirt.

It felt like a luxury mattress compared to the brutal stone behind him. He lay there, chest heaving, staring up at the night sky. Stars twinkled above, bright and impossibly close.

"Thank you," he whispered, lips cracked, voice fading.

He didn't know if he was speaking to the mice... to the mountain... or to God. But something, someone, had led him here... and it felt like mercy.

As the cold night air began to settle, Ari curled up on the ground, his cold body trembling with exhaustion and pain. The wind whispered softly through the peaks, carrying a strange mix of calm. His eyelids grew heavy, and sleep began to overtake him before he could think any further. And under the silent, watchful moon, he finally slept.

Sunlight of Hope

The following day, as the first rays of sunlight stretched over the Andes, the rescue team resumed their search. Guided by the tracker, they eventually reached the open area near the cliff. There, lying curled up on the small patch of ground, was Ari.

Raúl rushed forward, kneeling beside him. "¡Lo encontramos!" (We found him!) he called out, his voice echoing over the rocks.

Ari stirred, his body stiff and writhing with pain, but his eyes fluttered open at the sound. Relief flooded him as the familiar faces of the rescue team came into view.

"You found me," he croaked, his voice hoarse.

"We always do." Santiago smiled. "We got you, amigo."

Ari tried to sit up, wincing at the pain in his broken ribs and limbs. He glanced toward the cliff's edge, where the mice watched him. Ari shook his head with a faint smile. "I owe a lot to some mice; the rodent squad," Ari chuckled, his voice raspy, drawing puzzled looks from the rescue team.

Raúl raised an eyebrow, exchanging a glance with Santiago, who shrugged.

Ari let out a hoarse chuckle, his gaze drifting toward the rocky crevices where the tiny creatures had vanished. "I had some unexpected guides," he added softly. "Tiny determined little guys. Smarter than I gave them credit for."

The team exchanged uneasy glances, unsure if exhaustion and a concussion had made Ari delirious, but he didn't elaborate further, leaving the strange remark in the air.

Raúl shook his head and muttered under his breath, "Creo que el frío lo ha vuelto loco." (I think the cold has made him crazy.)

The team exchanged curious glances but didn't press him. Raúl's voice was sharp and commanding as he directed the team. "We need to stabilize him before we move."

They worked quickly, layering Ari in thermal blankets to combat his hypothermia. Raúl placed a hand on Ari's shoulder, his tone firm but encouraging. "You are going to be okay. We will get you down this mountain."

One crew member spoke in clipped Spanish as he assessed Ari. "Hypothermia, possible concussion, fractured ribs, fractured ankle, and multiple lacerations... Ready for transport."

Pulling out his radio, Raúl called Bryan at mid-camp. "Bryan, this is Raúl. We have Ari ready for transport. He is alert but injured. Send emergency transport. We are at a clearing near the ravine. We have found a landing zone. Coordinates coming now. Over."

Raúl adjusted the straps of his pack, scanning the narrow, rocky clearing they'd reached. The area was flat enough for a skilled helicopter pilot to attempt a landing, though the tight space and surrounding cliffs posed a challenge. The weather, fortunately, was holding steady, clear skies and minimal wind, a rare gift in the Andes.

A crackle of static answered before Bryan's calm voice broke through. "Copy that, Raúl. How's he holding up? Over."

Raúl glanced at Ari, who was wrapped snugly in silver thermal blankets, resembling a hot dog at a street carnival. "He is alive, but he needs medical attention, fast. Tell the pilot the landing zone is tight. Over."

"Understood," Bryan said. "I'll relay the details to the rescue team. Hang in there, Raúl. Help is on the way. Over."

Raúl ended the transmission and turned to his team. "Prep the area. Clear as much debris as possible and make sure everything is stable. The helicopter will be here soon."

The guides worked efficiently, clearing rocks and marking the perimeter. Soon, the faint sound of helicopter blades reached his ears, growing louder as the rescue craft approached.

The Helicopter Evacuation

As the helicopter descended, its rotors stirred up a storm of snow and dirt. Raúl waved the pilot toward the flares, marking the landing site. The medics hurried, quickly transferring Ari onto the chopper's stretcher. The lead medic nodded, securing Ari and signaling the pilot. With a final look at Raúl, they lifted off, the helicopter ascending swiftly into the bright blue sky.

At mid-camp, Bryan approached Elinor, his steps brisk. "Raúl's team secured him in the helicopter and is en route to the hospital now."

She stood outside the tent, watching the helicopter in the distance as it flew towards the hospital. The tension in her chest felt as sharp as the mountain air, but her faith served as her anchor.

"Thank You, Lord, keep him safe," she prayed softly. A wave of relief surged through her, filling her with gratitude. Then she looked back at Bryan; her voice was more steady. "And Raúl? The team?"

"They're fine," Bryan reassured her. "They're heading back to mid-camp now."

Elinor nodded, her determination returning. "I suppose we'll start packing up and move to base camp once Raúl and the others return?"

"Yep, that's the plan," Bryan said, giving her a smile. "Ari's tough, Elinor. He'll make it through."

"I know," she said, her voice quiet. "I have faith."

While in the helicopter, Ari drifted in and out of consciousness. The rhythmic thrum of the blades was strangely soothing, though every jolt sent fresh waves of pain through his battered body.

As the mountains blurred below him, flashes of the encounter with the Spirit of the Fear of the Lord filled his mind. The piercing gaze and thunderous voice exposed his pride and left him vulnerable in a way that still unsettled him. The Spirit had seen him for what he truly was, and that truth gnawed at him.

But amid the fear and pain, another memory surfaced... Elinor's face, her teasing smile, her voice calling him to something greater than himself. He clung to the thought of her, wanting her badly. But Stolz worked hard in the recesses of his mind, urging him to dismiss the vulnerability she inspired.

As the helicopter banked toward the hospital, a flicker of humility stirred within him, battling against Stolz's influence. Ari Keshet, who had spent much time climbing to prove his strength, was beginning to see the limits of his own power.

Chapter 10

Celebrating the Rescue Heroes

The helicopter had taken off from the rugged mountain clearing near mid-camp two days earlier, carrying Ari Keshet to safety. Though battered and semi-conscious, Ari had been transported, leaving the SummitTek team and Peruvian guides to finish their descent in his absence.

At base camp four days later, the remaining members finally returned. The relief of reaching the lower altitude was palpable, but an unspoken tension lingered.

"Any updates on Ari"? Elinor asked quietly, standing near the main tent as Bryan unpacked gear beside her.

Bryan shook his head. "Gottschall's been the only one in contact. She said he's stable since the surgery, but no visitors. Rest is priority."

Elinor nodded, biting the inside of her cheek. She couldn't help but feel frustrated at being left in the dark, though she knew Gottschall's no-nonsense approach was probably the best thing for Ari.

Raúl and the Peruvian guides arrived at base camp alongside the SummitTek team, their faces etched with exhaustion but satisfied with the rescue efforts. The group worked together to dismantle the remaining structures.

As Raúl helped secure supplies, Elinor approached him, her expression a mix of gratitude and curiosity. "Thank you for everything you did," she said. "I know it wasn't easy."

Raúl nodded, his tone steady. "It is what we do. On the mountain, you take care of each other."

She pressed, her voice softer. "Did he... did he say anything?"

Raúl hesitated, then gave her a reassuring smile. "Not much, señorita. He was fighting to stay awake. Although, he is stronger than he looks."

Santiago, standing nearby, joined in, his English accented but clear. "Your boss, very lucky. That storm... wow! Like mountain had it out for him. Teaching him big lesson!"

Bryan, overhearing, raised an eyebrow. "What do you mean?" Santiago shrugged. "Sometimes, Andes will test. It is not the climb, it is when mountain chooses to challenge."

Elinor crossed her arms and shot Bryan a look. "Oh, great. So now the mountains have agendas? Maybe next time, they could send a memo before nearly killing someone."

Raúl chuckled, shaking his head as he stepped closer. "Señorita Elinor, the mountain does not send memos. It sends lessons."

She raised an eyebrow, her voice dripping with sarcasm. "Well, I hope Ari kept his notes because I'm not climbing back up there to get them."

Raúl, sensing her underlying worry despite her sharp words, softened his tone. "He will be fine. Señorita Gottschall is with him." "Of course she is," Elinor smirked, although the tension in her shoulders didn't ease.

Packing Up

As the sun dipped below the horizon, casting long shadows over the camp, the team worked steadily to prepare for their return to Denver. The air was heavy with exhaustion but carried an undercurrent of accomplishment, tinged with a lingering worry for Ari.

Carlos, ever the comedian, wiped his brow dramatically as he heaved a crate into the truck. "I will tell you something, Raúl," he said, turning the words into a melody of humor. "¿Señorita Gottschall? She is not just running this mountain expedition; she is the mountain."

Raúl stopped mid-step, raising an eyebrow. "The mountain?"

Carlos nodded enthusiastically, gesturing toward the towering peaks. "Sí, big, immovable, and commanding respect. You do not climb a mountain like that; you admire it from a safe distance. But me? I would risk it all. Maybe she is my Mount Everest."

Raúl snorted, shaking his head. "Carlos, she is not a mountain; she is an avalanche. And if you do not watch yourself, she will crush you."

Carlos grinned, remembering her poise and competence. "Then I will die a happy man. There are many ways to go; I will go under the power of that woman."

Raúl rolled his eyes but couldn't suppress a chuckle. "You would be buried in seconds."

"And what a burial it would be," Carlos shot back, a dreamy look overtaking his face. "I would have no regrets."

From a few feet away, Bryan smirked, catching the tail end of the conversation. "Careful, Carlos. She might find out what you said, and then you'll find out just how much of an avalanche she really is."

Carlos shrugged, still smiling. "Maybe she already knows. She did not correct me when I called her 'Majestic Maria' the other day."

Raúl shook his head, giving Carlos a hard slap on the back. "One of these days, Carlos, your mouth will dig you a grave."

Carlos winked. "And maybe she will lay the first stone. What an honor."

The laughter eased the tension in the air, giving the team a brief reprieve from the weight of the expedition. As the last of the gear was secured, Elinor stood near the edge of the camp, her gaze fixed on the peaks looming behind them like silent guardians. She thought of Ari, his cocky grin, his relentless ambition, and the cracks in his armor she'd glimpsed before the disaster.

Raúl approached, his tone gentler than usual. "Señorita Elinor," he said, his accent softening his words, "It is time to go. You will see him soon."

Elinor smiled faintly. "I would like to get to the hospital as soon as possible."

Raúl gave her a small nod of reassurance. "He is a strong man. Stubborn, like the mountain itself. But he will make it."

She nodded, taking a deep breath, before joining the others for the journey back. Behind her, the peaks stood silent. Their mysteries were left for another day. But in her heart, she carried the hope that Ari had gained something valuable from the mountain's test.

Meanwhile, Carlos watched her leave, then leaned toward Raúl with a playful grin. "What do you think, does Elinor have an avalanche in her, too?"

Raúl smirked, shaking his head. "Careful, Carlos. Too many avalanches in one expedition might be too much for even you."

Hospital Hijinks

Days later, Ari lay propped up in a hospital bed, his left ankle encased in a thick cast after the most recent surgery. The room was quiet except for the faint hum of medical monitors, but Ari's mood was anything but subdued. The effects of the pain medication were evident; his usually sharp, composed demeanor had melted into a relaxed, goofy state.

His dark hair was messy, sticking up in odd directions, and a lop-sided grin spread across his face. He looked nothing like the confident, prideful billionaire who had set out to conquer the Andes. Instead, he resembled someone blissfully unaware of their predicament, chatting away with a carefree ease that was entirely out of character.

Elinor arrived breathless, as though she had run straight from the mountain. She sat by his bedside, watching him with amusement and concern. "You're going to be okay, Ari," she said, squeezing his hand.

"I know," he replied, his voice slurring. "You're here. And the mice are here. They led me to you, Elinor. There was a parade of mice. Brave little guys. And the purple cloud, it talked to me. Told me scary stuff."

Elinor blinked, struggling to follow his rambling. "Mice parade, a purple cloud?"

"Yeah," Ari said, nodding his head like a 5-year-old. "Very wise. Very scary. And you know what it said?" He leaned closer, his expression suddenly serious. "It said... you're the best thing that ever happened to me... and you smell nice."

Elinor bit her lip, holding back a laugh. "That's quite the revelation."

"I'm serious," Ari continued, his words spilling like a flood. "I love you, Elinor. Like... not just love, but love-love. You know? Like... I'd climb another ravine and break my leg for you... with the mice parade, of course."

Stolz stirred in Ari's mind, attempting to reassert his influence. *"Don't embarrass yourself, Ari. Pull yourself together. You're losing your edge."* But the medication kept Stolz's whispers at bay, reducing his influence to a faint hum in the background.

Ari, oblivious to Stolz's frustration, turned to Elinor with a dreamy smile. "Did I ever tell you how pretty your eyes are? Like, so green. Like the rain forest... or kale."

Elinor blushed, laughing softly. "Kale? You need rest, Ari."

"No, no, no. I need you," he insisted, reaching for her hand. "You and the mice. You're my team."

Gottschall to the Rescue

At that moment, Gottschall entered the room, clipboard in hand, her expression sharp and unreadable. She paused inside the doorway, looking at Ari's lovestruck, loopy grin as he sighed audibly. "Oh dear... what is he saying?"

"Nothing too damaging," Elinor replied, her cheeks pink though her amusement was hard to hide.

Gottschall frowned, stepping closer to Ari's bedside with a deliberate air of authority. "Mr. Keshet, this is neither the time nor the place to discuss your... feelings."

Ari waved a hand lazily, his grin widening. "Maria, you're amazing. Did I ever tell you that? You're like... a bear. No, wait. A beautiful, cuddly mama bear. The kind that scares the wolves but hugs the cubs. That's you."

Gottschall's eyebrows shot up. "No, and I'd prefer you didn't."

"But it's true!" Ari insisted, his voice rising with excitement. "You're the backbone of SummitTek. You keep us all from falling apart. And the Titan Tent? Brilliant. That was mine, right? Oh, wait, I shouldn't say that. Trade secrets."

Gottschall's eyes narrowed. "Yes, Mr. Keshet, and let's keep it that way. No more trade secrets." She glanced at Elinor, her tone shifting into something dryly amused. "I hope you can manage over-talkative and over-medicated patients."

Elinor stifled a laugh, though her lips twitched. "He's... quite expressive right now."

Ari, oblivious to their exchange, leaned forward conspiratorially. "Elinor, did you know I can't drink scotch? Not because I don't want to, but because it messes with my superpowers of decision-making skills. And it causes my brain to do wheelies, like... really bad wheelies. My brain is my greatest superpower. Except, you know, Ari flipped his index finger in the air. "When Stolz is talking... being Stolz."

Gottschall's head whipped toward Elinor. "Why is he talking about Stolz?" she asked sharply. "What has he said?"

Elinor shrugged, playing it off. "He hasn't really said anything that makes sense. It's just something Ari mumbles about when he's feeling stressed."

"Wonderful," Gottschall replied dryly. "Well, let's not add corporate espionage to his drug-induced revelations. Keep him hydrated. And if he starts talking about company mergers, call me immediately."

Ari's face lit up. "Maria, you're so good at this. We should give you a raise. And a medal. And, like, a really, big vacation. Somewhere sunny... with alpacas!"

Gottschall's lips tightened as she slowly turned to Elinor. "Good luck. I'll be back in an hour."

Later, Ari's rambling slowed, and he drifted into sleep. Elinor adjusted the heated blanket over him, brushing a stray lock of hair from his forehead. She smiled and momentarily allowed herself to savor the vulnerability he rarely let anyone see.

Gottschall lingered by the door, her sharp gaze softening just slightly. "He's lucky to have you here," she said quietly, her voice uncharacteristically warm.

Elinor raised her gaze, locking eyes with Gottschall. "We're fortunate to have one another," she responded calmly.

Gottschall nodded once, her expression unreadable as she stepped out of the room. But just as she reached the door, she paused and glanced back. "For the record," she added, her tone dry but with a hint of a smile, "I'll consider... the alpacas."

Elinor chuckled as Gottschall walked away.

Homeward Bound

Ari's return to Denver was far less triumphant than expected. The SummitTek Gulfstream touched down smoothly, but instead of the usual fanfare of staff and press, an ambulance was waiting on the tarmac to whisk him away to his mansion.

Gottschall ensured every detail was handled with military precision, from Ari's transport to his temporary homebound setup. She had set up her command center for SummitTek at the mansion so she could keep an eye on Ari and give command orders to the SummitTek crew. When the ambulance doors closed, she was already on the phone, coordinating with the staff to prepare for his arrival.

Days later, Ari sprawled across the plush leather sofa in his Denver mansion, looking less like a billionaire tech mogul and more like a half-mummified crash test dummy. His left ankle, now encased in a thick cast, rested atop a precarious tower of designer pillows that had not been intended for orthopedic support.

His ribs were wrapped tightly in layers of post-surgery gauze, and a bandage circled his head like a makeshift crown. Rumor had it that one of the hospital interns, a nervous med student on her first rotation, had practiced her bandaging technique on him like he was a mannequin from an EMT class.

Judging by the uneven wrapping and the faint scent of cherry-scented antiseptic, the rumor wasn't far off.

Gone was the polished figure in a tailored SummitTek suit. In his place was a man in a rumpled T-shirt and oversized sweatpants. His usual tailored elegance had been replaced by sweatpants two sizes too large and a mop of bedhead that looked like it had lost a fight with a pillow, and his ego was more battered than his body.

He shifted uncomfortably, the movement sending a sharp jolt of pain up his leg. His face twisted into a grimace as he let out a groan. The brace dug into his skin, and the cold ache in his ankle throbbed with every heartbeat. Even the pillows felt like an insult. His patience was unraveling rapidly.

"I'm a damned racehorse stuck in the stall," he muttered, running a hand through his messy hair. The urge to move, to do something, anything, gnawed at him. His body might have been forced into stillness, but his mind raced a hundred miles an hour.

Meetings he couldn't attend, projects he couldn't oversee, mountains he couldn't climb, all of it buzzed relentlessly in his thoughts.

The sound of the clock ticking on the wall became unbearable. His fingers itched to grab his phone or laptop, but Gottschall had confiscated them, citing "doctor's orders." Even the television remote was suspiciously absent.

"Imprisoned in my own home," he grumbled, shifting again and immediately regretting it as pain flared. "This is ridiculous."

But it wasn't just the physical confinement that irked him. It was the helplessness. The sense that, for the first time since childhood, he wasn't in control, not of his body, not of his business, not even of his schedule. It was a feeling he hated that clawed at his pride with relentless aggression.

From her station in the adjoining room, Gottschall's sharp ears caught the sound of his complaints. She didn't miss a beat as she walked in, clipboard in hand. "Mr. Keshet, if you move that ankle one more time, you will undo all our progress."

Ari glared at her, but it was useless. "I can't just sit here, Maria."

"You don't have a choice," she replied, precisely adjusting the pillows under his leg. "You might be used to conquering mountains, but right now, you're conquering rest. And judging by your attitude, that is the harder task."

Ari sighed, leaning his head back against the sofa. His body might have been confined, but his mind was still a battlefield of memories, one where his impatience and pride waged war against the growing realization that, for once, he had to comply.

Family Visit

The sound of footsteps and muffled voices echoed down the hallway. Ari barely had a moment to brace himself before his mother, Iris Keshet, swept into the room like a whirlwind. Her warm brown eyes immediately softened when they landed on her son. Following closely, his father, Abner, strode in with his distinctive New Yorker gait, clad in a perfectly tailored suit and a precisely knotted tie.

"Oh Ariel, my son, look at you," Iris exclaimed, rushing to Ari's side. She placed a hand on his forehead as if checking for a fever. "You're pale! Are you eating enough? Drinking water? Maria, why does he look like he's been living on crackers and tap water?"

Standing near the doorway with her clipboard, "Mr. Keshet is being monitored carefully, Mrs. Keshet. His meals are prepared according to strict nutritional standards. I assure you, crackers and tap water are not part of the menu."

Abner, already scanning the room with his scrutinizing gaze, sat heavily in a chair opposite the sofa. "An outdoor expedition," he said, his thick New York accent slicing through the air. "And this is how you come back? Broken body? Dragged out of some ravine like a rookie? I told you, Ari, stick to the boardroom. You are a CEO, not some adrenaline junkie."

Groaning sarcastically, "Good to see you too... Dad."

"Don't get smart with me," Abner gruffed, wagging his finger. "This wouldn't have happened if you had listened to me and stayed where you belong... behind a desk. Let your team handle the dangerous fieldwork."

"Abner," Iris interjected sharply, shooting him a look. "He needs rest, not a lecture."

Abner huffed but leaned back in his chair. "Uggh... I'm just saying."

Iris ignored him and returned to Ari, gently smoothing the blanket over his legs. "Sweetheart, this is why I keep telling you to settle down. Find a nice Jewish girl, get married, and have some babies. Enough of this mountain climbing and jet-setting nonsense."

Ari shifted uncomfortably, adjusting the pillows under his propped-up ankle. "Mom, I don't think a wife and kids would've saved me from an avalanche."

"They'd keep you off those mountains," she countered, her tone unwavering. "You're 40, Ari. It's time. A family would ground you, give you purpose beyond all... this." She gestured vaguely to the room. "A mix of fancy possessions and exhaustion."

Gottschall, standing nearby, cleared her throat with perfect timing. "Perhaps, Mrs. Keshet, that's a discussion for another time. Right now, Mr. Keshet needs to focus on his recovery."

"I don't see what's so hard about finding the right girl. He's got the looks and the money..." Abner muttered.

Ari felt his jaw tighten. His parents meant well, but their incessant push for him to marry a "nice Jewish girl" grated on him. What would they say about Elinor? He could already imagine his father's skepticism and Iris's disappointment at her being a Christian. He wasn't ready for that conversation... not now, not like this.

"Can we not?" Ari said, his tone edged with irritation. "My personal life isn't exactly a priority right now."

Iris sighed, patting his arm gently. "Fine, fine. But don't think you're off the hook. I'm your mother, I'll keep bringing it up until you listen."

"Shocker!" Ari complained.

Gottschall's sharp gaze flicked to Abner, who was poised to say something more. "Mr. Keshet needs rest. That means no more discussions about his marital status or his career decisions. Doctor's orders."

Abner threw up his hands in mock surrender. "Alright, alright. We're just saying what every parent would say."

Iris stood, leaning down to kiss Ari's forehead. "We just want the best for you, darling. That's all."

As his parents exited the room, they were muttering something about "kids these days," Ari let out a long breath. He loved them, but their well-meaning intrusions felt heavier than his physical injuries. He glanced at Gottschall, who was already rearranging his pillows with the efficiency of a drill sergeant.

"They mean well," Gottschall said, her voice softer than usual.

"I know," Ari replied, his voice low. "But sometimes it feels like they're rooting for a version of me that doesn't exist anymore."

Gottschall looked at him but said nothing, her silence more comforting than any words. In the quiet that followed, Ari couldn't help but think of Elinor, her wit, her beautiful eyes, and her ability to challenge him without tearing him down. She was nothing like some of the "nice Jewish girls" his mother envisioned.

But maybe, just maybe, Elinor was exactly what he needed.

Gottschall the Gatekeeper

Later, in the grand foyer of Ari's Denver mansion, a cluster of SummitTek executives gathered near the base of the sweeping staircase, resembling a group of eager teenagers at a rock concert jostling for a glimpse of their favorite boy band backstage. Their polished leather shoes tapped lightly against the pristine marble floor, and they leaned toward each other, whispering in hushed, excited tones.

Above them, a crystal chandelier cast shimmering light across the scene, shining off brass fixtures and the executives' anxious faces that mirrored the star-struck glow of adoring fans.

The tension in the air was palpable, like a tightly wound spring, ready to release at the slightest provocation. They were on edge, each hoping to slip past the gatekeeper and gain a moment of Ari's time, much like fans clutching memorabilia and hoping for an autograph.

"Do you think he'll see us?" one murmured, anxiously tugging at the knot of his silk tie.

"Not if Gottschall has anything to say about it," another replied, eyes darting at the imposing figure near the corridor that led deeper into the mansion's private rooms.

Gottschall stood like a sentinel, and her steel eyes narrowed as she took in the group. She resembled a formidable headmistress or perhaps a military officer surveying raw recruits. The executives straightened instinctively under her gaze, their confidence waning.

One of the men stepped forward, clearing his throat. "We just need a few minutes of Mr. Keshet's time," he said, attempting a diplomatic smile. "He's... unavailable by email, and this matter is quite pressing."

Gottschall's heels clicked once against the marble as she stepped toward them, silencing him with her presence before words left her lips. She began, her tone calm but unequivocal, "Mr. Keshet is unavailable for meetings. If you have business that requires his immediate attention, you may forward it to me."

The bold executive's brows drew together. "But this is urgent," he insisted, his voice cracking slightly as he tried to maintain his composure. "We need his input on...,"

Gottschall raised her hand, and the protest died in his throat. The foyer's hush deepened, and the faint hum of distant ventilation could be heard.

"I decide what is urgent," she said, clipped and precise. "Unless the building is on fire, you are not getting past me."

Several of the executives exchanged uneasy glances.

Their shoulders slumped, and a few stepped back, acknowledging defeat. Under Gottschall's unwavering stare, they realized resistance was futile. Muttering quietly, they retreated toward the double doors that led back outside, intending to regroup and reconsider their strategy.

Gottschall watched them depart, not a flicker of doubt crossing her face. Once they were gone, she allowed herself a small, satisfied exhale. Her gaze shifted upstairs toward the private wing where Ari Keshet rested, injured but safe from interference. No matter how critical these executives believed their agendas to be, Gottschall would ensure that Ari's recovery took precedence.

Ari's Reflection

As the room settled into a gentler rhythm, his mother's soft laughter drifting across the space and his father's voice responding in its usual tone of sage disapproval, Ari turned toward the panoramic windows overlooking the Denver skyline.

Beyond the glass, the city sprawled out like a gleaming circuit board, highways snaking around glowing skyscrapers. It all looked neat and orderly, unlike the chaotic peaks he loved.

He let out a slow breath, one part longing and two parts irritation. This was supposed to be his downtime, but sitting still wasn't in his DNA. Rest was an enemy he couldn't out-climb, out-think, or out-fund. Sure, the view was nice, with soft evening hues and twinkling lights, but something about his sterile luxury felt stifling, like being stuck in a gilded cage... with orthopedic pillows.

The itch to climb nagged at him. He could almost hear the crunch of snow beneath his boots, the whistle of the wind through icy crevices. He longed for the sting of cold air, the thrill of being one misstep away from disaster. But no, here he was, grounded by a bum ankle that currently looked like a swollen eggplant.

He shot a glare at his propped-up foot, now wrapped, stitched, and braced like a fragile museum piece. A swollen, throbbing mess. Narrowing his eyes, he muttered, "One little storm, and now I need a tactical plan just to get to the toilet."

Frustrated, he exhaled sharply, deciding his foot had stolen enough of his attention. Instead, he let his thoughts drift to something far more pleasant..., Elinor.

He pictured her at home, maybe surrounded by those absurdly cheerful plants she kept alive with ease. What would she think if she saw him now? She probably tilted her head in that infuriatingly understanding way, as she could see right through him.

The thought made him shift uncomfortably.

It was bad enough to be stuck in his current state; it was worse to imagine her quietly shaking her head at his impatience.

He smiled faintly, though, at the thought of her laugh. It wasn't just a laugh, it was sunlight in sound form. She'd probably tell him to enjoy the downtime, maybe hand him a book about something botanical he didn't care about but would pretend to read just to make her happy.

And just as his thoughts turned dangerously pleasant, Stolz's voice slithered into his head like an unwelcome party guest who wouldn't take the hint to leave. *"Rest? Really? You're Ari Keshet. You don't rest. You conquer. You prove them wrong. Weakness is for lesser men."*

Ari rolled his eyes, his jaw tightening. "Lesser men don't have purple ankles," he muttered, but Stolz didn't care. The voice prodded, oozing pride and disdain in equal measure, trying to coax him back into its grip.

He forced the voice to the background, letting his parents' chatter fill the space instead. His mother recounted some glowing tale of his childhood achievements, and his father was quietly correcting the details, as usual. It should have been comforting, this warmth, this safety, but to Ari, it was like being wrapped in bubble wrap and told to sit still. Necessary, maybe, but suffocating all the same.

His gaze returned to the skyline, the lights shimmering like a challenge. He could almost hear the mountains calling him back, daring him to try again. He sighed heavily. For now, he was stuck in this gilded recovery room. But soon enough, the ankle would heal, and he'd be back where he belonged, on the edge of brilliance or catastrophe, just as he liked it.

Ari smirked to himself. "Until then," he muttered, "I guess I'll practice the art of sitting still without losing my mind." It wasn't quite Mount Everest, but it might as well have been for a man like him.

Elinor's Reflection

Late evening light streamed through Elinor's apartment window, softening the chaos of books, potted plants, and the battlefield of half-written research notes scattered across her desk. She sat curled up on her love seat, hands wrapped around a mug of herbal tea, trying, and failing, not to think about Ari.

It had been a couple of weeks since she'd seen him. Bandaged and thoroughly irritated, while in the Peruvian hospital.

Even doped up on pain meds, he had spilled out a provoking amount of charm and ego... that made him, well... Ari.

She smiled despite herself, remembering his slurred words about heroic mice leading him to safety and a purple cloud that looked suspiciously like God. The man had been utterly delirious, his vocabulary a mix of tender confessions and drug-induced nonsense. But somewhere in between, he'd called her beautiful and "the best thing that ever happened to him." This was so un-Ari that she laughed and cherished the memory.

Still, the words stuck with her like sticky honey she couldn't quite wash off. Had he meant it? Or was it just the morphine talking? Knowing Ari, it was 50/50; he'd either accidentally stumbled into the truth or his painkiller-fueled brain had been workshopping movie clichés.

Elinor sipped her tea, staring at the potted plant on her windowsill, the same one she'd once tried to give him as a gift. His reply? "I don't do plants, Miller." Ari was about scaling impossible heights and conquering metaphors but give the man a houseplant and suddenly he's helpless.

Her lips twitched at the memory, but the ache in her chest deepened. Their worlds were so different. She was used to faith and humility, where success was measured in kindness and trust. Ari was a man of skyscrapers and summits, charging at life as if it owed him something.

Yet somehow, they found a way to laugh together, to see each other in those rare, unguarded moments.

She could imagine him at home in his luxurious estate, probably scowling at his propped-up ankle for having betrayed him. He was likely pacing, or at least trying to, refusing to let something like a broken bone slow him down. Knowing Ari, he was probably plotting his next adventure amid documents on how to "dominate" nature and texting his assistant about gear upgrades.

And then there were those moments. Those other moments, like the way his gaze softened when he looked at her, even when he pretended not to. She replayed his hospital bed confession. Was there truth buried in it, or just Ari's way of filling the silence? She sighed, placing her tea on the table and reaching for her Bible.

Her fingers traced the embossed foil letters slowly before opening and flipping through the pages, seeking the wisdom she always turned to in times of doubt. She mused that love was no simpler than scaling a mountain; it required courage, balance, and the ability to trust that the other person wouldn't let you fall.

And Ari? He was as wild and unpredictable as the Andes, a man who seemed more comfortable dangling off cliffs than holding onto someone's heart.

She sighed, setting her mug aside. Falling for Ari felt a little like standing too close to the edge of a cliff. Exhilarating but incredibly stupid. *What if he didn't catch me? Worse, what if he didn't even notice I was falling for him?*

He was all sharp edges and restless ambition, a man who saw the world as a series of mountains to climb. She, meanwhile, was the girl on the sidelines, clutching her heart and wondering if he'd ever notice it was his for the taking.

Did she want him? Absolutely. Did she also want to protect herself from being flattened by Ari Keshet's force? Oh, yes. She suspected that the man didn't do anything halfway, not even in relationships.

For now, though, she would wait, letting hope bloom while keeping her heart tethered.

If Ari ever figured out that conquering wasn't the same as connecting, maybe, just maybe, there would be a future for them. Until then, she'd stay grounded in her quiet faith, praying that someday the man she saw beneath the bravado would finally see her.

And if he didn't? She'd always have her chamomile tea and thriving plants to console her. At least they knew how to appreciate a little tender loving care.

Chapter 11
Hanukkah

The Keshet mansion glowed with the warmth of Hanukkah. The menorah's golden candlelight danced against polished marble and burnished wood. The scent of fried latkes mingled with fresh-cut evergreens, creating a festive and comforting atmosphere. Ari reclined in his favorite armchair, his injured ankle propped on a plush ottoman. The soft crackle of the fireplace and the hum of conversation in the background made him feel more like a boy in his parents' home than the Boss who commanded global attention.

Ari's parents had flown in from New York, determined to celebrate the Festival of Lights with their son, injured or not. Abner spun the Dreidel with an expert flick of the wrist, the move practiced from decades of holiday gatherings. Iris hovered near a tray of sufganiyot, carefully dusting them with powdered sugar as though each pastry were a masterpiece. They embraced tradition with polished ease, and at this moment, Ari could almost forget the complexities of his life beyond these walls.

"Come on, Ah-ree!" Abner boomed with his New York accent. "You're never too old to win a few chocolate coins. Spin the Dreidel!"

Ari gave a good-natured chuckle, leaning forward to oblige. "Alright, Dad, but when I empty your gelt stash, don't say I didn't warn you."

"We'll see who cries, kid," Abner smirked.

Iris clapped her hands lightly. "This is exactly what I wanted, us together, laughing." Her tone held genuine delight, but Ari noticed a slight nervousness beneath her bright smile. Perhaps it was the knowledge that they would not be alone tonight, that Ari had invited someone who mattered to him.

As if on cue, Elinor entered the room with a tray of fresh cookies. She wore a warm Christmas sweater and jeans, her hair neatly braided, and a hesitant smile that brightened at Ari's encouraging nod. She stepped forward, unsure where to place herself in this tight-knit family scene.

Abner noticed her and her sweater immediately. He raised an eyebrow as though sizing her up and being disappointed with the results. "And who's this?" he asked, his tone not quite hostile but certainly not welcoming. "Home healthcare staff?"

"Dad! Ari stiffened. "This is Elinor. She's been helping me," he paused, searching for the right words, "...with my recovery. She's a very close friend."

Iris, with her hostess instincts kicking in, extended a hand. "Oh! Elinor, is it? Lovely to meet you. We appreciate you keeping Ari on track with his healing." Her voice was pleasant, but there was an inquisitive edge to it; she seemed to be waiting for Elinor to say something that would place her in a comfortable category, preferably a "nice Jewish girl."

Elinor shook her hand gracefully. "It's a pleasure, Mrs. Keshet," she said softly. "Ari's been an easy patient, for the most part."

Abner leaned back in his chair, his arms folded. He eyed Elinor's simple cross necklace and the absence of any hint of Jewish tradition about her. "So, Elinor," he began, voice casual but probing, "where did Ari find you? At the rehab center or something?"

Elinor smiled, refusing to be rattled. "Actually, we met some years ago in Israel. I was involved in a sustainable botanical project in the Negev, and Ari was one of the donors."

Iris's face brightened slightly; Israel was a good sign. "Israel? How wonderful! Ari, you never mentioned that part."

Ari shrugged, feeling trapped by their expectations. He loved his parents, but he knew what they wanted: for him to settle down with someone who shared their traditions. He glanced at Elinor, silently apologizing.

Elinor, reading the tension, chose honesty. "Yes, I'm a geologist and a botanist, and the Desert Bloom Initiative perfectly fits my interests. It also had a personal draw for me, spiritually speaking. I'm a Christian," she said evenly, meeting Iris's eyes before continuing. "I was curious about the land and the rich history of my faith; it was meaningful to me to be there."

A tense silence took hold. Iris's polite smile faded. Abner's brow furrowed, and then his face changed, confusion giving way to a slow, dawning realization. "Wait a minute... This is the 'consulting geologist' you brought with you to the Andes?"

Ari met his father's gaze. "Yes. This is Elinor Miller."

Abner leaned back, the muscles in his jaw working. "You told me you were assembling a field team of specialists. I thought you meant vetted experts, not," He cut himself off, glancing at Elinor. "Not someone with a... personal mission."

Elinor didn't blink. "I was there to work, Mr. Keshet. I have two doctorates and years of field experience. My personal feelings for Ari don't disqualify my qualifications."

Abner's tone sharpened. "That wasn't the understanding I had when I signed off on the logistics. This was supposed to be a high-risk scientific expedition, not a romantic walk through the mountains."

Iris, breaking the tension, said, "Well... I'm sure the Andes are very beautiful. I'm glad it was... meaningful." She fumbled for her teacup, her voice brittle as porcelain.

Picking up the Dreidel and fiddling with it, Abner leaned in for the kill. "Elinor, do you know what the letters on the Dreidel mean? Or how to properly spin it?" He wasn't just testing her; it was a definite insult, and everyone in the room knew it.

Ari straightened in his chair. "Dad..., come on."

Elinor glanced at the Dreidel in Abner's hand. She knew some basics, but not enough to impress a man determined to find her lacking. "I know it's connected to the miracle of the oil and Hanukkah tradition," she said gently. "But I'll admit, I'm not an expert in the game. I'm still learning."

Abner snorted softly, spinning the Dreidel with a snap. "Learning, hmm."

"Dad, that's enough!" Ari set his jaw. "Elinor's not here for a pop quiz on Jewish customs. She's here because I invited her."

Iris attempted to smooth over the tension. "Ari, your father's just teasing," she said, but the strain in her voice hid her words. She changed the subject abruptly. "Would you like more sufganiyot, Ari? Elinor?"

Elinor smiled politely, but the damage was done. The disapproval in the room was palpable, hanging in the air like thick smoke from a stinky cigar. She half-expected someone to wave it away or cough, but the silence lingered, dense and heavy.

She had come hoping to share a peaceful holiday moment, but instead, she felt like a contestant on a cooking show, where the judges didn't even bother to taste her dish before voting her off the show.

She tried to keep her expression neutral, but the hurt was evident on her face.

A sharp anger ignited within Ari, directed squarely at Abner's rudeness. He leaned forward, his tone calm yet edged. "Mom, Dad," he said, his voice low and deliberate, "I think Elinor and I could use some fresh air. It's been a long day, and she deserves a break." His glare lingered on Abner longer than necessary; the unspoken message was clear.

Iris offered a strained smile. "Yes, of course. Rest is important." Elinor stood and handed Ari his crutches without comment.

She could feel the tension and disappointment flowing through the room like a current.

As they left, the warmth of the menorah's candles felt distant and unreachable. The hallway outside seemed cooler and quieter.

Ari hesitated, turning to Elinor, his voice low and apologetic. "I'm sorry," he said simply.

Elinor shook her head, her eyes kind but sad. "I understand. They love you and want what's best for you in their eyes."

Ari looked away, frustrated. "It shouldn't have ended like this," he muttered. The evening, which had begun with bright Hanukkah lights and familiar laughter, had turned bitter.

In the living room, Abner sighed heavily once the pair was gone, and Iris began tidying plates with restless efficiency. The holiday glow felt dulled. Even the menorah's steady flame seemed to flicker uncertainly, as if unsure of what this evening had accomplished.

Outside, Elinor and Ari stood in the quiet corridor. Stolz's whisper wanted to rise in Ari's mind, mocking him, but he shoved it down. He had Elinor beside him, and though the night had ended badly, her presence reminded him that life wasn't about pleasing everyone, not even his parents.

She reached for his hand, giving it a gentle squeeze. "Hanukkah is about miracles," she said softly. "And miracles don't always look like we expect."

Ari managed a small, sad smile. "You're right," he said, holding onto that thought as they moved away from the warmth of the menorah and into the uncertain future waiting beyond these walls.

Call for Understanding

A pale winter sun filtered through the mansion's tall windows the following day, illuminating the grand foyer and casting long shadows on the polished floors. Ari sat on the plush sofa in his study, cradling his phone in one hand. His injured ankle rested on a footstool, still sore but healing. The world outside remained calm, a stark contrast to the swirl of thoughts in his mind.

He hesitated, then dialed Elinor's number. The dial tone hummed softly. The memory of his parents' awkward encounter with her the previous evening weighed on him.

It wasn't just that they had mistaken her for staff; there was the unmistakable hint of disapproval, the unspoken expectations of who he should be with, who would be "acceptable."

When Elinor answered, her voice was warm but cautious. "Ari? Is everything okay?"

Ari exhaled, running a hand through his hair. "Hi, Elinor. I just... wanted to apologize again. About my parents. They can be a bit,"

"Protective?" she offered gently.

He managed a sneering smile. "That's a kind word for it. They were out of line, making assumptions. I'm sorry you had to deal with that."

The line was quiet momentarily, and Ari's heart tensed slightly. What if she were reconsidering everything? Finally, Elinor's gentle laughter came through. "It's alright. I've dealt with worse. Besides, I'm sure they meant well, even if it didn't come out right."

Ari relaxed, relieved. "I appreciate that. I just didn't want you to think you were the one who embarrassed me. My parents can be over the top. You're important, and your presence is helping me get through this rough patch."

Elinor's voice softened. "I'm glad to hear that. And for the record, I'm not offended. I understand family dynamics can be complicated."

Elinor's soft exhale drifted over the line. "Ari, it's okay. Parents can be protective. They don't know me, and I understand that. I just don't want to drive a wedge between you and your family."

Ari closed his eyes, relief washing through him. "It won't," he said, voice quieter now. "I care about them, and I care about you, too. I just... want everyone to get along. Eventually."

A gentle laugh from Elinor's end. "Eventually," she agreed. "So, how's your ankle feeling today?"

"Better, I think. The physical therapy is helping, but I'm still fighting restlessness and some pain. Gottschall is juggling her COO commitments and playing gatekeeper again, rationing my meetings." He tried to keep it light, but the frustration still seeped in.

Elinor's tone grew tender, "Patience, Ari. You've always been good at pushing boundaries; maybe now's the time to respect them. Give yourself a chance to heal."

Ari smiled. "Thanks for being patient with me. Maybe here real soon, when I'm walking better, we can... I don't know..., do something low-key. Like a walk in the Garden of the Gods? No climbing gear required."

Elinor's chuckle warmed him. "That sounds perfect."

Hidden Agendas

Abner and Iris Keshet bent their heads together in a guest suite like conspirators plotting a grand campaign. Iris perched on the edge of a chaise lounge, her hands folded primly in her lap. Abner rose and paced, his polished shoes muffled on the Persian rug. They spoke in hushed tones as though the walls might be listening.

"He needs a proper match," Iris said firmly, her voice brooking no argument. "Someone who understands our world, our faith, our traditions. Not just anyone..." She thought for a few moments, and then her face lit up with a knowing smile. "Diana! You remember Diana, don't you?"

Abner nodded, his expression reflective. "Of course, I remember her. She and Ari were together all through college. Back then, we hoped she'd become his wife someday. She was everything we wanted for him, brilliant, ambitious, and from a family that understood our world."

Iris's smile widened. "Exactly. We always said she was a perfect match for him. And now she's running her own law firm, practically a household name in corporate litigation. I've seen that she's had a bit of work done, Botox, fillers, a little nip and tuck. Her nose is a little smaller and she's... should I say... curvier now. Diana has clearly invested in herself, and it shows. She's polished, successful, and, well... let's say, impossible to miss when she walks into a room. Exactly the kind of woman Ari needs by his side."

Abner raised an eyebrow, his tone sarcastic. "Capable, yes. But their relationship was never about love, Iris. Diana was drawn to Ari's potential, his drive. And Ari... well, Ari was drawn to Diana for... let's say, less noble reasons."

"Don't be ridiculous," Iris said sharply, brushing off his comment. "Diana challenged him. She didn't just follow him around like some love-struck groupie; she kept him focused and motivated.

Abner leaned back, sighing. "But their relationship was all ambition and convenience. They both got what they wanted back then... status and a partner who looked good on paper. But marriage? That's not at all about looking good. You need love to make a marriage work."

Iris crossed her arms, "I know from experience that you don't need love to start a marriage. Love can grow with time."

Abner regarded her with a mixture of confusion and insult. He tilted his head slightly and stated, "What... Iris? Anyway... all I'm saying is that love holds great significance in matrimony."

He was uncertain of Iris's remarks.

"Diana was, and still is, exactly the kind of woman who could both keep Ari grounded and push him to greater heights," she continued, her eyes gleaming. "Let's invite her here. Think she'll come?"

Abner, knowing it was a losing fight, gave in, "Why not... Diana has had a soft spot for Ari for years. And now, with him vulnerable and at home, it's the perfect time." Abner thought about it, then advised, "Why don't you call her mother and tell her Ari's convalescing and could use a visit from a friendly face... before he gets too attached to that... *other girl*."

"Excellent," Iris said cheerfully. "Diana Metzenbaum will be perfect. Like Samson and Delilah, tempting him back into the fold of what is proper."

Abner cringed, "That's not exactly what I was getting at."

Iris took out her phone and dialed the number. Focused on the scheme. "I'm setting up a visit. Ari won't see it coming." Iris cleared her throat and waited. "Esther? It's Iris Keshet," her tone shifting into the confident, schmoozing drawl she used back in New York when arranging high-profile dinners for her husband.

"Long time, no speak. Listen, we were hoping you could do us a favor..."

Abner tried to ignore the red flags deep in his gut, signaling danger ahead. *"What could possibly go wrong?"* he mumbled.

Abner leaned in, straining to catch the murmured reply on the other end. He shot his wife a meaningful look as if to say, "Get to the point." Iris nodded, lowering her voice.

"Our dear Ari is back in Denver, laid up after an accident," she explained. "Poor boy's gone a bit off track. We think he could use some... encouragement. Someone who understands our world, his background." She paused, smirking as she imagined the reaction. "Yes, that's right, your daughter Diana. They were old college sweethearts. You remember how fond of her he was?"

"That sounds great! Thank you, Esther. Yes, that's perfect. Arrange for her to be in town soon," Iris continued, her voice like a knife wrapped in velvet. "A casual lunch, maybe a quiet evening together. I'm sure Ari would be thrilled."

The conversation ended, and Iris hung up the phone. "Done! We need to remind Ari of who he is. That *Christian girl*... whatever her name is... she might be nice, but she isn't right for him."

She continued, "We've known the Metzenbaums for years. Diana is well respected, and I've always known she was a great match for Ari!"

Abner internally groaned but chose to go along with his wife's scheme... despite his reservations.

Iris's eyes glazed as her mind pictured Ari's former lover, Diana, arriving at the mansion, gracefully walking in high heels, her dark hair perfect, and her lips carefully inflated and painted.

"Diana had charmed Ari once, and hopefully she could do it again. Guiding him back toward a proper match, away from distractions like that... whatever her name is... and her unpredictable influences."

Abner and Iris believed she could once again captivate their son. Iris didn't care if she was being manipulative; if it kept Ari on the right track with their family, then so be it.

Iris grinned, pleased with her plan. "Our boy's sharp, but he's been too distracted lately. This is for his own good."

They both stepped out of the guest suite, masks of propriety firmly in place, but awkwardly greeting a passing staff member in the hallway... trying to act "normal".

Meanwhile, in the main living area, Ari sat quietly, resting his head against the couch cushion. He felt lighter after talking to Elinor. Yet unbeknownst to him, the ground beneath him was shifting, bringing new challenges, orchestrated by people who claimed to know what was *best for him*.

For now, Ari enjoyed a few more moments of tranquility, cherishing the echo of Elinor's soft voice and the hope that he could somehow reconcile these conflicting forces in his life.

However, the world around him wasn't so easily controlled.

Chapter 12

The Dream

That night, Ari tossed and turned in his oversized bed, the Denver skyline glowing faintly through the curtains. His sleep was restless, and his dream was vivid and strange.

In this dream, Ari stood in a serene forest clearing, the air thick with an otherworldly amber light. In the center of the clearing stood a massive tree, its trunk wide and ancient, with branches reaching toward the heavens. Hanging from the branches were strange books, their covers shimmering with iridescent reddish hues. The leaves rustled gently, though there was no wind.

A red deer stood by a crystal-clear creek that wound around the roots at the tree's base. Its coat was deep crimson, almost glowing, and its eyes locked onto Ari. The deer dipped its head to drink, the ripples in the water creating mesmerizing patterns.

Then it looked up, beckoning him with a subtle tilt of its head. Ari stepped forward, drawn toward the tree and its mysterious books. The deer didn't move, its gaze steady as if waiting for him to act.

"READ," the deer seemed to whisper, though no sound came from its mouth. "SEEK GODLY KNOWLEDGE."

Ari reached toward one of the books, its cover glowing brighter as his fingertips grazed the surface. The moment he touched it, a surge of warmth rushed through him, and the tree's branches seemed to pulse with a living energy. The sensation was comforting yet powerful, as though the answers he sought were finally within reach.

But just as he began to open the book, a fierce, shadowy wind tore through the clearing. It howled like a living thing, whipping at the branches and scattering the glowing leaves into the void. The vision disintegrated into darkness, leaving him clutching at nothing.

Ari jolted awake, his chest heaving. The dream clung to him, vivid and unsettling, like an unfinished symphony haunting the edges of his mind. He sat up, rubbing his face and staring at the faint glow of his phone on the nightstand. A part of him ached to call Elinor, to share the strange dream and hear her steady, calming voice.

But he hesitated, his thumb hovering over her contact. What would I even say? Instead, he placed the phone back down, running a hand through his messy hair. The dream had left him with more questions than answers, but one thing was clear: something, or someone, was trying to show him a path he couldn't ignore.

He leaned against the headboard, staring at the faint city lights outside his window. The world out there was so predictable, so manageable compared to whatever this was. Yet, deep down, he felt it, the pull of something greater.

He planned to contact Elinor tomorrow. Perhaps she could help him make sense of this dream, or maybe just her presence would remind him why he needed to keep moving forward. For now, he let the night envelop him, its mysteries whispering softly in the quiet corners of his mind.

Morning Schemes

The sound of Iris humming a cheerful tune drifted through the mansion, her voice carrying a buoyant energy that immediately put Ari on edge. She rarely sang unless something was going exactly as she wanted. The upbeat melody floated through the hallways as she moved about, clearly in high spirits.

Ari sat on the edge of his bed, phone in hand, staring at Elinor's name on the screen. He pressed call, holding his breath as it rang, but it went to voicemail. It was early, and she was probably getting ready for the day. He left a quick message, his voice warm but tinged with hesitation.

"Hey, Elinor. It's me. I had this... strange dream, and I wanted to tell you about it. Call me back when you're available."

As he set his phone down, Iris peeked into the room, her face glowing with excitement. "Good morning, darling! Get up and get dressed. Something special is happening today, and I want you to look your best."

Ari raised a brow. "What's going on? Is someone coming?"

Iris just smiled, her humming resuming as she breezed out of the room.

The cryptic answer left Ari puzzled, but a flicker of hope stirred in him. Could it be Elinor? Was she the reason his mother was so animated? Maybe her early morning absence from his call meant she was on her way. The thought made him smile as he rose and began to get ready.

He showered quickly, picking out a crisp, button-down shirt and formal slacks for a surprise visit. His reflection in the mirror caught the faint excitement in his eyes.

When he reached the living room, his mother was already there, fluttering around like a hummingbird on caffeine.

She was plumping throw pillows, rearranging knick-knacks... that were perfectly fine where they were... and practically radiating with suspicious anticipation.

Ari narrowed his eyes. His chest tightened with the growing certainty that this wasn't about Elinor. His mother's buzz was too electric, too calculated. Something was up.

Before he could press her, the unmistakable hum of SummitTek's SUV pulling into the driveway made his stomach lurch. The doorbell rang. Moments later, Gottschall's sharp, no-nonsense voice echoed faintly from the foyer.

Then, his father walked in, flanked by none other than Diana Metzenbaum. She was a force to be reckoned with, like a typhoon dressed in designer fabric. Her tailored suit hugged every inch of her "*enhancements*." Her dark curls were perfectly styled. She looked like someone who had won the jackpot at a plastic surgery raffle.

Ari's excitement died a swift death. He turned to his mother, whose beaming smile could have powered the Christmas lights at Rockefeller Center.

"Surprise, darling!" Iris chirped, clasping her hands together like a game show host revealing the grand prize. "Diana's in town, and she simply had to see you!"

Ari's mouth opened and then closed. He glanced at Diana, who offered a smile so perfect it was probably trademarked. Her eyes sparkled with the confidence of someone who had already planned the seating arrangements at their imaginary wedding reception.

"Diana?" Ari forced a polite nod. "What... an unexpected surprise."

"Oh, Ari," she cooed, gliding toward him with the precision of a cat stalking prey. "Your mother told me you've been busy battling mountains, and you lost the fight. I thought I'd stop by to remind you there are people who care."

Ari shot a sidelong look at his father, who appeared to be studying the ceiling like it held the secrets of the universe. Abner wasn't about to risk Iris's wrath by showing even a hint of skepticism.

"Well...," Ari plastered on his most professional smile, the one reserved for hostile takeovers, "you have certainly brought excitement to the room."

"Isn't she stunning?" Iris interjected, positively glowing. "And so accomplished. Did you know Diana just expanded her law firm? She's practically a celebrity in corporate litigation."

"Impressive," Ari replied, his voice flat. "Though I'm not sure corporate lawsuits are a great conversation starter for a surprise visit."

Diana's laugh was as polished as her appearance. "Oh, Ari." She playfully batted his chest. "You were always so clever."

Ari suppressed a groan and glanced toward the door, silently wishing Elinor would miraculously appear to save him. The thought of her, with her messy, braided hair, cowboy boots, and genuine smile, would be a balm to his fraying nerves.

But for now, he was stuck, trapped in his mother's matchmaking circus, with Diana front and center. If the mountains had taught him anything, it was endurance, and he was going to need every ounce of it to get through this evening.

As Diana's presence filled the room, she beamed and embraced Ari with outstretched arms, wrapping him tightly and planting a kiss on his lips. Ari froze for a moment, feeling off guard. His mind raced. *Was I supposed to hug her back? Kiss her in return?*

The lingering warmth of her gesture left him feeling awkward and unsure, his confusion evident as he glanced toward his mother, whose delighted expression offered no escape.

Ari stood, wincing slightly as he shifted his weight off his painful ankle. "Diana," he said, his tone guarded but polite. "What brings you here?" he asked as he wiped his lips.

Before Iris could jump in, Diana smoothly took the lead, her voice as polished as her appearance. "Your mother thought it would be wonderful for us to reconnect, especially during the holiday season. As it happens, I was already in town for business and simply couldn't pass up the opportunity."

Ari's gaze flicked to his father, who looked too pleased with himself. His initial surprise gave way to a flicker of something else, nostalgia. Diana looked fantastic, and the memories of their college days together stirred old emotions.

And then Stolz spoke. *"She's perfect, Ari. Look at her, wealth, power, and beauty. Together, you'd be unstoppable. Elinor? She's holding you back. Diana? She's your equal."*

Ari's jaw tightened, the familiar whispers weaving through his thoughts. He forced a smile, gesturing toward the sofa. "Please, have a seat."

As Diana moved gracefully to sit near Ari, he felt a surge of conflict. He wasn't the man he'd been in college, not entirely. But Stolz's voice was relentless, fueling old feelings and tempting him with visions of a future built on power and lustful passion.

The conversation flowed easily at first, Diana's charm on full display as she recounted her latest legal victories and her admiration for SummitTek's recent innovations. Ari nodded along, his responses rhythmic, but his mind churned beneath the surface.

She leaned forward slightly, her dark eyes locking onto his. "You've built something incredible here, Ari. I always knew you were destined for greatness."

Ari chuckled lightly, though the sound felt hollow. "Well, I've had some help along the way."

"And you'll have even more help if you make the right choices," Abner added with an obvious wink.

The implication hung in the air, unspoken but clear. Diana smiled knowingly, her hand brushing playfully against Ari's thigh as she spoke. "The right choices can make all the difference in the world."

For a moment, Ari felt the weight of Stolz's words pressing against him. Old feelings of lust and passion that he and Diana shared years ago. But then, like a faint light cutting through the fog, the memory of Elinor's laughter and her natural beauty surfaced in his mind. He shifted uncomfortably, glancing toward the window. "Excuse me," he said abruptly, standing and limping toward the door. "I need a moment."

As he exited the room, Stolz's voice hissed in his mind, *"Don't let this one go... You deserve a woman like her."*

But Ari wasn't so sure.

Temptations

Ari shut the door to his bedroom with a soft click and leaned against it for a moment, exhaling deeply. He made his way into the adjoining bathroom, flipping on the light. The stark glow illuminated his tired reflection in the mirror. For a moment, he just stared, the image of Diana still vivid. He had to admit, she looked stunning, every bit the polished professional. Her hair framed her petite face perfectly, and her confidence radiated in a way that used to leave him spellbound.

Back in college, they shared a fiery, intoxicating relationship, the kind that thrived on frat parties, adrenaline, and unchecked passion. But it had also been reckless, immature, and, looking back, dangerously unbalanced.

Diana was thrilling and exciting, but she was never grounded. Their time together felt more like a scene from a coming-of-age movie than the foundation for something lasting.

Elinor, on the other hand, was different. She was solid, like the steady hum of a mountain breeze or the quiet comfort of warm sunlight. With Elinor, there was no pretense, no games, just a genuine connection that felt rooted in something deeper, something that could last.

His phone buzzed on the counter, pulling him from his thoughts. He glanced at the screen, and his chest tightened with relief. It was Elinor returning his call.

He answered immediately, his voice soft but eager. "Elinor, hey." "Hey," she replied, a hint of concern. "Sorry, I missed your call earlier. I just saw your message. You okay?"

Ari ran a hand through his hair, his thoughts briefly flickering back to Diana before he shoved them aside. "Yeah, I'm fine. I just...," He hesitated, not wanting to dive too deeply but desperate to hold onto this moment with her. "I had this weird dream last night. About a red deer and a big tree with books hanging from it. It... felt important somehow."

"A red deer?" Elinor echoed with curiosity. "That's... interesting. What do you think it means?"

"I don't know," Ari admitted. "I just thought of you when I woke up. Figured you might have some insight."

Her laugh was soft, reassuring. "Well, I'll need some time to think about it, but it sounds intriguing. Maybe it's something worth praying about."

"Maybe," Ari said, his voice lighter. "Thanks for calling me back."

"Of course," she said warmly. "We'll talk more about it soon, okay?"

Before Ari could reply, a knock sounded at his bedroom door.

His stomach sank as he glanced toward the sound. "Uh, yeah. Talk soon," he said hurriedly.

The knock came again, louder this time. "Ari, it's Diana," her smooth and familiar voice called through the door.

Ari closed his eyes for a moment, gripping the phone tightly. "I've got to go," he whispered to Elinor.

"Okay?" she said, her voice tinged with hesitation. "Take care."

As the call ended, Ari set the phone down with a sigh, steeling himself before heading toward the door. Ari barely had time to steady himself before the door creaked open. Diana stepped into his bedroom, her petite frame radiating self-assured elegance. Her dark curls bounced slightly as she moved, her fitted designer dress emphasizing her figure in a way that was impossible to ignore.

"Ari," she began, her voice honeyed and warm. "Your parents are quite the planners. They've already arranged dinner for all of us at the finest restaurant in Denver. No surprise there, right?" She chuckled lightly, closing the door behind her as she took a step closer. Dinner at the *Guard and Grace* restaurant sounds delish."

He nodded, trying to keep his composure. "That sounds... nice," he said, his tone deliberately neutral.

Diana smiled, her dark eyes locking onto his. "And maybe later," she said, her voice dropping an octave, "you and I can catch up properly. Just the two of us." She walked to the edge of his bed, smoothing it beneath her hand as she sat down. Her body language was casual but deliberately alluring. "It could be fun, don't you think? Like old times."

Ari's heart thudded heavily in his chest. Her words and proximity were a potent mix, stirring memories he thought he'd buried. Images of late-night parties, stolen moments, and a carefree passion flickered through his mind.

Stolz's voice slithered into his thoughts, its tone dripping with approval. *"She's perfect, Ari. She is beautiful and successful, and she fits the image. Reliving those days would be so easy. So satisfying."*

Ari swallowed hard, his gaze flicking briefly to Diana's hand resting lightly on his bed. He was tempted, more than he wanted to admit, but something felt... off. Diana was here, in his space, orchestrated by his parents, no less, and it all felt calculated, like a trap.

Before he could respond, the door swung open again with a decisive thud. Gottschall entered, clipboard in hand, and her presence was as commanding as ever. Her sharp eyes scanned the room, quickly taking in the situation.

"Mr. Keshet," she said briskly, as though Diana wasn't even there, "I need a moment to review the afternoon's agenda. There are pressing matters requiring your attention."

Diana stood up from the bed, her expression briefly flickering with irritation before she composed herself. "Maria," she said with a tight smile, "can it wait? We were just having a private conversation."

Gottschall raised an eyebrow, her lips curving into the faintest hint of a smirk. "I'm sure your conversation was fascinating, Ms. Metzenbaum, but business waits for no one."

Ari exhaled, the tension in the room shifting as Gottschall's presence broke the moment. "We'll talk later," he said to Diana, his tone polite but firm.

Diana straightened her suit, her smile still in place, though her eyes betrayed a hint of frustration. "Of course," she said smoothly, moving toward the door. "I'll see you at dinner, Ari."

As Diana left, Gottschall turned to Ari with a look. "You're welcome," she said flatly, her tone carrying the weight of unspoken warnings as she closed the door.

Ari slumped slightly, running a hand through his hair. "Thanks, Maria." unsure whether he was grateful or annoyed.

"You'll thank me more later," Gottschall replied, already moving on to her clipboard. "Now, about that agenda..."

A Public Spectacle

The restaurant buzzed with the hum of clinking silverware and lively conversation, its opulent décor practically screaming, "Denver's elite dine here." Crystal chandeliers bathed the plush booths and white linen tables in a golden glow. At the Keshet table, however, the glow was amplified by Iris and Abner, who beamed as though they'd already won an imaginary "Perfect Matchmaker" award.

Abner, always eager to be the loudest voice in any room, leaned back in his chair and practically boomed, "This is exactly what Ari needs, a sophisticated woman who understands his world.

Diana, you've always been brilliant. It's wonderful to see you two reconnecting!" His New York accent sliced through the hum of the room like a steak knife, drawing the attention of nearby diners, whose heads turned just slightly, ears perked.

Iris clapped her hands together, her excitement bubbling over like uncorked champagne. "Oh, absolutely! Ari, darling, don't forget to tell Diana about your latest investment plans. She's a lawyer, after all. Who better to give you advice?" She glanced toward a neighboring table, ensuring her voice carried. "And doesn't she look stunning tonight? Truly a power couple."

Ari, sitting stiffly next to Diana, offered a polite smile that barely reached his eyes. Diana, by contrast, was the picture of ease, graceful and composed, like she had choreographed this dinner herself. She laughed softly at Abner's remarks, her manicured hand brushing lightly against Ari's arm as she leaned in, perfectly aware of the attention they were garnering.

Around them, patrons whispered and shifted in their seats. A woman two tables over subtly angled her phone, her screen glowing as she tried to snap a picture without being too obvious. A flash went off, and Ari caught it out of the corner of his eye. His jaw tightened.

Iris leaned in, stage-whispering as though her voice wasn't already carrying halfway across the restaurant. "Ari, isn't Diana just radiant tonight? And so accomplished! Imagine what the two of you could achieve together. It's practically destiny." She turned to the woman with the phone, her voice still loud. "Isn't that right?" The woman was startled and quickly looked away, her face flushing.

Abner picked up where Iris left off, gesturing grandly as if delivering a TED Talk. "Ari's got the ambition; Diana's got the brains and the style. They're like Denver's own dream-team couple. Forget business deals, this is the merger everyone's been waiting for!"

Diana tilted her head, her curls bouncing perfectly into place as she smiled at Ari. "You know," she said lightly, her voice like silk, "your parents aren't wrong. We do make a striking pair. Don't you think?"

Ari opened his mouth to respond, but Stolz's voice slithered into his mind. *"Why fight it? They love this, and you should, too. Think of the headlines, the influence. This is the life you belong to."*

Ari's fingers tightened around his water glass, the cool condensation grounding him for a moment. He glanced at Diana, who gazed back with unwavering confidence, and then at his parents, who looked ready to start planning a wedding right there in the restaurant. He forced a smile that felt as mechanical as a vending machine. "It's certainly... a memorable evening."

Diana's hand rested on his arm again, her laughter as effortless as ever. "Relax, Ari. Enjoy the moment. Not everything has to be so serious." She gestured to the waiter passing by. "Another round of wine for the table?"

The waiter nodded, and Ari sighed inwardly. He could feel the pressure building, the room closing in as whispers and camera flashes swirled around them. This wasn't dinner, it was a spectacle, carefully orchestrated for maximum effect. And, like it or not, he was the main act.

The Evening Setup

Back at Ari's mansion, the night seemed to take on a life of its own. Iris and Abner were overly excited, giving directives to the staff as if they were orchestrating a grand symphony.

"Candles everywhere," Iris said, her hands fluttering like a conductor's. "The good ones, none of that synthetic stuff. And bring out the red wine. This is a special occasion... a reunion of love."

Abner nodded approvingly, his New York accent sharp as he added, "And don't forget the music, something classy but romantic. Frank Sinatra or Michael Bublé, maybe?"

Gottschall muttered under her breath, observing the spectacle from a corner of the room. "This isn't matchmaking... this is a siege!"

The mansion transformed as the staff worked efficiently. The grand living room glowed softly with the warm light of candles, the scent of fresh roses wafting through the air. A small table was set by the fireplace, adorned with a crisp white tablecloth and fine China. The ambiance was undeniably romantic, too romantic.

Ari and Diana arrived shortly after, stepping into the carefully curated atmosphere. Diana's eyes lit up as she surveyed the room, her appreciation evident.

"Wow," she said, her voice smooth as silk. "Your parents really know how to set a mood."

Ari felt his stomach twist. He glanced around the room, realizing just how intentional every detail was. He noticed the wine. "Yeah," he mumbled, his voice uneasy. "They think of everything."

Diana moved closer, grabbed the bottle, and poured their drinks. Her perfume was subtle but intoxicating. "It's nice, though," she said softly. "It feels... familiar."

She offered the glass of wine to Ari as they sat by the fireplace, the flames dancing in the reflection of their wine glasses. Diana leaned in, her dark curls catching the warm light. Her voice was low, almost a whisper.

"Ari, don't you miss this? The way we were? We had so much passion for each other. It was so much fun!"

Ari hesitated, her words stirring memories he thought he had buried. Their college days had been reckless and wild, a whirlwind of youthful energy and ambition. Diana had been the center of it all, her charisma as magnetic as it was dangerous.

"I don't know," Ari said, his voice conflicted. He put down the wine glass. "That was a long time ago. We were... different then."

Diana smiled as she tilted her head. "We are still the same where it counts. You've built an empire, and I've carved out my path. Together, we would be unstoppable."

Stolz's voice emerged in the quiet of Ari's mind, smooth and persuasive. *"She's right. Look at her. Smart, beautiful, and powerful. She's perfect. You've always needed someone to keep up with you, and she's right here."*

Ari's chest tightened as he glanced at Diana. Stolz's words echoed his thoughts, amplifying the heavy temptation in the air.

Diana leaned in closer, her fingers grazing his arm, her lips close to his. "Ari, you and I... we make sense. On paper, in real life, everything. We are perfect together."

He swallowed hard, her nearness overwhelming. Her lips were tempting. For a moment, he found himself nodding, his defenses slipping. "Maybe you're right," he admitted, his voice barely audible. "Maybe I've been overthinking everything."

Diana smiled triumphantly and leaned in to kiss him. Ari merged into the passionate kiss as old memories pelted his mind. Long forgotten scenes revived familiar feelings.

She whispered in his ear, "Remember the good times we shared. They will bring you back around."

As Diana's hand reached for his face, Ari sensed the pull of their shared history and the promise of what might be. Yet, as he was ready to give in to these feelings, the weight of the moment pressed upon him. A brief image of Elinor sliced through the hazy memories of his past college days with Diana.

Stolz hissed in frustration. *"Don't hesitate, go for it! Diana is what you need. What you deserve."*

But hesitation had already crept in. Ari pulled back slightly, his gaze searching Diana's face. "I don't know if this is a good idea."

Diana's smile faltered, her confidence wavering slightly. "Ari, don't overthink it... just let it go."

Before he could respond, a sharp knock echoed through the room. Fraulein Gottschall stepped in without waiting for an invitation, her expression unreadable.

"Mr. Keshet," she said crisply, her eyes flicking between him and Diana. "You are needed in the study. A matter of urgency."

Ari blinked, the spell between him and Diana was broken. He exhaled slowly, nodding. "I'll be there in a minute."

Gottschall lingered, her sharp gaze pinning Diana in place.

Diana leaned back, frustrated, her composure slipping.

"A matter of urgency... really, Maria?" she said, mocking, her irritation showing.

As he followed Gottschall, Stolz's voice panicked, *"Noo..., you're letting distractions ruin this moment. Go back to her."*

Ari stood there, his mind racing and confused about what to do next. "I'll be right back," he said, voice hesitant.

SummitTek Under Fire

Ari followed Gottschall down the grand hallway, his footsteps echoing like accusations on the polished marble floors. The encounter with Diana still simmered in his mind, Stolz's whispers fading away, like a mosquito you thought you had swatted but wasn't entirely gone. Gottschall's brisk pace and air of urgency snapped him out of his thoughts, though he wasn't sure what new storm awaited him in the study.

When they arrived, Gottschall swung open the double doors with precision and gestured for him to enter. Ari stepped inside, the familiar scent of aged leather grounding him. His study, usually a sanctuary of control, was now a battleground. Papers were stacked haphazardly on the heavy wooden desk, and the flickering light from the gas fireplace cast restless shadows across the room.

"Maria," Ari said, his tone clipped, "what's this about?" Gottschall handed him a thick folder, her expression grave.

"This came from SummitTek's legal team. It concerns the AndesCon's expedition."

Ari frowned as he flipped open the folder. His sharp eyes scanned the contents, but the images stopped him cold: the Titan Tent weathering a brutal storm. At first glance, it was a testament to his company's innovation. But then his gaze fell on the glaring issues, the kind that turned triumph into disaster.

"Is this what...?" he started, but Gottschall cut him off.

"Yes," she said, her voice even but heavy with meaning. "The testing was compromised. The equipment malfunctioned. AndesCon is claiming negligence."

Ari's stomach dropped like a climber losing its grip. He skimmed the accompanying report, the cold legal jargon practically jumping off the pages: "defective equipment," "failure to meet specifications," "potential liability."

"They're threatening legal action?" he asked, his voice tight.

"Not yet," Gottschall replied, folding her arms. "But they've contacted their lawyers. They're watching us closely."

Ari paced, each step sending a dull throb through his injured ankle. "How could this happen? The Titan Tent was flawless during our tests, even during that freak storm." His voice cracked with disbelief. "This is supposed to be our indestructible flagship product!"

Gottschall met his frustration with unflinching pragmatism. "It seems proper protocols weren't followed during setup. They're claiming human error on our end, insufficient field testing before deployment."

The accusation landed like a gut punch. If proven true, it wasn't just about money; it was about reputation. SummitTek wasn't just a company; it was Ari's identity. He had poured everything into building it, piece by relentless piece.

"This is absurd," he muttered, slamming the folder shut.

Gottschall's voice softened slightly, an unusual break in her iron exterior. "There's more."

Ari looked up, dread pooling in his chest. "What else?"

She hesitated, her usual efficiency tinged with rare hesitation. "A Peruvian climber went missing during a recent expedition near Huascarán. He was last seen not far from where the equipment was being tested."

Ari froze, the weight of her words pressing down like the mountain itself. His mind shot back to the Andes nightmare. The freak storm, the terrorizing Figure in the ravine, the absolute chaos.

The thought clawed at him: had his Pride, his refusal to heed warnings, played a part in this?

"This is on me?" he asked, his voice barely above a whisper.

Gottschall didn't rush to reassure him. Instead, she placed a firm hand on his shoulder. "What matters now is how you handle it," she said, her voice steady but not unkind. "You're the face of SummitTek, Ari. This is your moment to take responsibility and make it right."

Ari's jaw clenched as Stolz's voice oozed into his thoughts. *"Spin it. Turn this into your story of triumph. Blame others or the mountain, if you have to."*

He shook off the voice like an unwanted draft. The stakes were too high for ego. Ignoring Stolz, he turned back to Gottschall, determination hardening his gaze.

"Get me everything on the missing climber," he said firmly. "And I want a full investigation. No shortcuts. I want to know if there's even a hint of negligence."

Gottschall nodded, her approval flickering across her otherwise stoic face. "Already in motion."

As she exited the study, Ari sank into his chair, the folder still in his hands. The allure of the evening, Diana's glittering perfection, his parents' matchmaking circus, felt like a distant, petty distraction. What lay before him now was far more critical.

The flickering firelight cast long shadows on the room's walls, mirroring the weight of the decisions he had to make. He stared down at the documents. The night shifted from personal indulgence to corporate reckoning. Whether the summit he now faced was moral, professional, or both, one thing was clear... the climb ahead would demand every ounce of his strength.

The Turning Point

Ari closed the folder, his mind spinning with the weight of what lay ahead. The allure of his past, Diana, the easy distractions, and Stolz's whispers seemed to fade under the harsh glare of responsibility. He stood from his chair, slight pain waking in his ankle, but he ignored it. There was no time for distractions now.

Diana was waiting for him in the living room, lounging elegantly on the velvet chaise as if she belonged there. Her hair framed her face perfectly, and her dress caught the light from the chandelier above. She looked every bit the image of the total woman. Stolz stirred faintly in the back of his mind, feeding the image, but Ari silenced the voice.

"Diana," he began, his tone firm but not unkind.

She turned, her eyes lighting up when she saw him. "Finally. I was starting to think you got lost in this massive house of yours."

He forced a tight smile. "Something's come up, something urgent."

She pouted, sitting up straighter. "Ari, surely, whatever it is, it can wait."

"It can't," stepping further into the room. "I have a corporate situation that needs my immediate attention. It is critical."

Diana raised an eyebrow, her pout shifting into a look of disbelief. "You're ditching me for work? Again?"

"This isn't about prioritizing work over personal life," Ari replied, keeping his voice steady. "This is about my responsibilities. There's a lot at stake, and I need to be there to fix it."

Diana stood, her heels clicking against the polished floor. She closed the distance between them, her hand resting lightly on his chest. "Ari," she said, her voice soft, almost coaxing. "You're always working. Don't you think you deserve to take a break for once? With me?"

Her gaze was magnetic, her touch warm, but Ari didn't waver. The weight of the folder he had left in the study still pressed on his mind, and the memory of the ravine, the Peruvian guide, and his own near-death experience cut through the moment just like his pocket knife.

"Diana," Ari said, gently removing her hand from his chest. "This isn't the time. And honestly, this isn't right for either of us."

Her smile flickered, then flattened. "Excuse me?"

Ari exhaled, steadying himself. "I mean that we don't belong together, no matter how much sense it makes on paper. No matter what my parents say. No matter how good we look in public."

Diana blinked, her confidence barely wavering. "Ari, let's not be dramatic. We have a history, a connection..."

"We *had* a history," he corrected. "But I've changed. My priorities have shifted. I'm not the same guy from college who thought success and power were everything. This isn't about us anymore, it's about something bigger than me."

Diana crossed her arms, tilting her head. "Oh, please. You're not walking away from me over some 'work thing.' You and I are powerhouses together, Ari. We make sense. We could take over the world if we wanted to."

Ari's jaw tightened. "But that's just it, I don't want to... at least not with you."

A brief flash of doubt appeared on her face, but she swiftly covered it with a smirk. "You're dealing with something; I get it. Yet, we both know I don't back down... I always get what I want." She moved closer and dropped her voice. "In business, in life... and especially when it comes to you."

Ari sighed, running a hand through his hair. "Diana, you're incredible at what you do. But what we once had is over. We were chasing an image, not love."

She studied him, then let out a soft chuckle. "So that's it? You're throwing away a perfect match because of some epiphany? I don't believe that."

"It's the truth," said Ari.

Diana pursed her lips, tapping her manicured nails against her waist. Then, with a cool shrug, she straightened her blazer. "Fine," she said, her voice smooth and unreadable. "We'll put a pin in this...for now."

Ari frowned. "Diana... you still don't get it."

She held up a perfectly polished finger. "You're confused. I can see it in your eyes. But you'll come around."

With one last, slow glance at him, she turned and strode toward the door, her heels clicking against the floor. She paused before leaving, tossing her hair over her shoulder.

"Good luck with your... responsibilities. Let's hope they keep you warm tonight."

The door closed behind her, and the house fell silent. Ari let out a slow breath, pressing his palms onto the wall.

Then, like a shadow slithering into his thoughts, Stolz stirred.

"Fool!" The voice sneered. *"She is powerful, wealthy, and a force to be reckoned with. Everything you need to solidify your empire. And you just threw her away."*

Ari clenched his jaw. "No, Stolz," he muttered under his breath. "Diana is everything *you* believe I want. But she is not for me." Then Stolz retreated in silence.

The Gossip Spread

Ari's photo with Diana was plastered across several online gossip columns the following day. Headlines speculated about a rekindled romance between the billionaire and the stunning New York City lawyer. By mid-morning, the story had made its way to Elinor's office.

"Did you see this?" one of her co-workers whispered, sliding a phone onto her desk. The screen displayed the article, the headline bold and glaring: "Ari Keshet's New Flame? Spotted with Stunning Lawyer-Diana Metzenbaum!"

Elinor's stomach sank. She forced a smile and handed the phone back. "People always love to speculate," she said, her voice carefully neutral.

"Speculate?" the co-worker teased. "Look at them... she's gorgeous, and they look perfect together."

Elinor's smile faltered. She returned her attention to her work, but the words stung. Perfect together. She tried to shake it off, but the photos, Diana's flawless smile, and how Ari looked beside his mother's dream choice wouldn't leave her mind.

The next evening, Ari called Elinor, his voice warm as usual. "Hey, I've been meaning to check in. How are you?"

Elinor gripped the phone tightly, her voice short. "Fine. Busy day."

Ari frowned, sensing the distance in her tone. "Is everything all right?"

"Everything's fine, Ari," she replied, the words coming too quickly. "I'm sure you've had a busy day, too. With all the attention."

He paused, catching the bitterness she tried to mask. "What do you mean?"

"The photos. The headlines. Your parents must be thrilled," she said, trying to keep her voice steady.

"Elinor..." Ari began, but she cut him off.

"It's fine, Ari. You don't owe me an explanation. I get it, I don't exactly fit into your world."

"That's not true," he protested, but her words hung between them, heavy and unsettled.

"I have to go," Elinor said abruptly. "We'll talk later."

As the call ended, Ari stared at the blank screen, frustration knotting in his chest. He tossed the phone onto the couch beside him, running a hand through his hair as Stolz's familiar voice whispered excuses and justifications in his mind. He tried to ignore the pang of guilt that settled deep in his stomach.

On the other side of the call, Elinor sat motionless, her phone resting lightly in her hand. The room felt impossibly quiet, save for the distant hum of the radiator. She carefully set the phone down on the coffee table, her fingers lingering as though releasing it would solidify what had just happened.

The tears came before she could stop them, rolling silently down her cheeks as she pressed a hand to her trembling mouth. Her chest tightened with disappointment and the crushing realization that perhaps she was fighting for something Ari wasn't ready to give.

She pulled her knees up to her chest, wrapping her arms around herself as if trying to hold the pieces of her heart together. The vulnerability she'd shown him, the hope she'd nurtured, now felt fragile, too fragile to survive in Ari's relentless, self-centered world.

Through blurred vision, she caught sight of her Bible on the coffee table. For a moment, she hesitated, then reached for it, flipping through its pages until she found comfort in familiar verses. "CAST ALL YOUR CARES ON HIM BECAUSE HE CARES FOR YOU."

She whispered the words, her voice shaking. Still, the ache remained. Elinor leaned back into the couch, wiping her cheeks with the sleeve of her sweater. She wasn't angry, just profoundly hurt.

Heavy-hearted, the question lingered in her mind: *Could I ever truly belong in the whirlwind of Ari Keshet's life? Or would I always feel like an outsider, watching him climb higher and farther away?*

Tears kept falling, yet a small, stubborn determination grew inside. *If Ari couldn't see our worth together, I could try to encourage him to see it.*

Still, heartbreak remained intense.

Chapter 13
Tension in Calgary

Ari's day started with his typical blend of intensity and control. SummitTek's reputation was at risk following the equipment failure with AndesCon, and Ari was determined not to leave his team to handle it by themselves.

Calgary was home to one of SummitTek's key material suppliers, the company responsible for the advanced composites used in the Titan Tents. Ari wanted answers straight from the source if there was a flaw in the materials, so he had flown out with his legal team to address the issue directly.

Gottschall had argued against the trip. "You should be resting," she had insisted in her no-nonsense tone. "Your ankle isn't going to heal any faster if you keep playing superhero."

Ari had waved her off. "You're needed here, Maria. I need someone I trust keeping the ship steady while I'm gone."

She'd sighed but relented, though not without her usual sharp humor. "Fine. But don't break anything else while you're playing corporate detective."

Now, as the SummitTek SUV navigated Calgary's downtown, Ari sat with his legal team in focused silence. The stakes were clear: if the supplier's materials had caused the malfunction, it would be a PR nightmare and a financial hit. Worse, it would erode SummitTek's credibility, something Ari spent much time building.

The supplier's headquarters blended Canadian efficiency and modest professionalism. The conference room featured panoramic windows overlooking the Rockies, but Ari's attention was laser-focused on the task at hand. The meeting dove deep into material reports, testing protocols, and supply chain accountability. Ari led the discussion with his usual precision, his questions sharp and unrelenting.

The supplier representatives were cooperative, but Ari's instincts told him there was more to uncover. Then, during a lull in the conversation, something caught his eye: a small red deer pin on the lapel of one of the Canadian executives. It was a minor detail, but it pulled at his curiosity. Ari leaned forward. "Interesting pin. Is it a company symbol?"

The man smiled, glancing down. "No, just a nod to my hometown, Red Deer. A small city north of here."

Ari's chest tightened. The name stirred something deep and unsettling. The dream rushed back: the red deer drinking from the creek under a massive tree hung with books. He'd dismissed it as nonsense, but hearing the name now felt like a thread pulling at his subconscious.

"Red Deer," Ari repeated, his voice quieter. "Sounds... peaceful."

"It is," the man said warmly. "Quiet, scenic. A hidden gem."

The meeting continued, but Ari's focus faltered. The conversation moved toward finalizing resolutions, but the name lingered in his thoughts, gnawing at him... Red Deer.

When the meeting concluded and the documents were signed, Ari and his staff returned to their hotel. As the lawyers disembarked, they noticed Ari had remained in the SUV. One of them approached and asked, "Mr. Keshet, are you joining us?"

Ari shook his head, his decision already made. "Not yet."

He turned to the driver and said, "Change of plans. I want to go to the city of Red Deer."

The driver hesitated, surprised, but nodded. "Of course, sir."

The SUV pulled away from the hotel, leaving behind an astonished group, and sped onto the highway. Ari leaned back in his seat, adjusting his ankle as it complained. This wasn't just about a supplier or damage control anymore.

Something was drawing him toward that small city. Ari Keshet, ever the adventurer, couldn't ignore the call of the unknown.

Drive to Red Deer

The highway stretched out before them, cutting through the vast Canadian plains. Snow dusted the landscape, and the low winter sun cast long shadows over the rolling fields. Ari stared out the window, his mind racing. He couldn't shake the feeling that something, or someone, was calling him to this place.

After about ninety minutes, the modest city of Red Deer came into view. It was a stark contrast to Calgary's towering skyline. The driver navigated the quiet streets until they passed a building with a large sign: Red Deer Public Library, Closed for Construction. Despite being closed, a red glow outlined the front doors, catching Ari's eye.

"Stop here!" Ari said suddenly, his voice firm.

The driver pulled over and stopped, glancing at the sign. "It doesn't look like it's open, sir."

Ari stepped out of the SUV, taking his cane with him. He answered the driver with a distracted, "Wait here." He was drawn toward the building like an invisible thread. The red glow around the library's doors pulsed faintly, almost as if it were alive. The front door handle bore a "Closed" sign, but opened easily. He hesitated momentarily, glancing back toward the SUV, where the driver watched him with confusion. Then, with a deep breath, Ari limped inside.

Stolz chuckled darkly in Ari's mind. *"Ah, yes, chase the glowing lights like a moth with ambition. Let's hope there's no bug zapper waiting at the end of this genius plan."*

The air inside the library was heavy, as if the building was holding its breath. The red glow that had outlined the doors now filled the space, illuminating the rows of shelves. It wasn't natural light; it pulsed, alive and warm, casting shadows that danced across the floor.

Stolz's voice returned, sharper now. *"You're wasting your time. Leave this nonsense behind and get back to the real world, where you belong."*

But Ari took another step forward, brushing off Stolz's taunts like distant static. Despite the arrogance dripping from Stolz's every word, there was something undeniable about this place, a sense that he had stepped into a sacred threshold, one not crafted by human hands but destined specifically for him.

Revelation in the Library

Ari stood in uneasy silence inside the dimly lit library. The "Closed for Construction" sign mocked him as he ventured deeper into the supposedly vacant building. The red glow he had noticed earlier intensified, casting odd shadows along the shelves of books. He could smell dust and old paper, but beneath it, something new, an otherworldly fragrance that made the hair on his arms stand up.

Ari's feet moved as if guided by an unseen force, each step pulling him closer to the red light. A strange and disconcerting thing happened as Ari approached... Stolz fell silent.

The usual smug commentary, biting sarcasm, and incessant whispers of pride and ambition were gone. Ari's mind was left in an almost deafening quiet. It was unnerving, like walking into a room where the clock had stopped ticking. For a moment, Ari hesitated, his chest tightening at the absence of Stolz's familiar presence.

"Nothing to say?" Ari muttered under his breath, his voice barely audible over the sound of his heartbeat. But Stolz remained eerily still, retreating into the shadows of Ari's consciousness.

Then, a radiant figure appeared before him, wrapped in a warm crimson glow. This being didn't resemble typical ghosts or angels. There were no wings or flames; instead, he stood like a knowledgeable professor, pausing thoughtfully in a captivating lecture.

He wore a long, precisely folded robe, resembling an academic gown, adorned with glowing symbols shifting like animated writing. His gaze was piercing yet patient, as if he'd spent eternity studying, now ready to reveal the universe's final exam answers.

Ari accidentally dropped his cane, and he could feel his heart racing with excitement. This was more than just a simple encounter; it was no typical lesson. It felt like an invitation to discovery, and Ari was about to *"Get Learned!"*

"ARIEL KESHET," the Spirit said, his tone both assertive and gentle, "I AM THE SPIRIT OF REVELATION KNOWLEDGE. THE LORD HAS SENT ME TO TEACH YOU HIS TRUTHS."

The air around Ari thickened with presence, bookshelves shuddered as if bearing witness, and the light from the desk lamp bowed in reverence. Ari's soul quaked from fear and awe.

"THE LORD HAS SENT ME TO GUIDE YOU. YOU HAVE FEASTED ON THE WRONG FRUIT FOR TOO LONG, PARTAKING FROM THE TREE OF THE KNOWLEDGE OF GOOD AND EVIL AND FEEDING YOUR PRIDE, AMBITION, AND SELF-RELIANCE."

The Being's voice filled the library like a resonant echo through the halls. It carried the warmth of a favorite teacher and the authority of God.

As the Spirit spoke, the library around Ari began to shift, and though he knew his physical body remained in that building, his spirit was transported into another realm. The rows of books melted away, replaced by a boundless garden. Lush foliage and vines shimmered with living light. Ahead, Ari saw two mighty trees: one twisted, dark, and giving him the heebie-jeebies. Its fruits glistened with a dangerous allure; he knew this must be the Tree of the Knowledge of Good and Evil. The other soared heavenward, its leaves vibrant and evergreen, its trunk strong and ancient. Books hung from its branches, glowing with divine light. Waters, crystal clear and fresh, flowed from the foot of this magnificent Tree of Life.

Ari watched in awe as small red deer approached the stream flowing from the Tree of Life. They drank deeply, their coats shining like polished amber. Other creatures, such as lambs, doves, and woodland animals, gathered around the waters. Ari could feel their contentment radiating outward as they drank. Peace washed over him like a gentle wave.

The Spirit turned its gaze toward Ari, quoting softly from Psalm 42:1 of Scripture, "AS THE DEER PANTS FOR THE WATER BROOKS, SO PANTS MY SOUL FOR YOU, O GOD." Ari's chest tightened with an emotion he couldn't name. The Being also spoke of Isaiah's prophecies and Jeremiah's warnings, reminding Ari that true wisdom and satisfaction could only be found in surrender to God's Truth, not in man's crafty achievements or ambitions.

"YOU HAVE GROWN WISE IN YOUR OWN EYES, ARIEL," the Spirit continued, "YET YOUR SOUL REMAINS PARCHED. KNOWLEDGE WITHOUT GODLY, REVERENTIAL FEAR OF THE LORD IS A BARREN FEAST.

HUMBLE YOURSELF AND DRINK FROM THE LIVING WATERS OF THE TREE OF LIFE. THERE, YOU WILL FIND THE REVELATION KNOWLEDGE OF ANSWERS TO LIFE'S QUESTIONS. SEEK THE SPIRIT OF COUNSEL, AND HE WILL GIVE YOU THE DIRECTION YOU NEED TO FIND THE POWER AND WISDOM YOU CRAVE."

Ari's breath caught in his chest, a quiet, trembling acknowledgment of the regret coiled deep inside, the realization that he had been feasting from the wrong tree all along. Everything he had pursued, money, influence, summits both literal and metaphorical, suddenly seemed hollow. There was a thirst in him that wealth and intellect could not quench. He longed to drink from that stream, to ease the ache in his soul.

The Spirit smiled gently, as if seeing the flicker of yearning finally awaken in Ari's heart. He extended a hand, and from the sleeve of his robe, a small object materialized, a little red book, its cover embossed with ancient symbols that shimmered faintly in the crimson glow.

The book floated onto the ground before Ari, as though it were a treasure beyond price.

Then the Spirit spoke one last time, vibrating with eternal significance:

"KEEP IN MIND, ARIEL KESHET, THE GREATEST TRUTH IS NOT DISCOVERED THROUGH CONQUERING MOUNTAINS, BUT THROUGH KNOWING THEIR CREATOR AND HUMBLY SUBMITTING TO HIM."

As the words settled into the marrow of Ari's being, the garden around him began to dissolve. The towering Trees, shimmering waters, and even the creatures faded like mist under the morning sun. The crimson glow receded, folding inward upon the radiant figure until only a pinpoint of light remained, and then, it too vanished.

Ari gasped, the air rushing back into his lungs as reality snapped into place.

He found himself kneeling on the wooden floor of the dim library, the familiar scent of old paper and dust grounding him once more. The desk lamp flickered softly, reverently, as if it had experienced something holy.

And there, just inches from his hand, rested the little *Red Book*.

The Mysterious Red Book

The vision had vanished in the blink of an eye, but its weight lingered in the air like the final note of a sacred song. The crimson radiance of the *Spirit of Revelation Knowledge* had receded into memory, yet he had not left Ari empty-handed.

Before him was a small *Red Book* no larger than the palm of his hand. Its deep crimson cover was smooth like fine sheepskin leather, with an inexplicable glow beneath the surface. The book felt ancient and new at the same time, as if it existed outside of time itself. Its edges shimmered faintly in the dim light, a soft ember like flicker that reminded Ari of the Spirit's presence moments before.

Hesitantly, he reached for it. The second his fingers brushed the cover, a pulse of warmth spread through his hand, traveling up his arm, not scorching, not cold, but alive. This was no ordinary book. He could feel its presence as if the book itself was aware of him.

Curious, he opened it. The pages were impossibly thin, delicate as silk, yet indestructible beneath his touch. Despite its compact size, the text inside was small yet razor sharp, each letter perfectly inscribed in ink darker than night. And though it was no larger than a pocket notebook, somehow, impossibly, it contained every Scripture ever written.

Ari flipped through it in awe. He recognized verses from Genesis, Psalms, Isaiah, and New Testament verses, all there, all precise as if the entire Word of God had been woven into its pages.

But as he tried to read beyond a few lines, the words began to blur, shift, and fade as though they refused to be read out of curiosity alone.

Then he understood.

This was no ordinary book, nor merely a Bible; it was a revered guide, a living book revealing valuable insights at just the right moment. When the time was right, the words would sharpen and illuminate, not by Ari's own will, but by the Spirit's. It wasn't for idle study or casual reference; it was a supernatural gift, only unveiling Scripture when he required it most.

Ari exhaled, gripping the book tightly. This was his to keep, to carry, to live by. He had no doubt that it would change how he thought of the world and life.

The ordinary glow of the exit lamp above the doors spoke to him. He stood, his heart racing, his mouth dry. Physically, he was parched, as if he had been sprinting a marathon. He picked up his cane and noticed a water fountain near the wall, its spout gleaming under a dull bulb. Without hesitation, he gripped his cane and limped to the fountain, pushing the button before drinking greedily.

The water offered brief relief, soothing his throat, but it couldn't still the hunger and thirst deep within.

He wiped his mouth, the taste of earthly water emptying into a new understanding: his real thirst wasn't for success or control but for the Divine presence he had glimpsed moments ago.

Slipping the little *Red Book* into his coat pocket, Ari stepped out into the crisp Canadian air and made his way back to the waiting vehicle. The driver did a double take, his brows knitting together in confusion. Ari's face and shirt were damp, whether from sweat or some strange encounter, the driver had no way of knowing.

Ari said nothing, simply sliding into the back seat and sinking into the leather upholstery.

His mind reeled. The mansion, the corporate battles, and Diana's carefully curated allure awaited him back home. But something deeper tugged at him now, something beyond wealth, beyond power.

Ari was beginning to grasp a truth he'd never considered. Spiritual thirst was far more consuming than physical need... and he was parched.

He had tasted a hint of what his soul truly desired, and no earthly fountain could satisfy it. His body might be tired, drenched in sweat, and his ankle might still ache, but those pains were trivial compared to the hunger in his spirit.

"Drive... back to the airport," Ari commanded the driver softly, wanting nothing more than to be back at his home and, perhaps, to talk to Elinor.

The man behind the wheel raised his eyebrows, clearly curious. He'd seen his fair share of strange requests from high-profile clients, but this topped them all. Ari seemed disturbed. Unusually shaken. But the driver said nothing and pulled away from the curb, guiding the SUV back through the dim streets of Red Deer.

As they headed toward the highway, Ari called his legal team at the Calgary hotel to let them know he was being called back to Denver unexpectedly and that they would need to find their way home without him. He then called his private jet pilot and coordinated a return flight from Calgary to Denver that night.

The driver occasionally cast sidelong glances into the rearview mirror, noting Ari's distant gaze and the traces of water still clinging to his collar.

Ari stared out the window, the gray Canadian sky blurring into a backdrop for the turmoil in his mind. He replayed the vision, the encounter, the thirst, and the words that had pierced his soul.

The SUV engine's hum and the faint sound of tires on asphalt accompanied their silent journey to the Calgary airport. Each passing mile felt heavier with thought as if the distance they put between themselves and Red Deer somehow pressed more questions, more quiet revelations into Ari's heart.

By the time the SUV neared the terminal lights, Ari had peeked at the little *Red Book* in his pocket, knowing he wouldn't be the same man stepping onto his jet as he was when he'd left.

Chapter 14

Shift in the Wind

Ari sat quietly in the private jet's leather armchair as it soared above the snowcapped Rockies, heading back to Denver. Outside the window, the landscape stretched like a patchwork quilt, mountains and valleys cloaked in a winter's hush. The jet's engines hummed, a steady, comforting presence, yet Ari felt anything but comfortable.

His mind churned with the unexpected detour to Red Deer and the surreal encounter with the *Spirit of Revelation Knowledge*.

He gazed out the window. His thoughts were far from the present, tethered instead to the surreal memory of being transported into another realm. He could still see the vivid image of the crimson-hued Spirit, its voice resonating with a power that seemed to vibrate through his very bones. The reprimand echoed in his mind: he had been feeding from the wrong tree, absorbing the wrong knowledge, chasing illusions dressed as "wisdom".

His fingers tapped idly against his knee, his mind circling back to the red deer. The creature felt like a message wrapped in a mystery, its presence both comforting and unsettlingly intentional.

Why is it so haunting? What did it mean? The thoughts weaving themselves into the fabric of his curiosity.

Ari exhaled sharply, leaning his forehead against the cool glass. How do you explain to anyone that you stood before a divine Being and were called out for your ambition, your pride, your hunger for power disguised as purpose? He let out a dry laugh. "Yeah, that'll go over well in the next board meeting."

Stolz's whispers, usually so strong and confident, were quieter, though not entirely gone. Ari could still sense that lingering pride, that voice encouraging him to keep to the old ways of power and ambition. But the encounter in Red Deer had left a new impression on him, something that resisted Stolz's pull. He wanted to talk about it, to process it out loud, and he knew exactly who he wanted to share it with... Elinor.

The thought of her brought a mixture of hope and uncertainty. Their last phone call had been strained. She'd sounded hurt, and who could blame her. The gossip columns had splashed photos of him and Diana across the Internet as if they were the "perfect couple".

He hadn't told Elinor the entire story, how he'd turned Diana away and dismissed the urge to reignite that old flame. Perhaps if he explained everything and shared the details about the spiritual encounter, she might grasp that something had shifted within him.

He looked down at his phone on the armrest. He was still mid-flight, but he would call her as soon as he landed. Or he'd see her in person. Face-to-face would be better, but he suspected she might not agree to that easily. He would start with a call.

The flight attendant approached, offering sparkling water. Ari accepted a glass, sipping slowly. The taste reminded him of how thirsty he had been in that library, how desperately he had drunk from the fountain, and yet he realized that his spiritual thirst remained. It was a thirst that no fancy beverage could quench.

As the jet's engines hummed softly, Ari closed his eyes and attempted something he hadn't done sincerely since he was a boy... he prayed.

In New York City, years before SummitTek and global expeditions, he had attended a private Jewish school where prayers were routine. He remembered the synagogue where he had stood shoulder-to-shoulder with other students as they recited Hebrew prayers that had seemed quaint and childish at the time.

He'd dismissed them as traditions for the young or the overly devout. But now, thousands of feet in the air, his heart aching with questions, he realized that being childlike, open, trusting, hopeful, was not a weakness... it might even be the key. So, he bowed his head, whispered words in halting Hebrew, and invited the God of his youth back into his grown-up world.

The jet began its descent. Denver's skyline emerged on the horizon. Ari finished his water, straightened his tie, and prepared to face his company's troubles and his parents' misguided plans for his future. Tapping the small book in his pocket, he hoped to face them as a different man.

Gottschall's Secret Weapon

Meanwhile, at SummitTek, a different sort of revelation was unfolding. Staff were instructed to set up a station in a small conference room, turning it into their personal "mission control." Various monitors, the tap-tap-tap of keyboards, and the hum of the overhead fluorescent lights created a backdrop of modern detective work.

Susan Richard, Gottschall's Executive Secretary, had instructed them to find out everything they could about the missing Peruvian climber who had been involved in the expedition to test SummitTek's latest gear.

The initial reports had suggested negligence on SummitTek's part, but Ari had demanded a thorough investigation. Someone had mentioned possible sabotage by the climber, which raised many questions.

High above Denver's skyline on the top floor of SummitTek's headquarters, Susan sat behind a polished mahogany desk, her big blue eyes framed by dramatic eyeliner and a halo of blonde curls that seemed plucked from a 1980s fashion magazine.

She stood out like a vinyl record in an age of streaming playlists. Her style was out of place against the sleek, modern aesthetic of the glass-and-steel office environment, but no one questioned her presence. Her impeccable organizational skills were precisely why Gottschall had hired her.

In Susan's world, appearances took a backseat to results, which were the only things that mattered at the executive level.

Susan's desk told a quieter, more personal story. Amid the digital clutter of monitors and tablets, she proudly displayed a few cherished photos: a grinning husband with salt-and-pepper hair, grandchildren with goofy smiles holding up finger paintings. She would glance at these frames during her busiest moments, finding comfort in the reminder that life extended beyond corporate strategy and heated boardroom debates.

This morning, she summoned the research interns, Jacob and Emily, to her workspace. They had quickly earned themselves a reputation among the office staff, who, admiring and teasing, referred to them as "The Digital Duo." Word had spread that when someone needed a suspicious username traced or a cryptic social media trail deciphered, the interns were better than anyone to resolve the issue.

Jacob, who could mine data streams for hidden clues as easily as breathing, became known as Jacob "Hashtag Hacker" Reed for his uncanny ability to wrangle hashtags and trending topics into actionable intel.

Emily's knack for unraveling cryptic memes and obscure video comments for personal details earned her the nickname Emily "Meme Maven" López, a title she enjoyed.

In a realm filled with polished professionals and crisp collars, these two "cyber-sleuths" fully embraced their quirky titles, aware that their digital skills were capturing attention and changing the game for SummitTek's investigations.

They arrived bursting with energy, Jacob with a sling pack across his shoulder, while Emily tapped away on her smartwatch, her tablet peeking out from a bubblegum-pink tote decorated with tiny cherries, retro pixel hearts, and a vibrant anime sticker that exclaimed "*404: Not Today.*" She sported it like armor, half irony, half genuine love for everything playfully cute. The bag looked like it came from a cartoon, but it was packed with high-performance gear and an eerie number of charging cables.

They brought brains and bounce, cracking jokes as effortlessly as they cracked encryptions. Harsh environments like Alaska weren't exactly their element, but they were invaluable in the digital trenches of corporate warfare and exactly the kind of reinforcements Susan needed right now.

"Jacob and Emily," she said, leaning forward, her voice warm but authoritative. "We need more intel on this AndesCon situation. Ari wants every angle explored. Rumors, social media chatter, old mountaineering forums, anything that can shed light on what happened with that missing climber. We must clear SummitTek's name."

Emily nodded eagerly, preparing her tablet for action as Jacob whipped out and fired up his laptop. "We're on it," she said. "Do we have the climber's name and any known associates?"

Susan consulted her notes, a crisp, handwritten list in perfect penmanship, a contrast to Emily and Jacob's digital-first approach. "Julián Hurtado," she said. "Married, six kids, from Lima, Peru. Rumors suggest he fled to Colombia.

See what you can find: images, chat logs, or unusual activity on social channels. Anything that proves sabotage or personal motives will help us." His nickname, 'El Rompecorazones,' suggests he is a heart-breaker. Let us find out if his travels' rumors are true."

Jacob cracked his knuckles, already half-immersed in a search query. "I'll check the usual spots, encrypted mountaineer chatrooms, digital back-copies of travel logs, maybe even immigration databases, if accessible."

Susan watched them with satisfaction. While her style might be outdated, her instincts were spot on. She knew Jacob and Emily would never be comfortable lifting heavy gear on a glacier, but they could easily navigate the digital frontiers of the internet.

Gottschall admired Susan's ability to place the right people in the right roles, Jacob and Emily's talents were about to vindicate SummitTek's reputation.

"Remember," Susan said, folding her hands gracefully, "we need facts. Hard evidence. Ari relies on us to bring clarity. If we can prove that Julián Hurtado sabotaged the equipment and fled for personal reasons, SummitTek walks out of this lawsuit clean."

The Digital Duo nodded in unison, the hum of computers and clicking keys filling the space as they got to work.

Susan reclined slightly, letting a small smile appear on her fuchsia-colored lips. She might be a walking relic of another era's fashion, but she understood the modern corporate battlefield very well. Her job was to maintain order amid chaos, and as the interns set about uncovering the truth, she felt a renewed sense of purpose, and maybe just a hint of pride in knowing that she had chosen well.

Jacob cracked his knuckles. "Emily, check out these screenshots again on WhatsApp. The guy's name is Julián Hurtado, right? Aka, "El Rompecorazones"?"

Emily nodded, her blue-tipped hair swaying as she scrolled through a feed. "Yes, Julián Hurtado. Married with six kids. Officially listed as missing but look here." She turned her monitor to show Jacob a series of photos. "This is a social media account from a woman in Bogotá, Colombia. She's posted selfies with a man who looks exactly like Hurtado just a week after he supposedly disappeared."

Jacob whistled low. "He's not missing. He's on vacation with his sidepiece. That's messed up!"

Emily clicked through more images. "Check these timestamps. The days after he 'went missing,' she posted a picture of them kissing in front of a café in Bogotá. Also, I found a comment thread on a mountaineering forum where someone mentioned suspicious behavior from Julián Hurtado before the expedition, like he was strangely tinkering with the equipment."

"Sabotage," Jacob said, his eyes lighting up. "He must have tampered with SummitTek's gear to create an excuse for disappearing. Maybe he wanted everyone to assume he died or got lost so he could start a new life with his lover in Colombia."

Emily nodded with understanding. "That makes sense! He paints SummitTek as if they're responsible for faulty equipment, hoping to stir up a big scandal. Meanwhile, he's comfortably sipping Aguardiente in Bogotá, having a good laugh at everyone's expense."

Jacob pulled up an encrypted database of immigration photos and found that Julián Hurtado had secretly crossed into Colombia under a different name the same week he vanished. "Gotcha!" he said triumphantly. "Now we have proof he's alive and a total scammer."

Emily grinned. "We should notify Gottschall immediately. This clears SummitTek of negligence. The equipment failure was intentional sabotage."

Jacob tapped the final key on his laptop. "This is huge. Ari's going to be relieved. But man, what a jerk that climber turned out to be, leaving his wife and six kids? Unbelievable."

Emily shook her head, disgusted. "People do awful things. But at least we have the truth now."

The research team celebrated with high-fives and hugs, buzzing with the thrill of the breakthrough. Amid the flurry, Jacob instinctively hugged Emily, tight, warm, and... a beat too long.

When they pulled apart, both looked slightly flustered, unsure whether the moment had crossed from friendly to something more. Jacob, recovering first, flashed Emily with a crooked smile that said more than words.

Emily glanced away, cheeks-tinged pink.

Across the room, Susan raised an eyebrow, catching the entire exchange. Still, there was no time to dwell on office romance. This win was exactly what the company needed and gave Ari a break from the storm of bad press.

Ari's Return to Denver

The SUV left the airport and glided through Denver's streets, the sky dimming into the evening. As he drove back to his mansion and waiting parents, Ari stared out the window with his phone in hand. He contemplated calling Elinor right away. She had said, "We'll talk later," last time. But did she mean it?

He inhaled deeply and dialed. Her phone rang several times before her crisp but guarded voice came through.

"Hello?"

"Hey, Elinor," Ari said softly. He tried to keep his voice from trembling. "I'm back in Denver. I... I need to talk to you."

A silence. He could almost picture her tightening her grip on the phone. "About what, Ari?"

"Everything," he said, wincing at how vague that sounded. "I know you're hurt and disappointed. My parents are pushing the Diana situation. I didn't want that. I swear."

She sighed, a sound heavy with hurt. "I know your world is complicated. Maybe I'm just naïve for thinking I could be part of it."

Ari closed his eyes. He had to try another angle. "Elinor, please. It's not about that. I want to tell you something else, something... important."

He paused, searching for the right words. "I had an encounter..., a spiritual one. Something happened in Red Deer, Alberta. I... I met a Being that claimed to be the *Spirit of Revelation Knowledge*."

There was a short silence, and then her voice softened, curiosity creeping in. "*Spirit of Revelation Knowledge?*"

He nodded, then remembered she couldn't see him. "Yes. This Being showed me that I've been seeking knowledge from the wrong source, eating from the wrong tree, like the Tree of the Knowledge of Good and Evil in the Bible. It told me I needed to seek God's Knowledge, to drink from the waters of the Tree of Life. It quoted Psalm 42:1 and other Old Testament scriptures."

He took a deep breath, "I know this sounds crazy, Elinor, but it happened." He waited, heart pounding. If she laughed or dismissed him now, he wouldn't blame her. But instead, her tone softened further, turning thoughtful.

"You... Ari... you're talking about God now? The same Ari who never mentioned faith or God-stuff?"

He exhaled, relieved at her lack of mockery. "I know it's out of character. I've always relied only on myself. But after what I saw and the little *Red Book* I received from the Spirit... I can't deny something greater is at work."

Elinor was silent again, but this time, it felt different, like she was processing. "A little book? You said it quoted Psalms. 'AS THE DEER PANTS FOR THE WATER...' That's Psalm 42:1. It's about longing for

God, thirsting for Him. You never struck me as a man who recognized spiritual thirst."

Ari's voice grew quieter. "I know you're hurt from the things my parents have done but, I do want your help. I realize that I've always been thirsty. I just never understood it... what does that all mean?"

The line crackled softly. Then she said, "I appreciate you telling me this. I'm unsure what it means, Ari, but I will be a listening ear for you."

His chest loosened a bit. "I appreciate it. Maybe we can talk in person sometime... not now, I know you need space... but maybe soon."

She hesitated, then replied, "We can talk soon. I'll pray about this whole situation. And Ari... I'm glad you're seeing that there's more to life than what you can build by your own strength."

He smiled, feeling relieved as the call ended on a friendlier note.

Digital Duo Delivers

Ari entered the elevator at SummitTek's HQ the following day, limping slightly. His ankle still ached, but he refused to use a cane. The pain reminded him that not everything was under his control. As the elevator opened, he found Gottschall waiting at the Executive Suite, her clipboard against her chest, as usual. Unexpectedly, Susan stood proudly behind her with the Digital Duo: Jacob and Emily.

"Good, you're here," Gottschall said, her tone brisk as always. "Jacob and Emily have news," as they all followed Ari into his spacious office.

Jacob grinned. "Mr. Keshet, we've discovered the truth about the missing Peruvian climber. He's not missing at all! He fled to Colombia to be with another woman, leaving his family behind."

Emily nodded vigorously. "We found pictures of him on social media, WhatsApp messages, and photos posted by his lover. We also found emails insinuating that he sabotaged the equipment to blame SummitTek and vanish. The company isn't liable for any negligence. We have proof he tampered with the gear."

Ari's eyes widened in surprise and relief. This was the break he needed. "That's... incredible work... both of you. I'm impressed! It goes to show that knowledge is power."

The interns beamed at the praise. Gottschall allowed herself the tiniest smile. "This means we can present evidence to AndesCon and the Peruvian officials. We will be cleared of any wrongdoing."

Ari smiled and nodded. Just yesterday, he'd been weighed down by company upheaval and spiritual conflict. Today, the crisis showed signs of resolution. He also realized that even in chaos, God might be guiding him.

He turned to Jacob and Emily. "Put together a briefing for Legal. We're reaching out to AndesCon right away." They nodded and hurried out, excited to prove their worth in the company.

Gottschall lingered, her sharp gaze studying Ari. "You seem different," she said quietly.

"Different, how?" Ari sounded surprised.

"Less... frantic," she said, choosing her words carefully. "Less as if you're trying to bend the world to your will. More... open. I don't know what changed in Calgary, but I see it."

He smiled. "Ironically, a lot has changed. I'm still processing it."

Gottschall nodded once, her gaze steady. "If it helps you lead with clarity and conviction, then you have my full support.

But remember, wisdom isn't always loud, but it always leaves a mark." Ari chuckled. "You always have a way with words, Maria." "Someone has to keep you grounded," she retorted, turning to leave.

Quiet Evening Alone

Back at his mansion that evening, Ari sat by the fireplace alone. His parents had left for dinner with one of their influential friends at a predictably upscale restaurant; Ari didn't expect them back for several hours. The candles and romantic ambiance set up for Diana's arrival had long since been cleared away, leaving the house feeling cleaner and more honest.

He took out his phone and texted Elinor:

Hey, Elinor. I just wanted you to know that we found out that the missing climber was a scammer. It's a relief SummitTek.isn't at fault. Thank you for listening earlier. I'm still sorting things out, but I appreciate your willingness to hear me out. I hope we can talk again soon.

He hit send, feeling a cautious warmth settle in his chest. He didn't expect an immediate reply. Maybe she needed time to pray, think, and trust that his encounter was genuine and not some ploy. That was fair.

Outside, gentle snow began to fall, the flakes catching the mansion's exterior lights. The world seemed poised on a hinge, balancing past and future. Ari found himself whispering another awkward, halting prayer.

"God, I don't know what You have in store for me, but I'm listening. And I'm thirsty. Help me find the waters of life."

Stolz was silent or at least subdued. Maybe his hold was loosening. Maybe Ari's soul was taking its first real sip of something eternal, something he'd ignored his whole adult life.

He closed his eyes, imagining the red deer from his dream, the mighty tree with its glowing books, and the waters flowing endlessly clear.

He could almost taste that water in his mind, quenching not just physical thirst but something deeper. Perhaps Elinor would understand. Perhaps, with time, she might even join him on this strange new path he found himself walking.

For now, he accepted the moment's stillness, grateful for the lessons learned. He opened the little *Red Book*, its thin pages glistening with Bible scriptures. Chapters came to life, giving revelation to life's questions.

Chapter 15

Choosing the Higher Path

Ari spent most of the next morning unsettled, pacing the length of his mansion's library and running his hand along the spines of the carefully curated collection of books... that he'd never actually read.

He thought of the recent conversation with Elinor. She hadn't outright dismissed his spiritual account. Instead, she'd given him cautious hope that she might believe him or at least believe in the sincerity of his hope for transformation. He longed to see her, to speak face-to-face, but he sensed that patience would be key. The trust that his father and mother had damaged could not be repaired overnight.

Outside, a gentle snowfall drifted lazily, blanketing Denver's suburbs in quiet white. Inside, Ari felt the hush of something more profound, a silence that had settled since his return from Red Deer and the revelations there. He could feel that Stolz was still present, but no longer as dominant. The voice of pride slithered around the edges of his mind, seeking entry points. Yet, Ari found it easier to push Stolz aside, to refuse that old song of self-reliance.

His parents were somewhere in the mansion, a sprawling estate so vast it could almost qualify for its own zip code, but even with all that space, their presence seemed to linger like an unwelcome house guest who hadn't gotten the memo to leave.

Ari wasn't in the mood for another round of their passive-aggressive observations or not-so-subtle matchmaking schemes. His mind was still tangled in a web of thoughts he couldn't quite shake.

Just as he considered retreating to his study to avoid a "chance" encounter in one of the endless hallways. His phone buzzed, and the screen lit up with a text from Elinor:

> *Hi Ari. I've been thinking about what you said.*
>
> *Would you like to meet somewhere neutral?*
>
> *Maybe the park at the café?*
>
> *I'm free this afternoon.*

For a moment, the tension in his chest eased. The park café sounded like a breath of fresh air compared to navigating the emotional landmines under his own oversized roof.

Ari's heart leaped as he read Elinor's text message.

> *Coffee café near Washington Park.*
>
> *Quiet and cozy.*
>
> *Let's meet there at two.*

They confirmed the meeting spot, and Ari eased back, closing his eyes to murmur a brief, awkward prayer of gratitude... something that still felt unfamiliar to him.

Secret Meeting at the Café

At exactly two o'clock, Ari arrived incognito, wearing sunglasses and a gray hoodie, making his best impression of a man who was definitely trying to avoid being recognized. He had dodged his parents' probing questions about his future and slipped out unnoticed, feeling like an escaped corporate fugitive.

The café was small and charming, with creaky wooden floors, a chalkboard menu, and a quiet crowd of people engrossed in books and laptops. The scent of espresso and cinnamon pastries filled the air, grounding him in a moment of normalcy he hadn't felt in weeks. He chose a table at the back, away from the windows. Ari tapped his fingers anxiously as he waited.

Then, Elinor arrived. She wore a soft, warm sweater, jeans, and her favorite cowboy boots, the same boots Ari had teased her about years ago but had secretly loved. Her hair was pulled back simply, and she carried herself with the quiet confidence that had always captivated him.

She spotted him, hesitated for a second, then walked to him.

Ari stood, offering a tentative smile. "Hey."

"Hey," she returned, sliding into the seat across from him. Her voice was steady, but her eyes held the guarded edge of someone unsure where this conversation might lead.

"Tea?" Ari offered, already scanning the menu. She nodded. "Peppermint."

"Classic Elinor." He smirked. "No experimental flavors?"

"Last time I tried a 'seasonal special' from a café, I spent the next two hours regretting my life choices."

Ari chuckled and went to order, returning with his black coffee and her peppermint tea. As he set her cup down, she murmured, "Thanks."

"How are you?" she asked, folding her hands neatly on the table. Her tone was neither cold nor overly warm, somewhere between caution and curiosity.

Ari exhaled, rubbing a hand over his jaw. "I'm... okay. Actually, better than okay. I feel different." He hesitated. "I know that might sound vague."

Elinor studied him. "Different, how?"

He swallowed. "Less sure of the old ways. More open to something new. I know I said some strange things before, about the *Spirit of Revelation Knowledge*, about trees of knowledge and life." He looked down, fiddling with his coffee mug's handle. "I know it might sound crazy, but I can't deny what I experienced."

Elinor tilted her head, her green eyes searching his. "Tell me more about what you experienced. Not just the Red Deer moment, what you felt afterward."

Ari inhaled, gathering his thoughts. "I felt... thirsty. But not like normal thirst. No matter how much water I drank, there was something deeper I couldn't satisfy. And then I remembered the verse the Spirit quoted: 'AS THE DEER PANTS FOR THE WATER BROOKS, SO PANTS MY SOUL FOR YOU, O GOD.' I never really took it seriously. Now I do."

She nodded, her expression thoughtful. "Spiritual thirst is real. I've always believed we need God. No amount of worldly success, knowledge, or even human love can replace that connection."

Ari exhaled, feeling the tension in his chest ease up. "I realize that now." He reached into his pocket and carefully pulled out the small *Red Book*, its crimson cover gleaming softly in the café's ambient light. "And the Spirit left me this."

Elinor's brows furrowed as she took the book, turning it over in her hands. "What in the world...?" She slowly flipped it open, her fingertips brushing the impossibly thin pages. "This is fascinating."

Her eyes scanned the pages, lips parting in astonishment. The text was small, microscopic even, but somehow, each word was perfectly crisp. The more she turned, the more she realized the entire Bible was inside, every verse, every chapter, every book, compressed into this single, palm-sized volume.

"This..." she whispered, her voice barely above a breath. "Ari, this is the world's smallest Bible." She traced the delicate pages with reverence. "How is this even possible?"

Ari smirked. "Nothing about this journey has been normal."

She closed the book gently and handed it back to him. "I think I need to learn more."

Ari hesitated, feeling the weight of what was ahead. "The Spirit hinted that I'd need counsel, guidance... something about a *Spirit of Counsel*. Maybe that's my next step."

Elinor sipped her tea, considering. "In Scripture, counsel often comes from wise advisors... or directly from God. If you feel led to seek this Spirit, maybe you should pray again. Ask God to show you."

Ari turned the little book over in his hands, feeling its divine weight despite its size. He had a long way to go, but maybe, just maybe, he was finally on the right path. Ari huffed a small, amused breath. "Prayer. That still feels awkward."

Elinor smiled slightly. "Sometimes, we have to let go of pride to embrace trust in God. Prayer is just talking with God. Trusting that He hears you. Waiting for an answer from Him."

A pause stretched between them. Then, she hesitated before reaching out, placing a hand briefly over his. The warmth of her touch sent a current through him, a restrained passion lurking beneath the surface. Her fingers were soft, familiar, yet distant. 'I've missed you,' he wanted to say. But instead, he stayed silent, letting the moment settle.

"I'm willing to walk through this with you," she said softly, "but I need honesty. No half-truths or hidden motives."

"I promise," Ari said, voice low, almost hoarse.

They spoke a while longer, shifting into familiar conversations about SummitTek. He mentioned the discovery that cleared the company of negligence, and Elinor visibly relaxed. "Praise God," she said, her relief genuine. "And kudos to the interns for out-sleuthing corporate lawyers."

By the time they left the café, their tension had softened. Ari walked her to her car, the gray sky above them pressing low with the promise of more snow.

"I might try praying tonight," he admitted, glancing at her as she unlocked the door. "Seriously asking God for the next steps. If I learn anything... I'll let you know."

Elinor met his gaze, something flickering behind her eyes. Hope? Hesitation? "Of course," she said finally. "I'd like to know what you find out."

Ari watched her drive away, his heart full of things unsaid. He missed her. More than that... he realized that he loved her.

Meeting with the Spirit of Counsel

That evening, Ari had dinner with his parents. Diana was mercifully absent, and he skillfully avoided talking about her and how "wonderful" she was. Finally escaping, he retreated to a quiet room in his mansion, a study at the far end of the second floor that he rarely used and where his parents probably wouldn't track him down to browbeat their wishes into him.

He turned off his phone, dimmed the lights, and knelt awkwardly on the plush rug in his study, repositioning his sore ankle. It was an unfamiliar posture, both physically and spiritually. He cleared his throat, hesitant but determined. "God..." he began softly, the word feeling heavy and awkward on his tongue. "I don't know how to do this, but I'm goin' to try."

He paused, the silence around him pressing down like the weight of the mountains he had scaled. "You have shown me things... things I can't ignore. There was that strange creature in Alaska, and then the blue mist. It wasn't just luck that it appeared when I needed it. And Peru... that crazy storm, the *Spirit of the Fear of the Lord*, they shook me to my core. And then Red Deer..." He exhaled, his voice trembling. "The *Spirit of Revelation Knowledge*. That Being spoke truths I didn't want to hear but couldn't deny."

His fingers gripped the edge of the rug as if grounding himself. "God, all these experiences, what do they mean? Are You trying to tell me something? To change me? I don't even know how to change, but I can't shake this feeling that these encounters aren't just random. They are...pieces of something bigger."

Ari lowered his head, his voice dropping to a whisper. "Now, I'm asking for the *Spirit of Counsel*. I need guidance and direction. What do I do with everything I've seen and heard? How do I move forward when I feel like my pride and ambition are all tangled up in who I am?"

For a moment, the only sound was his ragged and uneven breath. Then, a faint memory surfaced in the stillness, the deer was drinking from the stream by the Tree of Life in his vision. Its serene grace and purity of the waters had stirred something deep within him. He whispered, "Help me find that peace. Help me drink from the right stream to choose what is right."

His words faltered, his throat tightening with unspoken fears. "And Elinor..." He hesitated, guilt creeping in. "She has shown me a different kind of strength. A faith I don't understand but can't dismiss. Is she part of what You are showing me? Am I meant to...?"

He trailed off, his thoughts spiraling. His heart felt exposed, raw in a way he hadn't allowed. "God, I'm not asking for a sign. You've already given me more than I deserve. But please, show me how to take the next step. I don't want to waste this chance. Not this time."

As he knelt there, a strange stillness settled over him, not the absence of sound but a profound quiet that seemed to touch the very core of his being. It wasn't an answer, not yet. But it was enough to remind him that he wasn't entirely alone in his struggle. He closed his eyes, breathing slowly. At first, nothing happened, but then a sense of warmth enveloped him. When he opened his eyes again, he was no longer in his study.

What looked like a distinguished law office, the kind one might see in a classic courtroom drama. Leather-bound books lined the shelves, their spines gilded with Hebrew letters. The scent of old parchment and ink hung in the air. On the shelves, not just law books but ancient scrolls, like the Mosaic Law, as well as volumes referencing the Prophets and Proverbs, and books on discretion and wisdom. There was a chessboard on a side table, pieces placed as though participants were partially through a game, and a set of balancing scales gleaming on a small stand. Every detail whispered of judgment, advice, and careful deliberation.

A large wooden desk stood at the center of the dimly lit space, polished and pristine as if waiting for an important case to be deliberated. Behind it, a figure rose, a golden, ghostly presence, yet solid enough to command authority. His tailored, light-colored suit was crisp, his posture poised with strong confidence. Ari's breath caught in his throat.

He resembled *Perry Mason*, the old television lawyer Ari remembered watching in reruns as a kid, with Ari's father murmuring comments about the legendary defense attorney's sharp mind and unshakable confidence. The realization struck Ari like a gavel pounding the judge's bench. This was no mere lawyer; this was the *Spirit of Counsel*. Ari felt it in his bones.

"WELCOME, ARIEL KESHET," the Spirit greeted, his voice calm and deliberate, carrying the weight of true Godly wisdom. "YOU SEEK COUNSEL, AND YOU NEED GOD'S DIRECTION."

Ari swallowed, shifting his weight. He wasn't used to this, admitting "need," acknowledging that he was lost. He had always been the man with the answers, the strategist, the one who dictated his own path. Asking for help had never been in his nature.

"I... I," His voice faltered, and for a moment, he considered bluffing his way through as he had in boardrooms and high-stakes negotiations. But here, in this sacred space, that arrogance felt hollow. "I don't know how to ask," he admitted, his voice quieter than intended. "I've always been self-sufficient. I lived by my own rules and climbed to the top with my own strength. But now... I see that's not enough. I need something more."

The Spirit's gaze held steady, unreadable yet kind. "YOU HAVE EATEN FROM THE WRONG TREE," he said, resting his ghostly golden hand on an open book. "YOUR AMBITIONS LED YOU TO WORLDLY KNOWLEDGE DIVORCED FROM RIGHTEOUSNESS. YOU BUILT YOUR EMPIRE ON WORLDLY WISDOM THAT SERVED YOU. NOW, YOU STAND AT A CROSSROADS. IF YOU TRULY WISH TO DINE FROM THE TREE OF LIFE, YOU MUST EMBRACE HUMILITY, OBEDIENCE, AND THE WILLINGNESS TO SERVE OTHERS RATHER THAN ONLY RULE OVER THEM."

Ari's throat tightened. The words cut deep because they were true. His entire life had revolved around control, managing his image, wealth, and power. Letting go and admitting he wasn't in control felt unnatural.

"I'm ready," he said, though the uncertainty in his voice betrayed him. He exhaled and steadied himself. "Or at least... I want to be ready."

The Spirit's expression remained calm, but there was something in his eyes, a knowing, an understanding of Ari's inner battle. "DESIRE FOR CHANGE IS THE FIRST STEP TOWARD TRANSFORMATION."

He pressed his golden hand against the book, and for a moment, the room filled with the soft rustling of unseen pages turning. The air around them shifted, thick with something ancient and weighty.

"I WILL GIVE YOU COUNSEL," the Spirit continued, his voice a measured decree. "YOUR JOURNEY DOES NOT END HERE. YOU HAVE ENCOUNTERED THE SPIRIT OF THE FEAR OF THE LORD AND THE SPIRIT OF REVELATION KNOWLEDGE. NOW, I OFFER YOU DIRECTION, GUIDANCE, AND WARNINGS. THE ROAD AHEAD WILL TEST YOU IN WAYS YOU HAVE NOT YET IMAGINED."

Ari exhaled slowly, absorbing the weight of the words. He didn't have a counterargument, a clever retort, or a backup plan. He simply nodded. He had faced challenges before, including hostile business takeovers, angry board members, and near-death experiences in the Andes, but this warning felt different. He stiffened slightly. He had expected advice, maybe even comfort. But this felt like something more... a *Call to Arms*.

The Spirit of Counsel leaned forward and spoke, "A BATTLE IS COMING, ARIEL. IT WILL TEST YOUR SOUL, YOUR PERSONAL LIFE, YOUR COMPANY, AND YOUR CALLING. YOU WILL STAND AT THE CENTER OF A CONFLICT YOU CANNOT AVOID."

A chill ran down Ari's spine. "A battle?" The Spirit nodded.

"DENALI MOUNTAIN AWAITS YOU. THERE, A SPIRITUAL WAR WILL BE WAGED. FORCES WILL SEEK TO BREAK YOU, TO REAWAKEN PRIDE, GREED, AND FEAR. BUT KNOW THIS: YOU WILL NOT FACE IT ALONE. THE SPIRIT OF POWER AND MIGHT STANDS READY TO ASSIST YOU AGAIN... IF YOU CALL UPON THE NAME OF THE LORD JESUS CHRIST.

DO NOT FORGET. THE DAYS OF CLIMBING MOUNTAINS FOR AMBITION WILL YIELD TO CLIMBING THEM FOR PURPOSE, GOD'S PURPOSE."

Ari's stomach tightened. Denali was one of his greatest ambitions and accomplishments, a test of his endurance, strength, and his company's inventions. He had always viewed it as a great conquest. But now... was it going to be a battleground for his soul?

He recalled the eerie, shadowy giant creature on the mountain and the dark mist that had suddenly appeared, scaring the giant creature away.

Ari swallowed hard. "Assist me again? What do you mean?"

The golden Spirit's eyes sparkled. "THE DARK BLUE PRESENCE YOU ENCOUNTERED WAS THE SPIRIT OF POWER AND MIGHT."

Yet the Spirit's command unsettled Ari more than anything. "CALL ON THE NAME OF THE LORD JESUS CHRIST."

Ari tensed. Not because of the mention of *Power and Might*.

Not at the warning of an impending battle.

But at that *Name... Jesus Christ*.

The Name wasn't unfamiliar. He had heard of Him in history books, in passing, even in curse words, but never like this. Never as

Lord. Never as someone he was meant to call upon. It felt... foreign. Uncomfortable. And Ari wasn't sure he could say it.

Ari's voice steadied slightly. "How will I know when to go? Or what to do?"

The *Spirit of Counsel* smiled. "First, you ask, then you must seek and learn, then while you are knocking at the door of opportunity, listen for God's direction."

He reached into a drawer, withdrew a scroll, and placed it on the desk with reverence. "The Lord directs the steps of the righteous. Do what is right in God's ways. Listen to the Spirit's guidance. Then you will know when and what to do."

"For now, prepare yourself. Seek direction in the little Red Book, the Holy Scriptures. The Mosaic Law and the Prophets are not relics but living words. Study Proverbs for discretion. Learn from history's mistakes. Heed the counsel of God's Spirit. Above all, remember: pride leads to downfall and death, but humility leads to life."

Profound and genuine feelings intertwined with thankfulness. He was offered an opportunity to reshape his journey.

The golden Spirit stood and extended his hand, palm up. In it lay a *gold compass*.

"You have chosen well by seeking Godly Counsel." His voice carried the weight of eternity. "Take this compass and go forth with strength. Resist the temptations that arise. Call on the Name of the Lord Jesus Christ, and He will send the Spirit of Power and Might to strengthen you."

The words lingered, heavy and undeniable.

Then, the vision began to fade. The office melted into a golden haze before dissolving into the dim quiet of his study.

Ari found himself still kneeling on the rug, breathing heavily like he had just sprinted a marathon. He opened his eyes. He was back. Physically unchanged, except... the *gold compass* lay on the table before him. Tangible. Real. It was unshakable proof that the encounter was not just a dream. His chest rose and fell with uneven breaths. Slowly, he stood with unsteady legs and left the study.

He poured himself a glass of water and drank deeply, but the thirst remained. Not the kind of water that could quench.

And still, that Name hung in the air. Pressing on his soul.

Parental Meddling

As Ari descended the sweeping staircase of his sprawling Denver mansion, the sight awaiting him at the base of the grand foyer made his stomach turn. His parents, Abner and Iris Keshet, stood in whispered conspiracy with Diana Metzenbaum, who, despite being uninvited, looked perfectly at ease. Her carefully sculpted figure and tailored designer dress screamed ambition and control, a walking billboard for "the right choice."

"Ariel!" Iris's voice rang out, dripping with saccharine sweet enthusiasm. "Look who stopped by! Diana wanted to say hello, so thoughtful of her, don't you think?" She flashed her most radiant smile, though her eyes betrayed a simmering panic.

Abner, his hands clasped behind his back in a pose of patriarchal authority, nodded. "We thought a quiet dinner, just the four of us, might be a good way to refocus. You've been... distracted lately."

Ever the performer, Diana stepped forward with a practiced laugh and a flick of her glossy curls. "Ari, darling," she cooed, "your parents were just telling me about your latest adventures. Very quaint. But we both know where you belong, at the top of our world. Deals, galas, power moves. That's the Ari I remember."

Ari paused mid-step on the staircase, gripping the banister as Stolz whispered in his mind, smooth and insidious. *"She's perfect. Gorgeous, accomplished, admired, exactly the kind of woman a man like you should have on his arm."*

For a moment, the old Ari wavered. Diana was everything his parents wanted for him and, if he were honest, everything Stolz had once convinced him he needed. But then he thought of Elinor, her quiet faith, her sincerity, and the *Spirit of Counsel's* words about humility and purpose. His grip on the banister tightened, and he silently prayed, God, give me the strength to see through this charade.

He exhaled and stepped down, his determination steadying with each movement. "Diana," he said, his tone polite but firm, "I appreciate you coming by, but this... reunion? It is not going to happen."

His mother's radiant smile flickered, panic flaring in her eyes. "Ari, don't be so hasty. You two were such a wonderful couple. Everyone could see it, your peers, your community. Why throw that away?"

His father grunted, stepping closer. "This isn't just about you, Ari. This is about your heritage, your future. You are risking everything, your legacy, for what? Some whim? Some girl?"

Ari's jaw tightened, but he forced himself to stay calm. "Dad, this isn't about throwing anything away. It's about stepping into something real. What I am pursuing is bigger than power or legacy, it's about something with purpose."

Diana crossed her arms, her carefully composed mask slipping into a glare. "Purpose?" she scoffed. "You are seriously throwing away what we had for that? I hope you know what you're doing, Ari. Because when you wake up and realize your mistake, I won't be waiting."

"Thank you for coming, Diana," Ari said evenly, refusing to rise to her bait. His heart pounded, but he held his ground, the silent prayer steadying him.

Diana's heels clicked sharply against the floor as she turned on her heel, her exit as theatrical as her arrival, as she slammed the door behind her.

Abner and Iris stood stunned, their carefully constructed plans unraveling before their eyes. "Ariel," Iris said, her voice trembling, "this *Christian girl*... she's not one of us. She doesn't understand our world. Do you really think she's worth wasting a proper relationship with Diana?"

Ari met her gaze, his tone unwavering. "Mom, Dad, I love you, but you need to understand something. I'm not throwing anything away." Ari took a slight breath and then continued.

"I'm finding something worth more than what you've been chasing for me. If you can't see that, then maybe you're the one who is blind."

Abner's face darkened, but he said nothing. Iris's lip quivered, her hands clasped tightly as if trying to hold onto her son's old self.

Ari turned and walked back toward his study, leaving them in stunned silence. He didn't slam the door behind him. He didn't need to. The quiet, purposeful click of it shutting was enough to make his point. Upstairs, in the near silence of his study, Ari exhaled deeply. The war wasn't over, but he had won a battle for now.

Glimmer of Hope

Later that night, Ari sat alone again in his study, thumbing through the little *Red Book*, reading Proverbs, and reflecting on the day's events. He had respectfully stood up to his parents and Diana without resorting to old defenses. He had resisted Stolz's tempting whispers. He had drawn closer to a spiritual truth he never knew he needed.

He picked up his phone, his fingers hovering over Elinor's number. He decided against calling this late. He didn't want to push her too hard. He decided to send her a short text:

> *I stood firm today. I resisted the old ways.*
>
> *I wanted you to know.*
>
> *Thank you for encouraging me to seek God.*

He set the phone down, his heart at peace. He didn't know how she would respond, but that was okay. He was learning patience. He had learned that he didn't have to control every outcome and didn't need to orchestrate every detail. That humility, that trust, a childlike openness to something bigger, was slowly becoming part of him.

Ari leaned back in his chair, recalling the *Spirit of Counsel's* warning about Denali. That fight still loomed, some kind of test of faith and purpose he didn't fully understand yet. He replayed the memory of that spiritual office, the golden ghostly figure resembling *Perry Mason*, the balancing scales, the shelves of biblical Mosaic Law and Prophets, all etched in his mind. He knew he needed to prepare by reading and memorizing more Scripture, investing more prayer time, and receiving more physical therapy.

Though storms lay ahead, he wasn't afraid. God was real, guidance was real, and he was learning to drink from the Tree of Life, letting divine knowledge and humility fill his soul.

His parents and Stolz would make another attempt, but he was growing stronger, rooted in something far greater than himself.

As the mansion's lights dimmed and the world outside fell into midnight silence, Ari would rest and allow himself a genuine smile, whispering a prayer of hope and gratitude.

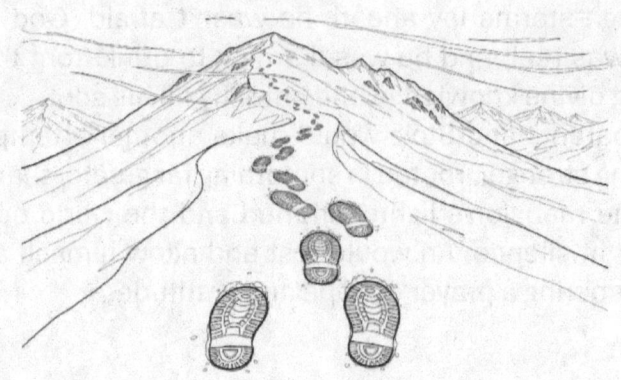

Chapter 16

Steps Towards the Summit

The day after Ari's quiet stand against his parents' manipulations, he called a meeting at SummitTek's Denver headquarters. The mood throughout the building was tense yet curious. Rumors had begun to swirl: Ari Keshet was planning something extraordinary, another field expedition, returning to Denali. His staff asked, "Why would he return there so soon?"

In the executive conference room, Ari waited for his key staff to assemble on the top floor. He straightened his suit jacket, still feeling the ache in his healing ankle. The pain reminded him that he wasn't fully recovered, physically or spiritually. Yet, he knew he had to go. The *Spirit of Counsel* had warned him that a war would be waged on the mountain at Denali, and he suspected this confrontation would prove pivotal for both his soul and his company's future.

A handful of executives, a few department heads, and his research leads filtered into the room. Gottschall entered last, clipboard in hand, her eyes sizing everyone up as if taking everyone's measurements.

Susan Richard moved briskly through the boardroom, distributing neatly stapled agendas like she was arming generals for battle. She was a force of her own. Beneath the glam exterior was a mind like a steel filing cabinet, fast, flawless, and terrifyingly organized.

Her towering blonde hair rose like a *golden warning flare*, a signal that something big was about to go down. It swayed as she walked, anticipating the tension in the air, a "glamorous barometer" for incoming corporate weather. But today, the hair was higher than usual... which is never a good sign.

Ari cleared his throat, drawing every gaze to him. He stood at the head of the table, shoulders squared. "I've decided we're going back to Denali."

A stunned hush fell over the room, more puzzled than alarmed. A few executives exchanged quizzical looks. After all, the last Alaska expedition had gone exceptionally well, SummitTek's cutting-edge gear had performed flawlessly, and the data collected had only bolstered their reputation.

The recent Peruvian scandal, now revealed as sabotage, had left the company unscathed and even more respected. With SummitTek's name cleared of all charges, no one saw any business or scientific reason to return to Denali's icy heights.

One brave researcher tentatively raised a hand. "Mr. Keshet, with all due respect... why are we returning? We've already proven ourselves in Alaska. Are we testing a new prototype, or is it something else?"

Ari paused. He hadn't prepared a neat corporate justification for this decision. He wasn't ready to speak of spiritual callings. "We have strategic interests," he said, choosing his words carefully. "There are certain... conditions I need to verify in the field. Consider it a follow-up study if you like. We'll finalize details soon."

The staff, perplexed but loyal, nodded slowly. Orders were orders, even if they didn't quite understand them.

Gottschall stepped in with her no-nonsense voice. "The orders stand. Prepare the necessary gear. Arrange logistics immediately. Our internal protocols will be followed, and we'll ensure everything is triple checked, as always."

There was another ripple of whispers. Some executives nodded, and others dared not question further. Gottschall was impressed that Ari was calm, decisive, and unmoved by skeptical looks. This was new. She sensed Elinor's influence had softened Ari, giving him a moral spine that resisted old manipulations.

Susan watched from the sidelines, approvingly noting how Ari carried himself. The top floor of SummitTek's HQ was her domain; she knew every personality at play. She'd already instructed the Digital Duo, Jacob and Emily, to keep their ears open. They might discover helpful chatter that justified the trip back to Denali.

The staff, for their part, assumed that some secret invention needed extreme-condition testing.

Let them think that, Ari thought. Better that they guess wrong than know the whole truth about supernatural battles.

When the meeting ended, the staff dispersed into purposeful motion. Orders from the top were rarely challenged. As they left, Ari remained behind, leaning on the polished mahogany table and massaging his still tender ankle. Fear gnawed at him. His body wasn't at peak performance. He wasn't sure if he could climb Denali again or face whatever spiritual monster lurked there.

He whispered an awkward, halting, but earnest prayer. "God, if You're guiding me, help strengthen my ankle. Give me courage."

The *Spirit of Counsel's* words echoed in his mind. "THERE WILL BE A BATTLE ON DENALI, AND YOU WILL RECEIVE MIGHTY POWER IF YOU CALL ON THE NAME OF THE LORD."

That promise both eased and alarmed him.

Training and Dread

Ari dedicated the next few days to physical therapy, hiring a top physiotherapist to come to his mansion every morning. They performed exercises to build strength, stability, and endurance in his injured ankle. The grueling sessions made sweat drip down his temples as he balanced on wobble boards, performed band-resisted movements, and stretched through pain that made him grit his teeth.

He iced the joint during breaks, staring out the window at the quiet sway of the garden. Could he climb Denali again? This time, it wouldn't be about headlines or corporate ego. This was different. This was a spiritual reckoning, and it would demand more than muscle and gear. The memory of the deep blue mist, the *Spirit of Power and Might*, lingered in the edges of his thoughts. Was it really true? That calling on the Lord's Name could summon strength not his own?

He dared to believe it. But at night, lying in bed, wrapped in surgical tape and questions, anticipation tangled with dread.

That's when Stolz crept in. *"You really think this is about surrender?"* the voice slithered through the dark. *"You think bowing and begging will win this battle?"*

Ari clenched his jaw.

"Denali doesn't care about your prayers. That mountain will chew you up and spit out what's left. Unless you take charge, show it who's boss. That's what you were made for. Power. Control. Command. Isn't that what got you to the top?"

Ari turned his face into the pillow, resisting the flare of agreement rising in his chest. He could feel it, that old fire, the desire to conquer, to dominate, to prove something. But instead, he whispered a prayer, "God, not my strength... but Yours."

Stolz hissed in disgust, retreating into the dark corners of Ari's mind and with each prayer, Ari felt the grip of Pride weaken... just a little more.

Elinor's Assistance

To steady his soul, Ari reached out to Elinor again. This time, he invited her to talk and help him understand the Scriptures. If his path involved embracing God's counsel and possibly calling on divine power, he needed to know who this God truly was, especially regarding the question of the Lord, the Messiah.

Elinor agreed to meet him at a quiet corner of an extensive public library in Denver. The building's lofty ceilings and hushed atmosphere provided a peaceful setting for study. She arrived with a worn Bible tucked under her arm, smiling softly when she saw him. They settled into a table near a window, sunlight filtering through old glass, illuminating dust particles.

"I appreciate this," Ari said, opening a notebook. "I feel like I'm stepping into unfamiliar territory. I need to understand more, especially about the Messiah. The Spirit of Counsel mentioned that I've been feeding on the wrong tree and need the Tree of Life. That implies I should learn from God's Word, right?"

Elinor nodded. "Yes, reading Scripture is a good start. I thought we might read from Isaiah 53 today. It's a key passage that points to the Messiah. It might help you understand why we see Jesus as the fulfillment of these prophecies."

Ari inhaled slowly. *Jesus*. That name triggered inner tension. He was Jewish by upbringing. He'd always known that Jews generally didn't accept Jesus as the Messiah. To even entertain the idea felt like betraying his heritage. But he had come this far; he had to be open-minded.

Elinor flipped to Isaiah 53, her finger tracing the text. She read the words, full of sorrow and depth, softly, speaking about a servant of God who was despised and rejected by men, a man of sorrows. Ari learned about a servant who bore the iniquities of many and was wounded for transgressions.

He listened, imagining this suffering figure. It painted a picture of humility, sacrifice, and redemption. The more he heard, the more he saw parallels to what he knew of Jesus Christ from cultural references. Christians believe Jesus fulfilled these prophecies. The idea both disturbed and fascinated him at the same time.

When Elinor finished reading, she looked up. "So... what do you think?"

Ari leaned back, heart pounding. "It's... haunting. Beautiful, but in a painful way. If I try to see it objectively, it could describe someone who willingly suffers for others. Christians say this is Jesus, right?"

She nodded. "Yes. We believe Jesus fulfilled this prophecy. He took on suffering to bring healing and forgiveness. He became the ultimate sacrificial Lamb of God, leading the way back to God the Father."

Ari's stomach twisted. The notion of Jesus as Messiah, as the Son of God, clashed with his cultural instincts. It felt too radical. He'd barely accepted that God was guiding him. Now, he was supposed to believe Jesus was the Messiah who set all things right.

"I, I'm not sure I can accept that," he stammered. "I mean, I only just started believing in God's involvement. Jumping to Jesus... It's too much."

Elinor placed a reassuring hand over his. "I understand. This isn't easy. I'm not pressuring you. You asked to learn, and I'm sharing what I believe. Take your time, pray about it."

Ari nodded and pulled his hand back gently, feeling confused. He wanted the truth, but this truth threatened everything he'd known. For now, he stepped back from the edge. "Let's leave it at that for now. I appreciate your patience."

They ended their session on a note of mutual respect but lingering tension. Elinor understood the difficulty of Ari's position. She would pray for him. Ari thanked her and left the library, his heart heavy and his mind churning.

Dream of the King

Late that night, Ari tossed in bed, unsettled by the day's revelations. His ankle throbbed dully, a persistent reminder of his limitations. He closed his eyes, trying to sleep, but his mind replayed Elinor's gentle voice reading Isaiah 53. It echoed in the silence: "HE WAS WOUNDED FOR OUR TRANSGRESSIONS..."

Drifting into slumber, Ari found himself dreaming. The Spirit of Revelation Knowledge appeared, radiant in a crimson hue, standing beneath a sky alive with swirling colors. The scene shifted, and Ari gazed upon a grand cosmic panorama: a throne nestled among the clouds, angels gathered around it, singing praises in a language he couldn't comprehend but felt deeply in his soul.

At the center, a figure emerged, wearing a crown that was brighter than the sun. This Figure rode on the clouds with authority as legions of angels bowed in reverence, and all creation seemed to quake. Ari knew, instinctively, that this was *Jesus Christ* as the sovereign King. This was the *Son of Man* the Scriptures hinted at.

In the vision, Ari was invited to step forward and join the throng in worship. He hesitated, fear and awe mingling in his chest. If he bowed now and gave in to this image of Jesus as Messiah, how would that change him?

As he stood there, torn, a sudden shriek shattered the harmony. A monstrous entity, taller than any giant, twisted and dark, lunged from the shadows.

Before Ari could call on the Lord, the creature grabbed his injured left ankle and pulled him downward. He screamed, feeling the ankle throb with excruciating pain. The vision of Christ and angels blurred above him as he was dragged into a cavernous abyss. Darkness closed in, and he heard Stolz's laughter echo in his ears.

"Nooo!" he cried, voice strangled by panic and regret.

He woke with a gasp, drenched in sweat, heart hammering. The mansion was silent, only the distant hum of the heating system reminding him he was in the real world. He sat up, his chest heaving, his ankle sore, and his soul rattled. The dream had forced him to confront the ultimate decision: to worship *Jesus as Messiah*... or to remain uncommitted?

He stumbled out of bed, limping to the bathroom to splash cold water on his face. The encounter had been too intense, too personal. He wasn't prepared to become what he mockingly referred to as a "*Jesus Freak*." He clung to his Jewish heritage and his intellectual pride. Accepting *Jesus as Messiah* felt like a bridge too far.

Yet, he couldn't deny the power he'd seen and that vision's majesty. Still, he would not yield, not tonight. He dried his face, his heart pounding. He decided to go to Denali, as instructed. Perhaps there, he would find the clarity he sought on that lofty peak of ice and wind. Maybe facing the spiritual battle on that mountain would bring him to a place of certainty.

Denali Awaits

Over the following days, preparations intensified. SummitTek's staff packed new equipment, gear that had been double-checked and triple-checked. The rumor that Ari had a secret invention needing field testing gained traction. Jacob "Hashtag Hacker" Reed and Emily "Meme Maven" López worked quietly under Susan's guidance to ensure no embarrassing leaks about Ari's quest made it into the media.

Gottschall oversaw everything, noting Ari's subdued demeanor, his steady determination, and the absence of cold logic that once defined him.

Ari tried to focus on logistics. This time, the team would be smaller, just a handful of trusted staff, some local guides, and minimal fanfare. He didn't want the world watching this endeavor, at least not yet. He worked daily with his physiotherapist, who reported incremental improvements in ankle stability. Still, Ari knew it wasn't at full strength, which scared him. But he placed that fear before God each morning in a halting prayer. If he were meant to go, strength would be provided.

Elinor and Ari spoke once more, briefly, over the phone. He told her about the dream, leaving no detail out about the monstrous creature or the glorious Christ figure in the clouds. She listened quietly, not pushing him to accept Jesus but gently suggesting that if this battle was spiritual, maybe Jesus was the ultimate ally he needed. Ari thanked her, voice thick with emotion. "Elinor, I can't promise anything. I'm still struggling. But... I'm grateful you understand."

"I'm praying for you," she said simply. "And be careful on Denali."

"I'll try," he replied. "When I return, I'll have answers... one way or another."

The Eve of Departure

Ari paced his living room the final evening before his flight to Alaska, staring at the crackling fireplace. His parents had left the day after the failed attempt to dictate his life. They tried several times to contact him, but he declined their calls. He loved them, but their manipulations with Diana had strained his relationship with them. He was getting his company ready for another expedition while his mind was bracing for... uncertain expectations. He needed no extra distractions.

Stolz attempted to whisper into his mind, but Ari shut it down, asking God for guidance as he remembered the *Spirit of Counsel's* words: "CALL ON THE NAME OF THE LORD, AND THE SPIRIT OF POWER AND MIGHT WOULD COME TO YOUR AID."

He clung to that promise. The upcoming struggle might decide his spiritual path for life. The idea both terrified and thrilled him.

Ari sat in silence, pen in hand, the room still around him. He wrote slowly, deliberately, as if carving the words into something eternal:

"I'm returning to Denali, not out of pride or profit. I go to find the truth, to face whatever separates me from God. Whether I come back or not, I will know the faith in God, in my life, or even in my death."

He paused, letting the weight of those final lines settle.

Then he folded the note and slipped it into the inner pocket of his climbing jacket, the one closest to his heart. It wasn't just a message for later. It was a surrender. A quiet covenant between a man and the God he was learning to trust, even in the shadow of death.

The night deepened into stillness, the only sound being the soft tapping of raindrops against the windows. Ari stood by the glass, watching the rain under the security lights.

His blurred reflection stared back at him, a hazy silhouette of a man on the edge of the unknown.

The glass felt cold beneath his fingertips, just like the uncertainty pressing around him, chilling and impossible to grasp. What awaited him on Denali was equally blurred. A battle loomed, and its answers were still shifting.

He thought to himself, "Am I really prepared? How can I even prepare for something I can't see?

He let out a slow breath, fogging up the glass. For now, the only thing clear was this... he was going.

"Alright, Keshet, tomorrow it begins." He exhaled, coaching himself. "You'll board the plane, go to Denali, and then you will climb. Not for self, but for truth. You're not climbing for glory; you're climbing for answers." He ran a hand over his face. "There's no turning back; you can do this."

Ari exhaled sharply, flipped off the lights, and headed to bed. His ankle throbbed, his heart pounded, and a simple prayer hovered on his mind, *"God help me."*

Chapter 17

Giant Trial on the Mountain

The flight north to Alaska occurred with far less fanfare than Ari's previous expeditions. SummitTek's expedition team... a select group of seasoned climbers, support staff, and logistics experts... boarded a small charter plane that took them from Denver to Anchorage, and from there, a rugged bush plane brought them closer to the gateway of Denali National Park and Preserve.

The mood was cheery. The daylight hours increased as the days went by, helping boost the mood of the locals. Questions persisted about why Ari had insisted on returning to Denali. They'd already proven SummitTek's gear under extreme conditions, and after the Peruvian sabotage scandal had been resolved, the company's name shone brighter than ever. Investors were pleased, the public admired the cutting-edge technology, and the market soared confidently.

Yet here they were, hauling crates of gear off a plane and onto sleds. Several local guides had been hired, men and women well acquainted with Alaska's harsh wilderness. They'd brought their sled dog teams, strong, brave huskies known for their tireless work ethic and loyalty.

These dogs had seen it all: storms, predators, avalanches. They rarely flinched in the face of danger. But on this journey, something would test their courage like never before.

Ari stood on the snowy airstrip as the last rays of afternoon sun slanted across the icy peaks. His ankle, though improved, still ached dully. He decided to apply a light brace to the injured limb, knowing he would have many miles of walking. Of course, he didn't share that with anyone.

He wore a serious expression that the staff read as determination. They noticed a shift in Ari since his return from Calgary. He carried himself differently, as though guided by some inner compass. Elinor's quiet influence was visible. Ari seemed calmer and less rash. The staff whispered that maybe Elinor had tamed his old ambitions. Whatever the cause, Gottschall found it a refreshing change.

Susan, under Gottschall's leadership, had arranged all the logistics. The Digital Duo had done their part to keep media speculation low. The team on the ground now set out with minimal fuss, just a few sleds, essential climbing gear, and some specialized SummitTek prototypes that Ari had half-heartedly mentioned but never in detail. The staff assumed he might be testing thermal sensors or advanced rope materials. They followed orders, but the air crackled with curiosity.

Moose

The journey into the park's interior began early the following day. The sled dog teams lined up, their bright eyes scanning the horizon. Marcus "Moose" Marcel, a professional climber with a laid-back, humorous personality known for his unwavering loyalty and knack for keeping spirits high in the harshest conditions, helped lead the way. The huskies barked, eager to run, their breath steaming in the crisp air. The summit of Denali loomed far away, a ghostly white titan under a blue sky.

Moose was the kind of mountaineer legend whispered about in base camps worldwide. Tall and broad-shouldered with an unruly beard tucked neatly into his wind jacket, Moose had been conquering peaks before he could legally order a beer. He got his nickname not just from his sturdy build but because he habitually let out a deep, moose-like grunt whenever he hoisted a heavy pack, much to the team's amusement.

When Ari Keshet assembled his lean crew for the return to Denali, Moose was the first name on the roster. Ari needed someone on the mountain he could trust. That was Moose: equal parts high-altitude expert and morale booster. He had that rare ability to crack a joke while hanging off an icy cliff or break the tension of a stormy night in the tent by singing off-key folk tunes until everyone was too busy laughing to worry about frostbite.

Moose's humor wasn't the forced, nervous kind but rather a quiet confidence that nothing nature threw at them could be so bad they couldn't smile about it later. He'd once told Ari, "Boss, if the mountain wanted to kill us, it'd send out a politely worded invitation first. Until then, we climb," delivered with a wink and a cheerful grin that made even the greenest recruit feel a bit braver.

Ari appreciated Moose's companionship and professionalism. Moose never asked too many questions about why they were returning to Denali. He figured if Ari wanted them up there, there was a reason, and he'd find out when needed. Until then, Moose was content to shoulder his pack, crack a joke when the silence got too heavy, and see this whole adventure through, at least until the mountain started playing by rules he had never learned.

Ari felt a growing heaviness as the expedition moved deeper into the wilderness. He remembered the *Spirit of Counsel's* warning: a battle awaited him on this mountain. He tried not to let fear show. Prayer slipped silently, a habit he was still forming: "God, guide me. Give me strength and courage." Every step forward edged them nearer to what awaited them.

The sleds glided over snow-packed trails. Guides shouted commands, and the dogs responded with disciplined energy. Hours passed, and the landscape transformed from gently rolling hills to steeper inclines, forests thinning into the tundra.

The team set up a base camp at the foot of a ridge, intending to ascend in stages. The weather reports were stable for now, but anyone who knew Denali understood that storms could appear out of nowhere.

Ari stood apart from the group at dusk, gazing at Denali's distant slopes. The sky was tinted lavender and gold. Stolz tried to whisper doubts: *"You've come all this way for what? A ghost story? Show everyone that you're the boss."*

Ari shook his head, quietly muttering a prayer of resistance. He could feel the curious eyes on him and turned to catch Moose's gaze, who offered him a respectful nod, recognizing his strong determination.

Night fell quietly. The team slept in sturdy Titan Tents while Ari lay awake with his throbbing ankle. He drifted into restless dreams, waking several times. The terrifying *Spirit of the Fear of the Lord*, with the gentle *Spirit of Counsel*, tried to warn him of what was to come.

The Husky Warning

Morning brought clear skies and a biting cold. The team pressed onward, using sled dogs to ferry equipment higher.

But as they gained altitude, something strange happened: the usually brave dogs began to whine and hesitate. Their ears flattened, and they pulled back on their harnesses. The guides frowned, puzzled.

"Never seen them act like this," said one guide, scratching his beard. "These dogs have faced wolves and survived blizzards. They don't spook easily."

Ari's heart sank. He understood why the dogs were frightened; they sensed something evil, a presence lurking in the spiritual air. He recalled the *Spirit of Counsel's* warning about a fight. Could the enemy already be near? He wondered.

The team attempted to urge the dogs forward, but the huskies resisted, some even snapping at each other in anxiety. A subtle tension wove through the ranks.

The SummitTek staff who had joined the trip, previously curious, now displayed signs of fear. Whispers rose:

"Why are we even here?" ...

"This is pointless." ...

"Ari won't explain himself." ...

A gust of wind carried distant howls, not wolves, something else, a sinister echo off the cliffs. The sled dogs trembled, refusing to advance. The guides, baffled, cursed under their breath. Ari's climbing party members approached him one by one with anxious faces.

"Mr. Keshet," said a researcher, voice quavering, "I'm sorry, but I'm not comfortable going further. The dogs won't move, and the atmosphere feels... I don't know... wrong?"

Another team member nodded, "I'm out, too. We finished our job last time. We have no reason to risk our lives again."

Ari wanted to urge them on, but he felt compassion. They didn't understand the true nature of this mission. How could they? He offered them no logical reason. Nodding, he told them they could return to base camp and wait.

The lead dog, a seasoned malamute with a grizzled coat, let out a soft bark, a signal to the rest of the team. As if understanding their new task, the dogs pulled at their harnesses, eager now to move, not out of fear, but with the relief of returning to the familiar safety of base camp. The sled creaked forward as the team fell into a synchronized rhythm, their powerful legs digging into the snow with renewed purpose.

One by one, nearly all the men retreated. After witnessing the dogs' fear, even the toughest guides decided it was unwise to continue. Only Moose remained, determined to go the distance.

Soon, they stood alone on the slope, the team's lights retreating down the mountain like scattered fireflies.

The Giant Battle

Ari felt naked before the vast, silent wilderness. The wind picked up, biting his cheeks. Without warning, a snowstorm formed, flakes swirling in furious gusts. Visibility plummeted. Ari stumbled forward, using a trekking pole, and every step was painful on his weak ankle.

He prayed, "God, if you're with me, guide and help me..."

The storm raged, and the two men marched on. The mountain's contours blurred until they were just feeling their way forward. Ari knew he must climb higher and face whatever awaited him. His arms ached from fighting the wind. Each breath came hard and cold.

Then, abruptly, the blizzard stopped. Ari and Moose found themselves in a crater amidst icy ridges, a natural amphitheater of snow and rock. The silence was eerie. He sensed a malevolent and immense presence approaching through the thinning veil of swirling snow. From behind a jagged spur of ice emerged a grim figure that nearly made Ari's heart stop.

Moose stood there, amazed and terrified. It was a giant, roughly twice his height. Its skin was gray like dirty snow, reddish hair was on its head, and its dark, hollow eyes burned with cruel intelligence.

This was no mere human; it bore the hallmarks of something ancient, Nephilim, as some legends might say. Its mouth opened wide, revealing teeth as sharp as daggers.

"Are you the champion of humanity, little man?" the giant roared, his voice echoing like thunder between the icy walls. *"You are half-hearted and weak. How pathetic you are."*

Ari's blood ran cold. He gripped the pistol at his waist, a small firearm he'd brought for protection or perhaps just for peace of mind. His heart told him bullets wouldn't help against a spiritual foe, but fear drove him.

Raising the pistol, hands shaking, he fired three shots. The bullets vanished into the giant's bulk with no visible harm. The creature laughed, a deep, mocking laugh that shook the ground.

"Foolish, little man. Your weapons mean nothing here. You think you can face a mighty giant with mortal tools?"

Ari stepped back, twisting his already weak ankle, which throbbed with pain. He thought of calling on the Lord, but fear and doubt choked his voice. The giant advanced, each step causing tremors that rattled Ari's bones.

Standing a few feet away, Moose froze as the massive figure loomed closer. His wide eyes darted between Ari and the advancing Nephilim, his face draining of color. "Nope," Moose muttered weakly, his knees wobbling like a newborn deer.

"Nope, nope, nope!"

Then, like a marionette whose strings had been suddenly severed, Moose's legs buckled, and he dropped to the ground with a heavy thud. His arms flopped at awkward angles, his head rolling to the side as his eyes fluttered shut. He was utterly unconscious and out cold, just like the snowy mountain surrounding him.

The giant shouted, *"Your fear is great, and your faith is weak,"* its voice dripping with disdain. *"You have no true faith, no Messiah to protect you. You are alone."*

Ari clenched his jaw. He tried to recall the *Spirit of Counsel's* words, the promise that he would be saved if he called on the *Name of the Lord Jesus Christ*. He opened his mouth and tried to speak, but the giant lunged and grabbed his injured ankle, wrenching him off his feet. Ari was then thrown back to the snowy ground. Pain exploded through Ari's leg. He screamed, tears of pain freezing on his cheeks.

The giant grabbed the injured leg again and dragged Ari through the snow, laughing. Ari's chest constricted. He was going to die here! The spiritual battle manifested in the material world, and he lost the fight!

Stolz mockingly hissed in his mind, *"This is what you get for chasing fantasies!"*

"Nooo...!" Ari gasped. "God, help me! Please!" he cried into the frigid air... but nothing happened.

The giant snarled, halting a moment as if listening for something to show up. Then it looked at Ari, *"Ha, ha, your god isn't coming."* It laughed mockingly.

Ari remembered the *Spirit of Counsel's* words: "You must call on the Name of Jesus Christ to be saved." But he wasn't ready to accept Jesus as Messiah. The very idea made his heart recoil as it went against all his family's teachings and the culture he had grown up in. Yet here he was in the end, with no hope left. If that Name could save him, he had to try and find out.

The giant's grip was merciless, bone-crushing. With a sickening snap, Ari's ankle shattered, pain detonating through his leg like an electric current. His scream tore through the air, raw and desperate. Before he could react, the monster twisted his leg like a pretzel, ligaments tearing, bones grinding, his knee bending in a way it was never meant to.

Ari's vision blurred, dark spots creeping at the edges. His ribs, already battered, splintered as the giant's other hand slammed into his torso, sending him sprawling across the frozen ground. The impact drove the breath from his lungs, his broken body skidding through the snow. His arm flopped uselessly at his side, dislocated and shattered.

I'm dying. The thought flickered through his mind, distant, almost detached.

His body was failing him, crushed under the sheer force of the enemy. Every heartbeat was agony. Every breath felt like dragging knives through his chest.

The giant towered over him, its shadow engulfing the last remnants of light. Ari attempted to move, but his limbs were unresponsive. His weary body refused to rise.

"Jesus!" he croaked weakly. With a raspy breath, Ari shouted with all his remaining strength: "In the Name of the Lord Jesus Christ, help me!"

In an instant, a blinding light ignited, so brilliant that Ari felt as though a nuclear bomb had exploded on the mountain. Startled, the giant roared in surprise. It shielded its eyes as the world became white-hot. A thunderous crack reverberated through the air, and Ari experienced warmth and power surging over him.

As the light faded, Ari blinked. The giant had disappeared, leaving merely a bare area where snow and ice had once rested, but now revealing the mountainside. The last thing he remembered was the giant's monstrous grip, bones snapping like twigs, the weight of inevitable death crashing down on him. But now... it was gone.

He blinked again. His vision cleared. The ground was scarred, clawed open like a wound, jagged rock, and torn soil lay bare. There were no footprints, no shadows, and no sign of the battle that should have killed him. It was as if death had changed its mind and vanished before finishing the job.

Except for a pathetic clump of burnt red hair.

Power and Might

The ground beneath him started to tremble. A new presence filled the air, like a storm brewing just beyond the veil of sight. Heat radiated through the frozen air, brushing against his broken body.

Ari gasped, his body jerking despite the pain. A figure stood over him.

No warning. No gradual approach. One moment, he was alone, clinging to the edge of consciousness. The next, raw, overwhelming power crashed into existence beside him.

Ari's breath caught, terror and awe slamming into him at once. The being radiated strength beyond comprehension, its presence sending shockwaves through the air. He wanted to crawl away, but relief flooded his soul at the same time.

Standing nearby was a Spirit unlike any Ari had yet encountered, an ancient warrior, tall and immovable, in gleaming armor. A dark blue aura pulsed around him like restrained thunder.

He held a massive sword gripped tightly in his hand, not raised, not threatening, but steady, as if judgment could fall at any moment without warning.

There was no smile, no softness; only silent strength. His face was unreadable, carved with the dignity of eternity. His gaze locked forward like a royal guard whose very posture declared, "Do not test me."

Ari, broken and gasping, felt the weight of the presence settle over him like a command. He lay there, gasping with his body in agony, overwhelmed by gratitude and reverence. He wasn't just in the presence of help... he was in the presence of holy authority. The kind that didn't ask questions. The kind that didn't make suggestions. The kind that delivered power... and expected surrender.

The Spirit's voice resonated like a hundred harmonious voices: "ARIEL KESHET, I AM THE SPIRIT OF POWER AND MIGHT. YOU HAVE CALLED ON THE NAME ABOVE ALL NAMES; JESUS CHRIST IS THE MESSIAH WHO SAVES. YOU HAVE WITNESSED IT THIS DAY."

Ari choked out a sob, both joy and shock mingling. He realized that in calling on Jesus, he had found deliverance. His old hesitations crumbled under the weight of this miracle.

The presence of the *Spirit of Power and Might* was unmistakably holy, and the *Name of Jesus* had vaporized the Nephilim giant as if it were nothing.

"Thank you," Ari managed. "Thank you... Jesus?"

The Spirit reached out a hand, emanating a fearsome yet awe inspiring energy. Ari lay there paralyzed, but he experienced a jolt of electricity as the Spirit made contact. As the Spirit lifted him to his feet, a wave of warmth enveloped him, radiating from the top of his head to the tips of his toes. The feeling was intense, both calming and invigorating.

Before he could comprehend what was happening, the *Spirit of Power and Might* raised its other hand, the sword glowing with brilliant light. The blade shimmered so vividly and intensely that Ari had to squint against its brightness. Without a word, the Spirit thrust the sword forward, not merely toward Ari's physical body but directly into his very being, piercing his spirit and soul.

Ari gasped as a rush of energy and clarity exploded within him. The sensation was terrifying in its intensity, unlike anything he had ever experienced. It felt as though every fiber of his being had been ignited with power, not his own, but something far greater, something divine. His heart pounded, his senses sharpened, and a God-given courage surged through him. This courage was different from the adrenaline rush he had always known.

As the Spirit withdrew the sword, its radiance lingered in his chest. Ari felt his injured body strengthen. His breath caught as he realized the pain was completely gone. He moved his limbs experimentally, stunned to find them healed and stronger than before. In fact, his entire body felt renewed. Every ache and bruise from the Nephilim's assault was erased, replaced with a vitality that hummed in his veins.

The *Spirit of Power and Might* regarded him with a solemn expression. "YOU HAVE BEEN RESTORED, ARIEL KESHET, NOT BY YOUR OWN STRENGTH BUT BY THE POWER OF THE LORD."

Everything Elinor had tried to show him about Isaiah 53, the suffering servant, the God of her faith, now came rushing back to him with undeniable clarity. Jesus Christ, the Christian God. It was all true. He could no longer deny it.

Ari's heart swelled, not with the Pride that had driven him, but with gratitude and reverence. The Spirit's words echoed in his mind as he met its gaze. He was not only rescued from danger but also healed.

The *Spirit of Power and Might* stepped back. Ari stood there, breathing deeply, feeling the weight of his transformation. He had been given new strength and understanding of the One who had saved him.

The sky, which had been storm wracked moments ago, began to clear. Soft sunlight filtered through thinning clouds. Ari could see forever, it seemed. As his gaze turned westward, far beyond what human eyesight should allow, he saw another great mountain range. Above the distant peaks, a green-glowing rainbow arched majestically. Ari thought it might be the Himalayas.

Ari's heart leaped. He was seeing in the Spirit now, given supernaturally enhanced vision. The *Spirit of Power and Might* nodded. "ARIEL, YOU HAVE PASSED THIS TEST. LOOK TO THE WEST. THERE, YOU MUST SEEK THE SPIRIT OF WISDOM, LIKE SEEKING TREASURE. THE JOURNEY CONTINUES."

Ari nodded, humbled and reverent. He was no longer the same man who had first climbed Denali in arrogance. He bowed his head. "Wherever the Lord leads, I will go," he said softly.

The *Spirit of Power and Might* stepped back into the blaze of divine blue light, his expression unreadable like a seasoned general giving marching orders to a recruit. There was no farewell, only finality. The command had been given.

In a blinding flash of glory, the Spirit withdrew.

Just like that, Ari was alone again, the memory of divine authority echoing like a drill sergeant's voice in his bones.

Ari scanned the snowy landscape, his eyes resting on the conspicuous area of melted snow and ice. His heart pounded, and his breath quickened. He had survived, but more importantly, he found faith in Jesus as the Messiah!

Remembering Moose, he started searching for him amidst the aftermath of the battle. Just then, as if summoned from hibernation, a bearded head popped up from behind a mound of snow. Moose's arms stretched overhead, fingers cracking as he yawned, looking for all the world as if he'd just risen from a long nap instead of having fainted at the sight of a literal giant.

Blinking his eyes, he glanced around, unaware of the colossal form that had vanished moments before in a blinding flash. He rubbed his eyes, shook his head, and muttered dryly,

"I swear I closed my eyes for one second. Did I miss anything good?"

Moose Tracks

Climbing down Denali felt strangely effortless this time. With his ankle fully healed, Ari moved with newfound peace and confidence, each step lighter than the last. Moose trudged beside him, shaking his head in quiet amazement at how the tables had turned. Where before the cold and fear pressed in like a vice, now the mountain seemed almost... cooperative.

Ari silently thanked God, marveling at how drastically his perspective had shifted. A short while ago, he faced a Nephilim giant, trusting in and invoking the Name of Jesus to save his life. Now, as the high winds eased and the ice fields offered firm footing, he knew he couldn't hide the truth from his team.

The snow crunched under his boots. He felt strong, as if every cell hummed with divine energy. Jesus, by His *Spirit of Power and Might*, had healed him fully, both in body and soul.

As they rejoined the base camp, the rest of the anxious crew who had huddled together during the storm to await their return came out to greet them with great relief. The storm's sudden appearance and even faster disappearance had left them baffled. They spotted Ari and Moose approaching, Ari upright and steady, Moose grinning in that lopsided way of his, and a wave of astonished relief rippled through the group.

"Mr. Keshet!" shouted one of the crew members, rushing forward. "We feared you were lost!"

"And you too, Moose!" another added, eyes wide. "We thought we'd never see you alive again after the storm hit."

Ari raised his hand to calm them. "We're both fine. Better than fine," he said, taking a deliberate step to show off his perfectly stable ankle.

The team questioned among themselves, "Wasn't Ari recently limping in pain?"

He surveyed their faces: confusion, fear, and relief danced in their eyes. He owed them honesty, at least as much as they could handle. Drawing a deep breath, Ari explained what had happened on the mountain, how he'd encountered a monstrous giant, something beyond human comprehension. He told them how calling on the Name of Jesus Christ had unleashed a power that saved him and annihilated the creature.

Some gasped openly, and others frowned skeptically. It sounded insane; he knew that. "It might be hard to believe, I know," he said softly. "But I can't deny what happened. I was injured before, and now I'm healed. We've returned safely, and you all saw the storm vanish as quickly as it had come. This is no coincidence."

A few members shook their heads, muttering about hallucinations or stress. But some, catching the sincerity in Ari's voice, looked intrigued. This expedition had already proven to be no ordinary mission, and Ari was no ordinary CEO.

A younger researcher dared to speak up, hesitating. "So... you're saying Jesus healed you? Literally... miraculously?"

Ari nodded, "Yes. I know it sounds impossible. I've doubted and struggled against this idea for so long. But now, I can't deny it. The Messiah is Jesus Christ."

Silence blanketed the camp.

Then Moose cleared his throat, stepping forward and brushing snow from his parka. "Uh, boss," he began with a lopsided grin, "I gotta admit something, I saw that giant, too. Big, ugly brute. I did the bravest thing a hero could do: I fainted. Dropped like a sack of potatoes before I could even squeak. When I came to, the giant was gone. Felt like I missed the final encore at a rock concert."

A few snorts of laughter broke the tension. Moose shrugged, grinning sheepishly. "Guess I owe you one, Ari. You saved my bacon while I was taking a nap. Next time, I'll try to stay awake for the grand finale."

His humor cracked the icy shell of disbelief. Some team members smirked, and others raised their eyebrows.

Moose added, "And about this Jesus stuff, I'm no priest, but if invoking His Name makes giant monsters go 'poof,' that's some top-notch customer service. Beats any gizmo SummitTek's ever designed."

The researcher who'd spoken earlier blinked, turning to Moose. "Wait, so you saw the giant, too? Ari's not just making it up or confused?"

Moose shrugged dramatically, spreading his arms. "Buddy, I wish he was makin' it up. I've climbed some nasty peaks and faced storms that'd freeze your nose hairs solid, but that giant?

Let's just say it's not in any National Geographic special I've seen. I'm putting it at the top of my 'weirdest life events' list, and I've got a pretty wild list."

The mood shifted. The team considered Moose's witness. If both Ari and Moose had seen something, perhaps Ari's story wasn't pure fantasy or delusion. Slowly, curiosity replaced fear. Ari realized Moose had handed him a precious gift: credibility wrapped in humor, easing the sting of the unexplainable.

Ari took a slow breath and addressed them again. "I know this is terrifying and beyond logic. You know me, I've never claimed to be a prophet or religious fanatic. I'm just telling you what happened. I never expected to believe in miracles or that Jesus is the Messiah, but here I stand, healed and convinced."

Moose tapped his chin thoughtfully. "Look, I'm as shocked as any of you, but we gotta face facts: Ari left limping like an old man and came back strolling like a marathon champ. That's gotta count for something. If he says Jesus healed him, who am I to argue? Looks like the Big Guy upstairs just staged one heck of a product demonstration, no offense to SummitTek's gear."

A few nervous laughs escaped. Some team members mulled it over, their expressions more thoughtful now. Not everyone would be convinced. The giant, Moose fainting, and Ari's miraculous return. It was enough that most would at least entertain the possibility of something extraordinary.

Some stood in silence, processing. A few bowed their heads, perhaps praying or pondering unseen truths. Others exchanged hesitant glances, unsure whether to call Ari's tale a miracle or madness.

Ari radiated a calm inner glow, as if some burden had lifted. Seeing this, one of the team members said, "Sir, we came here expecting corporate logic and got a miracle instead. I don't claim to fully understand it, but I can see you're different, truly different."

He smiled, grateful for her measured acceptance. Turning to the team, he said, "I'm not demanding that you all believe. I'm just telling you what I've witnessed. For me, this is real and life-changing...

Now, let's head home!"

Some grumbled quietly; others shrugged, relieved to leave Denali's heights. They began packing up camp. Ari helped, moving easily, no longer hindered by any injury. This silent testimony prompted a few to whisper their prayers, wondering if Ari's God might hear them, too.

As the group prepared to descend to lower ground, Moose sauntered over, nudging Ari's arm. "You know, boss, next time you plan on battling mythical giants, maybe give a guy a heads-up? I would have brought a camera. Could've gone viral!"

Ari chuckled, shaking his head. "Moose, I don't think the world's ready for that documentary."

Moose's grin broadened. "Probably not. But I'm glad you won, and I'm glad you're... healed."

Ari patted his shoulder. "Me too, Moose. Me too."

Looking West

Hours later, as the team descended and headed back toward the park's edges, Ari lingered at a vantage point above the silent Alaskan wilderness. The sky was serene, the air was crisp, and in that stillness, he paused, remembering the vision of distant mountains and a shimmering green rainbow. The *Spirit of Power and Might* had told him to go there next, to seek the *Spirit of Wisdom*. His spiritual journey was far from over.

As Ari stood alone on that snowy ledge, the *Spirit of Power and Might* reappeared beside him, still in the guise of a mighty, armored warrior. No one else seemed to see it, nor did they notice Ari's quiet communication with something divine.

The Spirit turned to him, its voice resonating in the silent air:

"YOU HAVE FOUGHT WELL, ARIEL. YOU HAVE CALLED ON THE NAME ABOVE ALL NAMES AND SEEN THAT NO DARKNESS CAN WITHSTAND IT. BEFORE YOU LEAVE THIS MOUNTAIN, I OFFER YOU A TOKEN OF COURAGE AND STRENGTH FOR THE BATTLES YET TO COME."

Ari inclined his head, his heart pounding softly in awe. Then slowly, shimmering into view, came another sword. Its handle was a deep, dark blue, and the blade was a radiant white light that did not hurt his vision. It hovered, weightless as if made of pure light.

"Take this *sword of the Spirit*, forged of mercy and the Word of Truth, it is yours. It will become part of you."

Before Ari could reply, the Spirit raised the glowing blade and pressed it into his core, not cutting flesh and bone but merging seamlessly with his very being.

Ari gasped as warmth and courage rushed through him, his spine straightening, his heart growing light and free. He breathed heavily, eyes wide with awe at what he'd just experienced.

The Spirit regarded him calmly, nodding in approval. "THIS SWORD WILL GRANT YOU COURAGE WHEN FEAR CLAWS AT YOUR SOUL, CLARITY TO KNOW HOW TO ACT WHEN CONFUSION CLOUDS YOUR MIND, AND STEADFASTNESS WHEN TEMPTATION TRIES TO LURE YOU. CALL ON THE LORD JESUS CHRIST, AND REMEMBER THAT YOU DO NOT FIGHT WITH HUMAN WEAPONS BUT WITH THE POWER OF THE SPIRIT OF GOD."

Ari's voice trembled softly. "Thank you," he managed. He felt stronger and more secure.

The *Spirit of Power and Might* stepped back, its radiant form beginning to fade into the swirling light of the mountaintop. Before vanishing completely, it spoke once more, its voice carrying both authority and caution.

"GO FORTH, ARIEL KESHET. RETURN TO DENVER AND SHARE WITH ELINOR WHAT YOU HAVE SEEN AND EXPERIENCED. LET YOUR BOND DEEPEN IN FAITH AND TRUTH, FOR THE PATH AHEAD WILL REQUIRE STRENGTH NOT BORN OF YOUR WILL BUT OF HUMILITY AND RELIANCE ON THE LORD. THEN, JOURNEY WEST, WHERE THE SPIRIT OF WISDOM AWAITS.

BUT TAKE HEED, ARIEL; DO NOT RELY ON YOUR OWN UNDERSTANDING. IN ALL YOUR WAYS, ACKNOWLEDGE THE LORD, AND HE WILL DIRECT YOUR STEPS. THE SWORD I HAVE PLACED WITHIN YOU WILL REMAIN, A REMINDER OF THE POWER AND MIGHT THAT COME ONLY THROUGH SURRENDER. YET IT IS WISDOM, NOT MIGHT, THAT YOU MUST NOW SEEK."

The Spirit's words hung in the air, but Ari's mind caught on "journey west." His thoughts raced as he recalled the vast, towering, and majestic mountains he had glimpsed in the Spirit. He assumed with growing certainty that the Himalayas had to be the destination. It was logical, and logic had always guided him in the past.

The Spirit's gaze lingered on Ari, perceiving his thoughts, but it offered no further explanation. Instead, it spoke one final time. "SEEK THE LORD'S GUIDANCE, ARIEL, FOR WISDOM IS FOUND IN SURRENDERING TO THE LORD'S GUIDING PRINCIPLES, NOT IN MAKING ASSUMPTIONS."

With that, the Spirit dissolved into a cascade of light, leaving Ari alone on the mountain. The air felt clearer, the wind gentler, and his body, miraculously, whole. His ankle, once a source of pain, felt strong and stable, and he stood tall, a surge of boldness coursing through him.

As Ari looked westward, the Spirit's warnings faded into the background, overshadowed by the rising tide of his own ambition and self-reliance.

Convinced he had understood the message, his confidence distorted it, casting the distant peaks in his mind as the Himalayas. And with that image fixed, he took his next steps, not in obedience, but in assumption.

Down below, his staff waited. Some were unsettled by the change in Ari's demeanor and story; others were curious and intrigued. He wouldn't force belief on them, but he would speak honestly and let God work in their hearts as He had in his.

As the plane lifted off, carrying them away from the rugged Alaskan wilderness, Ari gazed out the window, the snowy peaks of Denali fading into the distance. His team exchanged uncertain glances, unspoken questions evident in their sidelong looks at Ari and whispered conversations.

They didn't understand what had happened on that mountain. How could they? Ari knew he would face their confusion and skepticism in the weeks ahead, but it didn't unsettle him. Denali had tested him, stripping away layers of pride and revealing something deeper within.

Always the steady anchor, Moose eased the tension with his signature humor. But even he had seen enough to stand solidly beside Ari, his jokes a cover for the awe he couldn't fully express.

Ari leaned back in his seat, his heart strangely at peace. He had faced a giant beyond comprehension and emerged victorious, not by his own strength but through a power far greater.

The spiritual sword now embedded within his soul was a reminder of that victory, a blazing emblem of courage and faith.

For the first time, Ari felt a strength that was not self-made but divinely gifted, and it was more exhilarating than any peak he had ever climbed.

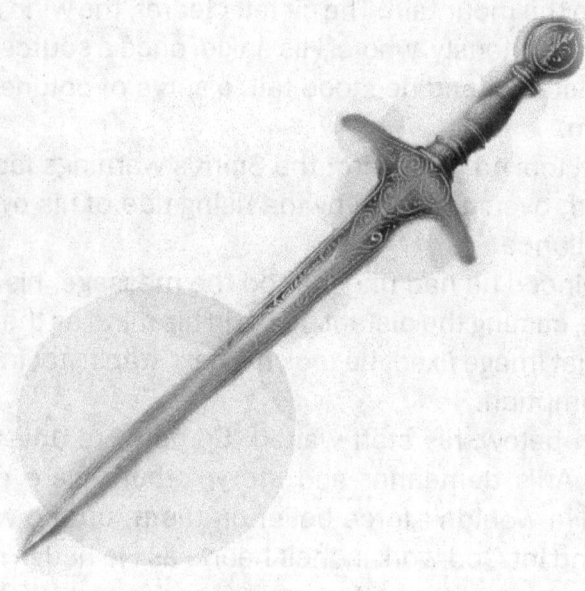

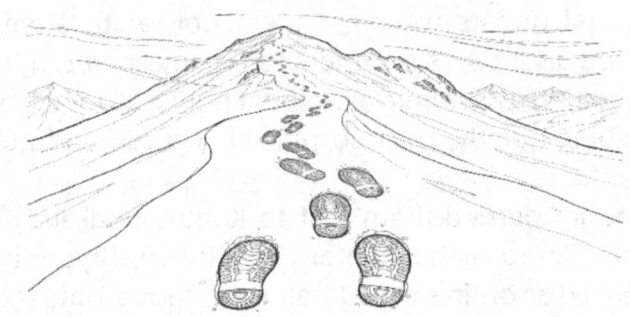

Chapter 18

Preparing to Search Everest

A week had passed since Ari had returned from Alaska. Memories of the battle with the giant and the miraculous healing of his ankle circled his mind. The halls of SummitTek's Denver headquarters whispered of his recent trials, though few knew the truth. Upon his return, Ari had only told Gottschall, Susan Richard, and Bryan Carter the specifics of his encounter on Denali.

Ari moved through his routine with renewed purpose, yet his heart was not fully at ease. The *Spirit of Power and Might* had shown that he must go to the mountains in the west. He began planning a trip to the Himalayas, and specifically Mount Everest, the highest peak on Earth. While the Spirit didn't specifically state the location of the *Spirit of Wisdom*, Ari had little doubt in his own mind.

He confided this plan to Moose and Bryan late one evening in his private office at SummitTek. They knew better than to question him outright. Ari's spiritual journey had already proven itself beyond ordinary logic. If Ari said he needed to go to Mount Everest, then they would follow.

The next morning, Ari arranged a secret trip with a small crew: Moose, Bryan, and a couple of trusted climbers.

Gottschall oversaw Susan handling logistics without comment, her piercing eyes aware that something was off with Ari, that his spiritual quests were not mere corporate stunts. She secretly worried about Ari's absence, too many secret trips could weaken his position at SummitTek. Yet her duty was to him, and Ari insisted on going quietly, with no official records and no grand announcements.

A private jet carried them first to Kathmandu and then to Everest's Base Camp by helicopter. Ari, Moose, Bryan, and the climbers, dressed as ordinary mountaineers, slipped into this high-altitude world without fanfare. The biting cold and thin air reminded Ari of Denali and the giant who had nearly claimed his life. But he walked now without pain, remembering Christ's healing power in his every step. If God had saved him then, what prevented him now from finding the *Spirit of Wisdom*?

Days passed in the shadow of Everest's towering summit. The crew established a modest camp and tested the Titan Tent and Rope System again, impressing even the grizzled Sherpas who guided them. But Ari had not come to impress anyone; he had come to find *Wisdom*. Each morning, he rose early, climbing higher, scanning the ice and rock for any sign of the Spirit. Stolz still lurked in his mind, whispering that he must claim Wisdom by force, by cleverness, by daring.

Bryan, ever practical, asked discreetly, "Ari, what exactly are we looking for?" Moose, leaning on his ice axe, nodded in agreement.

Ari gave a vague answer, avoiding Moose's skeptical gaze. "A sign, a presence... I'm not entirely sure." His cheeks flushed with embarrassment as the words left his mouth, sounding hollow even to himself.

He clung to the memory of the *Spirit of Power and Might's* command to go west to the mountains. Mount Everest was west of Alaska, and it seemed logical as the world's highest peak.

Yet, deep down, a nagging uncertainty gnawed at him... Logic. Once his trusted guide, he felt fragile now.

For a week, they climbed, navigating less-traveled paths that seemed to challenge them at every turn. Ari's anticipation turned to frustration as they pushed higher into the unforgiving landscape.

He had envisioned a divine encounter, a celestial figure waiting in radiant splendor, a whisper of guidance in the thin, icy air.

But there was nothing, just endless stretches of ice and rock, buffeted by relentless winds that seemed to mock his efforts.

When they descended to base camp, Ari's disappointment was palpable. The trip began with hope and determination and now felt like a wasted effort. He avoided the critical glances of his team, unsure of how to explain the absence of the "*spiritual revelation*" he had so confidently expected. Frustrated and humiliated, Ari was left questioning his assumptions and his readiness to truly seek the Wisdom he so desperately needed.

Meeting Mgon Po

On the eighth day, they stumbled upon a small clearing near a hidden valley. The crew had split to cover more ground, yet they kept connected through radio checks. As Ari and Moose circled back to camp, they spotted a little old man sitting on a rock beside the trail. He wore tattered, layered robes and carried a wooden cane. His face was lined with countless winters, his eyes bright and knowing. He seemed so out of place at this altitude and terrain.

Ari approached cautiously. "Hello? Are you well? Do you need help?"

The old man smiled, revealing surprisingly strong, beautiful teeth. "Mgon Po," he said, tapping his chest with the cane and then pointing to Ari. "You seek *Spirit of Wisdom* but find nothing, yes?" His English was heavily accented but clear.

Ari's heart leaped. "You... know why we're here?"

Moose watched silently, hand near his ice axe in case of trickery.

Mgon Po nodded. "You look for *Spirit of Wisdom*. But you cannot find her here. You have not the key."

Ari's throat tightened. "The key? What key? Nobody told me anything about a key?"

Mgon Po tilted his head. "You encounter *Fear of the Lord*, yes?" He spoke slowly. "It showed you *orb* but you not humble enough. Without *orb*, you cannot find *Wisdom*."

Ari remembered that the *Spirit of the Fear of the Lord* had once shown him a magenta *orb*, but he had failed to receive it. He shuddered at the memory.

Ari's stomach dropped. He had come all this way for nothing! "I thought I was supposed to come here," he muttered, anger and disappointment mingling in his chest.

Mgon Po shrugged. "You assume. You not ask." He tapped Ari's chest lightly with the cane. "Prideful hearts follow assumptions, not divine guidance."

Stolz's whisper rose in Ari's mind: "*He mocks you. Show him who you are!*" But Ari resisted.

Moose exhaled, "So we wasted our time?" His voice was gentle, and he empathized with Ari's disappointment.

Mgon Po smiled sympathetically. "No waste. Failure teaches humility. Failure best teacher. Now you know; to find *Wisdom*, you must first bear the *orb* from *Fear of the Lord*. Return home. Humble yourself; then you will find *Spirit of Fear of the Lord*. Remember, humble yourself."

With that, Mgon Po rose and walked away with surprising agility, disappearing among the rocks... as if he belonged more to the mountain than the human world.

Ari stared after him, fists clenched. He felt stupid and misled. He wanted to shout at the sky for the *Spirit of Power and Might* for being unclear. He thought he was following God's direction, but had not prayed, asked *Counsel*, or listened carefully to God's instructions. He had gone west on an assumption. Now, they will return empty-handed.

"Ya know what they say, "Moose chuckled, "When you 'assume,' you make an as..."

"I know, I know, "Ari interrupted. "Too soon?" Moose cringed.

The crew began their descent in heavy silence. Ari felt demoralized, yet Bryan held back the dreaded phrase, "I told you so," despite his disappointment being clear in every sidelong glance. The team moved with the efficiency of seasoned climbers, packing up their gear and signaling for the helicopter. The flight back to Kathmandu was subdued, the thrill of adventure replaced by the sting of unmet expectations.

By the time they returned to Denver, Ari hardly had a moment to process the trip's failures, trouble was already brewing at SummitTek's headquarters.

The Coup

Abner Keshet, worried about his son and the company's direction, was inflamed by Ari's absence and motivated by Diana's vengeful emotions, pushed the SummitTek board to declare Ari mentally unfit for the CEO role.

Rumors circulated of Ari's erratic trips, secret journeys, and talk of spirits and divine encounters. Things easily framed as delusions in a boardroom setting.

Diana played her part beautifully, whispering in certain board members' ears and offering hints of Ari's instability.

Gottschall fought fiercely against this coup, leveraging favors and presenting data that showed Ari's decisions remained profitable and his leadership was visionary. But Abner and Diana had something else, legal documents, even forged or twisted evidence, that would allow them to remove Ari at the next board meeting. They invoked old bylaws and mental fitness clauses. The more Gottschall fought, the more entrenched they became.

Iris watched from the sidelines, anxious and torn. She loved her son, but her husband's arguments were persuasive. She asked herself, "Ari had always been stable before; what were these secret trips? These talks of spirits and orbs? It all sounded unhinged."

Gottschall threatened to resign if Ari was removed without just cause. That rattled Iris. After all, Gottschall had served the Keshet family loyally for decades. If she was willing to leave over this, what did that say?

When Ari's jet touched down in Denver, he returned to SummitTek, expecting business as usual. Instead, he found his father, Abner, seated at the CEO's desk in Ari's own office, Diana standing behind him, arms crossed.

Ari froze in the doorway, Moose and Bryan Carter trailing him. "Dad?" he asked, his voice tight with confusion and anger.

Abner glanced up, appearing calm and self-satisfied. "Son... good... you're back. We need to talk."

Diana's eyes gleamed. "The board met this morning. Given your... recent behavior, they've decided a leadership change is necessary."

Ari's eyes widened. "You can't be serious. I'm the CEO. You can't just remove me."

Abner sighed as if disappointed. "We can, legally. You've been absent without proper notice and conducting secret ventures unaligned with the company's interests. Shareholders are concerned. We have documents proving questionable decisions and erratic behavior."

Gottschall stood nearby, arms folded, furious. "This is a travesty. Ari's leadership has always benefited SummitTek. I have records."

Abner raised his hand. "Maria, let's not make a scene. We appreciate your service, but this has been decided. Ari is out, effective immediately."

Diana smirked. "I'm sure you understand it's in the company's best interest. Remember, '*business waits for no one.*'"

Gottschall's voice trembled with controlled rage. "If Ari goes, I go. This is unacceptable." She turned to Iris, who hovered near the door.

Iris's face was strained. She'd never seen Maria so upset. This wasn't just corporate reshuffling... this was a personal betrayal. Iris found herself rethinking the entire scheme. Was pleasing Abner worth shattering Ari's future and losing Gottschall's loyalty?

Abner ignored Gottschall's threat, focusing on Ari. "Son, this is for your own good. You've become unstable. Chasing fantasies? Spirits? Jesus healing ankles? This is not rational. You sound insane!"

Ari clenched his jaw. Anger and betrayal flared inside him. He wanted to shout, to throw the accusations back at them, but the weight of his recent failures and Stolz's mocking voice made him feel hollow. He said nothing, glaring at his father and Diana before turning on his heel and leaving. Moose and Bryan followed him silently, fists clenched at their sides.

In the hallway, Gottschall stepped out, catching Ari's arm. "I threatened to resign, but they didn't care," she said, voice tight. "I'm sorry, Ari."

Ari shook his head. "It's not your fault, Maria," he managed. "I'll figure something out."

Gottschall's eyes softened as she saw Iris hesitating in her thoughts. Turning back to Ari, she encouraged him, "There can be a chance to stop this scheme if we can show you are mentally stable and still capable of running this company. But for now, Ari, go home. I'll keep you informed."

The Orb of Fear

That evening, back at his mansion, Ari paced the length of his study. He'd come home expecting comfort but found a knife in his back. His parents' betrayal stung deeper than any corporate maneuver. He remembered the Hanukkah evening months ago and how awkward it was... Now this.

He sank into his leather chair, head in hand. Stolz's whisper rose: *"Look at you now. Stripped of power, humiliated by your own family. You should have relied on no one but me."*

Ari closed his eyes, fighting the voice. He was tired of Stolz's poisonous counsel.

Where was Elinor? He wanted to call her, but shame and confusion held him back.

He tried to pray but felt too unworthy. He had failed to consult God about Mount Everest. He had followed his own assumptions and self-confidence. Now, he paid the price.

A soft presence filled the study, the *Spirit of Counsel*. A golden shimmer appeared. Ari was startled and sat up straight.

"YOU WENT WITHOUT CONSULTING GOD," the Spirit said gently. "YOU RELIED ON YOUR OWN UNDERSTANDING. THE RESULT? DISAPPOINTMENT AND LOSS."

Ari swallowed, "I know," he whispered. "I thought I knew what the *Spirit of Power and Might* was saying."

The *Spirit of Counsel* nodded, compassionate yet firm. "HUMILITY IS LEARNED THROUGH FAILURE, ARIEL. YOU MUST REMEMBER THAT TRUE DIRECTION AND INSIGHT COME FROM GOD, NOT YOUR GUESSES. PRAY AND ASK; DO NOT ASSUME."

Ari hung his head, a heavy sadness pressing on him. "I feel so low, so lost. My parents betrayed me, I failed to find *Wisdom*, and I can't even keep my company... I have nothing left."

A chilling presence drifted into the room. Ari's heart pounded as the *Spirit of the Fear of the Lord* materialized before him. This Spirit was towering and frightening, draped in a magenta-colored aura that radiated holiness and reverence.

Ari trembled, his soul remembering their last encounter. He had not been humbled enough then, but terror seized him now. He fell to his knees, then to his belly with his face pressed to the floor, not daring to look up.

The Spirit's voice resonated through his entire being: "ARIEL KESHET, NOW YOU FEAR GOD. NOW YOU UNDERSTAND YOUR SMALLNESS. GOOD."

Ari's body shook. He wanted to cry out for mercy, but his throat was tight.

The *Spirit of the Fear of the Lord* continued, his voice both terrible and merciful: "THE LAST TIME YOU SAW THE ORB, YOU WERE TOO PROUD. NOW, HUMILITY WEIGHS IN YOUR HEART. YOU HAVE LOST WORLDLY POWER BUT GAINED THE RIGHT POSTURE TO RECEIVE GOD'S GIFT."

The Spirit extended something into Ari's spirit, a magenta-colored *orb* of shimmering light with swirling currents resembling a fountain of water, contained in a perfect sphere. Liquid light flowed within it, surging as if seeking release.

Ari felt it merge with his soul, filling the void pride had left with warmth and holiness. He was unable to lift his head.

"BOW TO THE LORD GOD ALMIGHTY, GOD OF THE UNIVERSE," the Spirit commanded. "TO HIM ALONE BELONGS ALL WORSHIP AND GLORY!"

Ari nodded, his heart crying out in silent adoration. He finally understood that all his conquests, achievements, and wealth were meaningless without God's favor and guidance. At that moment, he surrendered, trusting in the One who held all truth.

The *orb* settled within Ari's spirit. A powerful, eternal flame of reverence and awe for God. A Fountain of Life and a Fountain of Living Waters surging inside of him. The *Spirit of the Fear of the Lord* nodded once, satisfied, and faded from view. Ari remained prostrate, breathing heavily.

Later, he gathered the strength to sit up. The *Spirit of Counsel* was still there, smiling.

"WITH THE ORB, YOU MAY NOW FIND WISDOM," *Counsel* said.

"BUT YOU WILL NEED REVELATION KNOWLEDGE TO GUIDE YOU."

As if summoned by name, the *Spirit of Revelation Knowledge* stepped forward, appearing as a seasoned college professor. Its form shimmered with a soft, crimson light, and its eyes were warm and bright. Ari inhaled sharply. This Spirit emanated insight like a thousand books had been read and understood in an instant.

Revelation Knowledge spoke calmly, measured, carrying both authority and grace: "THE FEAR OF THE LORD IS THE BEGINNING OF KNOWLEDGE AND WISDOM. YOUR JOURNEY TO MOUNT EVEREST WAS MADE IN ERROR, DRIVEN BY ASSUMPTIONS RATHER THAN SEEKING DIVINE DIRECTION. WISDOM DOES NOT DWELL WHERE YOU PRESUME. INSTEAD, FOLLOW THE EMERALD RAINBOW. SHE AWAITS YOU DEEP WITHIN THE EARTH, IN THE EMERALD MINES OF YUNNAN, CHINA."

The Spirit's glowing form pulsed with emphasis as it spoke: "NOW THAT YOU POSSESS THE ORB OF THE SPIRIT OF THE FEAR OF THE LORD, YOU ARE READY TO ENTER THE HIDDEN REALM WHERE WISDOM RESIDES. SHE AWAITS YOU IN THESE CONCEALED PLACES, AND REVERENCE FOR THE LORD SERVES AS THE KEY. WITHOUT THE ORB, YOU WOULD NOT HAVE BEEN ABLE TO APPROACH HER, FOR IT IS HUMILITY THAT UNLOCKS THE DOOR. WITHOUT IT,

YOU WOULD NOT HAVE ENDURED HER PRESENCE, FOR HER LIGHT REVEALS AND REFINES. YOU CAN STAND BEFORE HER ONLY THROUGH HUMILITY AND REVERENCE FOR THE LORD."

The words settled in Ari's heart like a steady flame, illuminating the path ahead while reminding him of the power of surrendering to the Lord, especially surrendering his own understanding and assumptions.

Counsel and Revelation Knowledge both smiled, fading gently. Ari was left alone in the study, kneeling in the lamp's soft glow. The weight of betrayal and humiliation still pressed on him, but something far greater had taken root: humility, reverence, and a guiding light from God Himself.

He rose slowly, wiping his cheeks. Outside, the world kept turning. His father might sit in his office, and Diana might plot destruction, but Ari had gained something eternal, a path forward illuminated not by pride but by the *Fear of the Lord* and the promise of *Wisdom*.

He took a deep, shaky breath, knowing he would find *Wisdom*, not by scaling the tallest peaks on a hunch, but guided now by divine direction. But would he reclaim SummitTek?

Ari desired to reclaim it, but right now, finding the *Spirit of Wisdom* was his top priority.

Chapter 19

Emerald Paths and Hidden Treasures

Ari Keshet stood in the Denver mansion's study, the *orb* of the *Spirit of the Fear of the Lord's* gift glowing faintly inside his spirit. He could sense its warmth deep in his chest, a quiet reminder of the humility and awe he had finally embraced. The instructions from the *Spirit of Counsel* and of *Revelation Knowledge* echoed in his mind: "FOLLOW THE EMERALD RAINBOW. YOU WILL FIND HER DEEP WITHIN THE EARTH, IN THE EMERALD MINES OF YUNNAN, CHINA. NOW THAT YOU BEAR THE ORB, YOU MAY ENTER THE HIDDEN PLACE WHERE THE SPIRIT OF WISDOM AWAITS."

He sighed, pulling an old leather satchel from a closet. He had traveled so far and returned empty handed, humbled. Now, he would go westward, not to climb skyward but to dig downward into the earth. The *Spirit of Revelation Knowledge* had told him to seek the mines in Yunnan, China, a place he had never considered. He needed no heavy climbing gear this time, no expensive expedition. He needed only the little *Red Book* and the *Golden Compass* he had received from the Spirits. He tucked them safely in his vest pockets. His faith was still fragile but growing stronger every day.

Days earlier, Ari would have summoned the SummitTek jet and crew by phone. But since Abner's and Diana's coup at SummitTek, Ari had been stripped of corporate privileges. Standing in his lavish study, he shook his head at its absurdity. He was the visionary who had built SummitTek into a global power, yet now he couldn't sign out a company plane without approval. Abner had blocked all his credit cards, cutting off corporate accounts with ruthless efficiency.

Ari suspected Diana's hand in these petty humiliations.

He approached the wall safe, hidden behind a painting on the wall. With a code entered and a twist of the hidden knob, the safe door swung open. Inside lay some emergency cash, crisp bills he had stashed for unforeseen crises. He never thought he'd need it for something as simple as traveling. He scooped up a thick bundle of bills and tucked them into his satchel.

Moose would accompany him. Of all his associates, Moose had proven loyal and unflinching. Though Moose lacked the corporate finesse of Bryan Carter or the cool scrutiny of Gottschall, he had a heart of gold and was unshaken by Ari's spiritual quests. He'd come to trust Ari beyond reason.

The next morning, Ari called Moose and asked him to come to his residence. Upon his arrival, Ari met him in the foyer.

"Moose," Ari said, "We're going to China." Moose blinked. "China? We climbin' over there?"

Ari managed a thin smile. "No, not climbing, but mining. We will be searching underground for *Wisdom*... It's complicated." He didn't elaborate, but Moose had stopped questioning Ari's strange missions. If Ari said they were going, Moose would follow.

Ari quickly discovered that booking a last-minute commercial flight to China was a trial. Without SummitTek's private jet and VIP handling, he was required to navigate endless phone calls and websites while sitting through interminable hold music.

He grumbled quietly, "This is insane. I once had a fleet at my disposal." Yet he stopped himself, recalling the orb's presence, realizing that Pride was a trap. He had to embrace this new humility.

Ultimately, he purchased two economy tickets on a major airline, paying cash at the airport because his credit cards were blocked. The young ticket agent looked baffled at the wad of bills he offered, but eventually processed the purchase. So now, Ari and Moose would fly with everyone else, no lounge, no special treatment. As they boarded the plane for the long flight across the Pacific, Moose smiled and asked, "You okay, boss?"

Ari shrugged. "Sure, just... not used to this."

Moose chuckled. "C'mon, it'll be fun. Maybe we'll make new friends." He winked, sitting beside a middle-aged Chinese man who smiled politely and offered them candy from his pocket. Ari smiled back stiffly, trying to appear at ease.

The flight was long and cramped, and Ari's knees pressed uncomfortably against the seat in front. He felt each hour passing, far different from the spacious comfort of a private jet.

Moose dozed off, and Ari prayed silently as he held the Golden Compass in his hand. He wanted to ensure he was truly following God's direction this time, not just assuming. The compass remained pointed ahead, indicating he was at least heading in the right direction.

Journey to Yunnan, China

They first landed in Beijing, then took a domestic flight to Kunming in Yunnan province. From there, after a tangle of language barriers and hurried translations on Ari's phone, they hired a local driver to take them toward the Dayakou emerald mine. The region was lush with greenery and mountains cloaked in mist, a far cry from Everest's starkness.

Could the "emerald rainbow" mentioned by *Revelation Knowledge* be a poetic reference to the emerald stones themselves?

As the car wound through narrow roads, Ari cradled the *compass* in his hand, periodically checking its bearing. It seemed to respond subtly. When he turned it one way, the needle swiveled gently, guiding him toward the mines. He prayed softly and consistently, "Lord, guide me. I'm listening this time."

Moose watched him. "Feels like we're on a treasure hunt."

Ari nodded. "We are. Buried treasure that's not gold or jewels, but something greater."

Moose grinned. "Well, I won't say 'no' to a few emeralds if we find them."

Ari chuckled. "Let's focus on *Wisdom* first."

They arrived near a mining settlement: a cluster of tin roofed huts, rusted machinery, and a guarded entrance to a tunnel slanting into the earth. Chinese workers moved about with practiced efficiency, carrying tools, chatting, and laughing. Armed guards lingered near the entrance, eyeing Ari and Moose suspiciously.

The driver spoke a few words to the guards, who nodded. Ari tried to present himself as a curious geologist (not entirely untrue), hoping to gain brief access. But the guards were not easily swayed. They demanded permits Ari didn't have and official documents he couldn't produce. Abner's coup stripped him of not just a jet but also corporate credentials and letters of introduction that might have eased this entry.

Ari sighed in frustration. He was so close yet barred by bureaucracy. He closed his eyes briefly, praying silently, "God, help me. *Spirits of Counsel and Revelation Knowledge*, help me."

Counsel Advises

As Moose attempted to distract the guards by asking questions, Ari slipped behind some rusted mining equipment. Suddenly, the *Spirit of Counsel* manifested quietly beside him, a luminous gold figure only Ari could see. Ari suppressed a gasp.

"Your approach is too direct," said *Counsel*. "You must be subtle. Your friend Moose can help distract the workers and guards. You must enter the cave quietly and follow the compass deep inside. *Wisdom* awaits in a hidden chamber."

Ari nodded. "I have no permits. No corporate clout. How?"

Counsel smiled gently. "Use what you have: friends, humility, resourcefulness. The *Golden Compass* will guide you through the labyrinth of tunnels. The *Orb of the Fear of the Lord* within you grants you the right to approach *Wisdom.*"

Ari understood.

The Spirit faded, leaving Ari alone. He emerged from behind the equipment and tapped Moose's shoulder. Whispering, Ari said, "Moose, I need you to keep them busy for a while. I have to get inside that mine."

Moose blinked, understanding instantly. "Distraction, got it. I'm the master of distractions!" Without further questions, Moose engaged the guards in broken Chinese and wild hand gestures, asking if they'd seen rare minerals or talking about a supposed film crew arriving.

While Moose distracted them, Ari slipped around the camp, ducking behind stacked ore crates and approaching a side entrance he'd spotted earlier, an old maintenance shaft. The *compass* glowed faintly in his hand, the needle urging him forward.

Inside, the air was damp and earthy, the space lit by sparse electric bulbs hanging from wires. The hum of distant machinery echoed softly. Ari followed the compass deeper, past junctions and side tunnels, stepping carefully over puddles and uneven ground. He heard distant voices but turned away each time, guided by the *compass's* silent directive.

Eventually, the tunnels grew quieter, older, and less maintained. Dusty beams and old tracks hinted at ancient excavations. The needle pointed steadily to a narrower passage, forcing Ari to duck and squeeze through. He prayed softly, thanking God for guidance and asking for courage.

He finally entered a small cavern lit by a phosphorescent glow. It wasn't electric light; some mineral in the walls glowed faintly green, painting the chamber in gentle emerald hues.

Ari gasped, "Emerald rainbows indeed."

Meeting the Spirit of Wisdom

In the center of the hidden chamber stood the *Spirit of Wisdom*. She appeared like a woman, but it was immediately clear she was not human. Her beauty defied age and time. Silvery-white hair flowed over her shoulders like liquid starlight, and her face, radiant and ancient, glowed with a grace that could only come from beyond the veil of mortality.

She wore a robe of light, softly pulsing with an emerald green glow. Embedded in its folds were symbols, ancient, celestial, shifting like living scripture. The writing wasn't merely decorative; it pulsed with meaning, like puzzle pieces finally locking into place.

Her eyes, a striking blue, held Ari in their gaze, not with judgment, but with knowing. Deep knowing. She carried within her the kind of wisdom that didn't come from learning, but from God Himself. She didn't just know things, she knew what to do with them. Every truth she possessed aimed at a single purpose: to glorify The Great God Almighty who sent her.

She seemed both impossibly youthful and beautifully aged, timeless, like a soul who had walked beside every generation. As Ari watched her, something stirred deep in his memory.

It was in the gentle tilt of her head, the knowing stillness in her eyes, the way her presence wrapped the room in quiet reverence.

She reminded him of his grandmother. Not in appearance, but in the gentle core of who she was.

His grandmother had been the kind of woman who could mend a torn sleeve while reciting a Psalm, who offered life lessons with a plate of warm cookies, and whose counsel always seemed to come at the exact moment when he needed it. She'd taught him how to tie a knot, how to speak the truth, and how to listen, not just with ears, but with the heart.

This Spirit carried that same essence, only deeper and eternal. Her presence didn't just command respect. It made Ari feel safe and known, as if God had taken the warmest parts of memory and woven them into something eternal to remind him: You have always been seen, and you have always been guided.

Around her swirled a quiet dance of light, spirals of galaxies, strands of DNA, and floating letters in languages older than time, all of it converged in her presence, as if the secrets of creation leaned close to listen when she spoke.

Ari fell to his knees, not out of terror but out of reverence. He felt a calm hush. In her presence, a sense that every question he'd ever asked could be answered here.

"ARIEL, YOU HAVE COME AT LAST!" Wisdom said with great joy and excitement. Her voice was like a chorus of gentle waterfalls. "BUT NOT BY YOUR OWN CLEVERNESS. YOU CARRY THE ORB OF THE FEAR OF THE LORD WITHIN YOU, THE GOLDEN COMPASS OF COUNSEL.

YOU HAVE HEEDED REVELATION KNOWLEDGE'S INFORMATION IN THE LITTLE RED BOOK, AND IN YOUR BEING, YOU BEAR THE SWORD OF THE SPIRIT OF POWER AND MIGHT. THIS SHOWS HUMILITY, OBEDIENCE, A HUNGER AND THIRST FOR TRUTH, AND THE COURAGE TO PURSUE IT."

Ari's voice trembled, "I...I tried Mount Everest... I failed. I...I failed to ask God first. I assumed...I've lost so much."

Wisdom's smile was comforting. "FAILURE IS A GREAT TEACHER. YOU HAVE LEARNED HUMILITY. YOU COULD NOT APPROACH ME WITHOUT THE ORB OF THE FEAR OF THE LORD. WITHOUT COUNSEL, YOU WOULD BE LOST IN THESE TUNNELS. WITHOUT REVELATION KNOWLEDGE, YOU WOULD NOT KNOW WHERE TO BEGIN SEARCHING. AND WITHOUT POWER AND MIGHT, YOU WOULD NOT HAVE THE COURAGE TO BOLDLY TRAVEL AND SEEK."

Ari nodded. "I want God's wisdom. I know I cannot rely on pride or logic... not anymore. Please, show me how to use the gifts and knowledge given to me."

Wisdom stepped closer, radiating a gentle emerald glow. "I WAS WITH GOD WHEN HE CREATED THE UNIVERSE AND THE EARTH," SHE SAID SOFTLY. "I CLAPPED WITH JOY AS HE SHAPED MOUNTAINS AND OCEANS, DELIGHTED IN EVERY CREATURE HE FASHIONED. HUMANS ARE HIS GREATEST CREATION, FORMING THEM INTO HIS IMAGE, CALLING THEM HIS SONS AND DAUGHTERS. HE BREATHED HIS LIFE INTO THEM, GAVE THEM HEARTS TO LOVE, MINDS TO THINK, SPIRITS TO COMMUNE WITH HIM."

Ari listened, his heart swelling with wonder. This was truth beyond any doctrine he had known. The Figure before him had witnessed creation's dawn and had known joy at the birth of existence.

Wisdom lightly touched Ari's chest. "I SEE THE ORB INSIDE YOU, THE MARK OF HUMILITY AND REVERENCE FOR GOD AND ALL THE TOOLS GIVEN SO YOU CAN WALK IN TRUTH."

Ari felt power and a calling stirring inside him. He understood now that the journey was not just physical. It was about aligning with God's ways, *Fear of the Lord, Knowledge, Counsel, Power and Might,* now *Wisdom,* Spirits he must embrace.

His newfound instinct helped him realize he must seek the *Spirit of Understanding* next.

Wisdom smiled as if reading his thoughts. "I WILL IMPART TO YOU GOD'S WISDOM, WHICH IS PURE, OPEN TO REASON, AND FULL OF TRUTH AND MERCY. THIS WISDOM IS NOT FOR YOUR EGO OR YOUR WORLDLY EMPIRE. IT IS TO LEAD JUSTLY, LOVE MERCY, AND WALK HUMBLY WITH GOD.

I WILL SHOW YOU HOW TO PROPERLY USE COUNSEL AND REVELATION KNOWLEDGE, NOT TWISTING THEM TO SERVE PRIDE, BUT LETTING THEM GUIDE YOU INTO RIGHTEOUSNESS."

Ari bowed his head. "I accept... Show me how."

Wisdom raised her hand, and a soft cascade of radiant light flowed into Ari's mind. The sensation was both soothing and invigorating, filling him with a sense of peace and clarity, unlike anything he had ever known.

Patterns and solutions unfolded before his inner vision, principles of leadership that honored God and served others with respect. He understood how to balance innovation with stewardship and wield power in service rather than dominance.

As the light bathed him, he felt a surprising sensation of tasting honey on his tongue.

"I taste honey?" Ari smacked his lips.

"IT IS A PLEASANT REMINDER OF THE GOODNESS OF GOD. WISDOM IS AS HONEY FOR YOU." Her voice softened, yet her words carried a profound weight.

"YOUR NEXT STEP AWAITS. SEEK THE SPIRIT OF UNDERSTANDING, WHO WILL GRANT YOU DEEPER CLARITY AND DISCERNMENT. TRAVEL TO MOUNT KILIMANJARO IN AFRICA, WHERE YOU WILL FIND UNDERSTANDING. BUT REMEMBER, ARIEL KESHET, THIS JOURNEY IS NOT ABOUT THE MOUNTAIN BUT ABOUT THE HOLY ONE WHO LEADS YOU TO IT.

PRAY FIRST. SEEK THE LORD'S GUIDANCE, FOR IT IS ONLY BY ACKNOWLEDGING THE LORD IN ALL YOUR WAYS THAT YOU WILL FIND THE TRUE PATH OF LIFE."

Ari's heart stirred with anticipation and reverence. Another journey, another mountain lay before him. But this time, things would be different. He would not rely on assumptions or self-direction. He would pray, listen, and prepare with humility. This was no longer about conquering peaks; it was about aligning himself with the will of the Creator who had called him to this extraordinary path.

Ari gratefully thanked *Wisdom* as she smiled warmly at him. Just before she vanished into an enchanting emerald glow, she gifted him a lovely *emerald stone*, about the size of a half-dollar. Ari accepted it with reverence, took a moment to admire its beauty, and then gently placed it into his pocket.

He retraced his steps, guided by the compass. At the main tunnel, he heard shouting. Moose distracted workers by claiming he had found something unusual, like a rare stone. Ari slipped behind the guards, who had rushed off to see the commotion.

In minutes, he was reunited with Moose outside.

He laughed. "You look like you saw a ghost."

Ari shook his head. "Not a ghost, something far better... *Wisdom*." He smiled broadly. "Mission accomplished!"

They hurried to the car, paid the driver, and then returned to Kunming before heading to Beijing. After what he'd gained, Ari didn't mind flying economy again. Every discomfort reminded him to stay humble. He prayed quietly, thanking God for guiding him step by step.

Chinese Christians

On the plane, Ari noticed something special about some of the passengers traveling. At first, he couldn't pinpoint it, but there was a subtle glow about them, nothing supernatural like he'd seen with the Spirits, yet undeniably special. They reminded him of Elinor's faith, her love, and peacefulness.

They wore simple clothing, nothing fancy. A few carried well-worn backpacks. They spoke softly among themselves in whispers, occasionally passing notes instead of speaking out loud. Their behavior was curious. They seemed both joyful and guarded, as if holding onto a precious secret in a place where secrets could be dangerous.

When the flight attendants were busy elsewhere, Ari leaned toward one of them, a middle-aged woman with kind eyes and streaks of gray in her dark hair. He kept his voice low.

"Excuse me, I don't mean to intrude, but I can't help noticing... You and your friends seem connected. Are you traveling together?"

The woman's eyes widened just a bit. She scanned her surroundings before responding in a hushed tone. "Yes, we are... friends. You could say, we are on a journey, *Back to Jerusalem*."

Ari smiled softly. "I've seen that glow before, in people who understand the love of God." He took a chance, gently testing the waters.

"You remind me of some close friends who believe in Jesus."

She tensed, and then her features softened into a cautious smile. "You must be careful what you say here, sir. That Name is precious, but not all can speak it freely in these lands. We are Christians, yes, followers of Jesus Christ. But we must be discreet. The authorities... they do not permit open worship. If discovered, we could face prison."

Ari's heart squeezed. He knew intellectually that oppression existed, but seeing these gentle souls forced into secrecy struck him deeply. "I'm so sorry," he whispered. "I never realized it was this harsh. You're so peaceful, so loving, why would any government fear you?"

She shrugged sadly. "Those obsessed with power fear what they cannot control, especially love and truth. We harm no one. We only want to worship the Lord. But to them, it is a threat to their world and their culture. So, we remain silent, secretly meeting, praying in whispers."

Another group member, a younger man, leaned over and quietly added, "We have learned to hide our Bibles. We memorize Scripture, so if our books are taken, we still have God's words in our hearts."

Ari felt emotions welling up. He had seen miracles and fought spiritual battles, but here was a different kind of courage: faithful souls facing daily worldly oppression. He realized their glow, that subtle radiance of the same Spirit guiding him on his journey, now shone in these believers who risked everything for their faith in Jesus Christ.

A pang of conviction struck Ari as he thought of his own family. His newfound faith placed him at odds with generations of tradition and expectation. He could almost hear his father's stern voice and see his mother's disappointed eyes, filled with the weight of heritage and obligation. To them, his faith might seem like a betrayal, an abandonment of his identity.

The cultural weight pressed heavily on his shoulders, yet at this moment, he drew strength from the example of these persecuted believers. Their quiet resilience reminded him that true faith often requires sacrifice, a willingness to stand firm even when the world pushes back.

Curious about the hush around them, Moose leaned into Ari's seat, "What's up, boss?" he whispered.

Ari explained in a few whispers that these people were Christians who couldn't freely speak of Jesus under the present Communist Chinese regime.

Moose's brows shot up. "You mean they get locked up for lovin' and talkin' about Jesus? Now that's messed up." He shook his head. "Never thought I'd say it, but man, that makes my run-ins with giant monsters sound simple. At least a giant is a direct threat. These good folks just want to serve their God in peace."

The older Christian woman nodded, grateful for their understanding. "We pray daily that China's leaders find mercy and wisdom, that they see we mean no harm. But until then, we must be cautious."

Ari whispered, "I have only recently come to know Jesus as the Messiah. The miracles I witnessed convinced me. And now I see you, faithful in secret. It humbles me. My struggles feel minor compared to yours."

The younger man smiled, eyes shining. "We each have our path, brother. God knows our hearts. We pray for you, too, that your journey is guided by His hand." Ari smiled. "Thank you. Your faith strengthens me."

A hint of tears shone in a few of their eyes. Although they couldn't speak openly, they were comforted that other Christians would remember them.

The plane droned onward through quiet skies. Ari and Moose talked in low voices with these Christians for as long as good judgment allowed, exchanging no last names and no details that could endanger them.

Before landing, they bowed their heads discreetly, praying silently for each other. Ari felt a weight in his chest, empathy and a deep respect for these believers who lived under oppression. Their love and courage shining in secret.

When the plane touched down, they parted ways with subtle nods and gentle smiles, careful not to draw attention. The secret believers melted into the crowd, anonymous travelers in a controlled society, yet carriers of heavenly light.

Cautious Conversation

Back in Denver, SummitTek was no longer Ari's. Thus, he wasn't shocked when his keycard failed at the entrance or when the security guards blocked his path with blank stares and professional indifference. Abner, with Diana's assistance, had obviously solidified their coup.

Still, Ari remained calm. The *Wisdom* he carried now was not his own. Fear and rage had lost their grip on him. Instead of fighting his way in, he took a detour, arranging a quiet meeting with Gottschall at a nearby café.

When she arrived, she looked relieved, but concern shadowed her sharp gaze. "I've tried everything," Gottschall said, sliding into the seat across from him. "Your father and Diana maneuvered brilliantly. But I haven't resigned yet. I was waiting to see if you had a plan."

Ari sipped his coffee, choosing his words carefully. He needed to explain his journey, the truth, but how much could he reveal without sounding... unhinged? Gottschall was a practical woman, grounded in logic and reality. Sharing his experiences about Spirits, visions, and supernatural encounters might stretch even her legendary patience.

"Maria, I left to find answers," he said finally. "To figure out who I am without all this... material fluff-n-stuff." He gestured vaguely, "Encompassing the world of SummitTek, wealth, and corporate wars. and I found something real. Something... bigger than me. I found God."

Gottschall observed him, an unreadable look on her face. "Go on."

"I feel different. I have peace now. I feel like I have true direction

in my life, like I've never felt before. So, with all this conflict with my Dad involving SummitTek, I need to trust God's plan, not mine. If the Lord wants to restore what's been taken, He will. If not, then He will lead me down another path."

"You've changed," Gottschall continued to observe him like a case file she wasn't quite ready to close. "I saw it happen. It's unnerving. You used to treat people like chess pieces. Now you," she waved a hand vaguely, "... smile at them. It's unsettling."

Ari chuckled. "Maybe I care about people now."

"Exactly. Highly suspicious behavior." She sipped her coffee and leveled him with a look. "What happened out there, Ari? And don't give me some vague spiritual speech. I want details."

Ari exhaled, stirring his coffee. "I had... encounters. Spiritual ones. I mean actual, undeniable experiences, not just abstract feelings or revelations."

Gottschall raised a brow. "You saw something, didn't you?"

Ari hesitated before nodding. "God's Spirits and a giant, to be precise." He carefully recounted some of his encounters with the Spirits. He added, "They've been guiding me, showing me where my pride has led me astray, how I need to change, how I need to..."

"Let me guess," Gottschall interrupted. "Be humble, be kind, and... stop terrifying the interns."

Ari laughed. "Something like that."

She shook her head, leaning back in her chair. "You're seriously telling me that ancient Spirits are mentoring you?"

Ari took a slow sip of his coffee, "Um...Yes."

Gottschall tapped a finger against her mug. "Well, that's just great... but did they mention how to get your company back? Or am I supposed to consult the *Ghost of Wall Street* for that?"

Ari grinned. "They told me to trust God's plan."

Gottschall sighed. "Fantastic... so now we're in a corporate takeover... with spiritual-based strategies."

Ari smirked. "Welcome to my new life."

He paused, then added, "I'm also being led to Tanzania... going to Kilimanjaro. The Spirit of Wisdom told me I need to seek the Spirit of Understanding there."

Gottschall's fingers tightened around her coffee cup. "Kilimanjaro?" A silence stretched between them. Her stare was sharp, evaluating. "And this... Wisdom told you this?"

Ari nodded. Sincerity in his eyes.

She stared at him for a long moment... then let out a dry chuckle. "Well, this ought to be interesting."

A Mother's Regret

Later that evening, as Ari approached his mansion, he expected emptiness. Instead, he saw his mother. Iris stood waiting for Ari at the edge of the driveway, wringing her hands, her face pale with worry.

When she looked up at him, her eyes filled with tears. "I never wanted this," she started dramatically, blubbering.

Ari's chest tightened. "Mom...? What are you talking about?"

She swallowed hard, her voice shaking. "Your father... he worries about you. Diana has gotten into his ear and twisted things. And I... I let it happen." Iris continued weeping.

Ari frowned. "What do you mean... you let it happen?"

Iris exhaled shakily as if forcing out years of regret. "I brought Diana into this family, Ari. I convinced your father to trust her. I thought she would be good for you, for the company." She hesitated before admitting, "I even hoped you would marry her!" Ari's jaw tightened, but he stayed silent, letting her continue.

"I was wrong," his mother admitted, her voice thick with remorse. "She's ambitious, but I see it now, she never truly cared for you. She only cared about power. And I handed her the keys to this family's empire." She shook her head, grief and frustration mingling. "I should have listened to my instincts, but I let family pride and tradition cloud my judgment."

Ari didn't hesitate. He stepped forward and wrapped his arms around her. Not in anger. Not in accusation. But in forgiveness. "I forgive you, Mom." His voice remained steady. "I'm trusting God's plan... even now."

Iris clung to him for a moment before pulling away, wiping her tears, and blowing her nose. She searched his face, recognizing something different in him... Peace. And she longed to experience it, too.

Finally, she whispered, "I'll try to reason with your father. Don't lose hope." Then she turned and walked away, shoulders slumped.

Ari watched her leave. Strangely, his heart felt both heavy and light all at the same time.

The struggle for SummitTek wasn't finished. However, he recognized that he wasn't facing it alone.

Directions In the Study

Once again alone in his study, Ari prayed, expressing gratitude to God for the lessons learned. Pride had cost him dearly, but humility had opened doors to true power, God's power. He pondered how he would travel to Africa without SummitTek's resources and with his accounts frozen, yet he would trust God regardless. Besides, flying economy class wouldn't kill him.

The *Spirit of Counsel* appeared, nodding in approval. "You seek God's guidance before deciding to go, and He supports your journey. Get ready for Kilimanjaro. The *Spirit of Understanding* awaits there."

Ari felt relief wash over him. He would not move without confirmation. "Lord," he whispered aloud, "I trust You. Show me, and I will go."

A soft red glow signaled *Revelation Knowledge's* arrival. "Your finances are blocked, but remember, you have friends outside SummitTek: Bryan, Marcus, Elinor, and even Maria. The path will open. Understanding does not require luxury, only obedience."

The Spirits faded, leaving Ari gazing out the window at Denver's city lights. He closed his eyes, imagining Kilimanjaro's flat, snowy crown as the *Spirit of Understanding* waited there for him.

Chapter 20

The Path to Understanding

Ari Keshet stood at the large window of his Denver mansion's study, gazing out at a dusky sky that offered no comfort. His accounts were completely frozen. His father had set up a legal and financial blockade so tight that Ari couldn't buy a coffee without rummaging for spare change in the couch cushions.

SummitTek's board had replaced him as CEO, and the media had had a field day. He could almost hear the chatter: "Ari Keshet dethroned! The visionary turned erratic mystic!"

Ari stared at his phone like it was a venomous snake. He hadn't spoken to Elinor since his humiliating Everest retreat, and avoiding her calls had become his new full-time job. But the weight of his silence pressed down on him, shame, regret, and an uncomfortable dose of Stolz whispering in the back of his mind, reminding him that calling her now would make him look weak.

Still, he was out of excuses. Taking a deep breath, he pressed the call button before he could change his mind. The phone rang. Panic washed over him. What if she didn't answer?

What if she did? What if...,

"Ari?" Her voice was warm, familiar. No accusation. No irritation. Just... Elinor.

Ari exhaled, rubbing his forehead. "Hey." He hesitated, then blurted out, "I lost everything."

There was a pause. Then, calmly, "Yes, Ari. I know." Ari blinked. "Wait... what?"

"Gottschall told me."

"Of course she did," he said half-jokingly. "Did she also mention that since my father has put my staff on temporary leave here at the mansion, I'm surviving on tap water, canned tuna, and deep reflections?"

"She might have," Elinor said dryly. "She also mentioned you're too stubborn to accept help. How's that working out for you?"

Ari sighed, slumping against the window. "Not great." He swallowed. Admitting weakness wasn't his strong suit. "I need to go to Tanzania. The Spirit of Understanding is waiting on Mount Kilimanjaro. I just don't know how I'm going to get there."

Elinor was silent for a moment. Then, instead of the judgment he expected, she chuckled. "You do realize most people take a quiet retreat or read a self-help book when they hit rock bottom. But you decide to climb another mountain."

Ari smirked despite himself. "At least I'm consistent."

She sighed, her amusement softening into something more serious. "Ari, you don't have to do this alone. You have people who care about you, who want to help. Including me."

Ari grimaced. "Gottschall already shoved her credit card at me. Moose and Bryan pooled their money. Do you know how humiliating that is?"

"Oh yes," Elinor said, mocking deep sympathy. "It must be awful, having friends who love you. How do you bear it?"

"Elinor...,"

"And let me guess," she continued, ignoring his protest.

"Your Pride is telling you that taking money from your friends makes you a charity case?"

Ari gritted his teeth. "Something like that."

"Well, tell Pride to sit down and shut up. This isn't charity, Ari. It's teamwork. Remember? The thing you preached at SummitTek?"

Ari groaned. "I really should be more careful with my motivational speeches. I never know when they will be used against me."

"Oh, definitely," Elinor teased. "But since you weren't careful, 'We the Team' are booking your flight. No private jet, just you in a middle seat, hopefully next to a snoring seatmate who drools on your shoulder."

Despite everything, Ari laughed. "This is revenge, isn't it?"

"Absolutely!" she said sweetly.

His smile lingered as he ran a hand through his hair, feeling lighter than he had in weeks. "Elinor..., thank you for everything."

"You're welcome," she said, her voice gentle. "Ari, God's grace isn't about what you deserve. You don't have to earn it. God gives it freely."

A lump formed in his throat. He wasn't used to receiving grace, but maybe... just maybe it was time he learned.

"Alright," he sighed. "Book me the worst seat on the plane. Let's get this over with."

Elinor chuckled. "That's the humility we've been waiting for."

Booking Flights to Tanzania

Ari planned to follow the Spirits' leading, whether that meant climbing a mountain or setting up permanent residence among the Tanzanian wildlife. Elinor and Gottschall orchestrated logistics like a tactical operations unit, booking Ari and Moose two round-trip economy tickets to Kilimanjaro International Airport.

"Pooling funds was a humble effort, and Moose made some sacrifices," Elinor noted.

"I was saving for a hot tub," Moose sighed, tossing bills onto the table. "But who needs relaxation when there's a constant threat of mortal danger?"

Ari looked at him. "That's not the mindset I wanted." Moose shrugged. "Minor details."

With Elinor's savings, Moose's hot tub-turned-adventure fund, and Gottschall's credit card, which she gave with a stern warning about "absolutely NO impulse purchases", they secured their travel, lodging, and local transportation.

Ari tried to focus on the spiritual significance of it all. But with every agonizing click of the "purchase" button, he felt another piece of his billionaire ego wither and die.

There was no private jet, no first-class gourmet meals, no personal attendant refilling his espresso, just economy coach seating next to Moose, who was already plotting his in-flight snack strategy like a high-stakes expedition.

"You know, this kind of reminds me of that old song," Moose mused as he scrolled the airline's menu.

Ari arched a brow. "What song?"

Moose grinned. "Two Tickets to Paradise, except instead of paradise, we're headed for altitude sickness and questionable airplane peanuts."

Ari joked. "What have I gotten myself into?"

As reality sank in, Ari exhaled. This was it... another adventure with Moose by his side. No titles. No corporate power. Just Ari on a mission from God... and stuck in economy with Moose.

Departing Denver

They left Denver on a sunny morning. Ari carried a modest backpack with essentials: the compass, the little Red Book, and a change of clothes. This time, there was no climbing gear; the Spirit of Understanding's meeting wouldn't require a technical summit attempt, just a guided tour.

In the airport, Ari recognized a few SummitTek employees, who gawked at him in line at the baggage drop. One whispered to another, "Isn't that Ari Keshet? The ex-CEO of SummitTek?"

Ari forced a smile, feeling Moose's reassuring presence beside him. The agent eyed Moose's battered duffel while going through security and checking their luggage. "Any lithium batteries?" she asked.

Moose grinned. "Only the battery of hope charging our spirits."

The agent blinked, confused. Ari patted Moose's shoulder, whispering, "Let's not confuse airport security."

Later on as they boarded the plane, Ari tried to keep a "good attitude" as he forced himself to sit in the middle seat on their long flight to Amsterdam. Ari felt like a packed sardine as he wedged himself in between Moose's large frame and a petite Chinese lady.

Sensing Ari's discomfort, she offered him ginger candies, speaking little English but consistently smiling. After trying a piece,

Ari coughed; the ginger was extremely spicy. Moose tried the candy. He chewed and nodded politely while his eyes watered profusely.

Halfway through the flight, Ari tried to read his little *Red Book*. The lady gently poked at him, pointing at the book. She nodded with approval and said something in Mandarin. Ari recognized the words, "Shèngjīng?" (Bible) and "Yēsū" (Jesus) in her sentence and smiled, giving her a thumbs up. She smiled widely, patting his hand.

Moose raised his eyebrows. "Making friends?"

Ari whispered, "I guess Christians are everywhere."

Joy in Tanzania

After a long layover and a lengthy flight, they finally touched down at Kilimanjaro International Airport. The warm African air greeted them as they stepped outside, the scent of distant forests and earth washing over their senses. Ari felt lighter somehow. This was new territory, but the *Compass* and the *orb* in his spirit steadied him.

He prayed quietly, "Lord, guide me again. I'm listening."

The *Spirit of Counsel* had advised him to book a hiking tour with a family-owned business. Ari had done just that via email from Amsterdam: a local Tanzanian family, the Juma family, offered personalized trekking tours. Their email replies were cheerful and in broken English, promising a warm welcome.

Ari and Moose took a taxi through lush green landscapes, children playing by the roadside, and bicycles rattling along dusty paths. At last, they reached the Juma family homestead, a small cluster of modest huts, a larger communal area, and a yard where chickens pecked and a lonely goat eyed them suspiciously.

Mrs. Juma, a short, round-faced black woman in a bright, patterned dress, greeted them with open arms. She hugged Moose, who stumbled back laughing. Her husband, Mr. Juma, taller and leaner, shook Ari's hand vigorously.

"Karibu! Welcome!" he said, grinning broadly. His English was clear enough, and what he lacked in vocabulary, he made up for in warmth.

Seven children ranged around them, peeking from behind doorways, giggling. The oldest, a boy of about twelve, stepped forward shyly. "Hello," he managed, offering his hand.

Ari glanced at Moose. "They seem so... happy?"

Moose nodded. "They have so little in material things, yet so much joy."

They were shown to a small guest room, featuring simple mats on the floor, mosquito nets, and a wooden table. Ari thought of his mansion and swallowed a lump in his throat. These people didn't have wealth, yet their smiles outshone any luxury he'd owned.

That evening, they gathered around a worn wooden table and shared a humble supper of rice, beans, and a green leafy stew fragrant with ginger and spice. The meal was simple and nourishing but not extravagant.

Ari ate slowly, savoring the flavors with genuine appreciation. The food was good, comforting, and honest. Yet, he felt a tug in his gut even as he tasted it.

A hunger gnawing inside him began to shift, not for fancy gourmet flavors, but for something deeper, something real.

"This might be it?" Ari searched his thoughts. "Could this possibly have the taste I'm searching for? Something eternal."

"What do you mean, boss?" Moose inquired.

They exchanged an uncomfortable silence before Ari dismissed it with a shake of his head.

"Oh, it's nothing..." Ari said, wiping his mouth.

Moose, still puzzled, concluded the odd moment with, "Alrighty, then..."

As the meal ended, the Juma family lifted their voices in song, a joyful hymn of praise to the Lord Jesus, sung in flowing Swahili. Though Ari didn't understand the words, the spirit behind them resonated in his bones, and faith poured out like pure living water. He closed his eyes, letting the melody wash over him. His heart swelled with something he hadn't felt in a long, long time... a belonging.

No pretense. Pure faith. Pure love.

Moose, usually full of jokes, sat quietly, absorbing the peace.

Later, they played soccer in the yard. Ari tripped over a root and landed face-first in the dirt. The kids burst into laughter. Despite being covered in dust, Ari couldn't help but laugh as well, a once arrogant CEO now enjoying barefoot soccer with children beneath the warm African skies.

He recognized their lack of material wealth, but they remained content and joyful. They had found a deeper joy than he had ever experienced. And he sensed that true understanding was close at hand.

Mount Kilimanjaro

At dawn, Mr. Juma and two of his older children got ready to take Ari to the starting point of the arranged Kilimanjaro hiking tour. The *Spirit of Counsel* had directed Ari to go alone this time. So, Moose stayed back with the Juma family.

As they were leaving, Moose shrugged with a grin that stretched from ear to ear. "Guess I'll stay back and take one for the team. I'm gonna show these kids how a real soccer pro does it," he said, winking dramatically. "Pray for my knees, my back, and my dignity, and God have mercy on me if they've improved their game!"

Ari chuckled, giving him a hearty pat on the back. "You're going to need divine intervention, Moose. These kids play like they've got rocket fuel in their veins."

The Juma kids burst into laughter, already buzzing with excitement. "You're going down, big man!" one of them teased, while another started mock dribbling an invisible soccer ball.

Moose clapped his hands together and declared, "Oh, it's on now!" He jogged onto the makeshift field. "Let's see if you can handle Moose Mania!"

The children erupted into giggles, chanting and cheering as they surrounded him, tugging at his arms and daring him to take the first kick.

Ari shook his head, grinning as Moose stumbled theatrically, faking defeat when the kids swarmed him like a pack of determined lions. Moose's exaggerated groans and dramatic dives had the kids roaring with laughter; their strategy was now more about outsmarting his antics than scoring goals.

It wasn't long before Moose, panting but clearly enjoying himself, called out, "Time out! You guys are relentless! Did someone sneak energy drinks into your water bottles?"

The kids just laughed harder, one of them holding up a banana as if it were the secret weapon. "This is our fuel!"

As the van pulled away, Ari glanced in the rear-view mirror, catching sight of Moose in full comedic glory. Moose struck a dramatic pose, pretending to be a soccer superstar, only to clutch his back in mock agony. The Juma kids doubled over with laughter, already plotting their next move on the field.

Mr. Juma chuckled. "Your friend knows how to entertain my children."

Ari smirked, leaning back in his seat. "That's Moose! He's always willing to embarrass himself just to bring a smile, whether it's for kids or adults.

The scene faded behind them, but Ari couldn't help smiling. Even in the midst of a weighty journey, Moose always found a way to bring lightness to the moment.

The Trek Begins

With minimal supplies in his backpack, trekking poles, and the compass tucked safely in his pocket, Ari followed the Jumas' directions to the trailhead. There, he was greeted by a small group of local guides and fellow hikers, a lively mix of accents, backgrounds, and energy levels that made the group feel like a mini–United Nations summit convened on Kilimanjaro.

Steady trekking awaited the small group, and, apparently, some cultural diplomacy along the way. The guides were seasoned, while the hikers ranged from a cheerful American couple in matching safari outfits to a tech executive from Tokyo armed with gadgets for every possible situation. An overly enthusiastic Australian aimed to capture every moment with his selfie stick, hoping his podcast vlog would go viral.

The air was crisp, the trail surrounded by lush greenery that whispered promises of higher, more sacred grounds. Ari adjusted the *compass* in his hand, its faint glow a reminder of the divine direction guiding him onward.

Over the next few days, as they hiked and camped, ascending through lush rain forest and then moorland, Ari marveled at the diversity of life. He prayed quietly with each step, feeling the *orb*'s gentle glow. At higher elevations, the air thinned, but not as severely as on Everest. He wasn't here to test his products but to seek *Understanding*.

As the sun set below the horizon, painting the sky in hues of gold and lavender, Ari felt the *Golden Compass* pulling at him once more. Its glow intensified, guiding him away from the group. The guides exchanged uneasy glances and observed in silent curiosity. Their voices lowered to hushed tones as they watched him walk away from the camp. Concern flickered in their eyes as Ari ventured farther away, attracted to something only he could sense, the distance between him and the group widening with every step.

Ari moved forward, the crunch of gravel beneath his boots the only sound in the oppressive silence. Once a constant companion, the wind had fallen unnaturally still, leaving the air heavy as though the mountain was holding its breath. His ears strained, catching faint whispers that might have been the rustle of leaves, or something else entirely.

Shadows stretched and twisted across the rocky terrain, their shifting forms playing tricks on his eyes. The compass in his pocket radiated warmth, its pulse syncing with his pounding heartbeat. Each step forward felt like a plunge into the unknown, and every instinct screamed for him to turn back. Yet, something unseen and unrelenting drove him onward.

Then, after a long silence, Stolz's voice slithered back into his mind, smooth yet edged with scorn.

"Ah, yes, brilliant strategy, charging into the middle of nowhere like some lost kitten. Very grand. Very noble. Tell me, why are you not listening to me? I have your plan for greatness. Listen to me."

Ari's jaw tightened as he pressed on, refusing to engage. But Stolz wasn't finished. His tone sharpened, laced with mock amusement.

"This is almost painful to watch. The great Ari Keshet, master of mountains, ruler of boardrooms, reduced to some wandering mystic, chasing ghosts and fairy tales. Tell me, what's the endgame here? Enlightenment? Or just one more attempt to prove you're better than the rest?"

The air pulsed with an unexplainable energy, a presence that felt alive and was watching. Stolz's voice faltered, momentarily muted, as if its arrogance couldn't withstand the weight of what lingered just beyond the veil. Ari gripped the *compass* tightly, and the *sword of the Spirit* in his spine steadied him, grounding him against the chaos within.

Stolz finally went silent. There wasn't even a faint hiss in the background of his mind.

"Idiot or not," Ari muttered under his breath, "I'll see this through."

As Ari rounded a jagged outcrop, he stopped short. The landscape beyond stretched vast and was shrouded in twilight hues, its contours unfamiliar and surreal as if they belonged to another realm.

His breath hitched, the eerie quiet now deafening as if the mountain awaited something monumental. The air seemed alive, charged with an unexplainable energy, wrapping him in awe and unease.

Ari paused, his heart pounding so loudly it nearly drowned out the sound of his own breathing. He scanned the area, his eyes flicking over jagged rocks and sparse grass, but nothing moved. And yet, he felt that something was here, just out of sight.

The *compass* in his pocket felt hot, and he sensed the *sword* from the *Spirit of Power and Might* bolstering his courage. An insistent pull was drawing him onward. He took another cautious step, then another.

And then, without warning, the mountain atmosphere erupted!

Encounter with the Spirit of Understanding

Light exploded around him, vivid and electric, cascading in every spectrum color and yet somehow blending into a radiant cyan glow. It wasn't just brightness; it was life, pulsating, crackling, filling the air with an energy that sent every hair on his body standing on end. It was as if a thousand firecrackers had burst in unison, illuminating every shadow, every crevice, every secret hidden in the mountain.

Ari instinctively shielded his eyes, his breath stolen by the sudden brilliance. The light didn't just illuminate the area..., it seemed to penetrate him, reaching into his very being, warming his soul, and filling his mind with a clarity he had never known.

And then, as his vision adjusted, he saw a figure.

The Spirit of Understanding stood before him, radiant and full of joy. She was luminous, her cyan aura shimmering like sunlight on water, her presence both startling and inviting. She clapped her hands together, her laughter ringing out like a playful melody that filled the air with joy.

"SURPRISE!" she exclaimed, her voice musical and full of delight. "YOU FOUND ME, ARIEL KESHET! I'VE BEEN WAITING FOR YOU."

Ari could only stare, caught between awe and disbelief. His heart raced.

The Spirit's playful exuberance was a stark contrast to the solemn grandeur of the other Spirits he had encountered. Here was someone who seemed to light up the world with her presence, a Being who turned even the most daunting revelation into a moment of joy.

"Did you think I wouldn't make an entrance?" she teased, her laughter filling the space like sunlight breaking through clouds. "I am Understanding, after all. And what is Understanding without a little surprise, a little light to illuminate the mind?"

Ari found himself laughing softly despite his shock, the tension in his chest easing as her radiance wrapped around him like a comforting embrace. But even as the joy of her presence settled over him, a new anticipation stirred in his heart.

Ari staggered back, shielding his eyes. When the glow softened, there she stood, the *Spirit of Understanding*.

Her laughter bubbled like a lullaby, giggling into the wind, melodic and contagious. Every word she spoke seemed to dance with a sing-song rhythm, as if her words were skipping rope. Her smile could have brightened the darkest cavern, and her very presence pulsed with playful wonder, like a child humming secrets only heaven understood.

"WELL, IT'S ABOUT TIME!" she exclaimed, continuing to clap her hands in a rhythmic beat. "I KNEW YOU WOULD MAKE IT. WELCOME TO YOUR 'AHA' MOMENT!"

Ari blinked, momentarily stunned. "I..., uh,"

"OH, YOU DON'T HAVE TO EXPLAIN," she interrupted, her voice a delightful mix of mischief and warmth. "I ALREADY KNOW. YOU'RE HERE, AND THAT'S WHAT MATTERS. NOW, LET'S GET THAT LIGHT BULB IN YOUR BRAIN TURNED ON, SHALL WE?" She twirled in place, her cyan aura dancing with her movements. The rocky ledge around them seemed to glow with her energy.

Ari felt an irresistible pull toward her, like a sailor drawn to a lighthouse, not one warning of danger, but one guiding him to safe harbor.

"YOU'VE BEEN COLLECTING PIECES TO GOD'S PUZZLE, HAVEN'T YOU?" she said, her eyes twinkling. "FEAR, KNOWLEDGE, COUNSEL, POWER, WISDOM. WONDERFUL, DIVINE COMPANIONS, BUT LET'S FACE IT, YOU ARE LACKING SOMETHING. YOU DON'T UNDERSTAND THE "WHY." YOU CAN'T SEE THE REASONING BEHIND WHY THE PIECES WORK TOGETHER. THAT'S WHERE I COME IN!"

Ari knelt, overwhelmed by the sheer joy radiating from her. "I'm honored to be here," he said, his voice thick with emotion.

Understanding crouched down to his level, her grin widening. "OH, ARIEL, IT'S NOT ABOUT BEING HONORED. IT'S ABOUT KNOWING THE LORD GOD ALMIGHTY AND WHY YOU HAVE BEEN CALLED TO WALK WITH HIM. AND YOU'RE READY NOW! LET ME LIGHT UP THAT MIND OF YOURS." She tapped his forehead lightly, and a cyan light surged into him.

Ari gasped as his thoughts shifted and aligned. It felt like puzzle pieces he hadn't even realized were scattered had now clicked perfectly into place. Questions about God, creation, and who Jesus really is, which had plagued him for years, were suddenly clear. He understood how to balance reverence with joy, approach challenges with faith and reason, and lead with *Wisdom* that served others instead of himself. It was exhilarating, like standing under a waterfall of pure clarity.

"OH, THERE IT IS!" she said, beaming. "THAT SPARKLE IN YOUR EYE. THAT'S THE LIGHT BULB TURNING ON! FEELS GOOD, DOESN'T IT?"

Ari nodded, his heart pounding. "It's... incredible."

"OF COURSE!" she replied, her hands on her hips. "BUT THIS ISN'T JUST FOR YOU TO HOARD AWAY IN YOUR SHINY LITTLE EMPIRE. THIS IS UNDERSTANDING FOR SHARING, LEADING, AND DOING IT WITH HUMILITY. GOT IT?"

"Got it," Ari said, feeling a weight lift from his shoulders.

With a snap of her fingers, a small, light *blue key* appeared, dangling from a silver chain. She handed it to him, her expression serious, though her eyes still danced with joy. "THIS IS YOUR NEXT STEP. CAPERNAUM, ISRAEL. YOU'LL FINALLY RECEIVE THE MOST IMPORTANT PART OF YOUR JOURNEY THERE."

Ari took the key reverently. "Capernaum?"

"YES, CAPERNAUM," she said, leaning in conspiratorially. "IT'S GOING TO BE FUN! JUST DON'T FORGET TO PRAY, SEEK GOD, AND KEEP THAT LIGHT BULB SHINING. OH, AND REMEMBER: REVERENCE TO GOD. IT'S STILL THE FOUNDATION. DON'T GET SO CAUGHT UP IN YOUR 'AHA MOMENTS' THAT YOU FORGET WHO'S GUIDING YOU."

Ari smiled, feeling a deep peace settle over him. "I won't forget."

She stepped back, her aura growing brighter. "Good. Now, go light up the world, Ariel Keshet. And remember, the best leaders are the ones who understand how to follow."

With a final burst of joyous laughter, *the Spirit of Understanding* vanished, leaving Ari standing on the ledge. The

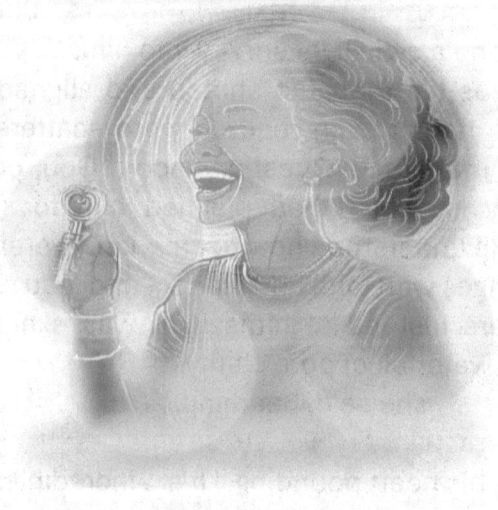

cyan glow faded into the deepening twilight, and the *key* felt warm in his hand, a tangible reminder of the revelation he had just received.

As he turned to walk back toward the group, Ari felt a new energy coursing through him. This journey was far from over, but its uncertainties no longer overwhelmed him. He was ready to move forward, his mind illuminated, his heart light, and his trust in God stronger than ever.

The Hikers Get Nervous

After the *Spirit of Understanding* had vanished, Ari stood momentarily in awe, the warm key still clutched in his hand. The cyan glow lingered on his skin, and he realized he felt different. His mind was clearer and sharper, but it wasn't just internal. His body seemed to radiate a faint, ethereal light.

He looked at his hands, turning them over in wonder. "Okay," he murmured to himself, "this is new."

The wind whispered around him as he tucked the *key* into his pocket and began the short trek back to the hiking group. They hadn't seen the radiant figure or heard her playful yet profound words. They only knew that Ari had wandered off alone and now returned... glowing.

As he rounded the rocky outcrop, their eyes widened in unison, their expressions frozen somewhere between amazement and terror.

"Monsieur Ari... you are glowing!" Mathieu, the very superstitious Frenchman, stepped back, crossing himself and kissing his crucifix necklace.

Ari stopped, realizing the cyan light was still faintly visible. He raised his hands, palms out, trying to appear non-threatening. "It's not what you think! I'm fine, really."

The group didn't seem convinced.

Remo, the Spaniard, muttered in panic, "Radioactive... él es radioactivo..."

Another hiker nervously edged toward the back of the group as if ready to make a swift getaway. One of the hikers whispered loudly to another, "Do you think it's, like, fallout or something? Maybe he rolled in some radium."

Ari sighed, rubbing the back of his neck. "It's not radiation, I promise. It's... uh... spiritual. Long story."

Mathieu blinked, his jaw slack. "Spiritual or not, Monsieur, you are glowing like a Christmas tree."

Ari tried to keep his composure, but their nervous glances and whispered conversations made the rest of the trip awkward at best. Around the campfire that night, no one sat next to him. When he reached for the coffee pot, someone quickly passed it down the line with trembling hands rather than letting him touch it directly.

Mathieu pulled Remo aside and whispered, "Maybe he is not a man at all. What if he is an angel... or worse?"

"Worse than an angel?" Remo retorted. "Diablo?" "I do not know," Mathieu hissed. "A glowy... thing!"

The group maintained a comically cautious distance as they set up their tents, their movements quick and deliberate, like they were racing against some invisible, glowing clock.

Whenever Ari tried to explain, someone interrupted with a muttered prayer, a hurried gesture of protection, or a sidelong glance at his faintly shimmering skin. It was as though they believed his glow could leap across the camp like static electricity.

The tension was thick enough to cut with a knife, causing nearly everyone to "turn in early." But it wasn't sleep they sought, it was a refuge. The hikers ducked into their tents with an urgency that suggested they thought the thin fabric was woven from "radiation-blocking threads."

Mathieu zipped up his tent flap, peeking out just long enough to hiss at Ari. One of the more superstitious hikers quietly taped a small crucifix to the inside of their tent wall, while another piled their belongings near the entrance as a makeshift barrier.

Meanwhile, Stefan, the Australian and ever the opportunist, adjusted his selfie stick inside his tent, whispering dramatically into the camera. "Live from Kilimanjaro: The glowing man phenomenon. Don't worry, folks, I'm documenting this for the sake of humanity! If anything happens to me... #GlowingMan." He glanced nervously at Ari by the campfire and said, "Perhaps we should use #PrayForStefan, just to be safe."

Ari sat by the fire, shaking his head in amused disbelief as he sipped his campfire coffee. Every time he shifted, heads poked out of tent flaps, only to disappear again with gasps and hurried zipping noises.

By the time the glow faded completely, the camp was eerily quiet except for the occasional muffled whisper inside the tents. The hikers clung to their makeshift bunkers as if protecting themselves from an alien invader.

Ari leaned back, staring at the stars overhead, a grin tugging at his lips. "Radioactive? The shunning continues," he muttered to himself. "Well, that's one way to make an impression," shaking his head. "At least I'm keeping things interesting."

They descended the mountain swiftly over the next few days, Ari's heart lighter than air. The hiking group kept their distance from Ari in case he was hazardous to their health. He didn't mind. He understood where they were coming from. He figured he probably would have kept his distance if the tables had been turned.

Mathieu gave him a cautious wave as he crossed himself. "Uh... safe travels, Monsieur Ari. And maybe... see a doctor?"

Ari chuckled, shaking his head. "Don't worry. I'm fine."

As the group disappeared into the distance, Ari couldn't help but laugh softly to himself. The Spirit of Understanding had certainly lit him up, both inside and out.

He glanced at the *key* in his pocket and the distant horizon beyond. Despite the bizarre reactions, his heart was happy. The journey continued, and he was ready, glow and all.

Returning to the Juma Family

Back at the Juma family home, Moose was in the yard, children hanging off his arms and shoulders as he pretended to be a "mountain giant" they must conquer. Mrs. Juma laughed from the doorway; Mr. Juma invited Ari in and offered him a cup of spiced tea.

Ari took the tea, smiling. "Your family is so joyful, so content. You have shown me what true wealth looks like."

Mr. Juma nodded. "We have the Lord Jesus and each other. That is enough."

They sat on a rustic bench, watching the sunset glow pink and orange over distant fields. Ari said he must leave for Israel to follow a calling.

Mr. Juma said, "We will pray for you. Wherever God leads, He provides."

Moose joined them, panting lightly from the children's games. "Leaving so soon, boss?"

Ari nodded. "Yes, I must. I'm going to Israel now."

Moose shrugged. "I guess I'll head back to Denver and keep an eye on things. Maybe I can help Gottschall and Bryan figure out how to restore your position."

Ari smiled softly. "Please do. And thank you for everything. I would've been lost without your help."

They embraced like brothers. Moose sniffed dramatically, wiping an imaginary tear. "You'd better find what you're looking for, or I'll start charging interest on that borrowed money."

Ari laughed. "Deal."

From Tanzania to Israel

The next day, Ari warmly bid farewell to the Jumas, expressing his heartfelt gratitude for their excellent hospitality, joyful singing, and laughter. He offered them a small sum of money, what was left of the borrowed funds, and they sweetly protested, saying it was just too generous. But Ari, with a smile, insisted on sharing it with them.

"Call it an investment in your family," he said. "Your witness of joy has inspired me."

Before parting ways, they shared a prayer, and Ari hailed a taxi to the airport, concentrating on the road ahead. He booked his flight to Israel with Gottschall's credit card, a humbling challenge for him as he was not used to depending on other people's money.

Stolz's voice slithered into his thoughts, dripping with mockery. *"Reduced to borrowing from your COO? Truly the pinnacle of success. Abner was right, you've lost it."*

Ari gritted his teeth, refusing to let Stolz's taunts take root. He knew the truth. His father had frozen all his accounts, claiming Ari was mentally unstable, but Ari wouldn't let Pride or humiliation derail his mission.

As the transaction went through, he pocketed the card with quiet determination. God provides, he reminded himself, tuning out Stolz's venomous whisper.

The flight was crowded. A crying baby screamed behind him, and a chatty student in front of him tried to guess his nationality. Ari handled it with grace. After facing giants, losing fortunes, meeting Spirits, and borrowing money from friends, what was a little discomfort?

Ari was seated next to a burly Russian tourist who snored loudly throughout the flight, his head rolling onto Ari's shoulder. Ari surrendered a smile and allowed the man to sleep, believing this was also part of his humility training. The flight attendant apologized and offered Ari extra peanuts.

He chuckled, "Peanut compensation for a stranger's drool on his jacket." Accepting the gift, he recalled God's words: Be thankful in all things.

He glanced down at the *key* he was holding and traced the address on the key chain. The address felt strangely familiar. "Capernaum?" He remembered family vacations from his childhood. That ancient town by the Sea of Galilee brought back good memories of a simpler time with his parents. "What will I find there?" Questions swirled in his mind. He knew better than to make assumptions, but he would pray and trust each step of the journey.

While in flight, Ari prayed, thanking God for *Understanding*'s gift, the Juma family's example of joy, and his friends' financial support. He also prayed for his parents, despite their betrayal, and asked God to soften their hearts and restore his relationship with them at the right time.

Journey to Capernaum

Arriving at Tel Aviv's Ben Gurion Airport, Ari felt a sense of warm familiarity. He had visited Israel numerous times, including several family vacations and work projects. It was also where he first met Elinor. Here, he sensed God's presence strongly. He passed customs without issue; after all, he was just a weary traveler with a backpack and a curious *key*.

The shared taxi to Capernaum meandered through the fertile hills of northern Israel. American pilgrims filled the van, animatedly discussing their plans to visit the Mount of Beatitudes and other holy sites. Ari listened quietly, the flutter of expectation in his chest growing stronger with every mile. The *Compass* in his pocket gave the faintest hum, like a pulse syncing with his own.

Arriving at a modest guesthouse near the Sea of Galilee, Ari was greeted by a kind Christian family. They offered him tea and a warm smile, sensing perhaps that he was a man on a special journey.

Ari walked toward the shoreline as the sun dipped lower, where the Sea of Galilee shimmered like molten gold under the evening sky.

He paused by the water, the sound of gentle waves brushing against ancient stones. The air was warm, carrying the scent of eucalyptus and jasmine. Childhood memories surfaced, his younger self swimming in the sea, taking boat rides with his cousins, and skipping stones across the water with his father. It had been so long since he'd let himself remember the simple joys of those days.

Ari clutched the small key bearing the Capernaum address, turning it over in his hands. The smooth metal was cool against his skin, yet it felt purposefully charged. The anticipation was electric. His losses, his corporate throne, wealth, and reputation seemed insignificant now compared to what lay ahead. He had traveled humbly, flying economy, borrowing money from friends, and enduring his father's scorn. Every step had been a stripping away, yet he felt unusually stronger for it.

As dusk painted the horizon with vibrant shades of orange and gold, Ari sat on the seashore, enjoying a rare moment of calm. He had removed his shoes, feeling the warm sand flow between his toes, an unusual sensation for someone accustomed to boardrooms and mountaintops. He rested his face in the soft warmth of the sun.

As he leaned back, exhaling, something small slipped from his pocket and tumbled into the sand. He turned. *"The emerald?"*

It glinted as it rolled, catching the dying light like it was a living thing. Ari scooped it up, brushing off the grains of sand, and turning it slowly between his fingers. Holding it toward the horizon, the last rays of sunlight pierced through the gem.

That's when he saw it... tiny inscriptions, delicate and ancient, etched within the *emerald*'s depths as if the stone had been waiting for the right light... or the right eyes.

Faint symbols shimmered like secrets whispered across centuries. Ari thought to himself, "Had they always been there? Or had I finally become still enough to notice?"

Ari drew in a breath, the weight of the moment pressing gently on his chest. Then, he whispered, "Lord, I'm here. You've given me the gifts, the tools, the calling. Now what? Show me the next step."

A breeze stirred, cool and sudden, carrying with it a faint melody, gentle and unplaceable, like a song half-remembered from a dream. He sat still, letting it wrap around him like a soft blanket.

"I'm listening, Lord."

The sky darkened, creating a quiet, intimate atmosphere. There was no booming voice, no glowing sign in the sand... just him, the gentle surf, and the old stones. It was a moment of holy silence, filled with peaceful stillness.

Behind him, the lights of the guesthouse flickered on. Ari glanced toward them, then back at the sky.

"So... that's it. No burning bush?" he laughed. He tucked the *emerald* in his pocket and headed toward the guesthouse.

As he walked towards the house, he could smell something cooking... or rather, *burning*.

"Oooh, they better not be ruining my supper!"

Chapter 21

House of Encounters

The next day, Ari Keshet took a taxi around the streets of Capernaum, Israel. The midday sun warmed the ancient cobblestones, and a mild breeze carried the scent of the nearby Sea of Galilee. His heart thumped faster as he clutched the light-blue *key* in his hand, its tiny inscription etched with an address he realized he knew well. He hadn't recognized it immediately, but as he followed the streets, memory stirred like distant laughter echoing through time.

When he rounded the corner, he saw a modest white house with blue shutters framed by olive trees and a low stone wall. He inhaled sharply. This was his childhood vacation home. He remembered coming here with his parents, grandparents, and a few cousins during summer breaks. Back then, he had lived simpler moments: no corporate empires, no shadowy spiritual battles, no Stolz whispering in his ear.

As a boy, Ari ran barefoot through this courtyard, the warm stone heating his feet while soccer balls flew between cousins, and laughter echoed off the walls. He had begged his father to stay "just one more day" before the corporate world beckoned him back to New York. And here, in this sun-soaked corner of his childhood, his father had been different, less executive, more dad. He would crack jokes. Chased the ball once or twice. Smiled more.

His mother, Iris, thrived here too, especially in the kitchen, though she was still learning. The real culinary magic had come from her mother, Sophia, a woman whose cooking felt like scriptures written in spice and olive oil. She moved through recipes like a rabbi through Torah scrolls, every dish infused with tradition and intention. And now, Ari understood, this was where it had all begun.

His lifelong pursuit of fine food had never truly been about wealth, status, or impressing clients. It was a private pilgrimage, a secret hunger that no Michelin star or truffle-infused dish could ever fully satisfy.

Below the refined dishes and lavish menus he demanded at SummitTek, he was seeking something much more profound... the recollection of his grandmother's kitchen, where affection was gauged in olive oil and joy bubbled in each pot.

He wasn't just chasing flavors. He was *chasing home*.

Now, he stood before that same house, *key* in hand, sent here by the *Spirit of Understanding*. He was sure it had been sold long ago. The paint was more faded, the roof edges softened by time, but the bones were unchanged. Slowly, he slid the key into the lock, half expecting resistance. Instead, it clicked easily.

The door creaked open, and the past rushed in like an old friend. The same tile floor, the same furniture arrangement, sunlight filtered through familiar curtains, and dust drifted lazily in the quiet air, a smell, an aroma. He paused.

Someone was cooking, but not just cooking... *creating*.

From the kitchen came the soft clinking of dishes. Drawn by curiosity and something deeper he couldn't name. Ari approached quietly, peering around the door frame. What he saw made his breath hitch and his knees weaken.

Standing at the stove in khaki pants and a plain white shirt, there was a figure wearing a cheerful apron that read *"Kiss the Cook."* At first glance, he looked like any ordinary Israeli man, olive-toned skin, shoulder-length brown hair that curled slightly at the ends, warm brown eyes, and a sturdy, average build. Someone you might pass on the streets of Capernaum without a second glance.

But it was the light that gave him away.

A halo of white light enveloped him, a soft flame, beneath his skin, and a shimmer danced. His tone was easygoing, and his movements were calm.

This was Him... It was Jesus!

The same Jesus who had appeared in his dream like the *King in Glory*, now stood here in this kitchen, quietly rinsing dishes, sleeves rolled up, as if He had... all the time in the world.

Ari staggered back a step, then slid down the door frame, unable to hold himself up. He sat on the floor, leaning against the frame as if it were the only thing keeping him upright. His chest heaved, but he couldn't look away. Reverence arrested him. The King of Glory hadn't come with thunder... but with a dish towel.

The weight of majesty hidden in such a humble form was overwhelming yet approachable.

"HELLO, ARIEL," the Figure said, turning from the counter where He was slicing fresh bread. His voice was gentle, calm, carrying a warmth that somehow felt eternal. "I'VE BEEN EXPECTING YOU."

Ari's breath caught mid-throat. His brain tried to form a sentence, but all dignity exited stage left. He stood there gaping, stammering like a malfunctioning GPS.

"L-Lord... I, I'm s-sorry, I didn't mean to, I wasn't trying to.., this is, uh, was..., I mean, it used to be, my family's house, the vacation one, I didn't..., uh," He pointed vaguely toward the doorway like it was going to help explain anything. "I didn't know... You'd be... making toast."

The Jesus Figure smiled warmly, setting the bread knife down with a gentle grace. "ARIEL, YOU HAVE COME TO WHERE YOU WERE GUIDED. NO APOLOGY NEEDED."

He gestured to the small, familiar dining table, a simple spread of soup, salad, fish, pomegranates, a small pot of honey, and a loaf of freshly sliced bread beside a single glass of wine. Then, with a nod and a wipe of His hands on the apron, He added, "COME. SIT. LET'S SHARE A MEAL."

Ari's legs trembled as he rose and approached the table. He glanced at the same worn wooden chairs from childhood, each sparking memories of family meals and laughter. He finally sank into a chair, heart pounding. "Lord," he managed, "This... is overwhelming."

The Spirit set the plate before him with quiet reverence, as if laying down something sacred rather than food. "NOW, LET'S EAT!" The Spirit of the Lord urged, serving Ari a piece of fish. "WE HAVE MUCH TO DISCUSS."

There were no gourmet flourishes, no gold leaf, no truffle oils or imported wines, only simple, humble fare, steaming gently in the air.

Yet the moment Ari leaned in, the aroma wrapped around him like an embrace he hadn't felt since childhood, warm, rich, achingly familiar.

His chest tightened before he even lifted the fork.

Somehow, he already knew.

Ari whispered, "This is it." He then sat up straighter and declared, "This is it... at last! This is it!"

He lifted the fork to his mouth, the scent pulling at something deep inside him. Ari took a bite, astonished at the flavor, like nothing he'd tasted since his grandmother's homemade cooking back in childhood. The fish was fresh, the pomegranate seeds bursting with sweetness, and honey drizzled golden threads on the plate. It was truly soul food. Every morsel carried nourishment beyond the physical, filling cracks in Ari's soul.

One bite, and the years peeled away. He was no longer a CEO or a conqueror of mountains and markets. He was a boy again, barefoot in his grandmother's kitchen, the smell of roasted herbs and warm bread filling the tiny, sunlit room.

A single thought rose in Ari's heart, as the truth finally broke through: I've been starving my whole life, and I never even knew it.

The ache in his chest gave way to something deeper: not hunger, but *home*.

Ari sat frozen, the fork still in his hand, as wave after wave of memory and longing crashed over him. Across the table, the *Spirit of the Lord* watched without a word, a tender smile playing at the corners of His mouth. Not the smile of a chef proud of his meal. But the smile of a Father welcoming a lost son home.

The Spirit's eyes shone with compassion, waiting patiently as the moment soaked into Ari's soul. Then the Spirit explained: "I AM THE SPIRIT OF THE LORD. YOU SEE ME AS JESUS OF NAZARETH BECAUSE I HAVE REVEALED MYSELF TO YOU IN A WAY YOU CAN UNDERSTAND.

JESUS CHRIST WAS CRUCIFIED, DIED, RESURRECTED FROM THE DEAD, AND THEN HE ASCENDED TO HEAVEN. HE IS NOW IN HEAVEN, SITTING WITH THE FATHER ON HIS THRONE. I WAS SENT TO DWELL WITHIN CHRIST'S BODY OF

BELIEVERS HERE ON EARTH TO HELP COMMUNICATE THE FATHER'S WILL AND PURPOSE FOR HIS PEOPLE."

He continued, "MY PRESENCE IS WITHIN GOD'S PEOPLE. I DWELL WITHIN THOSE WHO LOVE AND TRUST THE LORD, LEADING THEM INTO TRUTH, EMPOWERING THEM, AND BRINGING THEM COMFORT IN DIFFICULT SITUATIONS. I REMIND THEM OF THE WORDS THAT GOD HAS SPOKEN THROUGH THE AGES. WHEN YOU SEEK GUIDANCE AND LONG TO UNDERSTAND, SPEAK TO ME, FOR I AM NEAR TO THOSE WHO CALL UPON THE NAME OF THE LORD JESUS."

Ari swallowed, nodding. He recalled Elinor telling him that God was omnipresent through His Holy Spirit and could appear and guide as He willed.

At that moment, vibrant swirls of color shimmered into existence, weaving gracefully through the air like living ribbons of light.

The hues pulsed with a rhythm that Ari could feel, all merging and separating in a breathtaking display of movement and harmony. The air felt charged with life, as if creation had paused to witness this moment.

The Spirit smiled and lifted His hands. The luminous colors gathered around the Spirit of the Lord, their brilliance reflecting in His eyes. "MY SPIRITS ARE REJOICING WITH US," He said. "EACH OF THEM HAS WALKED WITH YOU, GUIDED YOU, AND PREPARED YOU FOR THIS MOMENT. THEY CELEBRATE WITH ME FOR WHAT HAS BEEN ACCOMPLISHED IN YOU."

As they ate, the Spirit asked about Ari's journey. Ari recalled at length Alaska, Peru, Red Deer, Mount Everest, the trip to China's emerald mines, and Mount Kilimanjaro. He also talked about the Spirits who guided him: *Fear of the Lord, Revelation Knowledge, Counsel, Power and Might, Wisdom,* and *Understanding*.

The *Spirit of the Lord* smiled and explained, "THE SPIRITS ARE INTEGRAL PARTS OF MY BEING. THEY RESEMBLE THE SIX WINGS OF THE SERAPHIM ENCIRCLING GOD THE FATHER'S THRONE AND REFLECT THE SIX CANDLES BESIDE THE CENTRAL SHAMASH OF THE MENORAH. ALL WORK TOGETHER TO SERVE GOD AND ACCOMPLISH THE FATHER'S WILL."

He paused, the light around Him deepening with gravity.

The Spirit paused... "YOU HAVE GATHERED WHAT WAS NEEDED. NOW, YOU STAND AT A TURNING POINT. YOU NEED TO MAKE SOME DIFFICULT

DECISIONS. WHAT COMES NEXT WILL REQUIRE COURAGE... AND THE WILLINGNESS TO CHOOSE."

The Painful Memory

The *Spirit of the Lord* touched Ari's shoulder, and the light in the room dimmed, softening into hues of memory. Ari blinked, finding himself transported into a vivid scene from his childhood. He was on the sidewalk of their brownstone house in New York on a sunny afternoon, filled with laughter as he played with two neighborhood friends. They were taking turns flying a remote-controlled airplane. A birthday gift Ari had cherished.

He watched as the smaller version of himself smiled widely, running alongside his friends as the airplane soared into the air. The joy was real, the kind of unburdened happiness only children know.

But then, the front door to the house suddenly opened. Abner stepped out onto the stoop, his face etched with disappointment. His presence cast a shadow over the lighthearted scene, and the children froze in place.

"Ariel!" Abner's voice boomed. "What are you doing? Didn't I tell you to finish your homework before you could go out and play?"

Young Ari's smile sank. "I-I'll do it after this, Dad," he stammered, glancing nervously at his friends, who now stood awkwardly, eyes wide.

Abner marched towards Ari, his steps deliberate. "After this?" he repeated, his tone biting. "You think life works like that? You think you can play first and worry about responsibility later?"

Before Ari could respond, Abner snatched the airplane from his hands. "If you can't follow simple rules, then you don't deserve this." And with a sharp, deliberate motion, he broke the airplane in two.

Ari's friends gasped, their shock only deepening Ari's humiliation. Heat rose in his cheeks as tears pricked his eyes, but he refused to cry, not in front of them.

"You'll never amount to anything if you keep acting like a child," Abner spat. "Stop wasting time and start thinking about your future."

His father turned and walked back into the house, leaving Ari standing there holding the controls. His friends muttered awkward goodbyes, avoiding eye contact as they left.

The laughter was gone. The sky, once bright with sunlight, now felt heavy and gray. The memory rippled with pain, and Ari's adult self watched the scene unfold with a sinking heart. He saw the humiliation, anger, and shame etched into his younger self's face. But there was something else, something darker.

It was the moment when Stolz, like a snake, twisted into Ari's thoughts. Ari's fists clenched, his nails digging into his palms. Inside him, something broke, and something else took root. A quiet, searing vow.

In the shadow of his father's harsh words, the young Ari clenched his jaw, his small hands tightening around the airplane's controls. "One day, I'll show him. I'll become so powerful, no one will ever be able to take anything from me again."

It was a vow born of hurt and pride, a seed that took root deep in his soul. Ari's drive for wealth and control and his relentless ambition all stemmed from this moment. Like a cunning predator, Stolz slipped into the cracks of that vow, whispering promises of power and independence.

The *Spirit of the Lord* stood beside Ari, His presence steady and comforting. "NOW, ARIEL," HE SAID SOFTLY. "LOOK AGAIN, BUT NOT THROUGH YOUR OWN EYES. SEE IT FROM YOUR FATHER'S PERSPECTIVE."

The scene shifted, and Ari stood inside the house, watching Abner from behind as he gazed out the window at the children playing. The man's shoulders were tense, and his thoughts conflicted about how to handle this situation.

Abner sighed heavily, muttering under his breath. "I can't let him grow up soft. The world doesn't care about dreams or toys. He needs to learn... or the world will crush him."

Ari's heart twisted as he recognized the fear hidden behind his father's anger, the fear of failure, the burden of wanting his only son to succeed in a harsh world. Abner wasn't trying to destroy him; he had been clumsily trying to protect and prepare Ari for his future.

"FEAR," the Spirit said gently. "YOUR FATHER'S LOVE WAS CLOUDED BY FEAR. HE DIDN'T KNOW HOW TO SHOW IT, SO HE TRIED TO SHAPE YOU THE

ONLY WAY HE UNDERSTOOD, THROUGH DISCIPLINE. HE THOUGHT HE WAS PROTECTING YOU."

Ari's breath caught as a soft cyan light surrounded him, glowing and otherworldly. The *Spirit of Understanding* had come, not with thunder, but with quiet clarity that wrapped around him like an embrace. It sparked within him that unmistakable 'Ah-ha moment', like a key turning in a long-forgotten lock. Gentle waves of understanding washed away the fog in his memory.

Then it hit him. "He was scared," Ari whispered, his voice barely audible. "Scared for me... and for what? Someone that I might become."

Ari didn't speak with bitterness, but with a new understanding, new insight. He saw for the first time not the burden of his father's expectations, but the fear behind them. Fear of failure. Of weakness. Of losing a son to... perhaps... the very pride he himself was battling.

Closing his eyes, he felt the soothing cyan light pulsing gently around him. He sensed the heavy weight of blame beginning to lift, bringing relief to his soul.

The *Spirit of the Lord* nodded. "AND NOW YOU MUST FORGIVE HIM. NOT BECAUSE HE WAS RIGHT, BUT BECAUSE MERCY IS THE ONLY WAY TO HEAL THIS WOUND."

Ari's breath caught as the weight of reality overwhelmed him like a tidal wave. For years, he had held onto the sting of humiliation, the slow burn of anger, and the unending need for his father's approval, which he believed would never arrive.

But now, he saw it. His father's fear. His brokenness. His flawed, human love. It hadn't been enough. It had never been enough. But it had been real.

Ari didn't break down with tears. He didn't sob or collapse to the ground.

No, his undoing was quieter and deeper.

His chest convulsed in tight, breathless shudders as the fortress he had built around his heart for decades finally cracked wide open. The boy he had been, the man he had become, they both stood there now, stripped bare.

Through his blurred vision, he caught sight of the *Spirit of Revelation Knowledge* standing nearby, silently watching like a wise teacher who understood that some lessons could only be learned through revelation and surrender.

Ari clenched his fists, the words scraping from his throat: "I forgive you, Dad," he rasped, his voice raw and broken. "I forgive you for the pain... for the shame... for not loving me the way I needed. And..." he choked back a sob that refused to fall, "I'm sorry for the resentment I carried all these years."

The moment hung there, suspended between heaven and earth. And then, like a gentle wind, peace swept over him, not because his father's failures had vanished, but because the chains around Ari's heart had finally shattered.

The *Spirit of Revelation Knowledge* smiled, and its crimson hue slowly faded from view along with the vision. Then Ari found himself back at the dining room table, sitting with the *Spirit of the Lord*.

"YOU NEEDED TO RELIVE THIS PAINFUL MEMORY SO THAT YOU WOULD UNDERSTAND THE ROOT OF THE PAIN YOU CARRY. NOW YOU CAN TRULY LOVE." The *Spirit of the Lord* smiled. "YOUR FORGIVENESS WILL SET YOU FREE TO LOVE. LEARNING HOW TO LOVE IS THE GREATEST THING YOU CAN DO IN YOUR LIFE."

A dam that had been holding back years of suppressed emotions, anger, and pain burst inside Ari, and he dissolved into tears, much like a child, his voice trembling uncontrollably. He stammered, wiping away the unfamiliar tears that felt so strange. The Spirit smiled, handing him a napkin.

"I never thought I'd borrow a napkin from the Lord of the Universe."

The Spirit chuckled softly, "I MEET PEOPLE WHERE THEY ARE. YOU NEED A NAPKIN. I PROVIDE ONE."

Ari laughed through tears. Humor amid holiness. He liked that.

The *Spirit of the Lord* reached across the table and touched Ari's hand. "YOUR FATHER, ABNER, LOVES YOU IN HIS OWN WAY. HE TRIED TO SHOW LOVE THROUGH WORK, DISCIPLINE, AND BUILDING AN EMPIRE.

YOU FEEL JUDGED BECAUSE HE MEASURED SUCCESS BY WORLDLY STANDARDS. BUT YOU MUST RISE ABOVE THAT PERSPECTIVE. LOVE HIM DESPITE HIS FAILINGS, SHOW MERCY AND COMPASSION."

Ari's thoughts drifted to childhood summers in this very house, memories of his father laughing as he spun him around, his mother calling them to dinner, cousins giggling on the floor. Memories Ari had suppressed into the corners of his mind. But now he sees those times differently.

Abner wasn't the controlling and ruthless corporate raider in those moments. He was his Dad. Ari missed those simpler times, before the striving and expectations, when love felt pure and safe. He whispered to himself, "He was just Dad... not a tyrant... just my Dad."

The *Spirit of the Lord* continued, "I KNOW IT'S HARD, BUT FORGIVENESS IS THE PATH TO HEALING. YOUR FATHER'S HEART MAY CHANGE OVER TIME. EVEN IF IT DOESN'T, YOUR FREEDOM LIES IN RESISTING RESENTMENT."

At that moment, Ari felt nothing but love for his father, remembering his childhood without harboring any anger or resentment toward him.

Stolz Comes Back with a Vengeance

Just then, a disruptive presence intruded. Stolz rushed in like a dark shadow. Ari stiffened. In Ari's mind, Stolz sneered: *"You can't forgive him! He took your company, your money. Get back at them! Reclaim your power! Don't you miss your luxuries, your jets, your control?"*

Ari's heart pounded. He looked to the *Spirit of the Lord*, his voice shaking. "Lord, Stolz is here... telling me to hold grudges, to use my power and money to dominate again. I feel the temptation stronger than ever before. It's influence is getting to me. I need help!"

His mind swirled with images of his mansion and executive office, where he ordered employees around and enjoyed gourmet meals at the snap of his fingers. The comfort of being revered and being the center of attention was very tempting.

The *Spirit of the Lord* slowly stirred the pot of honey, his eyes filled with compassion yet firm. "ARIEL, CAST DOWN THESE VAIN IMAGINATIONS," HIS VOICE STERN. "DO NOT LET PRIDE RULE OVER YOU AGAIN. PRIDE HAS BOUND YOU IN A PRISON OF SELFISHNESS. SELF-CENTEREDNESS HAS ROBBED YOU OF THE FREEDOM TO TRULY WORSHIP THE LORD GOD ALMIGHTY. YOU HAVE TASTED THE SWEETNESS OF THE SPIRIT OF WISDOM, A SWEETNESS LIKE THE HONEY IN THIS POT. SO, RESIST STOLZ, AND IN DOING SO, YOU WILL RESIST PRIDE."

As the Spirit stirred the honey, the very act seemed to stir the battle within Ari's soul, urging him to decide to cast down Pride and embrace the divine *Wisdom* that would set him free.

Stolz hissed, *"You fool! You'll live like a pauper! They'll laugh at you. Take back control. Money is power!"*

Ari trembled and stood up suddenly, causing his chair to topple over. "I... I need to go outside," he stuttered, hurrying out the door and leaving the Spirit at the dining room table.

Outside, the scorching Israeli sun watched Ari as he paced the courtyard where he had once played tag with his cousins. Stolz swirled in his mind like a swarm of angry hornets.

Ari shouted into the air, causing his voice to crackle. "No, I won't listen to you, Stolz!"

A passing neighbor was frightened as he eyed him like a madman. But Ari didn't care. He yelled into an empty corner of the yard, "Get out of my mind, Stolz! I renounce you! In the Name of Jesus Christ, leave me, now!"

The struggle felt endless, with visions of money and power tempting him and anger at Abner and Diana simmering. But as Ari prayed desperately, the *sword of courage* glowed hot, reminding him of the *Spirit of Power and Might*. He could feel the *sword of the Spirit* in his backbone, strengthening him with boldness. He invoked the Name of Jesus Christ over and over until Stolz's voice faded, replaced by a profound quiet.

Standing upright, Ari took a deep breath and then walked back to the dining room, where the Spirit sat waiting and holding the honey pot in His hand.

"YOU HAVE WON ANOTHER BATTLE," the Spirit smiled. "PRIDE NO LONGER CHAINS YOU; FREEDOM IS SWEET, JUST LIKE THIS HONEY. YOU ARE

FREE TO TRULY CHOOSE TO FOLLOW THE LORD JESUS, BUT ONE THING REMAINS TO BE ADDRESSED."

"What one thing?" Ari sighed with concern as he picked up his chair and sat back down. His body was weary, but his spirit was strangely lighter.

"ARIEL, YOU'VE LEARNED MUCH, BUT YOUR JOURNEY CANNOT MOVE FORWARD UNTIL YOUR HEART IS FULLY DEVOTED TO THE LORD."

"What do You mean?" Ari tilted his head, curious.

"YOU HAVE COME A LONG WAY." The Spirit said gently, "BUT ONE THING STILL NEEDS TO BE ADDRESSED FOR YOU TO HAVE YOUR FULL DEVOTION." He continued, "SELL EVERYTHING YOU OWN AND GIVE IT TO THE POOR." His eyes pierced into Ari's soul.

The words landed like a thunderclap. Ari froze, his mind spinning. He thought of the SummitTek empire he helped build with his family, the wealth he had compiled, his properties, his accounts (although frozen by his father, but still undeniably his. A flood of memories washed over him: the luxurious mansion, the boardroom victories, the admiration of peers. It was all tied to his identity and his wealth. Could he really let all of it go?

Stolz's voice was heard outside the house window. *"You've lost your mind! Everything you've built, everything you are, gone? For what? A promise you can't even see? Don't be a fool!"*

Ari glanced out the window. There, outside the house, Stolz appeared, his face twisted and distorted with rage, his form flickering in and out of the shadows. The embodiment of Pride ranted, pounding on the glass with furious indignation. *"Do you hear me? This is lunacy! You'll be nothing! Nothing! They'll laugh at you, your father, your enemies, the world. Do you want to be a pauper, a beggar?"*

The *Spirit of the Lord* said nothing, waiting calmly, His gaze steady and patiently looking into Ari's eyes. "IS A RELATIONSHIP WITH GOD MORE IMPORTANT THAN YOUR TREASURES? ARE YOU WILLING TO GIVE THEM ALL UP?"

Ari shut his eyes and thought of the Tanzanian children and their joy despite their poverty. He remembered the Juma family's laughter and the quiet humility of those he'd met on his journey.

He thought of Elinor, beautiful, steadfast Elinor, whose love was as patient as it was unshakable. She had seen him at his best and worst, yet she never flinched or demanded more than he could give.

Ari looked up, locking eyes with the Spirit. "Yes, I will do it," Ari declared, his voice firm despite his sweaty hands shaking.

"I'll do it. I'll give it all away, I'll sell everything. I will donate it to the poor. I will follow the Lord Jesus!"

The Spirit nodded approvingly. "MONEY WILL NO LONGER BE YOUR MASTER." The Spirit proclaimed, "BUT YOU, ARIEL, WILL MASTER THE MONEY. SERVE GOD, NOT THE SPIRIT OF MAMMON."

Stolz released a guttural scream, his figure outside the window fading into nothingness. Ari's heart felt even lighter, and his mind was clearer. He had made his choice, and it felt right.

"GREAT JOB, ARIEL. YOU ARE FREE NOW, FREE FROM THE HOLD OF PRIDE, FREE TO FOLLOW THE LORD WHOLLY."

The *Spirit of the Lord* motioned to the loaf of bread and the glass of wine on the table. "IF YOU ARE IN AGREEMENT WITH ME, THEN WE WILL SEAL THE DEAL BY SHARING COMMUNION."

This reminded him of the marriage contract; the signing of the Ketubah in Jewish tradition. In ancient ceremonies, the two parties would share a cup of wine to seal an engagement or agreement.

Handing Ari a piece of bread, "TAKE AND EAT. THIS SYMBOLIZES THE BODY OF JESUS, BROKEN FOR YOU." As Ari sat chewing the bread, his spiritual eyes were opened. He noticed what looked like holes in the Spirit's hands. The crucifixion wounds of Jesus seemed to glow faintly, as if they contained eternal light.

Ari struggled to comprehend the significance of the moment. The weight of those scars bore down on him. They represented more than just scars or wounds; they embodied the ultimate cost of our sin debt, a price that only the Lamb of God, the Suffering Servant from Isaiah 53, could pay for us. That sacrifice serves as a testament to boundless love.

The *Spirit of the Lord* continued by lifting the glass of wine. "THE NEW WINE..." His voice was joyful. "THIS SYMBOLIZES THE BLOOD OF JESUS, THE NEW COVENANT, THE NEW AGREEMENT BETWEEN GOD AND HIS PEOPLE, SEALED BY THE BLOOD THAT JESUS CHRIST SHED ON THE CROSS. THIS

IS NOT FOR WORLDLY INTOXICATION; IT IS A BOND, A SPIRITUAL SEALING OF OUR COVENANT. NOW, DRINK!"

Ari's hands trembled as he accepted the glass, the weight of this moment's commitment pressing on him. He sipped the rich, sweet wine that filled his body, soul, and spirit. Ari continued to drink, savoring the experience as he finished the glass. This was an engagement with God, His purposes, and His promises.

Suddenly, Ari was swept into another vision: a celestial wedding banquet with endless tables stretching beneath a radiant sky. The Bride of Christ, the Church, was clothed in splendor, and Jesus sat at the head of it all. Ari saw himself among the guests, not as an outsider but as part of the radiant body, welcomed and beloved.

In the vision, Jesus reached out and touched Ari's shoulder. "NOW, ARIEL, FOLLOW ME. YOUR JOURNEY IS FAR FROM OVER. BUT TODAY, YOU HAVE PASSED A TEST THAT MANY FAIL. TRUST IN ME, AND YOU WILL SEE THE FULLNESS OF MY HEAVENLY FATHER'S PLAN FOR YOU."

Feeling the Love of God infuse into his very being made every cell in Ari's body do a happy dance. "Thank You, Lord. I will follow You, always."

As the vision of the wedding banquet faded, Ari found himself cradling an empty glass of wine. He felt the weight of his decision and, oddly enough, its freedom. His wealth would no longer define him, and Pride would no longer be his master. His future was tied to something eternal and glorious, and possibly to the woman Elinor.

"NOW, LET'S TALK ABOUT ELINOR," the Spirit of the Lord interrupted in a light, playful tone, cutting through Ari's deep, contemplative moment.

Ari chuckled softly, feeling lighter in heart. "She's incredible, Lord," he said. "Her faith in You is truly inspiring. Her love for me... It's genuine, fierce, and spunky. She's always stood up for what's right, even when it wasn't easy. And wow, is she beautiful!"

The Spirit's gaze remained steady, his voice becoming tender yet firm. "BUT... DO YOU LOVE HER?"

The question struck Ari like a lightning bolt slap upside his head. He shifted uncomfortably. "Of course, I love her," he replied quickly, almost defensively.

The Spirit leaned forward, His expression serious yet friendly. "No, Ariel, not in the way you've been telling yourself. I'm asking if you truly love her. Not as a friend you admire or someone you drag along while figuring out your path in life. I'm asking if you love her with a deep commitment." Then the Spirit of the Lord asked, "Do you see her as the one you cannot live without, the one you will cherish, honor, and be one with for the rest of your life?"

The words hung in the air, stifling Ari's immediate reply. He felt the weight of the question settle upon him.

The Spirit continued, "True love is neither casual nor convenient; it is the foundation of God's covenant. It involves giving your heart fully and committing to love someone despite their flaws. True love isn't about dragging her through the chaos of your life, but rather about standing beside her as one, with God as your foundation."

Ari's thoughts raced. He remembered the spark in Elinor's eyes when she stood up for her beliefs, her fiery determination wrapped in grace. He reminisced about her laughter and the playful moments they shared.

Then he envisioned life without her. The clarity of that thought hit him so powerfully that his chest ached.

He exhaled deeply, and the realization settled in his soul as he looked at the Spirit. "Yes, Lord," he said. "I love her. I love her deeply. She's the one. I can't imagine my life without her."

For the first time, he truly understood that Elinor's love wasn't merely a nice gesture; it was a treasure, a divine gift, and a blessing he had been blind to for far too long. His heart swelled with gratitude and a renewed determination to love and cherish her as she deserved.

The *Spirit of the Lord* smiled, His face radiant with approval. "If you love her, then marry her! Your union will reflect the covenant love I have for both of you. She understands your calling, and you have my blessing, so... go ahead and propose!"

The Spirit playfully leaned in, "AND YOU KNOW WHAT... I LOVE A GREAT WEDDING!"

Ari's heart soared at the Lord's blessing, and for a brief moment, he reveled in the joy of being granted permission to marry Elinor. However, that euphoria was quickly overshadowed by a sobering thought: he couldn't access his frozen finances.

The harsh reality hit him like a cold shower. He frowned, his voice filled with regret, "But I don't even have the money to buy her a proper engagement ring right now."

The Spirit lightly touched Ari's chest. "YOU HAVE CARRIED THE GIFT OF THE SPIRIT OF WISDOM WITH YOU."

Before Ari could respond, a sudden weight in his shirt pocket caught his attention. Confused, he reached inside and felt something cool and smooth. His breath hitched as he pulled out an intricately designed ring made of gold, set with the emerald gifted to him by the *Spirit of Wisdom*. It gleamed with an otherworldly brilliance, the facets capturing the light like tiny stars.

He examined the ring closely and gasped upon noticing an engraving on the inner band. The words were in Hebrew, etched with perfect precision:

אהבת עולם אהבתיך
(*"I have loved you with an everlasting love."*)

Ari's throat tightened, his words catching as he looked back at the Spirit, his eyes wide with a mix of curiosity and wonder.

"This... this is the emerald," he whispered, his voice trembling. His gaze fell to the shimmering ring in his hand, and a wave of realization crashed over him. His breath quickened, excitement bubbling to the surface. "And now... It's a ring, an engagement ring!"

The Spirit nodded. "ARIEL, THIS IS MY GIFT TO YOU, A SYMBOL OF GOD'S COVENANT AND A REFLECTION OF THE LOVE YOU ARE MEANT TO SHARE WITH ELINOR. ITS VALUE LIES NOT IN ITS MATERIAL WORTH BUT IN THE TRUTHS YOU'VE GAINED ON YOUR JOURNEY. FURTHERMORE, ELINOR EMBODIES WISDOM; SHE IS A TREASURE TO HOLD DEAR."

Ari held the ring in his palm, mesmerized by its beauty and significance. "It's perfect. She'll understand and appreciate its meaning."

"LOVE HER AS I HAVE LOVED YOU, ARIEL, WITH PATIENCE, SACRIFICE, AND JOY. THIS RING IS MORE THAN JUST A GIFT; IT'S A REMINDER OF THE JOURNEY YOU'VE TAKEN AND THE PROMISES YOU CHERISH."

Ari's heart swelled with gratitude, and he felt genuinely prepared to embrace the future God had in store for him, with Elinor by his side.

They finished their meal. The Spirit gazed at him affectionately. "YOU HAVE CHANGED, ARIEL. YOU ARE MORE EQUIPPED TO CONTINUE YOUR JOURNEY. GO HOME. FORGIVE YOUR FATHER AND DIANA; SHOW THEM MERCY.

REMEMBER, ALL THINGS WORK TOGETHER FOR GOOD TO THOSE WHO LOVE THE LORD AND ARE CALLED ACCORDING TO THE FATHER'S PLAN AND PURPOSE." The Spirit of the Lord smiled as He rose from His seat. "GO AND DO AS I HAVE INSTRUCTED YOU. THEN, PREPARE FOR WHAT COMES NEXT.

FORGIVE THOSE WHO HAVE WRONGED YOU. BE PATIENT WITH THOSE WHO DO NOT UNDERSTAND. AND REMEMBER, LOVE THE LORD YOUR GOD WITH ALL YOUR HEART, SOUL, MIND, AND STRENGTH. KEEP AND OBEY GOD'S COMMANDS."

Ari nodded, tears again. "I will. Thank You, Lord."

Leaving the House

They parted with a solid embrace, a moment steeped in warmth and holy wonder. Ari could scarcely believe he was hugging the *Spirit of Jesus*... God the Father's love made near.

As he stepped outside, Ari took a deep breath and looked at the world in a different light. It seemed hushed, bathed in peace. Everything felt different, even the ordinary seemed changed. He perceived his journey was going to take a radical turn for the better and the idea of proposing no longer felt impossible... but right.

"One thing is certain," Ari murmured, glancing back over his shoulder. "I'm ready to commit to Elinor and... Lord?" Ari turned, looking around as if the Lord was hiding. But the *Spirit of the Lord* was gone, leaving behind a stillness that felt sacred rather than empty.

The encounter had left a divine fragrance of almond blossoms and freshly baked bread in the air, a warm, comforting aroma. Quietly assuring that what had transpired was no mere dream.

A sudden jolt of panic surged through Ari as he reached into his shirt pocket, his fingers fumbling desperately.

Had it been real or just another dream?

His breath caught until his fingertips brushed against the cool metal. He pulled it out, and there it was: the *engagement ring*, gleaming in gold with the exquisite *emerald* at its center.

The weight of it in his palm steadied him, serving as a tangible reminder that this experience was real and not just a figment of his imagination. It was a gift from the *Spirit of the Lord* and the *Spirit of Wisdom,* symbolizing the love he was now ready to share with Elinor.

Ari lingered in the courtyard, allowing the warm, fresh air to fill his lungs. His heart ached as he reflected on what had just occurred, replaying the milestones of his journey in his mind.

He had forgiven his father and had been released from his childhood pain and years of bitterness. Stolz was defeated, its whispers now silenced by the strength of humility and surrender to the Lord.

The grip of money, once his master, was shattered, and now he was free to give without any strings attached. Most significantly, he had embraced God's eternal covenant and the call to follow Jesus wherever He would lead.

His thoughts turned to Elinor, the one who had been his steady anchor throughout this storm. He could see her smile and hear her voice, filled with encouragement. Now, he not only wanted to be with her, but he was ready to honor her as his wife and build a life together rooted in God's love and respect.

Meshuga!

The *Golden Compass* in his shirt pocket hummed softly, confirming his direction: return to Denver, follow the Lord's instructions, plan how to give away his wealth, and prepare his proposal for Elinor. There was no hesitation in his heart, only excitement and a sense of peace he had never experienced before.

The journey wasn't over. There would be many more challenges, lessons, and mountains to climb. But he felt truly free. A laugh escaped his lips... then another, until he couldn't hold it in any longer as a belly laugh rumbled out loud.

He raised his arms to the sky and shouted, "Thank You Lord, Thank You Lord! You're so good! So, so GOOD to me!"

As he bellowed his praise, a movement caught his eye. He turned to see the same neighbor from earlier. The one who had seen him yelling at the voices in his head, walking by again with his dog.

The poor man froze mid-step, his face showing a mix of concern and sheer terror. With eyes darting, the neighbor quickened his pace, dragging his confused dog along.

"First yelling at the sky, now shouting about God..." Ari caught him murmuring in Hebrew.

"Meshuga! (Crazy man!)"

Ari bent over laughing. "I promise, I'm not crazy, I'm just finally free! Free in my soul!"

The neighbor didn't care... neither did his dog.

Chapter 22

Storms at Home

Ari Keshet stepped out of the taxi and gazed up at the imposing facade of his Denver mansion. Memories of lavish company galas and entertaining high-powered clients flooded his mind, but today, those memories were overshadowed by the turmoil that had recently upended his life.

Clutching the *emerald engagement ring* gifted by the *Spirit of the Lord and the Spirit of Wisdom*, he took a deep breath and approached the grand entrance. He braced himself for the challenges that his company would throw at him. He also readied himself to confront his parents, who had recently taken up residence in his home like squatters.

As he pushed open the heavy front door, Ari's staff welcomed him back from his trip. As his butler retrieved his bag from the taxi, Ari made his way into his mansion to find his mother, Iris, bustling in the kitchen. Her face lit up as she spotted her son. "Ariel, you're home!" she exclaimed, embracing him warmly. Her eyes sparkled with genuine happiness, reflecting the peace Ari carried in his spirit.

Ari and Iris made their way into the grand living room. Abner was relaxed, reading the *Wall Street Journal*, and Diana was sitting nearby, hovering over a stack of legal documents, plotting her next move at SummitTek. They both looked up, startled.

Ari was calm. His old anger would have flared up, but now he breathed, calling on God's presence. He commanded attention as Abner and Diana looked at each other.

They squirmed in their seats. The air was heavy with unspoken tension, but Ari's heart was steady, buoyed by the peace in his heart.

"Mom, Dad, Diana," he began, his voice calm but firm. "I have some important news."

Diana perked up immediately, her perfectly manicured fingers resting lightly on the arm of the couch. She leaned forward, her eyes gleaming. "Important news?" she repeated, her tone laced with expectation.

Ari took a deep breath, a hint of anticipation dancing in his eyes. "Alright, I'm going to get straight to the point... I've made a big decision... I'm getting married."

Diana's reaction was instantaneous. She leaped from her seat, a radiant smile lighting her face as she rushed to embrace him.

"Ari! Finally! I knew you'd come around."

Ari instinctively stepped back before she could touch him, holding up his hand. Her smile faltered, confusion flashing across her face. "I'm going to ask Elinor to marry me, not you." His voice steady.

Diana froze, her hands hovering in mid-air. For a moment, she looked as though she hadn't heard him correctly. Then her eyes widened, disbelief and fury conflicting on her face. "Elinor?" she spat, her voice trembling. "No. No! No, you are supposed to marry me..., not to that... that *wallflower*!"

"Diana.., Elinor is not a wallflower. She's the most remarkable woman I've ever met. She's kind, sweet, and intelligent. She's everything I want and more."

Diana staggered back, collapsing onto the couch, her expression stunned. "This can't be real," she whispered, her voice barely audible.

"I'm sorry, Diana," Ari said, his tone soft but firm. "But my heart belongs to Elinor."

The room fell into an uneasy silence with Diana's shock hanging heavily in the air. Abner's face was boiling red, and his brow furrowed, but before he could speak, Ari continued.

"Wait, there's more," his gaze sweeping over all of them. "I've also decided to sell SummitTek and give away my money." Drawing deeply on the courage of the invisible *Sword* in his soul, Ari remained steadfast. "I am seeing this more clearly than I ever have before. I've learned that God loves me and my faith in Him will sustain me. My thirst for worldly possessions has only kept me from my happiness."

For a heartbeat, Diana just stared... eyes blinking, mouth hanging open, as if her brain had short-circuited. Then, with a sharp gasp and a theater-worthy lunge, she launched off the couch like a ballistic missile.

"Sell SummitTek? Are you insane?" she cried, clutching her chest as though fending off a heart attack. "Is this a joke?" Her voice climbed an octave. "You've already turned us into a circus headline, and now you're just... what? Walking away like nothing happened?" She threw her hands wide, pacing dramatically. "What's next, humm? Shaving your head and living in a monastery?"

The room trembled... not from anger, but from the sheer force of Diana's dramatics. Her voice grew shrill as she paced the room, her heels clicking sharply against the marble floor. "You can't do this, Ari! 'We'... do you hear me, 'We' were supposed to be the power couple to run the SummitTek empire. You and me Ari... It was supposed to be you and me! Now, you are ruining all our plans! Everything you've built! Everything your father and I have been working on! For what? Some delusional spiritual journey?"

Abner's anger gradually rose..., his countenance fuming. "Ariel, what is the meaning of this absurdity? Are you seriously contemplating selling the company? Have you entirely lost your rationality? My initial assessment regarding your removal as CEO due to mental delusions was indeed justified."

Ari stood his ground. He remained unshaken. "I've never been more certain of anything in my life," he said. "SummitTek was never mine to keep. It's time to let it go and use what it has to make a real difference in the world... helping others."

Diana's uncontrolled fury reached its peak. She started grabbing anything within reach and hurling them at Ari. She grabbed an expensive oriental vase from the side table and smashed it into a million pieces. "You've embarrassed us, Ari!" she shrieked. "You're destroying everything for that... that *nobody* and her *Jesus!*"

Abner, visibly rattled by Diana's outburst, struggled to maintain his usual composure. His voice, usually firm and commanding, quivered as he raised a hand in a futile attempt to restore order. "Diana, enough of this!" he said, the authority in his tone undermined by an edge of uncertainty.

But Diana wasn't done. "This isn't over, Ari!" she hissed, her face contorted with a rage that nearly ruined her Botox treatments. "You'll regret this. Mark my words, you haven't seen the last of me yet. I will make sure you regret making these decisions!"

Hearing the glass items shattering onto the floor, Ari's staff hurried to the living room, crowding the doorways with wide eyes and slack jaws as they took in the chaotic scene.

Iris, clearly startled, instinctively pulled a housekeeper in front of her, using the poor woman as a human shield against Diana's rampage.

With one last venomous glare, Diana stormed toward the exit, her heels clicking sharply. She flung the door open with such force that the glass panels cracked and shattered. The sound echoed throughout the grand halls like an explosive crescendo to her tirade. The reverberation lingered, leaving an uneasy silence in its wake as everyone stood frozen in disbelief.

Ari exhaled slowly, turning to his parents as Iris peeked out from behind the housekeeper, watching him with a mix of pride and worry. At the same time, Abner's expression was a storm of emotions. Anger. Confusion. And perhaps a flicker of regret for involving Diana in the ploy.

"Dad, I know this is hard for you to understand. But I've found something greater than all of this, greater than money, power, or ambition. I've found peace with God through *Jesus the Messiah*, and I choose to follow the path He's set for me."

Abner said nothing, as if he didn't even hear him. All he could do was stare at the shattered vase on the floor and think about his father, Reuben, and decades of hard work that built the company. Now, it was suddenly coming to an end.

Iris brushed down the front of her dress, took a deep breath, and stepped forward, resting her hand on Ari's arm. "I'm so proud of you, Ariel," she said, her voice warm and brimming with maternal love. "You must follow your heart, darling... even if that heart has apparently decided to marry a *Christian girl* and sell the company our family has bled for over the decades..." She mumbled, "... like it's a slightly used sofa on *Facebook Marketplace*."

Ari cocked his head, questioning what she was getting at. But then decided to put it aside and offered her a grateful smile.

She patted his arm again, smiling bravely while her left eye gave a tiny, involuntary twitch.

Standing his ground, Ari turned to his father, who appeared torn, anger simmering just beneath the surface, but something softer flickering behind his sharp gaze. It wasn't approval, not yet, but perhaps the faintest seed of respect.

"Dad, I need a favor," Ari said, his voice steady yet urgent.

Abner's eyes narrowed as he sighed heavily. Gripping the arm of the couch, he sat down with the weariness of a man who had weathered too many storms. "Ari, what now? Haven't you caused enough chaos? What could you possibly ask of me now?"

Meeting his father's gaze, Ari pleaded, "I need to be reinstated as CEO. I have crucial decisions to make and plans to execute, and I need my position back to make it happen."

Abner leaned back, studying his son intensively. The silence in the room grew thick, everyone holding their breath. Finally, with a reluctant nod, Abner picked up his phone and called for an emergency board meeting.

"Fine," he said gruffly, his tone clipped. "I'll arrange it. But Ari, this is your last chance. I'm trusting your judgment."

Relief washed over Ari. He stepped forward and extended his hand. "Dad... I won't let you down."

Abner hesitated for a long moment before shaking his son's hand. "You better not let us down. I've already dealt with enough fallout to put me into an early grave."

As Ari turned to leave, a commotion outside caught everyone's attention. Staff and family members hurried to the grand windows, pressing their faces against the glass as Diana's red sports car roared down the driveway.

She tore off with an ear-splitting screech, leaving a trail of burnt rubber and fumes in her wake. The dramatic exit stretched for nearly a quarter of a mile, the echoes of her engine rumbling like distant thunder.

Abner groaned, pinching the bridge of his nose. "She is a tornado... dressed in Versace."

Ari was calm despite the tension. He placed a reassuring hand on his mother's shoulder. "It's going to be alright," he said softly. "You'll see. Everything will work out."

Turning to his father, Ari said, "I need to get started. There's a lot of planning to do, and time is not on my side."

"Please don't make me regret this." Abner raised an eyebrow and sighed.

Ari smiled faintly. "This is something big, Dad. Something that matters to me."

As Ari left the room, Abner slumped back in his chair, staring at the ceiling... like it might have the answers to his life questions. He muttered, "One minute he's a teenager grounded for missing curfew, the next he's on a deadline to 'save the world'. I really should've read the fine print on parenting."

The Surprise Gala

The SummitTek corporate gala had come together at lightning speed. The grand hallway sparkled with strings of twinkling lights, and elegant floral arrangements added bursts of color to the sleek corporate decor. Tables were lined with gourmet appetizers, and a live string quartet filled the space with soft, melodic music.

The atmosphere buzzed with excitement as employees mingled, speculating on what had prompted such a lavish event.

"Maybe it's a new product launch?" someone suggested.

"Or a surprise bonus?" another joked, their voice tinged with hope. Unbeknownst to them, the gala wasn't just a gesture of appreciation for their hard work. It was the stage set for a life-changing announcement.

Ari had planned it perfectly. He wanted this moment to be for the people who had built his empire, supported his journey, and stuck with him through the chaos of his spiritual transformation. The gala was a fitting backdrop for his bold plan to propose to Elinor in front of everyone who mattered to him.

The media, strategically positioned at the room's edges, captured the evening's grandeur, but Ari's focus was elsewhere. He adjusted his tie, glancing at the grand entrance's glass doors.

Standing nearby with a mischievous grin, Moose clapped Ari on the shoulder. "You nervous, boss?"

Ari chuckled, shaking his head. "More nervous than any climb in the world," he admitted.

"Well, don't trip over your feet," Moose teased. "She deserves a smooth proposal."

Ari's heart raced as the employees continued to sip champagne and speculate about the night's purpose. He glanced at the grand entrance, where Gottschall had arranged for Elinor's arrival.

Fairy Godmother

Earlier that evening, Elinor had been lounging in her apartment, comfortably dressed in leggings and an oversized hoodie, when there was a knock at the door. She opened it to find Gottschall, elegant and businesslike, holding a garment bag, a shoebox, and a jewelry case.

"Maria?" Elinor asked, eyebrows raised.

"No time for questions!" Gottschall said, sweeping into the apartment like a whirlwind. "You've been invited to a SummitTek gala, and I've been instructed to ensure you're dressed for the occasion."

"A gala? But I don't have...,"

Gottschall unzipped the garment bag, revealing a stunning floral dress. "Courtesy of Mr. Keshet himself. He thought you might need a little fairy godmother magic tonight. And voilà, shoes and accessories to match."

Elinor's eyes widened. "I..., I don't know what to say. This is... overwhelming!"

Gottschall handed her the dress and smiled. "Say thank you, Cinderella, and get ready. The SummitTek SUV is downstairs, and we must leave soon."

Elinor laughed nervously but hurried to change. Moments later, she emerged, the floral dress hugging her figure perfectly, the delicate heels elongating her stride. Gottschall added the final touch, a sparkling necklace with matching emerald earrings.

"Absolutely stunning," Gottschall proclaimed as she spun her around, admiring her handiwork. "Ari won't know what hit him."

The Proposal

As they pulled up to the corporate gala, Elinor was stunned by all *the pomp and circumstance*. She hesitated. "Is this... normal for a business gala?" she whispered to Gottschall, who gave her a knowing smile but said nothing.

As the staff opened the large glass doors, Elinor stepped into the flood of flashing lights from the media. In the grand hall, the air itself seemed to hold its breath. The room shimmered with golden light from cascading chandeliers and walls wrapped in gauzy, champagne colored drapery. The polished marble floors mirrored a constellation of candles that lined the perimeter, flickering like stars. The string quartet shifted subtly, their melody softening into a romantic swell as the moment drew near.

Clusters of SummitTek employees parted instinctively, forming a natural aisle.

And there, walking toward her, was Ari.

He advanced slowly and deliberately; his tailored suit was sharp beneath the golden glow of the chandeliers. In his hand, a small ornate gold box, intricately worked with filigree, gleamed like a sacred offering. And his eyes never left hers.

"Elinor," he said, his voice calm but thick with emotion as he reached her. He took her hand, gently lowering himself to one knee.

The crowd gasped. Cameras flashed. But to Elinor, the world had gone utterly quiet, everything moving in slow motion.

"Elinor," Ari began, his voice steady despite the thunderous pounding of his heart. "You've been my anchor, guide, and greatest blessing. Your faith in God, strength, and steadfast love have changed me. You've shown me what love is, God's love, and I want to spend the rest of my life showing you that same love."

He opened the box to reveal the emerald ring, which shimmered with a brilliance all its own. Light danced across its facets, casting tiny halos on Elinor's face and capturing the breath of the entire room. It wasn't just beautiful, it was otherworldly, as if heaven had whispered its color into the stone. Elinor gasped as the emerald pulsed with ethereal light, like a living flame cupped in gold.

"This ring isn't just a symbol of my love; it's a token of the lessons I've learned and the journey I want to share with you. I love you, and I can't imagine my life without you... Elinor." He inhaled, his heart pounding. "Elinor Miller, will you marry me?"

Her hands flew to her mouth, and tears welled instantly. One joyful tear broke loose, parading down her cheek like a tiny banner of joy, waving proudly for the whole room to see.

The moment pulsed with emotion; heaven leaned in to listen. She nodded through her tears, barely able to speak. "Yes," she whispered. Regaining her breath, she then bellowed, "Yes!"

The room erupted in applause and cheers, the employees celebrating as if it were their triumph. Cameras continued to flash, capturing the radiant couple as Ari slipped the ring onto Elinor's finger.

The Celebration

As the engagement was announced, the room transformed from formal to festive. Champagne flowed, a gourmet feast was unveiled, and toasts rose like confetti. Laughter and applause filled the air.

Although at the outskirts of the celebration, Ari's parents remained quiet. Abner's jaw was tight, his hands clasped behind his back as if holding in a reprimand. He didn't clap. His gaze stayed fixed on Elinor, not with hatred, but with the cold calculation of a man measuring an adversary.

He wasn't sure exactly what it was about the situation that made him feel as though he had lost the battle.

Standing beside him, Iris offered a forced smile, her eyes lingering on Elinor with growing curiosity. She really wanted to be hopeful for the future, but inside, she was unsure.

Gottschall stood nearby, saying nothing, but noticing everything. Moose, ever the life of the party, raised his glass high.

"To Ari and Elinor! And to Gottschall and Susan for pulling off the year's best surprise party!"

Gottschall leaned toward Ari, casually sipping her champagne with a satisfied grin. "Told you she'd say 'Yes'. Honestly, the only surprise here is that she didn't make you kneel twice for good measure." She raised her glass slightly, her tone dripping with dry humor. "Now, let's just hope she doesn't realize she could have done better."

"Hah...Haah." Ari mocked while glancing around the room.

Elinor crossed over with quiet poise, making her way toward Ari's parents. Abner stood stiffly beside Iris, his posture rigid, his expression unreadable. Though neither had fully embraced the idea of their son marrying a Christian woman, Elinor's warmth and sincerity made it difficult to dismiss her.

She extended her hand with a genuine smile. "Mr. Keshet, Mrs. Keshet, I'm truly honored you could be here tonight. It means a great deal."

Abner hesitated before taking her hand. His grip was firm, his tone formal. "You're very gracious, Elinor."

It wasn't praise, it was only acknowledgment.

Iris offered a tight smile. "We're happy for you," she said, the words gentle but not entirely settled. Then, as if searching for footing, she stepped forward and pulled Elinor into a brief and extremely awkward hug. "You seem... uh, very nice."

Elinor accepted the gesture with grace, sensing the tension but refusing to mirror it. "Thank you. I'm grateful to be part of your family."

For an awkward moment, no one spoke. Then, seeing the tension, Gottschall appeared at Elinor's side like a quiet breeze, gently redirecting the moment before it could stretch too far into regret.

As the evening wound down, Ari and Elinor stood on the grand staircase, the glow of the celebration below casting a warm light around them. Ari turned to her, his arm slipping securely around her waist, pulling her closer. His fingers traced gentle circles on her back as he gazed into her eyes.

"This is just the beginning. Are you ready for the most wild adventure of your life?" his voice filled with promise.

Elinor smiled, her hand resting against his chest, feeling the steady rhythm of his heartbeat. The *emerald ring* glistened. Elinor's eyes sparkled as she whispered, "As long as I'm with you." She tilted her head, her lips brushing softly against his jawline in a tender, sensual gesture.

"I still can't believe you said 'Yes!'" he teased, his tone warm and playful. Ari smiled, his free hand lifting to tuck a loose strand of hair behind her ear. "I don't want to wait a long time for the wedding. I want to marry you as soon as we can pull it together."

Elinor let out a soft laugh, her fingers curling into his lapel. "Well then, get your super party planners on it, and we might be able to have a lovely June wedding," she teased.

He leaned down, brushing his lips gently against hers in a kiss that held all the unspoken promises of their future. When they pulled back, he whispered, "I love you, Elinor."

Her smile widened as she reached up to touch his face. "I love you, too, Ari. Always and forever."

They lingered there, wrapped in each other's arms, the world below fading into the background as they shared a quiet moment of affection and anticipation for the life ahead.

Ari Shares His Journey with Elinor

The next evening, Ari and Elinor cuddled under a blanket on the mansion's terrace, with the Denver skyline sparkling in the cool night air. The scent of pine blended with the distant hum of the city, providing a peaceful backdrop to the conversation that weighed heavily on Ari's heart.

"Elinor," Ari began, his voice calm but weighted with something deep, something life-altering. "I've told you pieces of my journey, but I haven't told you everything."

She tilted her head slightly, curiosity flickering in her eyes. "I'm listening."

Ari exhaled slowly, gathering his thoughts. "I encountered all *Seven Spirits of God*, the ones Isaiah wrote about. They aren't just concepts or theological symbols. They're real, Elinor. They guided me, tested me, and broke me down before rebuilding me."

Elinor's grip on his hand tightened, her breath catching for a moment. "You met them all?" she asked, her voice barely above a whisper yet filled with eager anticipation.

Ari nodded, watching her expression shift, astonishment, wonder, a hunger to hear more. She leaned in slightly, her eyes locked onto him, like a child savoring the richest dessert, eager for the next bite. He could practically see her absorbing every word, her mind painting the stories as he spoke.

He recounted them, the *Spirits of the Fear of the Lord, Revelation Knowledge, Counsel, Power and Might, Wisdom, and Understanding*. Each Spirit had peeled back a layer of who he thought he was, revealing truths both uncomfortable and liberating. But then he paused, his voice growing softer and reverent.

"The last one, Elinor... the *Spirit of the Lord*." His voice was almost a whisper. "I met Jesus..."

Elinor interrupted, "You," Her voice caught. "You met Him?" She inhaled sharply, her fingers twitching in his grasp. "What...what do you mean?"

Ari stopped her. "Yes, but let me explain. I did meet Jesus, but not in the way you are thinking. The *Spirit of the Lord* is the *Spirit of Jesus Christ*. He told me that Jesus is in Heaven with the Father, so His Spirit is sent here on earth for His people. It's like... like a divine echo, a presence that is Him but still distinct." He exhaled, shaking his head. "Elinor, I looked into His eyes. I felt Him. I ate with Him. He knows us. The *King of the Universe* knows us intimately!"

Elinor's hands flew to her mouth, but instead of crying, she smiled, wide, joyful, utterly enraptured. "Ari, that's..." She shook her head, at a loss for words, her excitement bubbling beneath her skin. "That's extraordinary!"

Ari let out a small laugh, relieved she wasn't looking at him like he was crazy. "Yeah, it was." His tone grew serious. "But He didn't just meet me. He commanded me. He showed me who I really was. He showed me the time in my childhood when Stolz entered my soul and influenced my life. How pride, control, and money had chained me. Then He told me to let it all go. To sell everything, including SummitTek, and give it away to the poor. To trust Him completely."

Elinor arched an eyebrow, her fingers idly playing with the hem of her sweater. "Sell everything?" She let out a small, disbelieving chuckle, shaking her head. "Ari, that's wild. That's literally the *Rich Young Ruler* story from the Bible." She leaned back, studying him. "You do realize how that story ended, right? It didn't go well for the rich guy."

Ari laughed. "Oh, trust me, I thought about that too." He smirked. "I'd like to think I'll make a better decision than that guy."

Her teasing expression softened. "And you're really going to do it?"

He nodded. "Yes. Since the board reinstated me as CEO, I'll use that position to fulfill what Jesus asked of me. I'll sell my shares, ensure everyone in the company benefits, and then give the rest of the money away." His voice grew quieter. "Elinor, I don't feel like I have to do this... I want to."

Ari laughed, realizing something he never thought he would say, "I want to do it because I actually love Jesus! Me...the Jewish kid from New York, in love with Jesus Christ! It sounds crazy, doesn't it?"

She studied him for a long moment, a slow, radiant smile on her face. She exhaled, shaking her head in awe. "That's not just bold, Ari. That's beautiful," She squeezed his hand. "... and terrifying."

He chuckled. "You're not wrong. Everything I've built, everything I thought defined me, Jesus asked me to let it all go. But instead of feeling trapped..." He swallowed, his voice filled with something raw and authentic. "It's strange, but I finally feel free."

Elinor reached up, resting her hand against his cheek. She shook her head slightly, eyes glistening in the moonlight. "The man you're becoming... It's someone I admire and love." A small, mischievous smile graced her lips. "And, dare I say, someone I'm very, very attracted to."

Ari's breath hitched, his heart hammering in his chest. He leaned into her kiss, absorbing the moment, the weight of her words settling into his soul like a promise.

But then, his cell phone buzzed.

Ari groaned, reluctant to break the romantic moment, but his brow furrowed when he saw the name flashing on the screen. "Elinor," he said, holding up the phone. "It's AndesCon."

Her eyes widened. "Now that's unexpected."

Ari stared at his buzzing phone, lips pressing together in mild frustration. Of course. He sighed, throwing Elinor an apologetic glance before rolling his eyes dramatically and muttering, "Perfect timing, as always... uggh."

Elinor smirked, biting her lip to suppress a giggle. She leaned back, sipping her tea, clearly enjoying the moment more than he was.

Still, he composed himself and answered. "Mr. Diego Vargas," he greeted, keeping his tone neutral. "Good evening. Hope you are doing well."

Mr. Vargas, director of AndesCon, replied confidently yet pleasantly in his heavy Spanish accent: "Mr. Keshet, I hope I am not interrupting anything important."

Ari chuckled softly, glancing at Elinor, who arched a knowing brow. "Not at all," he lied smoothly, shooting her a playful grin as she shook her head in amusement.

"Bueno. I wanted to call you personally." Mr. Vargas continued. "We have been closely monitoring SummitTek's growth, and I would like to schedule a meeting to discuss something significant, a potential purchase agreement."

Ari, intrigued, straightened slightly. "A purchase agreement?" He glanced at Elinor, whose curiosity mirrored his own. "That's... unexpected. Tell me more." As Diego launched into the details, Ari, replying, leaned forward slightly, his heart racing. "You are interested in buying SummitTek?"

"Yes," Diego confirmed. "Let's meet to discuss the terms. We believe there is a strong synergy between our visions, and we would like to see if we can reach an agreement that works for everyone."

Ari paused, choosing his words carefully. "I'll need to bring this to the board, but I will arrange a time. Let's talk soon."

"Perfect. I look forward to it," Diego replied before ending the call.

Ari put down the phone and exhaled slowly. "That was unexpected," he murmured, turning to Elinor with a faint smile. "AndesCon wants to meet to discuss buying SummitTek. No numbers yet, just an invitation."

Elinor's eyes widened. "It sounds like a door is opening."

Ari nodded, his thoughts racing, but he felt calm. "It appears the next step is starting to align perfectly."

At the same moment, a brilliant shooting star darted across the night sky... signaling progress in the right direction.

Getting Down to Business

Over the next few weeks, Denver was abuzz with excitement as news of Ari Keshet's decision to sell SummitTek to AndesCon dominated the headlines. The city's corporate world was alight with speculation, while media outlets clamored for interviews and insider details. Every morning, Ari woke up to a flood of messages, but he remained composed and focused on the monumental task ahead of him.

In SummitTek's sleek boardroom, the tension was palpable as executives, lawyers, and AndesCon representatives worked tirelessly to iron out the finer points of the deal. Strategies were debated, contracts scrutinized, and tempers occasionally flared. Yet amid the chaos, Ari remained calm.

Sitting at his desk, reviewing the final documents, Ari felt the *Spirit of Wisdom* nearby, her aura a gentle reminder of how far he had come. The journey from a powerful CEO driven by ambition to a man seeking God's purpose brought a deep sense of gratitude to his heart. He wasn't smiling because of the billions he stood to gain, but because of the freedom he felt in surrendering his old life.

Meanwhile, Abner paced the executive suite, his brow furrowed, the weight of the moment carved into the lines of his face. To him, SummitTek was more than a business; it was the Keshet legacy, the culmination of decades of vision, sweat, and sacrifice. And Ari was about to give it up.

Finally, Abner stopped, turned, and faced his son, a mix of disbelief and pleading on his face. His voice was tight with frustration and concern. "Are you absolutely sure about this? Selling SummitTek isn't just a business move; it's your legacy, Ari. And it's my legacy, too!"

Ari looked up from the papers on the table, his gaze was calm. "Yes, Dad. I'm sure. It's time to move forward... to focus on what truly matters for this moment."

His father sighed deeply, rubbing his temples like he was trying to massage away the future. "I just don't want you to regret this. We have poured everything into this company. It was built to outlive us, to serve this family for generations."

"I know," Ari said, respectfully. "And I'll always be grateful. You and Grandpa Reuben didn't just build a company; you built a foundation. SummitTek was your vision, your legacy. But I believe

God's calling me to build something different on top of it. Something eternal. This isn't just a transaction, it's a turning point.

The wealth you created... I'm going to use it to plant something greater. Something that outlasts profits and stock charts. Something you will be proud of someday."

Abner's voice dropped to a near whisper. "But this was supposed to go to your children... their inheritance."

Ari smiled, lifting his hand in quiet reassurance. "If I ever have children, they'll receive something better than stock options. They'll get the truth. Integrity. A legacy built on faith, not just dollars."

His father stood frozen for a moment, then exhaled hard and threw up his hands in reluctant surrender. He didn't fully understand the path Ari was taking, but something in his son's conviction stopped him from pushing further. For now, he would accept it, even though he didn't understand it.

Later, as the ink dried on the final documents, the announcement went out: SummitTek employees would receive generous shares of the sale proceeds. Cheers erupted throughout headquarters. Shock turned to joy as the news spread, and people's lives changed in an instant. The building buzzed with celebration. Glasses clinked, hugs were exchanged, and phones lit up with calls home. For once, legacy wasn't just about the family name; it was shared with others.

Ari thought as he watched the joy ripple through the company, that was exactly how it should be.

Standing on the sidelines, Abner watched Ari with an expression no longer filled with anger but something closer to reluctant respect. He couldn't deny the transformation in his son; the peace and strength that radiated from him were undeniable.

With the sale complete, Ari wasted no time setting his following plans into motion. Once a monument to his success, the mansion became the center of new beginnings. He began selling his collectibles, ensuring that even the smallest items would find meaningful homes.

Family treasures, like the Hanukkah menorah and ornate Seder plate, were carefully packed for safekeeping, their sentimental value outweighing any monetary worth.

"It feels amazing to pay off my friends," Ari said with a chuckle, his voice brimming with gratitude. "With interest, of course. Although knowing Moose, he's probably already spent the money on... snacks."

Elinor laughed, shaking her head. "He probably has a spreadsheet titled, 'How Ari Saved My Snack Fund.'"

Ari grinned. "Honestly, I should've charged him for the trauma of hearing his campfire jokes on repeat. That's where the real debt lies. But hey, at least now he can finally buy that hot tub he's been rambling about."

Elinor raised an eyebrow, her lips twitching with amusement. "Wait, Moose? A hot tub? Seriously?"

Ari smirked, leaning back in his chair. "Oh, absolutely. He's convinced it's a 'multi-functional investment.' Recovery tool by day, conversation pit by night."

Elinor couldn't hold back her laughter. "Let me guess, he's already planning to host 'Hot Tub Summit Meetings' complete with snacks and questionable trail maps? Or is that trail maps and questionable snacks?"

Ari chuckled. "Exactly, knowing Moose, the 'meeting' will devolve into a *heated* debate over which hiking trail reigns supreme, fueled by corn chips and bad puns."

Elinor wiped a tear of laughter from her eye. "And probably some ridiculous plan to haul the hot tub up a mountain for 'altitude training.'"

Ari grinned. "Honestly, I wouldn't put it past him." He then picked up the little *Red Book*, its supernatural pages grounding him in the moment. His smile softened into something deeper. "This is just the beginning, Elinor," he said, his voice laced with conviction. Then, with a crooked smile, he added, "With God, and the patience to endure Moose's hiking stories, all things are possible."

Their laughter lingered, lightening the gravity of the moment and blending perfectly with the glow of the path that lay ahead.

Triumphant Transition

Before long, the big announcement to the media was set. Ari knew this was the final step in his transformation when his old life would officially give way to his new, purpose-driven life.

As Ari prepared for the press conference, his thoughts drifted back to his recent encounters, the persecuted Christians in China, the *Spirit of the Lord* in Israel, and the unwavering support of Elinor and his friends.

He had faced literal and metaphorical giants and emerged stronger and more grounded in his trust in God.

Ari felt a deep peace envelop him as he stood before the cameras, announcing his decision to sell SummitTek and devote his life to serving others. He had let go of his pride, pushing away Stolz's persuasive voice, and embraced the higher calling Jesus had called him to. In that moment, surrounded by the press and the people he loved and supported, Ari knew he was exactly where he was meant to be, ready to serve the Lord.

The week following SummitTek's sale to AndesCon was a whirlwind of activity and emotion. News outlets blazed with headlines: *"Billionaire Ari Keshet Sells SummitTek to AndesCon: A New Era Begins"* and *"From CEO to Philanthropist: Ari Keshet's Bold Move."*

Ari's mansion became a nerve center of corporate maneuvering, with AndesCon executives roaming the halls and conducting high-powered negotiations in every available corner.

Amid this chaos, Ari remained remarkably calm and content. He had orchestrated the sale meticulously, ensuring every SummitTek employee received a generous share of the profits. Watching his former colleagues celebrate their new fortunes brought him profound fulfillment. SummitTek would thrive under new leadership, and he was leaving behind a team poised for continued success.

Not everyone shared his enthusiasm, however. Abner still struggled to hide his disappointment behind a stoic facade. Forced into full retirement from the company he had nurtured so fiercely for several decades, he wrestled with a swirling tide of anger, confusion, and a reluctant respect for his son's daring change.

As the weeks passed, the business world marveled at SummitTek's seamless integration into AndesCon's portfolio. Employees rejoiced, and congratulatory toasts echoed through old and new corporate halls.

Quietly stepping out of the spotlight he had once reveled in, Ari found himself more prosperous than ever; several billion dollars still rested in his accounts. Yet, beyond the numbers, he felt freer than ever, ready to embrace his new purpose with open arms.

Chapter 23

Million-Dollar Garage Sale

Wasting no time liquidating his empire of excess, Ari embraced a simpler lifestyle with the determination of a man trying to undo years of bad shopping decisions. The mansion was listed for sale, not as a desperate move, but as a deliberate choice. The mansion, once a monument to wealth, hit the market with a price tag that could fund a small nation.

His prized art collection, the million-dollar paintings he once used to impress guests, who barely glanced at them, was all auctioned off. Their proceeds were funneled into charities and mission-based organizations. Prized collectibles, million-dollar artwork, rare sculptures, and antique furniture that once screamed, "*Look how rich I am!*", were now vanishing faster than a clearance rack at a luxury boutique on pay day.

Bidding wars erupted over his more eccentric items, a golden statue of a Greek god. Ari felt quite awkward about ever purchasing such a thing, even though the art museum was grateful to receive it.

His designer furniture, handcrafted by artisans with names he couldn't pronounce, was auctioned off for staggering sums. The best part was the stunned reactions of inner-city mission directors receiving unexpected million-dollar donations.

Local outreach directors choked on their coffee when a million-dollar check arrived from *The Keshet Foundation: L.O.A.F. Luxury Offered As Function, "Because our fancy stuff can help people."* "This must be a typo?" one mission director murmured, staring at all the zeros.

"Nope," his colleague whispered. "Ari Keshet just went full Apostle Paul on us."

"And if I read this right, we also now own two Rembrandts?" He scratched his head, wondering, "Do we hang them next to the soup kitchen sign?"

Meanwhile, the once-pristine office looked like a thrift store in transition. He picked up an old photograph of himself as a boy, standing next to his father during a long-forgotten family trip. He traced the edges, feeling the weight of what had once mattered to him and what matters now. Back then, success meant admiration. Now, it means surrender.

The mansion, the prestige, the need to impress... it had all been an illusion. Now, his wealth wasn't a badge of pride; it was a tool for service. A means to uplift others instead of himself.

Divine Encounter in the Mansion

Then, without warning, a faint white glow emanated from the room's corner. At first, Ari thought it was a trick of the light. But it grew brighter, radiating a warmth that wasn't physical but deeply spiritual. The magenta *orb* of the *Fear of the Lord* quietly stirred to life. Its strong presence was undeniable as Ari trembled.

He set the photo down and rose to his feet, his heart pounding. The light expanded, filling the room with a holy brilliance that made every shadow retreat. He could feel it, not just see it, an overwhelming sense of peace and reverence wrapping around him like a blanket. And then, the *Spirit of the Lord* appeared.

Radiant and majestic, He stood before Ari, an image unmistakably that of Jesus Christ in the Spirit. His presence filled the study with humbling, comforting holiness, as if heaven had drawn near. The air was charged, and the faint fragrance of frankincense and almond blossoms lingered like a sacred whisper. Ari's knees buckled, and he sank to the floor, overwhelmed by reverence and awe.

"HELLO, ARIEL," the Spirit spoke, His voice deep and powerful, carrying both authority and a love so profound it pierced through every corner of Ari's soul. "I AM PLEASED WITH YOUR OBEDIENCE, WITH THE STEPS YOU HAVE TAKEN ON THIS JOURNEY OF SURRENDER."

Tears welled in Ari's eyes as he lowered his head, unable to meet the radiant gaze that seemed to pierce right through him.

The weight of the Spirit's presence pressed on him, not as a burden, but as a purifying fire that lifted and humbled him simultaneously.

"YOU ARE LEARNING TO LET GO OF PRIDE AND WORLDLY ATTACHMENTS," the Spirit continued, His tone firm, "BUT YOUR JOURNEY IS NOT YET COMPLETE. THE WEALTH YOU HOLD IS NOT INHERENTLY EVIL. IT IS A TOOL, ONE THAT MUST SERVE GOD'S PURPOSE. LET THE MONEY SERVE YOU, BUT NEVER LET THE LOVE OF MONEY RULE OVER YOU AGAIN."

Ari glanced up, his voice trembling with emotion. "Lord, I wish to use it for good, for Your kingdom, and to help others. Yet... I have my worries. What if it traps me? What if I fall into worldly Pride again?"

The Spirit's face softened with compassion. His eyes twinkled with warmth and divine understanding. "YOUR NEWFOUND HUMILITY PLEASES ME. A WILLING HEART, THAT'S WHERE TRUE STRENGTH BEGINS... AND DON'T WORRY, I'LL GUIDE YOU.

NOW, I WANT YOU TO USE WHAT I'VE ENTRUSTED TO YOU. FOR EXAMPLE, THAT JET OF YOURS?" The Spirit gestured with amusement. "YOU ARE GOING TO NEED IT. EXCHANGE ITS INDULGENT PAST FOR A PRACTICAL FUTURE, A HIGHER CALLING, YOU MIGHT SAY.

THINK OF IT AS THE DIVINE DELIVERY SERVICE, SUPPLIES, PEOPLE, BIBLES, IT'S ALL PART OF THE FATHER'S MISSION."

Ari blinked, his mind momentarily short-circuiting at the thought of his prized Gulfstream G700, once stocked with caviar and imported wines, would now haul Bibles and humanitarian aid.

A surprised laugh escaped him despite the weight of the moment. "I hadn't exactly pictured it that way, Lord," Ari admitted, rubbing the back of his neck. "Who knew a luxury jet could be so useful...and holy?"

The Spirit chuckled. "WELL, YOU SHOULD'VE SEEN THE ORIGINAL BLUEPRINTS NOAH HAD WRITTEN UP FOR THE ARK, ALL THE SELECTED ANIMALS, AND HE STILL HAD ROOM FOR SOUVENIRS!"

Ari laughed; the unexpected humor lightened the moment and filled him with deep joy. Even in the weight of his calling, laughter found its place.

The Spirit's gaze softened, "I HAVE PLANS FOR ALL THINGS. JUST ASK THE BOY WHO GAVE TWO FISH AND FIVE LOAVES OF BREAD. WHEN YOU SURRENDER THEM TO GOD, NOTHING GOES TO WASTE. EVEN THOSE THINGS YOU BELIEVED WERE MERELY SUPERFICIAL OR EXCESSIVE, I CAN USE THEM, TOO."

As the Spirit touched Ari's shoulder, warmth spread through him, a holy fire igniting every fiber of his being. Peace and courage coursed through him, solidifying his commission. The light surrounding the Spirit grew brighter, filling the room with a brilliance that was almost too much to bear.

"GO, ARIEL, AND BE A FAITHFUL STEWARD. CARRY MY WORD, MY LOVE, AND MY LIGHT TO WHEREVER I SEND YOU."

The room shifted in response. A radiant swirl of light emerged, and colors danced like living entities.

As the *Spirit of the Lord* proclaimed each Spirit, "FEAR OF THE LORD," magenta rays shimmered with reverence. A vibrant red light pulsed boldly, brimming with energy, as He acknowledged "REVELATION KNOWLEDGE." Golden hues flowed steadily, their rhythm almost soothing, with the mention of "COUNSEL." Deep blue colors burst like waves of intense energy at "POWER AND MIGHT," while green spirals twirled softly, exuding the brilliance of "WISDOM." Cyan blue streaks darted playfully and joyfully as He declared, "UNDERSTANDING."

The colors were alive, weaving together in a symphony of harmony, each distinct yet blending perfectly into pure white light.

Ari watched in awe. His breath caught in his chest as the colored lights circled him. It was as if the Spirits rejoiced in his growth.

Swirling faster, their jubilant dance intensifying as if celebrating the *Spirit of the Lord's* words. Ari felt their energy coursing through him, igniting his spirit with a kaleidoscope of joy and divine strength. It was no longer just a vision but a mark on his spirit and his soul.

The room gradually returned to stillness, but the atmosphere remained charged. Ari locked eyes with the Spirit, feeling the warmth in those eyes reflect everlasting love and encouragement.

"JUST LIKE THE MEANING OF YOUR NAME, ARIEL, I WANT YOU TO MOVE FORWARD WITH THE COURAGE OF A LION." The Spirit's words resonated with deep power.

As the light faded, the room fell silent, yet it was anything but ordinary. The air held a familiar scent of frankincense and almond blossoms, serving as a reminder that heaven had touched earth in this space. Ari stayed on his knees, his heart pounding with unshakable determination.

This was not a fleeting moment; it was a commissioning, a sacred charge shaping every step of Ari's journey moving forward. Rising to his feet, he sensed a strange yet comforting sensation.

A tingling coursed through the soles of his feet, spreading upward like a warm current, as if the very floor beneath him had come alive.

If peace had a tangible presence, this was it. It flowed up his body, from his feet to his head. Steady and grounded. As he shifted his weight, the tingling didn't fade; instead, it deepened his sense of connection. He felt perfectly balanced. Ari recalled the scripture from Ephesians, "...FEET FITTED WITH THE GOSPEL OF PEACE..."

And in that moment, he felt the tingling in his feet anchor him. Ari knew he was now equipped to step into God's purpose.

Party Planning

The quiet stillness of Ari's study, filled with the lingering presence of holiness, gave way to a flurry of activity that would transform his life once more. Ari's encounter with the Lord had left him grounded and ready to embrace the next chapter of his journey.

That next chapter, however, wasn't just about moving forward; it was about celebrating the gift of love.

"All hands on deck!" Gottschall declared the next morning, practically dragging Ari from his bed. With the sale of SummitTek finalized, Ari had the time and the team to plan the wedding fit for a King. This was not going to be a simple matter. This would be a week-long celebration worthy of the God who united them and the love story that had defied odds, mountains, and corporate scandals.

The summer wedding began with splendor and a hint of chaos. Ari and Elinor had spared no effort or expense in crafting a magnificent Messianic Jewish celebration. Pentecost, a season symbolizing unity and renewal, provided the perfect backdrop for this lavish affair.

Once a symbol of excess, the mansion had undergone a remarkable transformation into a five-star resort. It was so magnificent it could have served as the backdrop for a royal prime-time drama. Hired staff swarmed like a well-oiled, highly caffeinated machine. The caterers wielded trays of gourmet delights with the precision of surgeons. Florists worked their magic on elaborate arrangements that looked like they might sprout legs and dance at any moment.

Gottschall, clipboard in hand, commanded the chaos like a seasoned general who didn't trust her troops. She issued rapid-fire instructions to decorators, servers, and even the professional wedding planners, whose carefully laid plans were no match for her relentless pursuit of perfection.

"No, no, no," she barked, gesturing toward a floral arch. "The roses need to be evenly spaced. Do I need to do this myself?"

The head wedding planner, a seasoned professional with years of experience in high-profile events, opened her mouth to respond, but Gottschall was already moving on, pointing at a server arranging appetizers.

"That platter should go on the right side of the table, not the left," Gottschall said, her tone leaving no room for argument. "We're not savages. Symmetry matters."

Moose, watching from a safe distance, smirked. "She's terrifying. Highly efficient, but terrifying."

"Think she's ever considered a career in the military?" asked one of the wedding staff, glancing nervously at Gottschall, who was now inspecting the placement of the aisle runner with the intensity of a bomb squad technician.

"She doesn't trust anyone to do it right," Moose laughed, leaning on a chair. "I bet she's got a backup clipboard in case that one breaks under the strain."

As the ceremony neared, Gottschall cornered the lead wedding planner. Her clipboard raised like a weapon. "Are the chairs perfectly aligned? Did the musicians rehearse one more time? And why haven't I seen the final dessert display? I need eyes on those cakes, people!"

The planner sighed, forcing a polite smile. "Ms. Gottschall, everything is under control. We do this for a living."

"Not under my watch," Gottschall quipped, adjusting her glasses. "This is the wedding of the century, and it would be over my dead body if a single petal were out of place."

Despite her relentless micromanaging, the event came together flawlessly, though not without a few exasperated glances from the professional planners. As the sun dipped lower in the sky, the venue glowed with fairy lights and a perfectly arranged floral canopy.

Moose crept up to Ari as the final touches were being made. "You owe Gottschall a bonus or a vacation. She basically took over the entire event."

Ari chuckled, watching Gottschall reposition a centerpiece for the third time. "She wouldn't have it any other way."

As the guests arrived, Gottschall finally set down her clipboard, surveying the venue with a satisfied smile. "Perfect," she muttered as if she'd single-handedly orchestrated this tiny universe. And in her mind, she had.

Invitations had flown far and wide, summoning loved ones and collaborators from around the globe. Overseas family members arrived feeling jet-lagged but delighted. Their luggage was packed with everything from wedding outfits to questionable "snacks" that had been smuggled past customs.

The Peruvian rescue team, who had once seen Ari at his absolute worst, showed up in awe of the mansion's grandeur. SummitTek and AndesCon employees, fresh off celebrating their generous stock payouts, turned the wedding into a networking event on steroids. The atmosphere was electric. Chandeliers sparkled like the night sky, and floral arrangements overflowed from every corner in a riot of vivid colors that even the hummingbirds paused to admire.

The buzz of last-minute preparations mingled with excited chatter and the occasional squeal of a decorator chasing down rogue helium balloons.

As the crowd gathered, Moose, dressed in a suit that barely contained his enthusiasm, or his love of hors d'oeuvres, leaned toward Ari and grinned. "This might be the biggest summit we've climbed yet. And I didn't even need a harness!"

Gottschall, overhearing, shot him a look. "Moose, if you touch one more canapé before the guests, I'm demoting you to bathroom duty."

Moose promptly saluted with a grin and made a theatrical exit.

The expansive lawn of Ari's mansion had been transformed into a breathtaking outdoor venue. Rows of white chairs adorned with delicate floral arrangements stretched out beneath a canopy of string lights that twinkled like stars. The scent of blooming jasmine mingled with the fresh summer breeze as guests eagerly filed into their seats, their hushed conversations a mix of anticipation and speculation.

Overhead, the late afternoon sun cast a golden glow across the scene, and the backdrop of the Rocky Mountains stood majestic as if nature itself had RSVP'd to witness the union. The soft hum of the string quartet added an air of elegance, their music weaving a serene atmosphere as everyone awaited the bride's arrival.

But Ari couldn't help but notice his father, Abner, was absent. A pang of concern crept into his thoughts.

Had the untraditional nature of the wedding, blending faiths and cultures, been too much for him to handle?

The Grand Wedding

At the front, Ari stood in place beneath a beautifully crafted chuppah adorned with cascading vines and white roses. He adjusted his tie for the hundredth time, his nerves dancing between excitement and impatience.

Standing proudly by his side was Moose. He leaned over and poked, "Relax, boss. She didn't change her mind... at least, not that I know of."

Ari shot him a glare. "Not helping."

"But, hey... I'm sorry about your dad, though." Moose tried to show sympathy.

The music shifted, and a ripple of silence swept over the crowd. Heads turned toward the grand staircase that led down from the mansion's terrace, the spot where Elinor would make her entrance.

The double doors opened... and there she was.

Her gown, simple yet breathtaking, cascaded like liquid silk, each step unveiling delicate lace details that seemed to dance in the sunlight. And then, with a touch of whimsy that only Elinor could pull off, a glimpse of fancy white cowboy boots peeked out as she walked, a charming nod to her down-to-earth roots amidst all the grandeur. It was uniquely her, blending elegance with the playful spirit everyone had come to adore.

But the real surprise wasn't just Elinor's radiant beauty, it was her escort... Abner Keshet.

The formidable patriarch stood proudly at her side. Known for his stern demeanor, he wore an expression of unexpected warmth and quiet pride.

The sight of Abner guiding Elinor down the staircase sent ripples of astonishment through the gathering, including Ari.

"Wait... is that Ari's dad?" someone whispered, their voice carrying just enough to spark a few chuckles.

Another guest muttered, "Never thought I'd see the day Abner would accept a Christian into his family."

Abner held his head high upon hearing the faint murmurs. This moment transcended past tensions, signaling the beginnings of a deeper familial bond.

Hidden cameras clicked furiously in the bushes as the media, desperate for an exclusive, captured every moment.

As they reached the white aisle runner, Moose leaned toward Ari again and muttered in a low voice. "Well, I'll be. The old man's got a heart, after all."

"I am pleasantly shocked," Ari whispered back at Moose.

The string quartet swelled into a joyous melody as Elinor and Abner made their way down the aisle. Guests craned their necks, some snapping photos and others watching in awe. The image of Abner Keshet escorting his soon-to-be daughter-in-law wasn't just unexpected, it was monumental!

Little did anyone know that Abner's heart had softened upon learning of Elinor's loss of her father years ago, leaving a void that no one could honestly fill. He couldn't bear the thought of her walking down the aisle without a father figure, so he chose to embrace that role, a gesture that revealed the quiet transformation within him, despite his initial concerns about the match.

As Abner and Elinor arrived at the front, Abner paused. For the first time in years, the tension that usually filled his eyes was gone. In its place was a serene acceptance, a recognition of the love his son had discovered.

He faced Ari, locking eyes with him. "Take care of her."

"I will," Ari's voice was thick with emotion, but confident.

Abner placed Elinor's hand in Ari's, lingering silently... taking in the moment. He took a deep breath and exhaled, turning slowly, and then sat next to Iris, who discreetly dabbed at her eyes with a tissue. A mix of both happiness and concern etched her face.

As Ari and Elinor stood beneath the chuppah, the golden rays of the late afternoon sun bathed them in a warm glow as though nature itself had joined in the celebration. The chuppah, adorned with cascading flowers, symbolized the home they would build together, a sanctuary filled with love, faith, and shared purpose.

The ceremony began, blending the rich traditions of a Jewish wedding with the faith in Jesus Christ. The rabbi and pastor alternated seamlessly, creating a union of heritage and hope, old and new, Jews and Gentiles together.

Ari's heart swelled as his eyes met Elinor's, her tears shimmering in the sunlight, matching the sparkle in her light green eyes. Their vows were simple yet profound, each word a promise of faith and love. "I do," their voices trembling with emotion, their gazes locked as though the world around them had faded away.

Joy sparkled at the moment of the breaking of the glass. Ari's bright smile appeared as the rabbi explained the deep meaning behind the custom. "This isn't just tradition," the rabbi said. "It's a symbol of the fragility of life, and the sacred weight of commitment. Once the glass is shattered, it can never be restored to its original state. The break is permanent, just like the vows made today. Marriage is a blessed covenant that changes you. There's no going back to what was before... only forward, into something new."

With one swift motion, Ari stomped on the wrapped glass, and the unmistakable sound of the shattering crunch reverberated through the crowd. The guests rose to their feet, cheering, "Mazel tov!" Their voices echoed across the sprawling lawn, mingling with the laughter and applause.

Then, under the open sky and the warm embrace of the setting sun, Ari and Elinor shared their first kiss as husband and wife. It was a kiss transcending words, a gentle yet fervent meeting of souls. Ari's hand cradled her face with reverence while Elinor's fingers lingered on his chest, feeling the steady rhythm of his heartbeat. Time seemed to stand still, the world narrowing to just the two.

The crowd, momentarily silenced by the sheer beauty of the moment, burst into applause and cheers once more. Elinor smiled against his lips, and Ari couldn't resist pulling her in for another brief, tender kiss. His forehead rested against hers as they laughed softly, overwhelmed by the joy of the moment.

Moose, ever the comic relief, leaned toward Gottschall. "I give them a 10 out of 10 for the kiss. The glass-smashing? Solid 8. Needs work."

Gottschall rolled her eyes, but even she couldn't suppress a smile.

The ceremony concluded with the newlyweds turning to face their guests, hand in hand, their love radiating as brightly as the golden light surrounding them. It was a day of faith, blended traditions, and sweet romance, a timeless testament to love, blessed by heaven and witnessed by all.

Just as the applause swelled, a breathtaking rainbow appeared in the clear, cloudless sky, an extraordinary sight given the absence of rain. Gasps rippled through the crowd, and Ari's heart swelled with awe. At that moment, he knew it was a sign from the Seven Spirits of God, their radiant approval woven into the vibrant hues arching above.

Seven Days of Celebration

What followed was a celebration unlike any other. For seven days, the mansion became a haven of joy and laughter. Guests danced beneath starlit skies, feasted on gourmet dishes, and toasted the couple with the finest wines. Elinor's warmth and grace captivated everyone, and her laughter was the soundtrack of the festivities.

Moose, true to form, dominated the dance floor, dragging reluctant guests into his whirlwind of energetic antics. But the real surprise came when Carlos, who had harbored a romantic crush on Maria Gottschall since Peru, seized the opportunity to invite her for a dance. With a mix of determination and charm, he extended his hand.

"Just one dance," Carlos pleaded, his smile as dazzling as the chandeliers above.

Gottschall hesitated, her usual composure faltering for a moment. "Fine," she said with a mock sigh, allowing herself to be led. "But if you step on my toes, I'm billing you for this."

As the music shifted to an upbeat salsa rhythm, Carlos twirled her with surprising skill, his excitement barely contained. "Maria, you are a natural!" he said, his admiration evident.

To everyone's astonishment, including her own, Gottschall relaxed into the dance, her laughter rising above the music. "I had no idea I could move like this!" she admitted, her cheeks flushed.

Carlos's eyes sparkled. "There is a lot you need to discover," he sported a playful grin, spinning her gracefully.

Gottschall saw beyond Carlos's usual demeanor and found him handsomely charming. As the dance ended, their shared laughter lingered in the air, and she caught herself thinking, Maybe there's more to this man than I thought.

Meanwhile, Moose, noticing their chemistry, gave Carlos a not-so-subtle thumbs-up before diving into his next over-the-top dance routine.

Reflection of the Celebration

Each day of the week-long celebration offered new delights: a poolside luncheon with laughter echoing over the water, a string quartet serenading under the stars, and even a surprise fireworks display that painted the night sky with brilliance. The festivities were not just about Ari and Elinor but a tribute to the friends, family, and faith that had carried them to this moment.

As the final evening wound down, Ari and Elinor stood hand in hand on the mansion's grand staircase, gazing out over the bustling scene below. The guests, full of joy and memories, mingled and shared stories while the Denver skyline twinkled beyond the windows like a quiet witness to their journey.

"This is just the beginning," Ari whispered.

Elinor leaned into him, her head resting gently on his shoulder. "With the Lord guiding us, it's going to be an amazing adventure."

They stood for a moment longer, savoring the last echoes of laughter and the warmth of the celebration. Yet amidst the joy, there was a bittersweet undertone. The mansion, filled with life and memories, would soon be sold. Its grand halls and sprawling grounds had been the setting for a transformative chapter in Ari's life, but now it was time to find a place they could call their own, a home that would be theirs to share.

As they stepped outside to take one last look at the moonlit grounds, Elinor leaned into Ari, her voice low and teasing.

"We'll find the perfect little love nest," she said, her eyes sparkling with a flirty gleam. "Something cozy, just big enough for us, and maybe a hundred houseplants."

Ari laughed, wrapping himself around her in a body hug. "As long as you're there, it'll be perfect. Even if it's a tiny cabin in the woods."

Elinor grinned, "A cabin might need some upgrades. Like a cozy fireplace, a big kitchen... and a greenhouse for all my house plants."

Ari raised an eyebrow, showing concern. "All your house plants? Elinor, you need more than a greenhouse. You'll need a massive conservatory!"

She playfully nudged him. "Don't tempt me."

The night settled into a peaceful hush as the couple reflected on their joy and the promise of a future built on love, faith, and the shared adventure ahead... complete with ample space for Elinor's plants.

A Divine Gift

As the last strains of wedding music faded and exhausted guests dragged their suitcases toward waiting cars, Ari and Elinor found themselves alone in the mansion for the first time... well, almost alone. The housekeepers still roamed like graceful phantoms, tidying up evidence of the week-long festivities. After seven days of nonstop celebration, the sudden quiet felt almost suspicious, like the moment after a roller coaster ride when your brain is still catching up.

"So... what now?" Elinor glanced around, taking in the vast, empty grandeur.

They looked around, half-expecting a mariachi band to pop out of a closet just to keep the momentum going.

Ari exhaled, running a hand through his hair. "Honestly?

I think this is the first time I've heard my own thoughts all week."

"Anything interesting?" she teased.

He grinned. "Mostly that I'm starving and slightly concerned that I might never get this confetti out of my hair."

They exchanged smiles, hands intertwined, as they soaked in the magnitude of what had just transpired. While strolling to the Mansion's study, the atmosphere began to shift, a sacred energy stirring in the air.

A soft, radiant light filled the room, and the magenta orb within Ari's spirit blazed with brilliance. Elinor gasped, her fingers tightening around Ari's hand as a divine presence enveloped them. Her heart raced, and she instinctively stepped closer to him.

Suddenly, the *Spirit of the Lord* appeared as the *Spirit of Jesus Christ*, His radiance majestic and awe-inspiring.

Elinor's knees buckled, her breath catching in her throat. She had always believed by faith, but now, standing in the presence of the Lord, she was nearly overwhelmed with holy fear. Ari gently guided her to kneel beside him, his own heart trembling with reverence.

"YOU BOTH HAVE DONE WELL, ARIEL AND ELINOR," the Spirit said, His voice tranquil yet majestic, resonating with love and authority. "I AM PLEASED WITH YOUR SURRENDER AND OBEDIENCE. AS A WEDDING GIFT TO YOU BOTH, I AM GIVING YOU THE VACATION HOUSE IN CAPERNAUM, ISRAEL. YOU ALREADY HAVE THE KEY; IT'S YOURS. MAZEL TOV!"

The light blue *key* suddenly appeared in Ari's pocket, glowing softly with divine energy. His voice was trembling with gratitude. "Thank you, Lord," he whispered.

Beside him, Elinor was speechless, her wide eyes fixed on the Lord in awe and wonder. "Is this... real?" she whispered, her voice barely audible, trembling with a mix of terror and awe.

Ari gave her hand a reassuring squeeze. "It's real," he whispered. "It's Him, It's the *Spirit of the Lord*."

As they knelt together, the *Seven Spirits of God* manifested in radiant harmony. The *Spirit of the Lord* stood at the center, exuding a holy, white light that radiated love and power. To one side stood *Wisdom, Counsel, and Revelation Knowledge*; their auras shimmered. To the other side stood *Understanding, Power and Might, and the Fear of the Lord*, glowing in ethereal light.

Elinor's breath came in shallow gasps, her mind struggling to comprehend the magnificence before her. "Ari..." she whispered, clutching his arm. "This... this is more than I ever imagined."

Ari's voice was steady despite the emotion brimming in his chest. "I know. I was terrified the first time I met them... and I still am, but look, they're here to bless us."

They had guided Ari on his journey from pride to humility, from worldly ambition to divine purpose. And now, they extended their blessing to Elinor, her trembling heart gradually filling with peace.

As the light faded, Ari and Elinor gazed at the ethereal vision before them. The *Seven Spirits* stood in radiant harmony, their luminous forms resembling the seven-branched menorah. Each branch shimmered with its unique color but blended into pure white light, forming a divine symbol of unity. This image etched itself in their minds, a sacred assurance they would never walk alone.

Rooted in the *Spirit of the Lord* and guided by six other Spirits, Ari and Elinor felt the weight of their mission. This moment was a commission, a heavenly mandate to spread the light and truth of the Gospel. After a last look at the newlyweds, the *Seven Spirits* faded, leaving Ari and Elinor awestruck with unprecedented joy.

Filled with excitement, they wasted no time packing for Israel, looking forward to a time of rest and romantic discovery.

"*Honeymoon in the Holy Land*, what an unexpected blessing!"

Romantic Honeymoon and a Divine Encounter

The summer breeze and the waves of the Sea of Galilee created a romantic atmosphere as Ari and Elinor returned from an evening walk along its peaceful shores. The serene beauty of their new life together in Capernaum felt like a continuous gift. As they entered their new home, they were greeted by a breathtaking sight.

A seven-candle menorah stood ablaze on the dining room table, its flames swaying gently as if responding to an unseen melody. Beside it, a freshly baked loaf of golden bread and a glass of deep red wine appeared, exuding a warmth that permeated the room. The fragrances of almond blossoms and warm bread enveloped them, creating an atmosphere so sacred that it felt like heaven had reached into their humble dwelling.

Elinor froze, her hand tightening around Ari's. "Did you, do that?" she began, but her voice faltered as she stared at the miraculous scene.

Ari shook his head, his eyes wide with wonder. "No... I didn't," he whispered.

Elinor gasped, sinking into a nearby chair. "It's Him," she said, her voice trembling with emotion. "The Lord is here. He's inviting us to communion."

Ari stepped forward cautiously, his heart pounding as the menorah's flames flickered with life. The sacredness of the moment pressed on him, heavy yet comforting, as if God Himself had entered their home.

He reached for Elinor's hand, his voice low and reverent. "Let's not keep Him waiting." Together, they sat at the table, overwhelmed by the Lord's presence.

Ari broke the bread, his hands trembling, and passed a piece to Elinor. Lifting the glass of wine, he spoke with quiet reverence, "This is His body... and this is His blood. Let us remember His sacrifice, the price He paid to save us from God's wrath."

They partook in communion, the bread's warmth and the wine's richness filling their spirits. It felt as though the very essence of love and grace had been poured into their hearts, sealing the covenant they shared with Him.

And then, the room began to shimmer. Lights swirled around them, the colors dancing in harmony. The *Seven Spirits* seemed to celebrate, their luminous presence forming a divine symphony of energy and joy.

Still chewing a piece of bread, Ari nearly choked as he exclaimed, "The Spirits... they're celebrating!" He coughed, quickly recovering as Elinor laughed softly, patting his back.

"Ari," she teased, "maybe finish chewing before you narrate."

He grinned sheepishly and coughed. "Didn't expect a light show with dinner."

The colors swirled faster, enveloping the room in a radiant embrace before gradually fading into stillness. The menorah remained steady, its light casting intricate patterns on the walls.

"This house isn't just a home," Ari said softly, his voice filled with awe. "It's a sanctuary, a gift from God to rest and prepare for what's next."

Elinor's gaze lingered on the glowing menorah. "And it's a promise," she whispered. "No matter where we go in the world, His presence will always be with us."

Sitting in the menorah's warm glow, they inhaled the sweet aroma. Their hearts swelled with gratitude. They realized this marked not just the start of their life together but also a greater mission guided by the Holy Spirit.

A Holy Dilemma: To Blow or Not To Blow?

Later that night, as they prepared for bed, Ari and Elinor stood side by side in the kitchen, staring at the glowing menorah like two detectives examining an unsolvable mystery.

"So..." Ari began, crossing his arms. "Do we blow it out? Or leave it?"

Elinor tilted her head. "What if blowing it offends God? It's not exactly your average candelabra."

Ari squinted at the menorah, his brow furrowing. "But if we leave it burning, that feels like a fire hazard. What's the divine protocol for this?"

They exchanged a glance, a mix of reverence and playful exasperation. Ari leaned in slightly as if studying the flames would provide a heavenly user manual. Elinor bit her lip to stifle a giggle.

And then, as if answering their unspoken debate, the menorah shimmered. The light grew brighter for a fleeting moment, the flames pulsing like a heartbeat, before the entire menorah began to dissolve. Its form softened into a cascade of light, fading into the air. Within seconds, the table stood empty, bathed in stillness.

Ari blinked, his arms dropping to his sides. "Well," he said with a dry chuckle, "looks like God handles His own clean-up."

Elinor let out a soft laugh, shaking her head. Ari slipped an arm around her waist, pulling her close as they turned to head upstairs. "Remind me to add 'divine fire safety' to the list of things I'm grateful for."

Continuing the laughter, she leaned into him. As they ascended the stairs, the house seemed to exhale, settling into a serene stillness. The quiet hum of divine presence lingered in the air, wrapping them in peace.

When they reached the top of the stairs, Ari glanced over his shoulder one last time. "Just making sure it doesn't pull a surprise encore," he muttered.

Elinor rolled her eyes affectionately, nudging him toward the bed. "If God wants a midnight light show, I'm sure He'll let us know."

They shared a moment before settling into bed, the memory etched in their hearts. Whatever awaited them on their supernatural journey, they knew they would confront it together, anchored in love and guided by the *Seven Spirits of God*.

Epilogue

Ari and Elinor Keshet

A few years later, life had settled into a strange but wonderful new normal for Ari and Elinor. High above the Atlantic, Ari reclined in the plush seat of his Gulfstream jet, though "plush" might have been generous since their two children had decorated it with stickers, snack crumbs, and the occasional crayon masterpiece. Elinor, radiant and relaxed, gently soothed their fidgety son while their curious daughter launched a series of important theological inquiries about whether alpacas prayed before grazing.

Moose had joined the journey this time, and as they soared above continents, their children alternated between giggling at Moose's jokes and asking if penguins ever attended church in Antarctica. The couple used their jet, as the Spirit of the Lord had permitted, to reach distant places where believers hid in secret, sharing Scripture softly in candlelit rooms. They brought relief supplies, offered whispered prayers, and witnessed miracles of faith flourishing in the world's shadows.

As their jet soared through the star-strewn evening sky, Ari's thoughts returned to the *Seven Spirits of God*, who had once stood as a living menorah in his study and later in their Capernaum home. Their silent blessings still illuminated his path. Seated beside Elinor, their hands intertwined, they exchanged a warm smile, marveling at how faith, love, and divine miracles had intricately woven their journey together.

Fraulein Maria Gottschall

Speaking of alpacas, somewhere in the misty highlands of Peru, Maria Gottschall, Ari's former no-nonsense COO, spent her time managing a successful alpaca farm named Heavenly Alpaca Hills. But the real twist in Maria's story isn't merely the career change; it's her whirlwind surprise wedding to Carlos in none other than Las Vegas. What began as a spontaneous weekend seminar culminated with an Elvis impersonator officiating their vows in a rhinestone jumpsuit.

"I came for a conference," Maria later joked, "and left with a husband. Talk about unexpected mergers."

Carlos had always admired Maria's sharp wit and commanding presence, but seeing her laugh uncontrollably at an Elvis-themed alpaca plushie in the gift shop sealed the deal for him. "She is terrifyingly brilliant," Carlos grinned, "but also has a soft spot for fluffy things. And me... apparently."

They had traded corporate boardrooms for quiet mornings in the Andean fog, her substantial wealth redirected to managing what they lovingly call "the fluffiest board of directors on Earth." While the alpacas lacked Maria's knack for spreadsheets, they excelled at producing luxurious wool and looking unbearably cute.

"Alpacas are way easier to manage than executives," Maria often said, sipping her morning Peruvian coffee.

Carlos would nod, pretending to type "alpaca minutes" into a laptop while occasionally muttering, "Chairman Woolington approves."

It was said that a notably obstinate alpaca, named Señor Stubbornhead, attempted to form a union, insisting on extended grazing breaks and top-quality alfalfa.

"It's like running a Fortune 500 company," Maria joked, "except the board occasionally spits at you."

Despite the humor of their new life, the surprise wedding and alpaca farm became symbols of a love neither of them had expected. From late-night strategy sessions to early-morning cuddles, Maria and Carlos embraced their new late-in-life chapter with as much passion as they once brought to the corporate world.

And as Carlos often said, "I may not understand alpaca code, but I know I hit the jackpot with Maria and the fluffiest team in the business."

Jacob, Emily, and Bryan

Back in the digital realm, Jacob, Emily, and Bryan had launched Cyber-Shield Security, "Keeping Your Faith Fire-walled!" as their slogan proclaimed. They had transformed their skills into a thriving business with the tagline, "Protecting the Faithful from the Faithless."

Their mission was serious: protecting underground churches and mission groups from cyber threats. When Ari and Elinor began working with persecuted Christians, the trio ensured their communications were secure, using cutting-edge encryption to outwit oppressive regimes.

Bryan kept the networks running seamlessly. "Paranoia is just good practice," he'd mutter, double-checking firewalls. Jacob, always the jokester, would add, "Gold medal in cyber Olympics, faith edition!"

Meanwhile, Emily, coding furiously, smirked. "And I'm clearly the brains and beauty here," she said, rocking fiery red hair. "Jacob has dubbed me 'Chili-Pepper.'"

Bryan joked, "We've gone from corporate drama to battling malware for God's Kingdom!"

Their work was vital, often tense, but deeply fulfilling. When a critical message to an underground pastor safely reached its destination, Jacob would lean back, hands behind his head. "Pizza for the win?"

Emily rolled her eyes with a half-smile. "Hackers run on carbs and caffeine. Some things never change." She tossed him the last breadstick, without looking, and he caught it one-handed and winked.

Their humor kept the weight of their work from becoming too heavy, but their passion for protecting the persecuted church worldwide burned with a steady fire.

During late-night coding sessions, soft glances were exchanged between Jacob and Emily. Encrypted prayers and shared silence. Something unmistakably tender, something like love, was quietly beginning to take root.

Their banter was playful and flirtatious. At times, when the screen's glow illuminated the room, and the code continued to flow into the early hours, their laughter would give way to quiet glances, just moments too long. They never spoke about their feelings for each other out loud... at least, not yet.

Marcus "Moose" Marcel

Moose had always been a man of action, and retirement wasn't in his vocabulary. After Ari and Elinor's wedding, he threw himself into their underground missions with gusto, becoming an indispensable part of their efforts. Whether smuggling supplies to persecuted Christians, navigating covert routes through hostile territories, or simply lifting spirits with his relentless humor, Moose was always in the thick of it. He had a knack for making the impossible seem manageable.

"Who needs a secret agent when you've got Moose?" he'd joke, flashing his signature grin as he hauled crates of hidden Bibles disguised as children's toys. He was a master of distraction, too, telling outlandish stories to suspicious border guards or slipping through checkpoints with a bag of snacks and a cheeky comment. Moose's good humor was as vital as his resourcefulness. In the darkest places, his laughter was a light. He'd organize impromptu sing-alongs on long journeys or tell ridiculous tales that left everyone clutching their sides.

"If we're going to risk our necks," he'd say, "we might as well have some fun doing it."

His presence was practical and a balm for weary souls. In secret gatherings of underground believers, Moose would tell stories of hope and perseverance, his booming laughter breaking the tension in rooms filled with fear. He'd sit with families, entertain the children, and remind everyone that joy wasn't just possible... but essential.

"Moose," Elinor once said, watching him share jokes with a group of children in a dimly lit church basement, "you don't just help people. You help them believe they can smile again."

He winked, leaning back in his chair. "That's because joy is a secret weapon; it works every time."

He became more than a helper; he was a symbol of hope, a reminder that even in the face of danger, laughter could be a shield and joy, a powerful act of defiance. Wherever Ari and Elinor went, Moose was right behind them, a steady presence, a loyal friend, and a living reminder that faith, love, and a good sense of humor could overcome anything.

Iris Keshet

Iris, Ari's mother, discovered a quiet Messianic Jewish congregation in New York City. She snuck out of the house, telling Abner she was "shopping for artisanal kosher pickles" when, in fact, she was enjoying music that blended Hebrew canticles and praise choruses. After service, she would bring home said pickles, just for authenticity, and chuckle to herself. Iris hummed new melodies learned in that congregation, praying Abner might join her one day, or at least taste the spiritual sweetness hidden behind those sour pickles.

Abner Keshet

Now retired and wrestling with a quiet house and an ungodly amount of kosher pickles, Abner had begun thumbing through a Bible Ari left behind. Curiosity led him to Isaiah 53, and as he read, he found himself strangely moved, almost intrigued by the idea that Jesus Christ might indeed be the promised Messiah. He hadn't admitted it to anyone, but he considered it more seriously than he ever thought possible. The thought hung in the back of his mind like a gentle, insistent whisper.

Diana Metzenbaum

Far from the joy and purpose Ari and Elinor had found, Diana's world spiraled into bitterness and obsession. Consumed by jealousy and rage, she watched Ari's work from the shadows, every public success feeding her desire for revenge. Her hatred became a dark mission: to destroy the man she believed had humiliated her and taken everything she deserved.

Diana's plotting reached a fever pitch when she caught wind of one of Ari and Elinor's covert missions to support persecuted Christians in a hostile communist country. Through her network of shady contacts, she devised a plan to sabotage the operation, exposing Ari to local authorities and an international scandal. But

Diana underestimated the loyalty and resourcefulness of Ari's allies.

Jacob, Emily, and Bryan, ever vigilant, picked up on the chatter of Diana's plot in encrypted communications. It didn't take long for the trio to unravel her plan. "Looks like someone's playing dirty again," Bryan quipped as they uncovered the sabotage details.

"When will she ever learn?" They said.

They intercepted her plot with precision and a touch of flair, thwarting her attempts before any damage could be done.

Their evidence, including emails, wire transfers, and surveillance footage, was compiled and forwarded to the authorities. It was airtight; Diana's involvement couldn't be denied.

Authorities moved swiftly. Diana was arrested at her luxurious penthouse, her protests and indignant outrage falling on deaf ears. The trial was swift, the evidence damning. Found guilty of conspiracy to sabotage a humanitarian mission, she was sentenced to several years in a women's prison.

Clad in an orange jumpsuit, Diana stalked the stark prison yard. Her manicured nails were chipped, and her once-flawless hair was pulled into a tight ponytail, the sterile walls and chain-link fences far from the designer elegance she had once commanded.

Despite the bars confining her, her mind was consumed with revenge, planning, seething, calculating.

"This isn't over," she muttered, her nails digging into her palm. "Ari thinks he's untouchable? Elinor can't save him." Her lips curled into a cold smile. "They have no idea what's coming."

The wind howled through the yard, but another voice, a familiar, silky whisper, slithered into her mind.

"They took everything from you, Diana," the voice murmured, smooth as glass, laced with venom. *"They humiliated you. Replaced you. Left you to rot in this... cage."*

Diana's breath hitched, her heart pounding. "Stolz," she whispered, eyes narrowing. "Where were you when I needed you?"

"Oh, my dear," Stolz cooed. *"I never left. You and I? We're the same. You were meant for power. Ari will pay for disgracing you."*

A slow, wicked smile spread across her lips.

While Ari and Elinor moved forward in faith, Diana remained ensnared in her self-made prison of pride and vengeance, Stolz whispering in her ear, feeding the flames of her twisted purpose. She turned from the fence, her mind sharpening like a blade.

"This game isn't over... It's just beginning."

To those who think you have everything under control...
The real journey begins the moment you let go.

About the Author

April R. Newton lives in a quiet Ohio farming community, where chickens, grandchildren, and a bustling household keep life anything but dull. She's a wife, mother of five, grandmother of six, and the founder of Newton Apple Books, a company dedicated to creating faith-filled books.

"Stories that make you think."

April serves as a Kids Church Pastor at her local church and is an author and illustrator, best known for her Christian children's series, *Popcorn the Wandering Little Lamb*, inspired by Psalm 23.

While writing *Seven Spirits*, she experienced what she describes as a supernatural encounter with the Lord. She believes the Holy Spirit led and inspired the story, giving her glimpses of His heart and direction far beyond her own imagination.

Through humor and spiritual insight, April seeks to point readers to Christ, the true Author of her story. When she's not writing or painting, she's likely in the backyard feeding chickens, sharing stories and wisdom with her grandchildren, or jotting down her next God-inspired idea.

For more information or to book an event, contact:
www.newtonapplebooks.com
email: newtonapplebooks@gmail.com

Table of Contents